SCAPEGOAT

Amy Dawson Robertson

Bella
BOOKS
2011

Copyright © 2011 by Amy Dawson Robertson

Bella Books, Inc.
P.O. Box 10543
Tallahassee, FL 32302

Printed in the United States of America on acid-free paper
First published 2011

Editor: Katherine V. Forrest
Cover Designer: Linda Callaghan

ISBN 13: 978-1-59493-262-5

Other Bella Books by Amy Dawson Robertson

Miles to Go

Acknowledgments

Towers of cupcakes and endless gratitude first and foremost to Alexandra Ogilvie who has been instrumental in the creation of this book. Her patience and kindness got me over many rough spots. I could only thank her adequately if I could confer upon her an uncle who was a jazzhead.

To S-H, who always has good ideas when I'm stuck and who reminds me that I can take things too seriously. Her help in entering edits into the manuscript was invaluable though it made me realize how slow a worker I really am.

Thanks to Mary Buonanno and Ella Schiralli for their support and always useful feedback. I'm so glad to have such good friends.

Thanks to Robin Eastman Caldwell for her unflagging support, friendship, feedback and for always being willing and wanting to read for me. And for all the nights chatting in the gazebo.

Thanks to Rana Choi for her Korean language help which as she knows was awesome, behind-saving, life-transforming and did wonders for my hair.

Thanks to Amanda Kyle Williams for always giving me a boost when I felt unable to meet my deadline. I wouldn't have made it through without the Bustelo.

Thanks to Katherine V. Forrest, a great lady, a great writer and editor and a pleasure to work with.

Thanks to my Dad, my siblings and my great sprawling family of aunts and uncles and cousins – your support means the world to me.

I feel fortunate to have so much interaction with so many of my readers on Facebook, in forums, and through email. It gives me a constant sense of purpose and inspiration. I thank you all.

And thank you, finally, to my mother, Sally Loy Woodward, who couldn't be more supportive and encouraging. She makes me believe, even when I am exhausted and feeling overwhelmed, that I can do it. She's also a darn good editor. Thanks, Mom, you truly are the best.

Once again and always for Mom,
And for Alexandra

About The Author

Amy Dawson Robertson lives and writes in the Washington, D.C. area. Connect with her on Facebook or check out her blog and website at amydawsonrobertson.com.

PROLOGUE

Saint Mary's Correctional Center
St. Mary's, West Virginia

The rain had been coming down hard for days all over the West Virginia Panhandle. Road conditions, with the flash floods and the poor visibility, had kept most people home, ordering in takeout and turning to their televisions for solace. Finally, the storm—a nor'easter, the weathermen said—had moved on, slipping over the mountain to torment the good people of Virginia, leaving only a fine drizzle behind.

West Virginians count themselves a hardy lot—especially the hunters. And a little bit of rain wasn't going to keep them from their quarry. The roads were already filling with trucks driven by men in camouflage and blaze orange. Neither was it going to keep the men of the Saint Mary's Correctional Center from their daily breath of fresh air and the great outdoors of the prison yard. They filed outside one by one in their thick hooded gray prison-issue plastic raincoats—useless against the cold but serviceable for a bit of water falling from the sky. Once in the yard the men assembled along the usual racial and gang lines. But basketball was colorblind and anyone who had decent moves could play alongside a man who might otherwise spit in his face. Or worse.

Those who weren't playing were either waiting to join the game or watching. And the rest milled about smoking cigarettes, talking trash and making deals.

Two white inmates stood about twenty paces from the action going on around them—close enough to the play on the court that they wouldn't draw the attention of the guards but secluded enough that they could talk without being overheard.

The two men were about the same height and build except that one was slimmer than the other. And they had such similar features that the other convicts called them The Twins. To many of the black and Latino inmates, the two white boys might as well have been identical, except that one was blond and one was dark. They were an unlikely pair. But prison can make for strange bedfellows and the two men—a skinhead and a rich boy who'd gotten himself into trouble—had struck up a kind of friendship.

They were together so much—and on their own—that some thought a prison romance had developed between them. Sex, of course, occurred between men in prison. But it was a kind of sex that almost never entered the realm of emotion and was required to fit neatly into the established prison hierarchy. Those who had power could demand it. And those who had none found it necessary to offer themselves up. Or suffer the consequences. Any liaison entered into on the basis of equality—and that happened only very rarely—was met with derision and violence. The man who had first uttered the suggestion that the skinhead and the rich boy were more than just friends was beaten so badly by the skinhead's crew that no one ever mentioned it aloud again.

It wasn't true anyway. The skinhead simply liked to talk to the rich boy. The rich boy listened to him, to his theories about the Zionist conspiracy and the coming New World Order. How the government of the United States had become a failed experiment. The skinhead thought he was getting through to him, converting him as he'd done with so many young men back home in Blanding, Utah.

He had big plans for when he got out of prison. And it turned out the rich boy had a few of his own and would be released just a week before him. The rich boy also said he had a car waiting for him on the outside. That would work out just fine.

"Yo! C.K., heads up!"

The skinhead and the rich boy both turned their heads at the same time to see a football spiraling toward them. The rich boy jumped and snagged the ball, tossing it back to Cruz, a short pockmarked El Salvadoran who'd slit the throat of a convenience store clerk during a botched robbery.

C.K.

Cainkiller.

Though the name had only belonged to one of the two white inmates when they entered the prison system, they had both come to identify with it.

The skinhead shoved his hands deeper into his pockets. It was damn cold and he'd have been just as happy to give up his rec time to stay warm and dry in his cell. But the delivery was today. He and the rich boy pretended to watch the game—the Kings were stomping the Gaylords—but the muscles along his back twitched like a horse at the gate, waiting.

The prison, past the checkpoints and the parking lots, was surrounded by miles and miles of woods—some parkland, some private. Hunters with a valid license were active this time of year. With overpopulation, they were allowed two bucks and a doe per season.

One hunter, hunkered down on his belly in the woods, crawled inch by inch over the wet ground till he reached a spot fifteen paces from the perimeter of the woods, the closest point he could get to the prison without drawing the notice of the guards and still have a clear shot. But today he wasn't carrying his .30-06. Feeling the damp through his thick camo raincoat, he held in his hands a potato rifle. And it was that potato gun that would fire the package over the concertina wire and into the yard. At the exact time.

The skinhead looked at his watch.

"Okay. Now."

The rich boy nodded once and strolled over to the basketball court, lighting a cigarette as he went. He walked without a care into the midst of the game. Chaos quickly erupted with ricocheting bodies and shouts of, "What the fuck you doing? Get off the fucking court!" He didn't hear the thunk of the package landing in the mud—and neither did the guards. He fell, took a few sharp kicks to the ribs and one bastard's boot caught the corner of his ear. He felt his body being lifted and tossed and then he landed with a wet *thwack* in the mud far enough off the court for the game to continue. He wiped the mud from his eyes and turned his gaze to the skinhead.

The skinhead was smiling and in the pocket of his raincoat was a bulge just larger than a pack of cigarettes.

CHAPTER ONE

Istanbul, Turkey

Rennie Vogel stepped into the courtyard closing the door behind her. She checked her watch before pausing to take in the moon, low and perfectly full, silhouetting the dramatic spire of the former Beyoglu hospital against the sky, clear tonight. The courtyard had come with the apartment and was double its size. The same pattern of green, white and coral red tiled her living space and extended into the courtyard and up six steps to a narrow rise lined with lush potted plants. A high stuccoed wall enclosed the courtyard and tonight, like most nights, a black cat sat on the wall eerily outlined against the backdrop of the city. She turned away from the flash of the cat's eyes to fit her key into the iron gate that led up a short flight of steps where she threw the bolt on the heavy door to the street.

It was just a few minutes to midnight and though the little

store just paces around the corner of her cobbled street was usually open till then, her American habits, accustomed to opening and closing times written in stone, nagged at her. She ran through logical scenarios in her mind in the thirty seconds it took her to round the corner. They should be open till midnight, she told herself. They usually are. But sometimes they close up early. She had been unable to discern any predictable pattern. The store's hours didn't seem to be aligned with the weather or the tourists carousing more than usual. Sometimes she thought she liked living in a world where the clocks ran more naturally, more in tune with human whim rather than a constantly thrumming capitalist machine. But not when she was thirsty.

A beam of light breaking the shadow of the Galata Tower told her she'd gotten lucky tonight and she hurried down the steps. Shops so tiny didn't exist at home and she found the intimacy of being with not one, but usually two, clerks in a store no larger than a walk-in closet disconcerting.

"Marlboro Light and an Efes," she said, holding up a finger.

American cigarettes were everywhere in Istanbul. American beer was not. But Rennie wasn't choosy and had grown to like the one lager to be had all over Turkey.

Back in the courtyard, Rennie sat with her feet up on the low brick wall, sipping her beer and taking in the skyline. When she could rouse herself to it, she was still awed by living in a foreign city. And Istanbul seemed to embody the foreign with its minarets and the keening call to prayer waking her every morning. She'd balked at the Istanbul assignment at first, suspecting it was the opening chime to the death knell of her time with the FBI. But then she found the foreignness suited her. She *wanted* to feel alienated.

Rennie stifled a yawn and watched as the ever-present courtyard cat slinked away as he always eventually did when she invaded his territory. She heard a window open above her and saw a man lean out, take a final drag on a cigarette and drop it to the courtyard below. She'd almost taken the sixth floor flat for its balcony and the sight of the Golden Horn in the distance. But the courtyard sold her, hemmed in on three sides by tall buildings where Turks hung out their hand-woven rugs to air on their windowsills. Rennie didn't like feeling enclosed, without an escape route, but she'd developed a habit of not shunning things she found unpleasant. Punishing herself seemed logical somehow.

And deserved.

Indeed, her guilt felt like an entity that had taken up residence in her body. An unexcisable and malevolent twin. She shook her head, wishing she could just stop thinking. She drained her beer and went into the studio to try, once again, to sleep.

Twenty hours later, Rennie sat at her desk in the FBI Legal Attaché Office in Istinye, tapping her heel against the cheap industrial carpet, staring, her eyes unfocused, at the cryptic Turkish document before her. It was eight o'clock and she would leave soon, walking slowly down the street to a pub frequented by Eastern Europeans. She wouldn't see anyone she knew there and would sit in a quiet corner drinking a much needed beer and pretending to read.

Her body had gone soft. She hadn't felt strong for a long time. Every morning she'd wake, thinking, *This is a new day.* But by evening she'd be filled with longing for the moment when the seal of the fridge door pulled away from the chill metal and she'd reach for the cool neck of the bottle, the opener at the ready. It was as if the woman she had been, the woman who felt she only had to reach out and could firmly grasp whatever she wanted, was always just ahead of her, out of sight, slipping around the corner into the shadows. She'd intend to get some exercise but the desire to calm her mind as she'd done since Tajikistan would be too strong. She'd done nothing more in the past six months than occasionally walk up the steep hill to her Beyoglu apartment after a stroll across the Galata Bridge to the Asia side of the city. Sometimes, she went to the baths. Stared at the copper ceiling, feeling her shoulder bones, her hips against the octagonal marble slab as she waited to be called and scrubbed perfunctorily by a robust Turkish woman. Afterward, she'd eat too many mezes and a fish and go home. It was strangely comforting somehow, cloaking herself in a layer of fat.

After Tajikistan, CT3—the special forces team she'd worked so hard to get onto—had been dissolved, supposedly temporarily, while the investigation took place. She was placed on leave with pay, enduring round after round of humiliation, failing to adequately respond to questions that were unanswerable unless the government admitted its role. And they were never going to do that.

In the midst of it all were the funerals.

Baldwin. Goode. Levin. Smythe.

Awkward conversations. Family members broken by grief.

The funerals had done nothing to heal the wounds from the death of her team. At each ceremony, family members had eyed her with confusion or sympathy or outright hostility. Only Smythe's wife—Smythe, whom she'd clashed with time and again—had approached her, irony of ironies, gripping her hand and saying the expected, "Thank you for coming. I know this is hard for you, too, and I want you to know I don't blame you at all."

And it was there that she finally cried. Not at Baldwin's funeral, her friend, whom she ached for, but at Smythe's. Rennie had gripped Fiona Smythe's hand so tightly. And then the woman had guided Rennie's head to her shoulder where she heaved once, and cried as silently as she could. For everything that had happened. And for Fiona Smythe too, who stroked her back and cooed in her ear, so kind and never to know what a bastard her husband was. When Rennie had finally lifted her face, she stared at the woman, certain an expression approximate to madness had twisted her features. She wanted to say, *Why don't you blame me too?*

Baldwin. Goode. Levin. Smythe.

Every day she recited their names like an incantation, only her lips moving. But on the bad days she could hear the words like a banshee scream in her head.

Where had her strength gone? Rennie had retreated into herself further than she ever imagined she could. Accepted whatever accusations were made in the interrogations. Fully expecting to be fired, she waited for it, patiently, longing to hear the words and go home and sleep. But they never came. She was to attend language classes, pack her bags and settle into a desk job—research and analysis—in the Istanbul office. Safely away from all that had taken place in those dark woods, sentenced to smother under reams of paper.

Rennie forced her leg to stop its incessant jumping. She shut down her computer. Locked her files in the drawer. She spoke to no one on her way out. The other agents and the foreign service staff had learned to keep their distance. They knew she was tainted and didn't want to be infected by whatever had tanked her career.

Outside the day was still hot and the city was busy and cosmopolitan. It almost buoyed her mood. This March was unseasonably warm in Istanbul and it only made her feel disjointed, the seasons all askew. She longed for the normalcy of a rainy spring in Washington—the coming of the cherry blossoms and the tourists. She stopped at a street vendor and bought a wrap—spiced meat and roasted eggplant—before she headed to the bar. She didn't want to get too drunk. Just a little.

Thoughts of Hannah Marcus crept into her brain. She couldn't go there. To the place where she imagined what might have been possible. it was too much. Too much.

Reaching her bar, she thought, I'll just walk by, go home, read a book, get a good night's rest. She stood before the door, a woman in a daze.

You should go for a run.

Every day she told herself she would run. Every day. But the lure of the bar and its easy comfort was too strong.

Or at least just go home.

But her apartment was too empty. And if she was there and coherent, she would think. And she must not think.

Rennie tried to remember who she was before the FBI, before she began running around that old track in college. But her mind wouldn't stretch back that far. She only remembered that first moment of clarity as she tore up her favorite trail on Old Rag Mountain, when she realized she could become whoever she wanted to be. And it had seemed like everything that came after that—getting into the FBI, being chosen for CT3—had only reinforced her unflagging sense that she could achieve whatever she set her mind to.

A finger of pain trailed along her throat.

You need a drink.

Rennie pushed through the heavy door, trading the thrum of the hot, muggy street for the clamor of the airless bar. The tension in her throat was almost unbearable. But release was close.

The light in the bar was entirely artificial. She could be anywhere except for the incomprehensible chatter in the background. Mainly Bulgarians, with a sprinkling of Czechs and Romanians, maybe even a Pole or two. It didn't matter. She couldn't understand them and they had no interest in her and that was what she wanted. She moved to her table in the back, waving to the bartender as she passed. She sat and found she was in a curious mood. Something new had crawled into her brain. Something that felt like action. She set her jaw against it, didn't have the energy for it. What was the point anyway?

There was a pay phone at the back of the bar. Her eyes kept returning to it. Before she could change her mind, she moved toward it pulling the calling card from her pocket—the one with no connection to her government. Several weeks before she left for Turkey she had stopped by a colleague's office, finding him absent and the database she needed open on his desktop. She quick-searched Hannah's name, memorized her number and performed her colleague's original search. Sometimes at night, when she tossed and turned in bed, she would visualize punching those numbers into a dial pad. It never once helped her to sleep. The numbers on the pay phone were sticky and Rennie had to try twice before reaching a dial tone. The 202 exchange—the D.C. area code—seemed a million miles away.

What if she answers? What could you possibly say? Without ruining your career?

But her career had felt over for a long time. If it wasn't, she wouldn't be where she was. She couldn't think. Was it a crime? Calling Hannah Marcus. When she'd been explicitly instructed to have no contact with her. She was about to hang up when Hannah's machine picked up.

Good. Yes. Just listen to the message and hang up. Just hear her voice.

The message was brief and to the point and Rennie could hardly take it in.

Oh, Hannah.

Just as the beep sounded, she heard Andrei calling to her from the bar.

"Vogel, you're up." Her beer sat frothing on the bar, scarred from years of abuse.

"I'll be right there."

Rennie replaced the receiver. It felt like the end, a conclusion to something she shouldn't have been thinking about anyway.

The walk from the phone to the bar seemed interminable. She heard Hannah's voice in her mind and the memory of their one night together rushed back, achingly vivid. She thought, What could it possibly matter? But somehow it did.

The bar was busy. It was Friday night. She drank half the pint in the first gulp, easing the tension in her throat.

Andrei, unshaven and handsome and always good-natured, stood smiling at her. Rennie was an unusual presence in the bar.

"Our friendly American," he said.

Rennie smiled back and lifted her glass.

"Cheers to that."

CHAPTER TWO

Washington, D.C.

Hannah Marcus walked down N Street, the high collar of her black knee-length trench coat shielding her face. It wasn't cold, but she was still recognized occasionally from cable news pieces during those first few weeks when the story broke that Ahmad Armin had been shot by an Iranian assassin and she had escaped in the chaos.

The story was laughable. As if she could have made it through those woods on her own.

The trench coat was belted and hugged her figure. Heeled black leather boots reached to her knee. Not the ideal ensemble to avoid attention. But this morning, standing in her closet, she'd made a decision, one a long time coming. To move on, to retire the past. And long black boots seemed to be the order of the day.

Hannah had just enough light to cut through the alley on

her way home. Knowing she probably shouldn't. But a mere kidnapping and a year and a half of captivity was not enough to keep her from doing what she wanted.

The walls of the alley were graffitied—mostly amateurish tags. Hannah concentrated on the exaggerated swirls of the oversized letters while her mind fixed on the Dumpster she was approaching and controlling her irrational fear of what might be hiding behind it. She moved slightly toward the opposite wall. With no place for the sound to go, her boot heels struck sharply on the brick and reverberated off the alley walls, but stubbornness made her refuse to change her pace. Suddenly she heard the clatter of glass on brick and froze. Her hand at her throat she skittered back against the wall as a rat shot across the alleyway and disappeared into a crack in the masonry by her feet. Looking for the source of the sound she saw an empty Heineken bottle rolling slowly across the uneven brick as if it were out for an evening stroll. There were other bottles on the ground next to the Dumpster. The rat had tipped one over.

Breathing hard, Hannah hurried out of the alley onto Sunderland Place. She stopped and leaned against the wall of an apartment building. Her hands shook violently as she pulled a cigarette from her purse and lit it. She took a long drag.

Steady, girl.

She shook her head and dropped the cigarette to the sidewalk, crushing it with the toe of her boot. For just a moment she could feel Rennie near.

Rennie Vogel, what have you done to me?

She shook her head again. This kind of emotional terrain was as alien to her as the moon and so full of craters she felt she might fall in and never find her way out again. It was a good day when she could think in such terms instead of wanting to hunker down in her apartment and never leave again. The shower was when she was most vulnerable, the warm water running down her face, so akin to tears. Hannah had never been one for sentimentality. And certainly never one to want what was impossible—and the FBI made it crystal clear that she and Rennie Vogel were never to see one another again. No Sunday morning brunches, no cocktails after work, not even a phone call. She tried to remind herself it was all for the best anyway. Relationships, commitment—she wouldn't say she was phobic but like everything else she preferred to keep such things in their proper place, and for her that had always been in the tiniest fraction of the totality of her life. She continued along Twentieth Street, thinking what a cliché it sounded, commitment problems. But it was what it was.

Rounding the corner to O Street, she hurried up the stone steps to the heavy oak door of her nineteenth-century apartment house. Two more flights of stairs and she fitted the key into her door and turned off the alarm. She stood just inside and took it all in, so very glad to be off the street. She hadn't taken her freedom for granted. Yet. She still found it strange to wake in the morning to such delicious comfort. The temperature just right, her body buffeted by the soft mattress and pillow, the lighting, warm and enveloping, filtered by the heavy curtains at her window.

After Tajikistan, when she flew into Andrews Air Force Base surrounded by servicemen, her parents had been waiting for her on the tarmac. It was incongruous. She had almost felt as if she had never seen them outside of the chaotic living room of their Baltimore apartment. They both wore brimmed hats and her mother clutched her brass-clasped pocketbook to her front. Seeing them, Hannah wanted to turn away. They seemed an anachronism, ripped whole from another time. Which in a way they had been. After a childhood in Ravensbrück, where they survived the concentration camp only by their wits, they'd come to the United States still inextricably rooted to the place they were so fortunate to escape. And it stayed that way. The horrors of the War—and there was only one in their eyes—were always present. It colored every part of their emotional life. That day, as she walked toward them on the tarmac, only moments back on home soil, Hannah had forgotten the prayers she whispered for them over the past year and a half and just wanted to be alone. When she reached them, they stood and looked at her for a long moment. Then they turned to one another and nodded and she realized that no one in her life would ever know what she went through better than they would. They finally had something in common.

Hannah dropped her keys in the bowl atop the table just inside her door. It still held spare coins she'd never bothered to exchange from countries she traveled to for Reuters before she was captured. Hard to believe she hadn't left the U.S. since she'd flown home in that air force transport jet. Yet another consequence of her time spent in captivity.

She crossed the old wood floor of her living room to her bedroom. Without bothering to switch on a lamp she sank down onto the bed and pulled off the long black boots. She dropped the rest of her clothes on the bed.

Changed into a black cotton V-neck sweater and a pair of pale wide-legged pants that hung, just barely, on her hips, she sat on her red sofa. She had bought it a month after she returned home. It was in Tajikistan, when her ordeal was finally over that she had promised herself she would acquire one. After visiting every overpriced showroom in the city, she knew this was the one the moment she saw it. Absurdly expensive, it was a decadent couch, but one of sublime beauty that stood out like a beacon in her monochrome apartment.

After she'd had a few months to adjust to a life not lived in a six-by-ten-foot cell, Hannah found she couldn't return to her old job for the wire service, covering politics in the Middle East and Central Asia. Her knowledge of her government's role in Armin's death had tainted her coverage of politics. She found she couldn't see any of it clearly; every mystery seemed to lead her to her parents' conspiracy theories. So, she'd applied for a job at the *Post* and they'd offered her the crime beat. Her ego balked at first. But soon the job's simplicity appealed to her. A break-in, a stolen car, a death. It seemed simple in a way politics did not.

She sat on her beautiful sofa and held a book in front of her as she did every night. She had no desire to go out. Her mind went to Rennie. Remote, maybe unknowable. She knew almost nothing about her. But she knew their hearts had opened to one another in those woods.

She wouldn't think of it. She wouldn't. She had no use for useless things.

Where are you? And why don't you come to me?

No.

This was not who she was. A woman who asked for things.

Her apartment was cold. She kept it that way. Too much heat roused the senses.

The phone rang and she ignored it. Either a solicitor or a reporter. She never answered the phone. Never had. Hannah didn't believe in the command performance and considered the phone a nuisance, a thing to be approached on her terms and her terms alone. But something nagged at her today. She stood and moved toward the sound. The machine picked up before she reached it. She heard her own outgoing message and thought, *You sound exhausted.* As the machine started to record, she heard a mix of voices in the background, the tinkling of glassware, a chair scraping across the floor. A restaurant, maybe a bar, she thought, her reporter's instincts kicking in. Then a heavily accented male voice.

"Vogel, you're up."

Before she could reach the receiver, she heard Rennie's voice, muffled and distant, but clearly Rennie's voice. "I'll be right there," Rennie said and the line went dead.

For a moment, Hannah's heart thumped hard in her chest.

I'll be right there.

But Hannah knew that Rennie had given up, was already hanging up, and those words weren't meant for her.

Hannah walked to the window, raised the blind and looked down into the alley. For a long time she stood, staring at nothing. Then she closed it again, walked back to her sofa and picked up her book.

CHAPTER THREE

Denver, Colorado

He'd just finished lunch with Lily when it happened. Another time long ago, in another place very far from Denver. The sound of tires screaming as a car driven too fast came to a very sudden stop. Masked men on the street...

He'd worn his best tie that day with his tweed coat and had enjoyed himself. He thought she had too. On the street, they stood together for too long as they said their goodbyes, holding one another's gaze. He was trying to imagine the texture of her hair, always covered by her headscarf, when she'd said, "Perhaps we could—" Then he'd heard the horrible sound of tires braking suddenly on pavement. Lily's face became wide-eyed and stricken. He turned and saw the doors flying open on a long black Mercedes sedan. Lily screamed—a sound that still cut him, he'd never forget it—as three men, their faces covered, leapt from the car. He threw his arms wide to shield Lily as the men—one of them very large—ran toward them. He could feel Lily's hands clutching his shoulders so tightly her nails bit into his skin. The large man reached them first and grabbed him by his tweed coat, jerking him forward and to the side while ramming his open palm into Lily's chest, sending her flying across the sidewalk.

It was over in less than thirty seconds and he was speeding down Fereshteh Street in the black sedan, watching Lily from the backseat through the tinted windows. Lily struggling to stand, Lily panicked and clamoring for the help of passersby, Lily pointing at the Mercedes. Inside the car, they flew past the shops, the overpriced restaurants and finally his own house, lost to him forever. When they blindfolded him, he'd felt that, surely, his heart must burst. His shirt had become soaked and with shame he could smell his own fear. And knew his captors could too.

Massoud Akbari still felt shackled by the terror of that memory even as he sat on the balcony of his tiny garden apartment smoking and drinking weak tea. Sometimes he made polite conversation with the old man who sat on the balcony adjacent to his own. Sometimes he thought to tell the old man his story. Would he even believe it? That his friendly, untroublesome Iranian neighbor had once been an important figure in Iran's covert nuclear program. That he'd been kidnapped by the CIA and turned into an asset under duress.

And now he had nothing to do. He'd cooperated with them at first. It was the easiest path he could take. He gave them information, his days filled with long and detailed interviews. But then he'd read in the paper that his brother had been killed. Poor Ahmad. He knew the Americans had to be responsible. His CIA handler swore they'd had nothing to do with it. But he didn't believe them. And he stopped talking.

Massoud had a bank account into which ten thousand dollars was deposited each month. Along with it, his other bills, his rent, his utilities, his car, were paid for by the American government. The money was his to do with as he pleased. Each month he converted it into cash and spent only a fraction of it on food and necessities, stowing the rest in a large zippered leather valise he kept in a safe in his closet. His only joy in life was to convert the smaller bills into larger ones as time passed, watching the money accumulate and hoping for something, what, he didn't know.

Since he'd refused to tell them any more, he was stuck, merely being, drinking tea and taking naps, languishing in an ugly room in a staid, unsophisticated city, in the middle of America.

It had been at his father's insistence that he and his brother focused on the nuclear elements of physics during their time at Harvard. His little brother had dived in head first, obsessed with returning Iran to its former glory at any cost. Massoud, always a better student than his brother, was less enthralled, uninterested in politics. His true love was theoretical mathematics—sitting in his worn leather chair with a pad and pencil, puzzling out the only truths he could ever believe in.

But the ties of family and country ran deep in him, and he and his brother returned home to government posts where the sins of the Americans were always pushed in their faces, where they were schooled that the Americans continually erred in their judgment about the Middle East by conflating modernity with Western culture. With that he agreed. But the illogic of the Iranian administration had nagged at Massoud. How could they rail against the Americans for intruding into Iran's affairs during the time of Mossadeq while ignoring the real tragedy—that the Americans' meddling had thwarted Iran's chance for democracy? Massoud had no desire for Iran to become a Western clone. But he longed for a true democracy. And peace. His role in propping up Iran's nuclear ambitions had never set well with him and over time he had become more and more uneasy. It was perhaps the only benefit that had come from the FBI snatching him away from his life. And since he'd been freed from considering the annihilation of the West, he found any form of war or violence both repellent and ethically unsupportable. Thus he found himself in a conundrum—though he'd loved his brother deeply, the savage turn he had taken blunted any blame he had for whoever had finally stopped him.

He would have liked to have prayed—he certainly needed help in sorting things out—but he had never found any solace there. He approached Islam with respect but also with skepticism. He believed that religion was inherently dangerous in the modern world. At humanity's infancy, it was necessary to tamp down fears of the unknown, to shine a light—however wavering—into the dark and shadowy corners of man's imagination. But in a perfect world, once society began to assemble itself, formulating and codifying laws, it would have fallen away, with logic and reason reigning supreme.

In a perfect world…

"Nonsense," Massoud said aloud, waving away such folly. Stubbing out his cigarette, he laid his head against the back of his chair and closed his eyes.

A week later, Massoud pushed through the heavy bank doors into the sunlight. Since he refused to provide them with any more information, his CIA handler said that his "service" to the agency was concluded. They were not happy about it. He was now, essentially, in the witness protection program though most "witnesses" didn't have such a generous stipend. They'd even agreed that he could leave Denver. *Thank Allah.* He'd already begun to pack up his little apartment. It wouldn't take long. He'd acquired only the bare essentials since he left Iran. Nothing held him back and now he only needed to decide where he would go, what sort of American life he would lead.

As he walked along the sidewalk toward his apartment, he was lost in thought. San Francisco perhaps. Or even Los Angeles. He would like to live somewhere warm. Sitting on his tiny apartment balcony these recent days, he had entertained fantasies. Becoming an adjunct professor of mathematics in some little college town. Sitting in the park and playing chess with other men with too much time on their hands. Getting a dog, maybe meeting a woman. Yes, he'd finally been seduced into conjuring his own American dream. But then, from the corner of his eye, something tugged at his attention. A long black European sedan with tinted windows drove slowly, keeping pace with him, fifty yards behind.

Fear coursed through him. The car was nearly identical to the CIA vehicle he had been tossed into in Tehran. He had an impulse to run. But where? There was no one he could turn to for help. *They've come for me, to finish me.* Just when he'd begun to imagine a new kind of life. He was a fool.

Massoud stopped at the corner and waited for them. He didn't have the energy to struggle, to try to save himself.

The sedan finally pulled alongside him. He could hear the gentle hum of its big engine. The tinted window receded, a cool blast of chilled air wafting from the interior, and Massoud saw a smiling, blond man. The man stepped out of the car, reaching out a large friendly hand and said, "Mr. Armin, my name is David Johansson. I know you are in a difficult position right now and I'd like to speak to you."

It was the first time Nasser Armin had heard his true name in years. He had even come to think of himself as Massoud Akbari. Nasser backed away from the car unable to puzzle out what it could all mean.

"Please." The man held up his hand. "I have no reason to ask your trust, but I think I can help you."

It all sounded so familiar, so like before. Nasser was responding to something honest in the man's tone, but it was true, he had no reason to trust him, would be a fool to, and he backed away farther from the car.

"You requested to meet your brother, Ahmad's assassin," the man said. "Her name is Rennie Vogel and I can facilitate that."

Nasser shut his eyes and felt the hot sun on his close-cropped head. He didn't believe the man. But it was the only thing in life he still desired—to know his troubled brother's final moments.

The man opened the door to the car and Nasser stepped into its chill leather interior.

CHAPTER FOUR

Somewhere in Ohio

He hadn't meant to kill him so soon. But he'd been strumming on his last nerve for the past two hundred miles.

I am Cainkiller. Yes, I am.

Cainkiller bent down to Slim's lifeless body and checked the pulse again. He couldn't feel anything. But it wasn't like he was any fucking doctor either. He stood and raised his big boot.

"You are now dispatched to the great hereafter, Slim, old pal." Cainkiller giggled. "And you can tell whoever's there to meet you that I'll be sending more that way soon."

Before his mind took off considering the relative merits of heaven and hell, he thrust the sole of the boot against Slim's windpipe with all his weight. The man's neck made a sickening crunch. No air would ever come through there again.

Cainkiller threw back his head. He wanted to scream. He

wanted to tear off all his clothes and run naked through the woods. Killing a man called for some sort of celebration. Cel-e-bra-tion. The word fractured in Cainkiller's mind. What did it mean? Really mean? He remembered taking Latin but almost none of it came back to him.

Sum, es, est

Sumus, estis, sunt

Cainkiller peered down at Slim, stared into his unseeing eyes. Dead. He sure *was* dead. As dead as one dude called Slim could be. Cainkiller slapped his palm against his thigh in rhythm, a tribal beat pulsing with his blood.

Sum, es, est

Sum, es, est

Slimus estis mort

Sum, es, est

Slimus estis c—

Cainkiller heard a sharp sound behind him and whirled, pulling the serrated hunting knife strapped to his thigh from its sheath. He squinted into the darkness. He saw the flash of a pair of tiny red eyes some twenty yards ahead. An opossum. Or an otter or something. Nothing to worry about. Cainkiller's eyeballs started to hurt. The sign that the drug was wearing off and he needed more. No problem. He could be back to the car in ten, fifteen minutes tops.

He turned back to Slim and bent down to him. The night was cool for summer and Slim's skin was already clammy. Cainkiller rolled him over and fished his wallet out of his back pocket, unsnapping the leather loop that chained it to his belt. From his own pocket, he pulled out the digital camera he'd stolen from the nice family he and Slim had encountered when they pulled off the highway at one of those scenic overlooks to pee. He zoomed in and snapped the picture.

"Sorry, kiddo. It had to be done," he said aloud. A splinter of regret pricked him unexpectedly. Where had that come from?

No apologies. Ever.

He didn't waste any time getting back to the car. He wasn't afraid of being alone in the woods in the dark. He wasn't afraid of anything. But he needed the drug bad. He should have brought some with him when he'd convinced Slim that it was a good idea for two men just released from prison to take a walk at three o'clock in the morning on private property. He hoped the rat-toothed animals would have their way with Slim before anybody found him. Maybe after the drug was in him, he'd go back and get rid of Slim's primary identifying marks. His teeth, his tats. What else? He should have paid better attention all those nights watching *CSI* reruns in the prison rec.

Cainkiller saw the car and almost shouted with joy. He climbed in through the passenger side and peeled up the corner of the floor mat.

"Come to daddy, sweetheart."

He tipped the powder from the vial onto the back of his hand and snorted. It hit his brain instantly and he let his eyes roll back in his head before washing the bitter taste out of his throat with the last dregs of Slim's Mountain Dew. Then he put the seat back and let the meth do its work. He hadn't taken enough to bring on the mania. No, he needed his wits about him for at least a little while.

Cainkiller felt the warmth on his legs and jerked awake.

Daylight. Not good. He looked at his watch. Just after seven a.m. and the sun was streaming through the windshield.

Christ.

He grabbed the vial from under the mat and took another snort. Then he crabbed over to the driver's seat, turned the key and gunned the engine.

He shouldn't have started with the drugs again. Had promised himself that he wouldn't look for them after he got out of prison. But then Slim had wanted some and he'd said, Okay, what the hell. Just a little bit now and again can't hurt, right?

He'd been so clearheaded in prison.

As clearheaded as a crazy fucker can be.

Cainkiller grinned as he put some distance between himself and Slim's rotting corpse. It was all going to be okay. Having the cell phone shot over the prison fence and setting things up with Keller ahead of time had been a stroke of genius on his part. And now he just had to turn up and take things one step at a time.

CHAPTER FIVE

Metropolitan Police Department
First District
Washington, D.C.

Rennie Vogel shivered on the bench in her cell. She wore a white cotton V-neck T-shirt and a baggy pair of jeans and she was freezing. The cot on the opposite wall beckoned, but she wouldn't allow herself to sleep. She had too much to work out, to think through how she came to be sitting on a rough, dirty bench in the D.C. jail.

At least she hadn't been put into the communal holding cell. Her FBI identification still afforded her a sliver of respect even though it indicated she wasn't active duty.

She had been processed hours before. She had no idea how many. She hadn't worn a watch in months, and even if she had it would have been taken from her. But she knew she'd been there long enough to sober up a little. And she had been working over the events of the night that brought her to where she was sitting.

It was a typical night for her since she'd returned from Istanbul, her evening routine. Trudging home from the bar around the corner on Pennsylvania Avenue, she had managed to drag herself up the steps to her apartment. She'd left all the lights on before she went out for the night and now stalked through the four narrow rooms swatting off the switches. In the bedroom, she sat down heavily on the bed. She wasn't ready to sleep. It wasn't dark enough.

It's never dark enough.

She rose slowly and made her way back to the kitchen. A single beer rattled at the bottom of the crisper.

I'm so tired of all of this.

She popped the cap and took a long pull off the bottle. Then back to the bedroom, stopping in the living room, swaying slightly. She patted herself down and found her pack of cigarettes in her back pocket. Lighting one as she stepped out onto the roof deck, she raised her hand to her eyes.

"You've got to be kidding me."

As soon as she saw the glaring security light across the street affixed to the lip of the roof, she became enraged. Her neighbor had put it up a month earlier and, in a more reasonable moment, she'd talked to him, tried to convince him that it disturbed her sleep and general well-being, shining like an interrogation light through her bedroom window.

A small bald man with an overgroomed beard, he'd said dismissively, "It's for the good of the neighborhood. Keeps crime down. Every spring, I've had my impatiens and petunias dug right out of the ground. This year it'll be different."

Tonight she'd had enough. She just needed to lay in the dark and feel blotted out. "Blotted," she said aloud in a low, even voice. She walked, wavering, back into her bedroom, to the ancient dresser with the blotchy mirror and got her gun. It was already loaded. For the smallest instant she thought, *This is not who you are*, before opening the squeaky screen door to the roof, holding it open with her foot. Squinting, she fixed the sight on the light and squeezed the trigger. It was late and the bullet exploded from the muzzle like a cannon, the retort resounding through the streets. The light went out and she heard the tinkling of glass as it fell to the brick below. The effort had exhausted her and she collapsed onto her bed still clutching the gun.

Darkness.

"Vogel." The guard unlocked the heavy door to her cell, interrupting her remorseful train of thought. "Wake up. You're done."

Rennie lifted her forehead from her knees. She was so cold and weary she had sunk in on herself. She opened one eye on the burly guard standing over her.

"Let's go. Unless you want to stay," he said taking her arm and pulling her to her feet.

The guard steered her down the long hallway past the other cells and into the front room of the station.

Will Jenkins, who'd served as agent in charge of command center operations for the Tajikistan mission, sat on a cracked teal vinyl chair reading the *Post*. Rennie snorted when she saw him.

Who the hell called him?

"Vogel." Jenkins' voice held no trace of goodwill. "Rough night?"

Rennie didn't respond.

It was Jenkins who'd been there during the investigation after she got back from Tajikistan. And at the hearing too—the kind that never makes the papers. It had felt more like a tribunal. And Jenkins had been doing nothing but saving his own ass.

"Captain Brown here was good enough to let us know you'd gotten yourself into trouble," Jenkins said, gesturing to the tall black cop behind the desk. "I'll be driving you home."

"I'll walk."

"That's not the deal."

"You're good at deals, aren't you, Jenkins?"

"This could have been much worse for you." He leaned in close to her ear. "A bit of gratitude might be in order, don't you think?"

Jenkins wore a navy track suit with a shiny stripe that ran from his shoulders to his shoes. His hair was slicked back as if he'd just showered. He seemed even more reptilian than usual, she thought as they crossed the street to the car.

"Oh yeah. I'll always be thankful for all you've done for me." Rennie concentrated on walking without swaying. "What are you doing here anyway?"

"You're still *officially* employed by the FBI, Vogel. At least you were before tonight. Did you remember that when you fired your service weapon at your neighbor's house?"

It was true. Rennie had been granted a leave of absence. But it had been six months and the existence she had led during that time did not lend to her thinking of herself as an agent of the FBI.

"Besides," Jenkins continued, "I'm sure you can understand that we'd like to make sure you don't do anything else we'll regret."

"Like tell the cell guard who makes ten bucks an hour that the United States government murdered Nasser Armin."

"We can pretend you didn't say that, that the drink has turned your brain to applesauce."

Rennie didn't respond.

"You do know you've just driven the final nail in the coffin that was your career in law enforcement, right?"

Rennie exhaled. The leaden sensation she'd carried in her gut since Tajikistan suddenly evaporated.

Maybe this is what I've been waiting for.

The final severing. She'd been so imperfectly knitted to her employer for so long, she'd felt she was living a half life. She and Jenkins sat in silence until he swung the car into the alley, his tires noisy on the brick, and parked in front of Rennie's apartment.

"Look, Vogel. I know you had a rough time in Tajikistan, but you really oughtta get your shit together. I never figured you for one to tank out like this."

Me neither.

"A rough time? That's a bit of an understatement don't you think?"

"We all play the cards we're dealt."

How fucking original. "Yeah, we do. And if we screw people over in the process, that's just part of the hand, right? Those shitty low cards we have to make the best of."

Jenkins put his hand on Rennie's thigh. She was still too drunk to determine whether the gesture was kind, condescending or some horribly inappropriate come on. She roughly shrugged him off and got out of the car.

"Go fuck yourself."

Rennie walked slowly up the wooden steps to her apartment. She wished she had somewhere else to go, to get away from herself. Inside, ironically, the Metropolitan cops had left all the lights on.

Redux.

Rennie slapped the off switch in the kitchen and opened the fridge door.

Christ.

The crisper was empty.

This should be a lesson to you.

Rennie paused only for a second before pulling the bottle of Jack Daniels from the cabinet over the sink and poured freely into a clear glass mug. The fumes were so intense she could almost see them.

This is a bad idea.

She took the mug and turned off the rest of the lights and stared at the still open drawer of her dresser in the bedroom. The cops had taken her sidearm, of course. She leaned heavily against the dresser and slowly closed the drawer. When she raised her head there was just enough light in the room to see herself in the mirror.

"Good God, you're a mess," she said in a whisper.

Out on the roof deck it was as dark as it could be, now that her neighbor's security light was no more. She sat in her old Adirondack chair and fumbled for a cigarette. She laid her head back and took a tiny sip of the bourbon and a long drag on her cigarette. The night was cloudy, swirling ghost-like across the moon.

So much lost.

And now she'd be a free agent, so to speak. She wouldn't be going back to Istanbul. Or Quantico. Or FBI headquarters. It was over. And she really did feel free. In Istanbul, she hadn't been doing the work she wanted to do, work that mattered. She had never been given interesting cases. And she suspected that the only reason she hadn't been fired was because she knew too much. Keep your enemies close.

And now? How could she put herself to use? It had been so long since she'd even thought of herself in those terms. As an actor in the world. She laughed under her breath. It was as if her country had broken her heart and she'd been drowning in her sorrows ever since. She laughed again. There must be a bad country song in there somewhere. Rennie stubbed out her cigarette and set the mug of bourbon next to her chair.

Most things in life were a choice. She had chosen to descend to the place she was now. She had always exercised control but this had been her time to let go. She would allow herself to wallow in self-pity a little while longer. She would know when that time was up and she knew it would be soon. But, she remembered, there was a time when she *hadn't* chosen her action. Everything inside of her had been compelled to climb over that balcony and go to Hannah.

Rennie wasn't good at relationships, she knew that. Had never even attempted one. But Hannah Marcus and she had been so powerfully drawn to one another that Rennie, against orders, found a way, with a prayer and leap, to be with Hannah that one time.

She couldn't bear to think about Hannah. She knew if she did, allowed her to reenter her mind, she would go after her. She'd pour the bourbon over the railing of the roof deck and find her. And she couldn't do that. Could she?

CHAPTER SIX

Washington, D.C.

Hannah Marcus exited *The Washington Post* building onto Fifteenth Street. It was mid-afternoon and traffic was moving quickly. With a banker's box in her arms and her briefcase on top, she stepped off the curb and failed to hail a cab with insistent jerks of her head. She set down the box to wave, and finally a morose turbaned driver pulled alongside her.

"Twenty-second and O," she said, settling into the backseat.

Inside the box were the contents of her desk and file cabinet. She had hauled another box home the day before. Hannah leaned her head back and closed her eyes. She wasn't sure she'd ever felt quite so free. Maybe that first night of freedom in the hotel room in Dushanbe. Then, though an FBI guard stood just outside her door, she could only revel in the looseness of her limbs. Gripping tension had bound her muscles for so long it had begun to feel normal. Those first breaths of smogged Dushanbe air, as she stood on the balcony taking in the city, had been as refreshing and mind clearing as any she'd ever taken. But then she'd come home and new tensions began. Daily phone calls from her parents, the endless debriefings with the FBI, the muddle her brain was in over what to do with her career. And whether or not she was relieved by the mandate that she would never see Rennie Vogel again.

Rennie Vogel.

Her lips silently mouthed the syllables. She didn't think of her every day. She thought of no one every day unless they intruded upon her line of vision. Perhaps the only living creature who did was the almost feral cat who visited her minute backyard every night. Without ever wanting such a connection, she found herself putting food out for him each night and swearing she would stop the moment he left any physical sign upon her pathetic lawn that he'd been there. He seemed to understand their deal. But Rennie remained only vaguely, a shadowy presence always clouding her mind. Now, without the prospect of work the next day and as yet unsure how she would approach her freelance career, she knew thoughts of Rennie, thoughts rounded and shaped with long buried clarity, might encroach upon her peace of mind.

She hadn't heard a word from Rennie since the aborted message—"I'll be right there"—from a number that Hannah had traced to a bar in Istanbul. Since then Hannah had often wondered if Rennie was still in Turkey or possibly back in D.C. She knew she had lived somewhere near the Supreme Court in Capitol Hill, and had stayed her hand countless times when she felt compelled to use her sources to find out exactly where. She would hate to have an ugly visit from a man in black with vague connections to the government politely but menacingly suggesting she refrain from further investigation.

Hannah paid the taxi driver, who had blessedly not tried to enter into a political discussion with her, and manhandled the box up the stairs and into her apartment. She dumped the box just inside the front door. Yes, she felt free. The hours she'd spent at her desk at the *Post* had begun to suffocate her. And though the crime beat had served her well, keeping her mind blunted when she needed it, now it was time for her to do real work again. And on her own terms. But this very moment was no time to be home alone.

She jogged down the stairs to the street, dialing a colleague on her cell. She was hungry to begin tracking down leads for a story. She walked the four blocks to a New Hampshire Avenue tavern, a regular haunt of journalists. Taking a table near the bar, she ordered a Chivas and soda and waited for the drink to arrive before she lit a cigarette. She had just lit her second when Lisbeth Harmon scooted into the booth across from her.

"That was quick," Hannah said.

"I was looking for an excuse to get out of the office. Mark is on the warpath today."

"I heard," Hannah said, glad the fallout from the managing editor's capricious moods wouldn't be her problem anymore.

Over her blouse and jacket, Lisbeth wore a roughly woven scarf of pale blue cotton tied in a complicated knot at her throat. Her makeup and hair were as crisp as ever and seemed to say *Don't fuck with me, I'll eat you alive.* Though she looked more broadcast than print journalist, Lisbeth was hard-hitting and ambitious and at thirty-eight sat at the head of the terrorism desk.

"So, freelance? I hadn't heard. That's what every journalist dreams about, isn't it?"

Hannah caught the implication.   Without guaranteed success, there had to be money in the bank. And there was. A lump sum payment from the U.S. government of three hundred thousand dollars. They said it was for her ordeal, for time lost out of her life. But all Hannah understood was hush money, confirmed by the agreement she had been coerced into signing. Whatever Rennie had gotten off the CIA operative in Shuroabad was very damaging to the United States and they could never be sure how much Hannah knew.

"So, knowing you, you'll head toward investigative work rather than fluff."

Hannah shrugged. "I haven't firmly decided on an angle yet. I've got my eye on corruption networks, religious extremism, nationalism."

"Sounds like my kind of girl."

Hannah felt a current of something and looked at Lisbeth anew.

They talked for an hour or so, going over the big stories on the horizon. Hannah's interest was piqued by one about an exclusive and secretive religious organization comprised of congressmen and other powerful political operatives that made regular trips to Africa, throwing money around and influencing policy and legislation. Hannah felt her mind coming alive again as they talked. She was ready to attack a big story, something that really mattered.

On the street after they'd paid their tab, Lisbeth leaned in, pressing her lips lightly on Hannah's cheek.

"You know, I'd hate to lose touch. Call me, we'll do this again," she said, holding Hannah's gaze longer than necessary.

Walking home, Hannah wondered if she had misread her. It wasn't the first time a woman had made a pass at her, but it was the first time since Rennie. She'd never considered a woman lover before Rennie who had been the first woman she'd connected with in such a way. Her most meaningful relationships seemed to be with whoever her translator had been at the time. She had dated, when she'd been in the U.S., and even wound up with a boyfriend of a sort. Nick. Who she'd somehow tolerated longer than any of the others. In a clichéd scene at the airport the night she left for Tajikistan, moments before she passed through security, he proposed to her out of desperation, knowing he was losing her. She had stared at him blankly, then reached up and kissed him lightly on the cheek. And then she was gone, through the metal detector and hurrying toward her gate, without looking back. He'd never called and she felt that she had barely escaped something that would have crushed her. She had always been the one to pull away first—to end a kiss, extract herself from an embrace, to turn her back to her lover in bed.

Turning onto O Street, she felt a twinge of guilt about Nick. At least she'd spared him the role of grieving boyfriend, long-suffering during her captivity. Before ascending the steps to her apartment, Hannah paused, her hand on the cool iron railing. She looked down the street. The old oaks and maples lining the brick sidewalks had lost the fresh green of spring and were now full and lush. She breathed in deeply, a trace of honeysuckle in the air suffusing her with a sense of how good things can be. Maybe she'd go for a walk after dinner.

I will no longer be afraid.

CHAPTER SEVEN

Somewhere in Minnesota

Cainkiller was sick of driving. He'd been on the road for eight hours and hoped he'd be seeing the back of Minnesota sometime real soon. He'd been listening to industrial electronica the whole way and he still wasn't sick of it, not one little bit. Drills and buzz saws in his brain felt like a natural state of mind. But now he'd heard the same tracks so many times he was starting to make up his own lyrics. He sing-songed in a wobbly falsetto.

Rich boy, poor boy
Highway, stretched along the sun,
Highway, thronged till day is done
Rich boy, poor boy
Highway, shrill with murderous pride
I am not my brother's keeper, no way, no how

"No way, no how. I sure as hell ain't."

"Ain't," he said again and started to giggle. "Ain't paint bobaint, bananafana fo faint."

He drove with two fingers on the wheel, driving fast, but not so fast to get himself into any trouble. He tried to remember more of the poem he'd just mangled, the name, the writer, anything. Didn't matter. He liked his version better anyway. He held his wrist up to admire his new tattoo. The wrist was still sore but it looked good—better than the shitty ink he'd paid for on the back of his neck. At least he didn't have to look at that one every day. But his new one was well done. It better be. He'd paid three hundred bucks for the ten Gothic letters encircling his wrist: C-A-I-N-K-I-L-L-E-R. Perfect.

Cainkiller tried to stretch in his seat. His accelerator foot had fallen asleep twenty miles back. He figured it'd only take two more hours before he got to the no-name town in Wisconsin where he had hopes of getting his hands on the merchandise he needed to fulfill his grand plan. The merchandise he'd so far failed to get at Keller's camp. Keller kept his shit locked up so tight he'd have to be some kind of Terminator just to get in the door. But that didn't mean he was giving up. Especially if Wisconsin didn't pay off.

He swung the car off of route I-94. The piece of shit Pontiac Firebird—nearly older than he was—was making more noises and probably wasn't long for this world. Cainkiller slammed the door on the car in the parking lot of a convenience store. He took a step and the tip of his shoe caught on a twisted rusty tie that used to keep in place a now absent concrete wheel stop. He caught himself before he fell but it ruined his mood. He pushed through the door and felt his leg brush against the twin bells looped around the handle on a dirty string. He couldn't hear anything over the soothing drone of Daft Punk coming through his earbuds. He glanced up at his distorted self in the round security mirror. *Vicious. You look fucking yummy vicious.* A glance at the expression on the greasy clerk's face confirmed it. He loved seeing fear in another man's eyes and knowing he was the progenitor of it.

"Greazy," he said out loud, seeing how it felt on his tongue. Since he'd been at the camp he'd barely talked to a soul. Just that dumb fuck Buddy Olsen. Hell, he'd barely talked to anybody since he'd left Slim cold and dead in those woods. He didn't even know what his own voice sounded like anymore. He'd once done a stint in Tennessee. Funny how that twang grabs a hold of you and won't let go. But he was in Minnesota now. "Easy, peasy." He craned his upper body toward the clerk. "Did you know that a man who doesn't continually reinvent himself is destined for obscurity?" The clerk only stared. "Who said that? Somebody famous for sure." Cainkiller put a finger to his lips and screwed up his face as if he were thinking hard. "Or maybe it was me. Maybe *I'm* the genius." The clerk turned away and Cainkiller made a show of slowly extending his middle finger.

Scanning the aisle for a box of minidoughnuts, his brain paused. You need to stop drawing attention to yourself. *Okay, no more drugs.* Or at least no more for a little while. But it would be a long time before he could sleep. He spread an imaginary map in front of his vision, and stretching his arms wide, placed one finger where he stood and another far to the southeast. Still a long ways to go. The track blaring in his ears hit one of his favorite grooves and he mimed rolling up the map and then exploded into ten seconds of wild thrash dancing. When he stopped, he felt so depleted he just wanted to lay down on the floor. He stood perfectly still, his head hanging, until the moment passed.

Where are the fucking doughnuts?

When he found them, he had to consider his options. Such a difficult decision. Powdered or chocolate? He loved them both. But the car was trashed enough and he settled on the chocolate. *Waxy chocolatey goodness.* He cut his eyes at the clerk who was still watching him close. He grabbed two giant sugar-free Red Bulls for when the drug wore off and dumped his quarry on the counter.

"I love the taste of aspartame in the morning—completely superior to the so-called 'natural' taste of sugar. And it's a myth, a total myth, that it causes cancer. Do you know how much they force-feed those rats the stuff to get those numbers? Do you even want to know? Do you?"

The clerk didn't respond. Cainkiller pried a Bic lighter out of a plastic display case and added it to the pile. It had a picture of a blonde in a cowboy hat with big fake-looking tits. He dropped his sunglasses lower on his nose so he could eye the clerk.

"What do the assholes smoke around here?"

The clerk's lips parted. Then he closed them and shook his head, irritated.

"The good old boys, the real assholes with the belt buckles and the thick necks."

The clerk shook his head again.

"I'm serious. Hey, I'm taking a poll. Their brand? Of cigarettes?"

Another shake of the head. "I don't know. Winstons, Camels, Marlboros."

"See, now how hard was that? A carton of Camels." Cainkiller pushed his sunglasses back up with his index finger. "This your dump?" He was pissed the clerk wasn't scared of him anymore.

The clerk glared at him, getting cocky now. "My father's," he said, ringing up the order.

Cainkiller leaned over the counter. "You tell your father he's gonna get his ass sued if he doesn't fix that parking tie out there. You get me? It's called a trip and fall and some prick cracks his head on the pavement and all your New World dreams go straight down the toilet."

The fear was back in the clerk's eyes and Cainkiller felt the tension ease from his chest. He collected his change and grabbed the bag. "Just a word of friendly advice."

CHAPTER EIGHT

Crane Technologies Building
Penthouse Suite
Portland, Oregon

Sam Crane was not a man to second-guess himself. And though he'd taken risks throughout his career, they didn't compare to the step he was about to take.

Six months ago, he had surrendered his position as CEO of Crane Technologies, the software security giant he'd brought from an idea hatched in a bedroom with walls still plastered in *Star Wars* posters to the most powerful company in the field. The reins of control weren't far from him though, since his more-than-capable wife, Ella, would steer the company as long as she wished. And now, for the next chapter of his life.

Crane drove his toes deeper into the bone-white carpet as he gazed out the window at the slowly moving traffic on the dramatically arched Fremont Bridge. His office, ten thousand square feet of teak and steel, was on the twenty-seventh floor in

Portland's City Center and boasted the best views the city had to offer. The floor directly beneath him housed the temporary offices of his newly created think tank, the Foundation for Liberal Democracy. The offices would move to Washington, D.C. once all of the key players were vetted.

The toy-like cars hundreds of feet below slowed and Crane performed a calculation in his head. His mind had always had a bent toward the quantifiable and traffic engineering was a private hobby.

"Sam?" Peyton Virgil entered Crane's office after a light rap on the door.

Crane lifted his hand to the imposing, nattily dressed man who'd been with him from the beginning.

"Pick up where we left off?" Virgil asked.

"Let's do it."

"Okay. We have the people who made it out of the Armin incident."

"Armin?" Crane narrowed his eyebrows. "That's the Iranian with the cell in Tajikistan who was supposedly assassinated by one of his countrymen?"

"Right," Virgil said. "And now as the countryman rots in prison, his family lives outside of London in a two-story house with vinyl siding."

"That's very thorough, Mr. Virgil."

"That's what we do," Virgil said, smiling.

"So," Crane said, dropping onto a sand-colored leather bench and clapping his hands, "who took out Armin?"

"CT3. The FBI international counterterrorism team."

"CT3? That was the unit that was refused funding unless women were allowed in?"

"Correct."

"Ella was following that story," Crane said. "The woman made the hit on Armin, right? Now I'm remembering what was reported about this story. This was just before nine-eleven."

"Right."

"And Armin had a hostage. A reporter, I think."

Virgil shuffled through the sheaf of papers on his lap. "Hannah Marcus," he said.

"That's right," Crane said. "The story was that she escaped in the chaos after the shooting. But she was brought out by the female CT3 operator who killed Armin?"

"Exactly. But it was even more complicated than that. First, Armin was motivated by the belief that the U.S. had kidnapped and murdered his brother, Nasser."

"Nasser Armin," Crane said, nodding contemplatively. "So when Ahmad Armin didn't get his way he began to follow through with his threats."

Virgil nodded. "Yes. At the end he had two things on the horizon. To procure material for a dirty bomb. And he'd connected with a CIA case officer who claimed to have photographic evidence that the CIA murdered Nasser Armin."

Crane raised his eyebrows. "Photographs, huh? Do we know the identity of the CIA man?"

"Yes. His name is Martin Garrison."

"And this Martin Garrison is on our short list?" Crane asked.

Virgil nodded. "We want to bring him in."

"Do all the analysts agree?"

"All the analysts do…" Virgil trailed off.

"You don't?"

Virgil shook his head. "It's Ella."

Crane trusted his wife's judgment implicitly. "I want to see everything we have on Garrison and the reports from the individual analysts—not just the final summary—before I give the final go-ahead."

"I'll have it all sent over when we finish here."

Crane went to the window again and stared down at the bridge. "You said 'people' from the Armin incident—who else?"

"The woman who made the shot on Armin—Rennie Vogel."

"She's not with FBI anymore?" Crane said, turning to face Virgil.

"That's right."

Crane shook his head. "This is about to get complicated."

Virgil snorted. "*This* has been complicated from the beginning."

"Indeed," Crane said. "So, Vogel's role will be operational?"

"If she's suitable."

Crane sat in the Eames chair behind his desk. "If you're skeptical why consider her?"

"I'm always skeptical. And as I told you going into this thing, you can't expect the type of résumé you're used to seeing. These are people doing extraordinary things and they are usually a bit damaged as a result. We'll have to overlook some things that we would never overlook in the corporate world."

Crane leaned back in his chair and laced his fingers behind his head. "You think this is a bad idea, don't you?"

Virgil exhaled, shaking his head. "Yeah, I do. We're assembling an army. We're going to be launching operations." He gave a humorless laugh. "Yeah, I think it's a really bad idea. You and I have worked too damned hard to build this," he said, stretching out his arms and taking in the expanse of the penthouse.

Crane nodded. "I'm hearing you, my friend. But if anything goes wrong, if the media gets wind of it, we're covered, right?"

"Supposedly," Virgil said. He rubbed his hand over his close-cropped head and laughed under his breath. "I *do* see the importance of this, especially in these times, I just never imagined we'd be getting into something like this."

"We've got the go-ahead to take it slow, get our sea legs before we jump into anything too big. Do we have a name for this group yet?"

"I've been calling it the Special Projects Section in my notes."

"Fine. Let's go with it."

Four hours later, as Peyton Virgil steered his car out of the underground garage of the Crane Building, his cell phone vibrated gently in his jacket pocket.

"Go home, old man. Take your wife to dinner," Virgil said.

"Ella's here with me now. We've been going over the Garrison file."

"And?"

"Bring him in."

"Will do." Virgil closed his phone and waited for the light to change.

CHAPTER NINE

Falls Church, Virginia

Martin Garrison sat in his well-appointed living room, a paperback copy of Dostoyevsky's *Notes From Underground* on his knees. He had begun the book two months before and was on page eighty-seven. He began each evening sitting in a plush chair in the corner of the room with a snifter of Armagnac. He would read a few pages and then stare at the china cabinet against the wall in the dining room. The dishes hadn't been used since his wife died, by her own hand, fifteen years before, and probably never would be again. The ramblings of the great Russian writer's narrator suited Garrison's mood though he preferred to ingest them in tiny gulps, one sentence at a time along with the Armagnac. This was how he spent his life now. Barely existing.

When he left Tajikistan, shackled and in custody of the very organization he had devoted his life to, he expected he would spend the rest of his days in prison. A career CIA case officer, he was considered the foremost operative of his generation. He had spent years in deep cover in the Soviet Union and with the failure of the August Coup, he'd moved on to the next battleground, the Middle East.

But then everything had gone wrong at home. His son, Jonathan, had had too little guidance given his long absences and his wife's instability. A sensitive boy looking for meaning and order in the world, he'd fallen into one cause after another until finally finding a calling in Islam. For him it was only a short walk to jihadism. When Garrison realized the path his son had taken, he finally chose family over career, broke from his employer and set out to find his son at all costs.

But he'd lost everything anyway. His son. His career. Regret sometimes nipped at his heels and sometimes swallowed him whole. A life with Jonathan on the run in Europe or Asia— though perhaps not the ideal way for a father to bond with his son—had held a deep appeal for him. But it was not to be.

For a long time, Garrison had sat in a cell, his status yet to be determined, until in a surprising show of reason he was finally pardoned by his government, an acknowledgment that he was no real traitor, merely a father trying to save his son and in the process securing the best intelligence on jihadist elements they'd ever seen.

And now he was adrift. A man who had always spent his infrequent vacations preparing for a return to his life underground, he didn't know what to do with himself. For him, life was work and he had never developed any hobbies or outside interests. So he sat and he stared at the china cabinet, never entirely sure if he should allow long-buried thoughts to rise to the surface.

On the table next to him lay the most recent letter from his son. Jonathan, in a maximum security prison in Colorado, was allowed to send one a month. It was the only thing Garrison looked forward to.

Jonathan had been in the facility for two years, in a single cell—no television, though he was permitted books and writing paper. Allowed one hour a day in the concrete yard penned by concertina wire, he had to endure a cavity search on entering and exiting his cell if he wanted to take advantage of this privilege. He seemed content, content as he could possibly be under the circumstances. He was reading Plato and Montaigne and Pascal, struggling to place himself and his actions in the context of his now very limited world. If he were a different man, Martin Garrison might have risen from his chair and, running his fingers along their spines, plucked the relevant texts from the shelf to place his son's quotations in context. He might have tried to puzzle out if the complex boy was returning to a state of mind that resembled normalcy—if such a thing were possible for him. But to do so would require Garrison to position himself in the world, reestablish a place for himself and then determine if the passages were ancient examples of a pathological angst that resonated with his son, or every human being's attempt to answer those unanswerable questions we all seem so compelled to ask. But Martin Garrison couldn't see where he fit into the world at all.

Garrison was torn from his stupor by a knock at his front door. He stood and slipped the 9mm Beretta on the end table beside him into the back of his trousers. Peering at the distorted image of a man through the peephole, Garrison opened the door and stepped outside closing it behind him.

"May I help you?"

The man was tall and blond and wore an English suit. He smiled, his hands clasped in front of him. It was an expression of such guilelessness that Garrison almost reached for his weapon.

"I'm David Johansson," the man said. "I work for Sam Crane."

Sam Crane of Crane Technologies, Garrison thought, the computer security giant based in Portland. Garrison suddenly had a vision of himself in an overdecorated office worrying over digital piracy and disgruntled employees.

"Not interested," Garrison said.

"I think you might be."

Garrison raised an eyebrow at the man's presumption. His fingers began to twitch.

"From what we've been able to glean about you…" David

Johansson continued. "I think you are a man who lives for the game."

And there it was. That all important key word. *The game.* The great game, of course, was over. Garrison still mourned it. There was nothing more exhilarating than hunting in Moscow, finding a crack in their defenses and exploiting it. There were other games—and though he suspected he'd never find them as enlivening as the one he'd cut his teeth on, he'd do anything to return to the fray.

So he stood on his portico and listened to David Johansson's offer. He didn't say yes. He said he'd consider it, meet with the principals and mull it over. But he knew even as he stood there with the sun sinking and the sky filling with showy color that he'd give his assent. A corner of the shroud that had seemed to cover his whole world lifted, just slightly, and began to let in some light. Yes, the next phase of his life had begun. Garrison would have to discover his hobbies in his old age. For now, he had something to do.

CHAPTER TEN

Capitol Hill, Washington, D.C.

Rennie's car rounded the corner of Fourteenth Street and Independence Avenue too fast, just catching the light. She stamped the accelerator of her 1994 Saab 900 turbo, knowing if she could catch the next one and traffic cooperated she'd hit the rest just right and be home in a few minutes.

And then the Capitol came into view. Its impact had never diminished but its symbolism continued to shift as her relationship to her government transformed. From a place of unabashed loyalty when she was a young recruit to where she was now, trying to keep an all-encompassing cynicism at bay. Corruption inevitably existed inside any large organization, but the way it had touched her had instilled a deep suspicion of the intelligence community as it currently operated.

Unlocking the door to her apartment, Rennie realized it had

been two months since she'd spent part of a drunken night in the substation holding cell. She'd been kinder to herself ever since. Not as many nights at the bar on Pennsylvania Avenue. She hadn't begun to consider her future yet but she wasn't getting herself into any trouble.

Sitting in the Morris chair in her bedroom with her feet on the sill of the open window, enjoying the breeze and Thelonius Monk's *Brilliant Corners*, she leaned her head back and let herself drift. Ever since she discovered jazz, almost by accident, and whenever she found herself overcome by all that weighed upon her, she'd slip a disc onto the turntable and feel measurably better. Sometimes it was only a shade, enough to make her feel like her world hadn't entirely imploded. Other times, as it did now, as she gave her body a reprieve from her attempts to poison it, she felt entirely swept up, carried along upon a lifesaving raft of horns and brush sticks.

Thank you, Uncle Gerard.

Rennie had an uncle who was a jazzhead. That's what her parents had called him. Gerard had a head for something else, too, and that's what did him in at the end. When he died, his body discovered after weeks in the loft of his house where he'd gone to partake in his addiction, Rennie's parents were charged with settling his estate. The house was a disaster, hadn't been kept up in decades and almost nothing was salvageable, certainly nothing in the loft. But then there were his record albums. He had over a thousand vinyl discs in wooden crates lining the wall of the one room that seemed to be cared for more than the rest. Most of the collection was jazz with a preference for West Coast cool and hard bop. Rennie's parents had disposed of everything in the house but the discs and these they'd trucked home and stowed first in the old stand-alone garage at the end of the gravel lane that ran alongside the house and, finally, in the basement. They'd intended to sell them but like many intentions they never got around to it. After Rennie's father died and her mother decided to move into a retirement community, Rennie had helped pack up the house and ended up bringing the heavy crates home with her.

Rennie shifted in the Morris chair as "I Surrender, Dear"

came over the speakers. Other than loving how it sounded, she considered what drew her to jazz. It was full of conundrums. And it made her mind churn. Both imagining its origins and listening to it unfold, double back, toss in allusions and jump back on track—like dancing on top of a train, touching down to ground occasionally but leaping back onto the chugging car at the final moment. For the first time in—she couldn't remember how long—she didn't want a cigarette. Draped in the Morris chair, she allowed her arm to swing, tracing her fingers on the rug she'd brought back with her from Istanbul.

I surrender, indeed.

A sharp knock on the glass of her front door startled her. Rennie's apartment was in a house built in 1910 with four small rooms, one after the other shotgun style—kitchen, dining room, living room, bedroom—with aligned doors from the front all the way back to the roof deck. Her front door led down a set of rickety wooden stairs badly in need of whitewashing to a bricked courtyard. Rennie never got many solicitors, religious proselytizers, or people looking for a different house. Neither did she get many visitors, and she hoped this one had made their way to her in error. She snapped off the music and heaved herself up, feeling the tightness of her muscles.

You really need to get some exercise.

Passing through the dining room, she saw the back of a man's head through a pane of glass in her front door. He turned and as she saw the beard and then the familiar cold eyes, she froze and her heart began to pound. Her thoughts flew to her service weapon sitting uselessly in an evidence bag at the MPDC property warehouse. She suddenly regretted not keeping an additional weapon. She could be certain that Martin Garrison, the ex-CIA agent standing just fifteen feet away on the other side of her door, was armed. He was the type of man who was always armed.

"Shit."

Without thinking, she turned and ran, tearing back through the house to the bedroom. She heard the sound of breaking glass as she swung open the door to the roof deck. She turned to see Garrison—his arm through the new opening in her front door—

in one efficient motion sliding the chain and throwing the dead bolt. She didn't wait to see him push into her kitchen.

What does the bastard want?

The last time she had seen him she was handing him over to the authorities. She'd never expected to see him again. How the hell did he get here?

On the roof deck, Rennie quickly surveyed her options.

Down, up, or over?

Down meant taking a five-foot jump off the deck of her third-floor apartment and hoping she could grab onto a limb of the elm that grew along the house. Rennie looked down at the hard uneven brick she'd slam into if it went wrong. Garrison's heavy shoes sounded on the creaky wooden floor of her bedroom. He was coming fast. Glancing back into her apartment, she could just make out his shadowy form barreling toward her before she wheeled and sped across her deck, his proximity making her decision for her.

Rennie hand-vaulted over the rail onto her neighbor's deck and darted to the other side just as Garrison exploded through her screen door. With her hand on the next rail she turned and looked at him about to maneuver over her deck railing. He held no weapon. They locked eyes then.

"What do you want?" she yelled.

His glacial gaze was inscrutable and his lips parted as if he was going to speak. But then he closed them and hopped deftly over the rail. Rennie followed suit, springing onto the adjacent roof. The next few houses were utilitarian. No railings, no deck chairs. Rennie raced across them, scanning the roofline for a way down, a fire escape, anything that could get her to the street.

There were only three more houses before the end of the block and a long, dead drop to the street. She could stop and confront Garrison. But what would that mean? Talking to him? He clearly didn't want to talk. Tossing him off the edge? He hadn't drawn a weapon but that didn't mean he wouldn't. She just didn't have enough information. Why had he come for her? Revenge? If so, of what form? If he wanted to kill her he could have pulled his weapon and done it.

Rennie swerved around an HVAC unit on the deck of the last house. She was out of options. She peered up at the roof squinting into the sun.

This is madness.

"What do you want?" she yelled again. But Garrison just kept speeding toward her.

Rennie forked to the right and clambered up the rusty fire escape. Just as she grasped the last rung, she jerked her hand back in pain. At the same moment her foot slipped and she wrenched her shoulder as she caught herself from falling.

"Dammit!"

Blood poured from her fingers so fast she couldn't tell how many were cut—her whole hand throbbed. Glancing down at Garrison pounding toward her she pulled herself onto the roof, this time avoiding the corner of razor sharp metal.

The blood was coming fast as she ran and she could feel her pulse in her hand. She had to get somewhere to assess her injury. She heard the clang of metal and knew Garrison was climbing the fire escape and would be on the roof any moment. The conjoined roofs were flat except for the occasional venting unit.

Garrison was moving fast but not as fast as Rennie. She heard a clattering and turned to see Garrison falling, his arms outstretched to catch himself. Rennie lunged toward him. Even at her distance, she could see the look of panic on his face. Too close to the edge, he hit the roof and skidded, his body careening over the side. He caught the lip of the gutter with one hand. It made a sickening groan as it pulled against its moorings.

Rennie ran toward him, dropping to her knees at the roof's edge. She reached down and gripped his wrist tightly with both hands. The bleeding from her fingers had slowed but the pain in her shoulder decreased her strength.

"I get you up and this stops right now," she said.

Was she really bargaining with a man who could plummet to his death at any moment?

Garrison finally, reluctantly—how painful it seemed for him to need help—said, "Yes."

"I've got you," Rennie said through clenched teeth. "Grab my arm."

Garrison didn't hesitate. She felt a sudden pull on the wrist she held as he shifted his weight and brought his free hand up, seizing her forearm. Pain shot through her shoulder. Rennie knew she'd have one chance to get him onto the roof. She didn't have the strength for a second try.

You can do this. You come through in the end. It's what you do.

"On three," she said. She met Garrison's eyes. They were uncannily calm now. He gave her the slightest nod of assent.

"One. Two…" Rennie filled her lungs, exhaled hard and heaved on the final count. Fully engaging every essential muscle, she pulled up and back, roaring as Garrison's full weight threatened to pull her over with him. Rennie's vision tunneled as she heard the gutter giving way. With the last ounce of her strength she continued rearing back, hoisting Garrison up and over. Then she felt her back meet the roof and Garrison was rolling over her.

They lay only inches from one another, their chests heaving. Rennie propped herself up on her elbows and blinked into the sun. She inspected her hand—the blood was nearly stopped now. She glanced down at Garrison. Pulling himself up into a sitting position, he wiped debris off his sport jacket. He studied the marks of Rennie's blood encircling his wrist as if he were tinkering with the innards of a watch.

Finally meeting her eyes, he smiled. "Long time, no see."

Rennie finished taping a piece of cardboard over the broken pane in her front door. She'd cleaned and bandaged her hand. She wouldn't need stitches but the pain wouldn't be subsiding anytime soon. She grabbed two bottles of beer out of the fridge and headed back to the roof deck.

"What the hell are you doing here anyway?" she said, handing Garrison a beer. They both stood leaning against the rail.

"That's no way to greet a colleague."

"No, breaking into a colleague's apartment is a much better way."

Garrison shrugged. "A little fun. No harm intended."

"Besides… a colleague? Is that what we are?" Rennie leaned her forearms on the railing. "Hardly. We're both out of the business."

"Did you want out?"

Rennie shook her head. "You just nearly killed yourself by falling off my roof. Now we're going to have a friendly chat?"

"Aren't you…" Garrison paused. "Bored?"

Rennie shrugged in response. It wasn't quite boredom that she'd been feeling. But it was akin to it.

"So. *Did* you want out?" Garrison asked again.

Rennie wondered why she was letting Garrison question her. But something made her want to talk. She hadn't talked to anyone from the Tajikistan episode and somehow it made her feel less alone. And maybe closer to Hannah too.

"No more than you did."

Garrison dropped his chin in what she thought was meant to be a nod.

"Quite the view," Garrison said, looking westward.

Rennie nodded, taking in the dome of the Capitol looming over them.

"You've been back from Istanbul, what, four or five months now?"

Rennie turned her head toward him wondering where he was getting his information since the CIA had cut him loose. "Something like that," she said. She supposed he still had friends, contacts.

"Magnificent city, Istanbul. Did you find it so?"

"I had a lot of free time." Rennie frowned. "And a pretty good view there, too."

"Well, there's our small talk, I suppose. It doesn't appear either of us are much good at it."

Rennie knocked a cigarette out of her pack and lit it.

"Nothing to be nervous about," Garrison said in an amused tone.

Rennie cut her eyes at him. "Don't flatter yourself. I'm just impatient."

"You have somewhere important to be? You're without employment and appear to have no personal life at all. It seems to me you have all the time in the world." Garrison half-smiled. "But I'll get to my point all the same."

Cheap shots.

Garrison was trying to get under her skin but she had no intention of letting him.

"I've been hired by a private military firm," he continued. "A *very* private military firm."

Rennie forgot her irritation, her curiosity stirring. "Like Blackwater?" she said, mentioning the private military company infamous for its misdeeds in the Iraq War.

"Something like that but even more private and less openly in concert with the U.S. government."

"What? Like some kind of mercenary organization?" Rennie was ready to toss Garrison out if he suggested such a thing.

"No. Nothing like that. Nothing like that at all."

Garrison went on to tell Rennie about the organization, which was being assembled as they spoke. And he mentioned a mysterious benefactor who was funding the whole thing.

"You have to know how this sounds," Rennie said. "Shady if not completely criminal. And other than your betrayal of the CIA and your country, for that matter, I don't know anything about you. I can't think of a single reason I should trust you."

Garrison turned and leaned both hands on the rail, staring into the distance.

"Real trust is a luxury few of us have and more often than not a delusion one should never latch on to." Garrison angled back to face Rennie and shrugged. "I guess you'll have to take a gamble. Could be your only shot to get back in to it. And to do something good."

Rennie shook her head. She had a feeling Garrison wasn't often motivated by a desire to do good. "Am I ever going to find out who this benefactor is?" she asked.

"Yes. But you'll have to jump through the same hoops I did."

Rennie's curiosity was piqued. "Which are what?"

Garrison smiled slightly. "Psychological tests. A lot of them. Probing psychological tests." He raised an eyebrow at her. "And then the analysts. They've got to make sure we're not crazy."

Given the slightly crazed look on his face, she was not reassured.

"When would this happen?" Rennie took a step and crushed her cigarette into a tin balanced on the arm of the Adirondack.

"It's known you're not at the top of your game."

That's an understatement. Rennie bristled all the same.

"There will be a physical examination as well," Garrison said.

"Of what variety?"

"The same you'd have to pass if you were just entering the FBI or a police academy. The work will be primarily in the field of intelligence gathering. There may be operations, but nothing on the scale of your shenanigans in CT3."

Rennie held her tongue. The physical test would not remotely compare to her trials for CT3 but she couldn't remember the last time she'd gone for a walk let alone a run.

"And you passed this physical examination?" she asked, cutting her eyes at Garrison and the slight paunch over his belt. Though she had to admit he'd handled himself pretty well hurtling across the roof deck.

"Indeed I did," he said without emotion. But something ugly had flickered in his face for just an instant. Typical, she thought. He can dish it out but he can't take it. Then Garrison looked as if he was about to say something.

"What is it?" she asked, at once wishing she hadn't. She had an instinct that she had just stepped into a trap.

"Armin."

"What about him?" Her uneasiness ticked up several notches.

Again, Garrison appeared to hesitate. "You won't be rid of him any time soon."

Rennie felt a rush of anger and gripped the railing until the wood bit into her fingers.

Don't let him bait you.

"Don't you want to know *why* you won't be free of Armin?" Garrison asked.

"Sadist," Rennie whispered under her breath. She took a breath before she responded. "He's dead. I couldn't be much more free of him than that." She lit another cigarette and drew the smoke in slowly. She exhaled and turned to him, leveling her gaze at him. "Look, I don't care what you think about me. I don't care that you feel humiliated by what happened in that hallway in Shuroabad." Rennie leaned closer to him. "But if I'm even to *consider* working with you, the game playing has to stop." Rennie took one last drag off her cigarette and crushed it in the tin.

Garrison shrugged, unperturbed. "You have six weeks." He buttoned his jacket. "And don't worry," he said, his voice slippery. "No need to run away next time you see me. We'll have loads of fun working together."

And with the slap of the screen door, he was gone.

CHAPTER ELEVEN

Washington, D.C.

The interview with Vogel concluded, Garrison drove down Independence Avenue as fast as he dared with the ever vigilant Capitol Police everywhere. Ever since the attacks, Washington was a different city. For that matter, the United States was a different country. From 1991 to 2001, the United States had enjoyed a peace it had never known and might never know again. Garrison felt no shame that he'd been a bit bored during those years. He had still been busy, certainly, but nothing seemed to have had the stakes that the Cold War had. Garrison swung a left into the Ninth Street tunnel, now driving fast and enjoying the claustrophobia of the enclosed space. He shrugged his shoulders and stretched his neck, wondering if he pulled a muscle during his dangle from the roof. The little sprint after Vogel had been the most fun he'd had in ages.

Turning onto the G.W. Parkway, Garrison switched on the CD player. It was nearly dusk and though it wasn't the most direct route home, Garrison would often take this tour with the city unfolding before him, Ravel flowing from his speakers. *Gaspard de la Nuit.* The great impressionistic piano piece. The work was both bleak and suggestive that much more lay beneath that bleakness. Garrison wasn't the type of man to have a signature piece of music but if he did, this would be the one. It was said to have inspired Poe, especially the delicious second movement, *Le Gibet.*

Garrison wasn't as optimistic about the new venture he'd just sold to Vogel as he'd been when he stood with Crane's emissary on his portico. When he finally met Sam Crane in his Portland penthouse office—an office Garrison considered a modernist nightmare—the old spy was as cautious as he was in every element of his life. He listened and said little until he was certain Crane had the fortitude to carry this thing through. Garrison had met with him repeatedly, sometimes with Crane's wife, a plain woman of exacting intelligence and the usual useless empathy of women.

It was a risk for both of them, Garrison pardoned and formally retired and Crane having only played the game on the straight and narrow. But Crane was deadly serious and wanted to do whatever he could to save his country from dangerous elements that threatened it from within. Unfortunately, he also had the tendency to lace every worthwhile argument with a load of utilitarian nonsense.

But Garrison could see how such an operational model, functioning freely, could be useful. It wasn't unlike what the CIA did on the sly but with even less oversight. Operating outside the usual parameters guaranteed a certain degree of risk, but the Foundation was doing everything it could to mitigate it. Garrison knew that once again he would be crossing over to a place devoid of safety where he could be denounced and arrested. But what other options did he have? Even the dreaded CIA desk job was beyond his reach. Here he could believe he was doing something effective again. Crane's ideals for the greater good were beyond him—Garrison could never believe or hope for some elusive utopian future. He could only respond to immediate threats.

Morality had its place, he knew. Civilized society was born of high-minded notions. But somehow he'd always found himself on the outside. Even as a boy.

He had been born Martin Alfred Garrison and as a too-serious adolescent he could remember the moment when he looked at those three words typed at the head of an English essay due the next morning and thought, *These words, these letters composed of curves and straight lines, these marks upon a sheet of pressed cotton fibers in some way define me. Can that be all there is?*

Garrison knew his conception of himself, of his identity, was complex. He first felt true freedom when he had his initial taste of being released from the tyranny imposed upon him by his name. That was how he'd first begun to lie. As a boy, whenever he was asked his name, at least when he could get away with it, he would make something up. He would cobble together the parts from film stars.

Grant Rooney.

Jimmy Holden.

Wayne Montgomery.

But that was as far as he went. It was later that he would construct whole identities to go along with the names. Backstory, education, career, personal attachments. He never felt freer than when he wasn't himself.

Garrison's path to the CIA was not the usual one. At the time he was recruited, the CIA was populated by third-generation Ivy Leaguers. Garrison had entered a master's program at Yale from a tiny college in Tennessee that was barely hanging onto its accreditation. That had been his first success, scrabbling out of the vocational school that was the pinnacle of accomplishment in his hometown.

He endured his early life in a farmhouse in western Tennessee along the Mississippi border. There seemed to be a thread stitched through his family that strangled any potential. There was susceptibility to drink, there were half-wits, and there was madness. Garrison saw much too much before he was ten years old. There were his cousins, boys he accompanied into the woods where they lured and trapped animals and prolonged their pain. There were his uncles and his father, who smoked and drank and groped any girl near them, kin or no. His mother he had never known. He'd sometimes listened to his aunts in the kitchen and he took two truths away from all he heard—that for all their desire for them, women despised men. And they'd do anything in the world to hold onto them.

Now, *Martin Alfred Garrison* was only three cryptic words upon a page and meant almost nothing to him. When he thought of himself, when he spoke to himself, he used no name, not even a pronoun. His wife was dead. He had no personal acquaintances. Only his son still roped him to the singularity of self that he presented as Martin Alfred Garrison. The only identifier that made any sense to him was that of actor, of operator—one whose sole purpose was to effect some course of events. He did have enough of a sense of himself as an inhabitant of the world that he hoped any effect he created at the very least didn't make things worse.

Garrison turned up the volume on the CD player. Vogel had called him a sadist. Had he been cruel to her by his allusion to Armin? Yes, he supposed he had. He had wanted to hurt the woman who had shown him his age, that he could no longer handle himself in any situation where physicality was required. Perhaps he should have argued for her exclusion.

No. He would sweep the grain of animus he still had for her into one of the dusty corners of his mind. It was only a grain after all and needn't chafe him unless he chose to allow it.

He'd had low expectations about his meeting with Vogel. He'd balked when he'd been urged to be the one to approach her. And though he had been instructed to set up the meeting in advance he had declined their suggestion. The Foundation was nothing if not bursting at the seams with psychiatrists, psychologists, psychoanalysts. But Garrison discounted the men and women of those questionable sciences and had wanted to see how Vogel would react to him turning up on her doorstep.

Now that the meeting had taken place, Garrison had no clear opinion of her and it would be some time until he formed one. He hadn't intended to menace her. Though she'd understandably fled his approach, she hadn't seemed particularly rattled by him forcing his way into her apartment. Only perplexed as to his purpose. Too bad he couldn't include the incident in his report to the Foundation. No, he was certain they wouldn't approve of his tactics.

He'd made a bet with himself beforehand as to whether she'd respond with cynicism or allegiance when he played the patriotism card. He hadn't made an argument for her to accept the position based on country loyalty, he just put it out there. "Your country needs you," he'd said, as he'd said countless times in his career, convincing others to betray their homeland for the supposed betterment of it. Vogel had disappointed him and answered like a rube. He considered it to be a wholly naïve position. But perhaps it was perfunctory, like flexing a muscle. She did seem to be in the grip of some sort of psychic anguish or just crawling out of it. Garrison had seen every sort of horror this world could offer, had taken it in and moved on, so he really couldn't relate.

He swung the car to the left and took the Spout Run exit onto I-66. It would be interesting to see if the little team they were forming would turn into what Sam Crane imagined it would.

CHAPTER TWELVE

Rennie had gone back out to the roof deck after Garrison left, snagging a beer on her way through the kitchen. Sitting in the Adirondack below the illuminated Capitol as the light of the day began to fail, she touched the St. Catherine medallion at her neck. It had been given to her as a child by her father. She wasn't entirely certain what it represented to her. But she did, without forethought, raise her hand to it on occasion. She leaned her head back on the hard chair. She felt staggered by Garrison's visit and his offer, his tentative offer. And excited. Though at first she'd been skeptical.

"I don't believe you," she'd said when he had offered a brief outline of the group he was representing. It sounded too much like a pipe dream. Rennie knew that there were a handful of private security firms that had their own agenda, that launched their own operations. But these weren't typically on American soil and Rennie had always considered such activity to be a dangerous kind of meddling. "I don't believe this thing can work."

"Then believe in what is asked of you," he'd said. "The mission, your assignments will be presented to you with absolute clarity. Nothing will be kept from you. This won't be like before. I know your job in Tajikistan was a fool's errand. But this can work. You'll come to believe it too."

Rennie had visibly flinched at his description of that time. *A fool's errand.*

"Here you will have every resource you require—including uncensored intelligence at your service. The organization is in its infancy but it will grow quickly and efficiently. You'll soon see that our only constraints are the inherent difficulty of our goals." He'd leaned toward her then. "Your country needs you, Vogel."

Rennie did believe him or, at least, suspected she might come to in time.

She lit a cigarette and pulled on it with a longing that she knew meant she would be leaving it behind soon. The late nights and all that went with them had pulled her down, worn away at her health and done nothing good for her brain. Even in the midst of it, she'd always told herself that there would be a reversal. That the day would come when she would just stop. Stop living the lie that she was a woman who allowed herself to wallow in drink, who allowed inertia to muddy her mind and turn her body to mush. She supposed that day had come. She thought again about what Garrison had said.

You'll believe…

She stayed up late that night. She drank and smoked and stared at the sky. She even thought of things she hadn't often dared to since Tajikistan. Of Hannah. Of her team. And, yes, of Ahmad Armin.

You'll believe…

The next morning, though her body begged against it, Rennie woke before the sun and dragged the rowing machine out onto the roof deck. She wiped down the rail and oiled the chain. Then she stood tall and stretched her arms wide. She moved her head from side to side, feeling the tightness in the shoulder she'd wrenched on the fire escape. It would take time, forcing her body back into shape.

Six weeks.

She wondered if the time was arbitrary or if Garrison had an insight into her, knowing she thrived on discipline and order and fulfilling expectations.

Rennie settled herself on the seat of the machine and slipped her feet onto the foot boards, pulling the straps tight. She rowed for twenty minutes, pulling hard with each stroke until her skin was slick with perspiration and the sky began to lighten. She felt the old familiar burn in her shoulders and legs and pulled harder. With each contraction of muscle she began the slow journey back to herself. She didn't transcend the pain in those twenty minutes. But maybe tomorrow, or the next day, she'd get to the place where she could just go and go forever. This is how it begins, she thought. Stroke by stroke, the resurrection of her body would keep the demons bound and gagged, murmuring incoherently.

CHAPTER THIRTEEN

Six weeks later
Herndon, Virginia

Waiting for traffic to inch forward, Peyton Virgil drummed his fingers on the steering wheel of his Alfa Romeo. Under ideal conditions it took ten minutes to get from the CIT building's underground garage to the departures corral at Dulles Airport.

"At this rate it would be faster to abandon the damn car and trek the five miles on foot," he muttered.

He checked his watch again. He was very close to missing his flight. Crane would be expecting a thorough briefing bright and early the next morning. Virgil wanted nothing more than to point his car in the opposite direction. Go home, have dinner with his wife and get a good night's rest.

It had taken some convincing to get Jackie to agree to the move back to D.C. The move to Portland had been bad enough.

But after initial complaints about the dearth of other black people, an inferior opera and the weather, of course, the little city had grown on her. When it came down to it, nothing would ever make her perfectly happy except living in Manhattan again. But at least being back in D.C. was allowing her to return to her other great love—politics.

Virgil sighed and shifted his six-foot-four frame. At last traffic was beginning to move. Maybe he'd make his flight after all. He would have liked to have handled Rennie Vogel's selection interview in D.C. and had argued for it. He hated to be flying back and forth to Portland and wanted to settle into the house he and Jackie had just bought in Shaw. A grin spread over his face. He *was* glad to be back in D.C. Shaw had been the African-American cultural and intellectual mecca before the great migration north and Virgil had never wanted to live anywhere else.

But Crane was right—Crane Technologies had the facilities and the staff in Portland to handle the interview process. No need for redundancies at this stage of the game. He and Crane had always had the most collegial relationship even when they disagreed—and though that wasn't rare, it was always in the spirit of worthwhile debate. They'd never been petty or grandstanded with one another. Not even once. It was a true partnership. Virgil chuckled as he remembered his skepticism when he first met Crane.

Virgil was a man most people—except maybe the street corner boys with their jeans hanging off their asses—would consider stylish. He liked his Kangol caps and good rough wools and buttery soft Italian shoes. Crane, on the other hand, tall and bony, made only a few concessions to fashion, if it could be called that, in his eyewear and the quality of his cotton. He persisted in wearing khakis every single day though they were perhaps less wrinkled now than in their early days together. A polo shirt and sport jacket rounded out his wardrobe.

Despite his lack of style, Crane quickly won him over. Now one of the wealthiest men in the world, Crane had made his fortune on brains and serendipity. And a particular intellectual entrepreneurialism colliding with a culture's readiness for a monumental technological advance in bringing security systems into being that helped safeguard the Age of Information.

Virgil had never once stopped feeling fortunate for being picked by Crane. Though he was ashamed to admit it, it had always scraped against his ego that his wife—with her partner's salary in an international law firm—outearned him. As a young man, he had gone from four hard years at Howard University where he had to surmount his shoddy public school education and learn to be a student, working evenings at the nearby Burger King and studying half the night to maintain his near-perfect grade point average—marred only by his shaky first semester—to a full ride at Princeton Law.

It was there that he met Jackie. And nearly fell in love at the first glimpse of her striding across the Yard, tall and dignified in her bearing. She'd scoffed at his initial attempts to capture her interest. A daughter of the black elite in upper Manhattan, she admitted later, "Yes, I was a snob back then." But her better instincts won out and though Virgil had never vacationed on the Cape, his perseverance finally paid off.

The law had interested him only as it pertained to crime and his goal: to enter the Metropolitan Police Academy and work his way to the top in hopes of turning around his beloved but troubled city. That D.C. was the blackest city in America was not lost on him. *This* would be his work, *this* would be his activism. After achieving part of that dream, in the summer of 1985 it all changed.

Virgil was assigned to a joint task force that included members of the FBI, CIA and Metropolitan PD. His performance and professionalism and exacting intelligence were noticed by the Feds and before he knew it, he was handing in his resignation to Metropolitan Police and driving south to begin training at The Farm.

Life in the CIA had been hard for him at first. He was a consummate family man and a bit of a homebody. He hated being away from Jackie. She'd already sacrificed a lot to follow him to D.C., which she considered a provincial backwater. Something she never let him forget.

He was sent to Somalia and was a natural at recruiting assets for the CIA. But then his old boss retired and his promotions and assignments stagnated. He was never sure if it was the color of his skin or just a basic personality conflict with his station chief, but then he met Crane who made a persuasive case for leaving the CIA. His role with Crane promised to be important and fulfilling and it was. As Crane's head of security, he eventually became his right-hand man. He'd entered the organization at a time when their caché was exploding on Wall Street and Virgil's stock options had made him a very wealthy man.

At fifty-five, he was in perfect shape and not nearly ready to slow down. He still planned, upon retirement, to focus his energies on his hometown. But when Crane called him into his office one cloudy day in June last year, again everything had changed.

"When you first came aboard," Crane had told him, "I wasn't much more than a kid. I saw how you kept your life balanced with a steady professionalism I knew I had to acquire to succeed in this game. You became a kind of mentor to me."

Virgil smiled, cocking an eyebrow. "It sounds like you're putting me out to pasture."

"Indeed, no."

Virgil had sat with Crane that day, no computers, no desks, just two men sitting across from one another, leaning forward, their elbows on their knees, in a huddle. Then Virgil had taken a deep breath, stood and paced as he listened to Crane outline what he considered to be a wildly radical venture.

Crane had already poured millions into the arts and established organizations, meeting places where people could come together and discuss ideas—political, literary, philosophical. He'd also established a think tank, the Foundation for Liberal Democracy, whose goal was to influence policy, issue papers every quarter and operate within the usual strictures. Using the technology his company had developed, the think tank focused on what Crane saw as the most dangerous threat to his country—extremist elements, religious and nationalistic, outside and inside American borders.

The data that emerged from the Foundation's work led him to consider *doing* something about the problems they outlined.

The analysts considered the consequences and ethics of such a course. These were the meetings where minutes weren't taken, when the room was swept for security intrusions. It began simply and organically, possible solutions to a series of threats that were receiving short shrift as the intelligence agencies focused their attention on al Qaeda and Iraq. Crane began tapping old contacts. One of those contacts set everything in motion. Two weeks later, Crane was calling Virgil up to the penthouse and informing him that they now had an operations division of the Foundation.

"Operations?" Virgil had said incredulously. "And you want me to run this thing?"

"We will have a silent partner that you will be in very close contact with."

Virgil had sat down in his usual place across from the man he sometimes thought of as a son. "You're crazy. You *do* know that, don't you?"

Crane didn't smile. "Ella thought so too."

"Of course she did," Virgil said. Ella Crane was the most logical, rational person he'd ever known and more times than not, her opinion counted more than anyone else's—his and Sam Crane's included.

"But she doesn't anymore," Crane added with a grin.

The two men locked eyes then and Virgil was certain each of them saw fear in the other's.

"Ella agrees," Virgil said aloud. It was somewhere between a statement and a question. "All right then."

And that was that.

Virgil shook his head at the recollection as he swung the Alfa into the overnight parking lot and collected his ticket. He slid the car into a spot and grabbed his overnight bag. Inside was the file he'd review on the plane on the woman who might become the final member of their nascent team.

CHAPTER FOURTEEN

Devils Lake, North Dakota

Cainkiller gripped the steering wheel tighter as he felt the razor blades wending their way through his veins like Pac-Man hell-bent on chomping every last pixilated dot. The razor blades ate the drug as they went. They needed it to live.

Waka, waka, waka...

And once they were finished with the last of the drug swimming so beautifully in his veins and in his arteries they would turn to his brain.

Veins and arteries.

And suddenly he wasn't driving a shitty car through North Dakota trying to keep from gnawing a hole in his wrist. He was sitting in ninth grade biology.

"Who can tell me the difference between veins and arteries, class?" the teacher said. The flowers on her dress were pulsing.

Cainkiller raised his hand.

"You there, with the purple Mohawk and the lip ring."

"The difference is that veins carry the drug to your brain. And arteries take it away." Cainkiller cleared his throat. "Arteries suck."

"You've almost got it, Cainkiller," she said.

Behind the wheel, he giggled at the notion of his teacher calling him Cainkiller. It felt so right.

"Veins carry the drug to your heart," she continued. She was clasping her hands together in front of the pulsing flowered dress and she was smiling, lipstick smeared over her mouth. "It's the arteries that carry the drug to your brain."

Cainkiller's face twisted and he felt tears prick his eyes. He wrenched himself from his little trip down memory lane and massaged the big artery in his neck with his thumb as if he could milk the last dregs of the drug, coaxing it upward to relieve the terrible pressure in his head.

Seeing lights for the first time in thirty miles, he said, "Fuck it," and pulled off the highway. He swung into a parking slot, his vision so blurred from his need of the meth that he couldn't tell where he was. But none of it mattered. Nothing mattered. And now that he'd made the decision to no longer deny himself, he took his time.

So many broken promises.

"Waaa, waaa, waaa," he said, mocking himself and leaned forward and slipped the vial from under the mat.

At least you haven't started smoking it again.

Fifteen minutes later Cainkiller pushed through the windowless door of what he could see was a roadside bar now that the meth had cleared his vision. Inside it was dark, the lights low, the neon of beer ads floated, one melding into the next each time he blinked. He envisioned each of them as a tiny red-hot brand imprinting itself permanently on the soft tissue inside his skull.

"You wanna drink or you just going to stand there all night?"

Cainkiller shook off the last of his stupor and forced himself to focus. He was still standing, squinting, just inside the door of the bar. The bartender spoke to him again.

"You all right, man? I won't serve you if you're already wasted."

Suddenly everything snapped into place. He shouldn't have gotten out of the car until the drug had done its work. But it was nice to be standing up when it hit him. Something about blood flow maybe. He felt himself...*growing*. His arms and legs, everything expanding until he towered over everybody and everything. It was the best feeling in the world. Cainkiller grinned at the bartender. "No worries, my friend. I'm not even close."

CHAPTER FIFTEEN

Rennie leaned over, her hands on her knees, breathing hard. She'd pushed herself on her run tonight. Along with her rowing regimen and working with free weights in her apartment, she ran at least a few nights a week. Usually about five miles from home to the Capitol across to the Lincoln Memorial and back. If it was a quiet night for the tourists—typically only when it rained or was bitterly cold—she'd pause at the memorial and climb the steps.

A temple. Yes. For a country where nothing was more sacred than the rule of law, civil society and separation of church and state. It never failed to move her. Before jogging back down the steps she would stand, Lincoln at her back and gaze through the two central columns at the proud monument and its shimmering reflection, the Capitol in the distance.

This night, knowing that soon a new stage of her life

would begin—she was to fly to Portland on Friday—that image resonated even more deeply than usual. She only wanted to serve her country in the most direct and honest way she could—the irony wasn't lost on her that she would be doing so outside of any official U.S. umbrella.

With one last look over her shoulder at the man's austere visage, Rennie jogged down the marble steps and took off at a full run with a wave to the parks employee whose head jerked up as she shot by.

When Rennie unlocked the door to her apartment, she could see the light on her answering machine blinking in the dark. There was no message, just a heavy sigh and a hang up. Rennie shook her head. No one could sigh as distinctively and recognizably as her Aunt Laurel. Her mother's sister, Laurel, was a strange and wild woman who had spent most of the sixties and part of seventies braless and barefoot on one commune or another in New Mexico and Arizona. She returned from her final experiment in the counterculture in seventy-six, bought forty-three acres in North Carolina, remained deliberately unmarried, and lovingly cared for a horde of chickens and peafowl. She seemed wholly content. Growing up, Rennie had visited her on her hilltop farm and most times she wished she could have stayed.

Punching in the familiar number on the cordless, Rennie had a suspicion—something about the tenor of that sigh—that this was not just a pleasure call. Laurel, who didn't have an answering machine, picked up, slightly breathless, after almost fifteen rings.

"Oh, Rennie, it's been too, too long."

Rennie smiled at the comforting cadence of her drawl.

"You still with the government?"

This was a joke between them. Laurel still carried a deep distrust of any political entity, though these days she only thought about her precious fowl and didn't give politics a second's thought.

"No, you'll be glad to know, I've finally entered the private sector. I'm doing consultation on security matters for a think tank." This wasn't entirely accurate but it would do for now.

"Hot damn and hallelujah! I always knew you'd get your head straightened out—so to speak."

Though she couldn't see her, Rennie could hear her aunt's wink in her voice. Laurel was, perhaps, Rennie's only truly liberal relation and was always attempting, without success, to get her niece to open up about her romantic life. But Rennie, private to the end, ignored her remark.

"Let's not talk about work. Tell me how you've been."

They caught up as they always did, Rennie mostly listening and laughing. But then they lapsed into an unusual silence.

"I heard from your mother."

So, this is it.

Rennie didn't respond for a long moment. Finally, she said, "And?"

"She wants to talk to you, to see you, actually."

"So, she calls you?"

"I know. But she didn't think you'd respond to her directly after the way things have been."

"What does want?"

"I don't know. But she's an old woman. Maybe she's ready to make amends."

"I'll believe it when I see it."

Rennie hadn't spoken meaningfully with her mother since the afternoon of her father's funeral. When Rennie had helped her move several years later, their conversation was kept to practicalities. Never a warm woman, when Mary Vogel understood that Rennie would never be a good Catholic girl— marrying a nice boy, settling down and raising a bunch of kids— she shut her out so completely that when she spoke to her only daughter, she would not meet her eye but focus her gaze just to the right of her. For years—they only saw one another at Easter and Christmas—this single detail, her mother's averted gaze, wormed its way deep into the part of Rennie that was rarely touched: rage. At that last Christmas, after too many eggnogs overspiked by her brothers, she'd wanted to reach out and grab her mother by the head and yell, *Look at me! I'm your daughter.*

She never went back. There were a few awkward telephone conversations after that, the last one when Mary called to say she had finally sold the house. Though she was mostly packed and ready, the house hadn't lured a buyer as quickly as anticipated and Mary had refused to leave it empty, postponing her move to a senior Catholic community in Virginia. Her voice on the phone was clipped, saying she was sending, by post, a box of Rennie's things she had found tucked in a forgotten corner of the basement. They lived six blocks from one another. And then, long years of silence. At times, Rennie almost forgot Mary Vogel existed.

The retirement community was several hours from the city and Rennie tried, and failed, to keep her mind blank as she drove, tried not to anticipate what news could be so important that her mother wouldn't tell her over the phone.

It must be bad.

Rennie swallowed hard. Though they had no relationship to speak of, she couldn't bear the thought that she might be ill.

Just outside of Harrisonburg, Rennie turned the Saab down a long gravel drive. In the parking lot, she switched off the engine and sat listening to it click as it cooled.

Okay.

Inside, she stopped at the public restroom and washed her hands and face before taking the stairs to the second floor and lightly tapping the knocker at Room 27. She heard motion inside and jerked her head down the hallway, thinking she could make it to the stairwell before the door opened.

You're a coward.

And then Mary Vogel was before her, small and birdlike yet seeming indestructible, telling her to come in, not meeting her eyes. Rennie accepted her offer of coffee, thinking they'd both appreciate having something to do with their hands.

Finally, they were seated, at an angle to one another, in

matching slipcovered wing chairs. Mary Vogel began to speak without preamble. "I thought you should know I am going to remarry."

Rennie breathed an internal sigh of relief. "I'm glad for you," she said automatically. But something shifted inside her. She'd had a mostly happy childhood. Though she sometimes felt isolated in her big family, never joining in as her rambunctious brothers tore around the house, she had felt safe and enveloped within the family dynamic. That had shattered with the sudden death of her father thirteen years ago. Even though she hadn't been the kind of daughter to come home for family dinners on Sunday, she had still felt herself a part of them. And now this. The rift between her and her mother would undoubtedly stretch even wider.

"You are, of course, invited to the wedding. It will be very small, just close family and a few particularly dear friends." Mary Vogel drew her fingernails across the arm of the chair in a rhythmic pattern. "But I would prefer that you don't attend." She didn't pause. "I will make appropriate excuses."

Stunned, Rennie couldn't think how to respond. She sat for a long moment, rubbing her palms on her jeans, a lock of dark hair shielding her eyes.

"I *am* very busy with work right now," she finally said, unsure why she was propping up her mother's…what was it? Insult? Snub? Slap in the face?

"Yes, I thought you might be." She said it almost as an accusation. As if she hadn't just made it clear that Rennie's presence was unwanted and that, now, Rennie was ignoring her family responsibility.

Rennie shook her head in disbelief, her chest so constricted that her head swam.

"Before you go, I have something for you."

Mary Vogel handed Rennie a handkerchief drawn together and tied with a blood-red velvet ribbon. Rennie could feel something cool within as it rested in her hand. She pulled an end of the ribbon.

"I thought you could wear it next to the St. Catherine your father gave you," she said. Rennie couldn't read her tone.

Inside the handkerchief was a Catholic medallion, but Rennie was so shaken that its image was only a blur.

Then for the first time in years, Mary Vogel, soon to be Mary McConnell, allowed her eyes to meet Rennie's.

"You must fight against whatever is disordered inside of you, Reneé."

The child within Rennie crawled into her throat.

Do not cry.

Rennie said nothing, holding her mother's gaze, as anger swelled inside her.

Her mother finally looked away into the air just to Rennie's right.

"I wish you well," she said as Rennie rose to leave.

In her car in the parking lot, the top down—it was a perfect day, no chance of rain—Rennie hunted furiously under the seat until she found a crumpled package with two bent cigarettes inside. She lit one and pulled on it ferociously, her heart pounding.

She turned her face to the sky. Feeling the sun's warmth, she began to calm. She remembered her mother's gift and reached into her pocket and pulled out the handkerchief—she wasn't sure what had happened to the ribbon. Unfolding it, she picked up the medallion. It was old and Rennie recognized it as one of many her mother had acquired over the years—she was a collector of sorts. This one was of St. Jude.

Rennie leaned her head back and closed her eyes. She had always been a good student. Perfect grades in all her courses, not the least of which was catechism class. St. Jude, she remembered, was the patron saint of hopeless causes.

Suddenly, she stuffed the medallion and the handkerchief back in her pocket and jammed the key in the ignition, tearing out of the parking lot, gravel flying, onto the winding, shaded road. She drove too fast, throwing the gears, making the car perform as it hadn't in years, deftly maneuvering the curves as if she were gulping down the road.

By the time she reached the highway back to the city, she

was calmer. When she got home, she sat on her bed and looked at the medallion again, thinking of unclasping her St. Catherine pendant and slipping the St. Jude next to it, as was her mother's wish. Instead, she folded it neatly inside the thin white cotton handkerchief and placed it in the corner of the top drawer of her dresser, to be retrieved another day.

CHAPTER SIXTEEN

Portland, Oregon

Rennie took a deep breath as she stepped out of the terminal, glad to be free of the canned air of the airplane. She wondered if she was imagining it but there was something of the scent of the sea. She set her bag on the concrete and rotated her shoulders, working out the kinks from sitting for six hours. It was hotter than she'd expected. She tilted her face to the sky and felt her skin warm. She took another breath. She hadn't smoked regularly in six weeks and her lungs were already clearer.

Time to reenter the world.

She felt good and strong. And perhaps more importantly—ready. Ready to recommit herself to a life of effectiveness. Ready to get back to what she was good at.

What is it exactly that you do?

Rennie shook her head at the prospect of defining such a

thing just as a black Chevy Suburban with tinted windows rolled to a stop and double-parked a few paces in front of her. An imposing man with a shaved head, wearing aviator glasses and a black suit, exited the vehicle holding a placard with the alias the still shadowy organization had assigned her for her travel.

Beth Forrest.

Rennie waved to the driver and picked up her bag. She hoped if she was hired on she wouldn't be stuck with "Beth."

"I am Evgeni," the driver said as he took her bag and stowed it in the rear of the Suburban. Rennie didn't detect any accent.

On the twenty-minute drive into the city to her hotel, she leaned her head back and tried not to think about the next few days. She couldn't know yet if this would be the right position for her. But she had hope. And this was a step in the right direction. Meet with them, find out more about the organization and decide if there was a place with them for her. Ever since Garrison stood with her on her roof and made his unexpected offer, she'd had a lot of time to consider what she wanted to do with her life. She'd never been one to think in terms of career. She never considered her working self as distinct from her personal life. It was all interwoven so thoroughly that she sometimes wondered if she had left any room for a self that existed outside of her work. Perhaps she was like a worker ant, meant to trudge along single-mindedly fulfilling her role. Whatever that was.

What must it be like to just 'be'?

She'd always had expectations of herself. It was hard to imagine a life with a regular job. Sitting at a desk, a cog in a machine oiled by the assurance of the next paycheck. A trace of a smile twisted one corner of her mouth. Government was certainly a bureaucracy, the intelligence community was certainly a machine, one that chuffed and wheezed and sprang leaks and vomited springs and loose bolts as it hobbled along. You didn't want to stand too close. Or you might get hurt.

Rennie opened her eyes. She glanced at the shielded eyes of the driver in the rearview mirror. She sensed he was looking at her. She reached into her messenger bag and slipped on her own sunglasses, pressed a button on the armrest and lowered her window. She propped her elbow on the door and let the cool breeze trail through her fingers. Yes, it was good to be back to the form of herself that she recognized. An image of Hannah sleeping quietly in the hotel in Dushanbe swept through her mind and her stomach flip-flopped.

Soon she'd have to do something about Hannah. What, she didn't know. Find out that she was well at the very least.

The driver swung the car into the drive of the hotel, coming to a neat stop. Handing her her bag just outside of the lobby, he said, "I hope your stay is to your liking."

Rennie raised her eyebrows in response. And odd thing to say, she thought. Or maybe just awkward.

"You are not to eat breakfast in the morning," he continued. "You'll be fed after your blood sample is collected."

Rennie nodded.

"I'll be here at seven a.m. sharp," he said closing the door.

In her room, Rennie stretched and then ran the shower hot and cold, feeling the fatigue from the trip evaporating from her body. She dressed in a fitted gray microfiber short-sleeved shirt and a light pair of black pants. Ten minutes later, after a brief call to the concierge for a recommendation, she was running along a gravel path in a park near the hotel. Though the light was fading, the evening was still warm as the path wound through trees that alternately provided shade or open spaces where the sun broke through. The air felt good flowing through her still damp hair. She still wasn't quite in top form but she was close. She only hoped she hadn't done any permanent damage to her body in the time she'd allowed herself to let go. She picked up her pace and pushed herself harder. The sound of her shoes on the gravel was rhythmic and comforting. The burn soon began in her thighs and she knew she'd have to focus there when she had time for weights. She glanced at her watch. Three and half minutes and the burn had evolved into something else. Something bearable. Almost pleasurable.

There were exercise stations along the path—wooden and steel structures for sit-ups, pull-ups, balancing and stretching.

Rennie smiled as she blew past a set of monkey bars. Her CT3 training winged through her mind and she turned and ran back toward them. There were, maybe, twenty rungs. Rennie didn't pause as she leapt to the top step and then upward, jumping and grasping a bar, one-handed, and swinging on to the next, negotiating them so quickly she never felt the full weight of her body. At the end she swung off the last rung, landed squarely in the dirt and kept running. Yes, she was ready for some action.

The building Evgeni delivered Rennie to the next morning was marked with the slightly ominous title *Corporate Solutions*. A slight shiver raised the fine hairs on the back of her neck. Evgeni, as taciturn as he'd been during their drive from the airport, led her down a long, carpeted hallway with subdued lighting emanating from sconces along the wall. The driver rapped lightly on a door marked Anthony Marietta, M.D., Psy. D.

Rennie heard a deep voice from within. "Come."

"Best of luck," Evgeni said. He took off the aviator glasses and slipped them into the breast pocket of his suit. His eyes were penetratingly blue. "Don't let them get to you," he said, tapping his finger soundlessly on the nameplate where it read "Psy. D."

Inside the office, a fifty-something man, very tall and fit in a white shirt and dark pants, stood as she entered. His skin was smooth and brown, his close-cropped black hair peppered with gray. He took a step forward and grasped her hand.

"Rennie Vogel. Thank you for coming all this way. This is Dr. Marietta. He'll help to guide you through the testing," he said, gesturing to the doctor, a stocky man in a shirt and tie. He didn't offer his own name and Rennie knew better than to ask.

He asked her how things were in the District. His warm smile suggested he might have a connection to the city.

"I'll leave you to it then," he said, clapping his hands once. "If you have any questions or concerns, Dr. Marietta should be able to take care of anything you need." He shook her hand again, holding it a beat longer than was customary. "Good luck."

And then he was gone. Rennie rued this somehow. His had

been a comforting presence. Dr. Marietta, on the other hand, exuded a manner that instantly set her off-kilter.

"Sit, please." He gestured to one of the chairs in front of his desk without looking up.

Rennie sat, her hands on her thighs, still sore from her run the day before, and waited. Marietta stared at his computer monitor, his finger manipulating the scroll wheel of his mouse. Rennie scanned the office. It was dim and there were no personal effects. At all. Not even a cup of coffee or a bottle of water on his desk. His lab coat was draped across the back of his chair and the sight of his arms, pale and soft, emerging from his short-sleeve shirt, made her think he rarely saw the light of day. He was balding and what hair he had he wore longish, oiled and combed severely back against his pate.

"All right then," he said, finally turning to her and folding his arms on the shiny surface of the desk. "So it begins."

What the hell does that mean?

In the pause that followed, a disconcerting smile spread across his mouth. Something defensive rose up in Rennie. She had expected mind games during her interview process but she hadn't anticipated any would occur outside of the polygraph. When she didn't respond to his ambiguous remark, his false smile faded and he handed her a sheet of paper.

"This is your schedule for the *next* two days. But there may *need* to be—" he paused, the strange smile returning, as if he were searching for a word "—adjustments here and there." Marietta emphasized certain words as he spoke, seemingly at random, imbuing his speech with a disjointed rhythm that made Rennie scramble to unravel his meaning. She wondered if it was an idiosyncrasy or a deliberate attempt to unsettle her.

Rennie glanced at the schedule which only indicated blocks of time and room numbers. She breathed in deeply, frustrated, but decided to play along. "I'll be as flexible as you need me to be."

"That's very good of you. A fine quality in an employee."

Is he kidding? Rennie stifled the desire to roll her eyes and only nodded.

"You haven't broken your fast?"

It took a moment for Rennie to grasp his meaning. "Correct."

"Good. Please direct yourself to the lab. There is a map of the facilities stapled to your schedule."

Marietta stood and handed her a thick folder. "After the *thorough* physical exam, you'll be fed. These forms should occupy the rest of your day. The initial fifteen or so documents are background. Each question must be addressed thoroughly as it has direct bearing on *your* security clearance."

No kidding, Rennie thought.

"The rest *of* the forms are your *psychological* assessment. You'll meet with Dr. Hauser tomorrow after *the* fitness exam."

"And what about the day after?"

Dr. Marietta looked away and shuffled through some papers on his desk. He raised his eyes to hers. "That *depends* on how things go today and tomorrow."

"And the polygraph?"

The doctor glanced at his watch. "The examiner *is* very busy. He'll fit you in *when* he is able."

Rennie reached out to shake his hand, guessing his response. He didn't disappoint. Ignoring her hand, he dipped his head, averting his gaze and turned back to his desk. Psy. D. indeed, she thought.

In the hallway, Rennie peered at the blurry map and realized it was useless. It didn't even seem to be for the building she occupied. It appeared that her interview process would be a game of wits meant to determine how easily she rattled, as well as whether she was hiding anything damaging or if she was mentally unstable. The polygraph would be the most harrowing. The device itself—as a lie detector at least—was famously unreliable. But that wasn't the point. The polygrapher was trained to use the machine to intimidate and unsettle the subject. It was nothing less than psychological warfare—some would call it torture— and it was the make-or-break moment for many trying to pass into the more sensitive regions of the government. This wasn't the government but Rennie assumed the Foundation wouldn't go any easier on its applicants—if they did she'd question their seriousness. But that didn't mean she was looking forward to it. A lot of things had happened to her since she went through the polygraph as a fresh FBI recruit and she wasn't confident that the experience would help her here.

She held the worthless map and thought for a moment. *Building codes.* Rennie jogged down to the end of the hall and examined the map affixed to the wall by the fire stairs.

Perfect.

At the lab there was nothing unusual in her physical exam. Her blood was drawn, her blood pressure taken, her hearing and vision were tested. The young female doctor was professional though not particularly friendly. Rennie wasn't surprised when, after her medical evaluation, she was delivered to a windowless room to begin her paperwork. They certainly could have provided her with something less spartan if they had wanted her to be comfortable. But they clearly didn't want her to be comfortable. She was told her breakfast would be brought to her there. It wasn't.

Several hours later, she had finished her background information and begun to work on the psychological tests. They were standard, which meant they were both lengthy and maddeningly repetitive. Being famished and verging on light-headedness—due to the eight vials of blood they'd drawn—she hurried through them faster than was probably prudent.

When she flipped the final sheet over onto the thick stack she'd already completed, she stood and braced herself against the edge of the table, trying to shake off the inertia she felt. She had no idea what time it was. Her watch had been removed during the physical exam and hadn't been returned to her. Stepping out into the hallway, she strained to hear any nearby movement. All was silent, unnervingly so. She passed down to the end of the hall, rounded the corner and tapped on Dr. Marietta's door. When there was no response she made her way back to the lab, but even before she reached the heavy door she could see that no light illuminated the white strip of paper covering the narrow window and obstructing a view into the room.

It must be late.

Pushing through the exit doors she had entered so many hours ago she saw Evgeni leaning against the dark Suburban, his arms crossed.

"Doesn't look like you had much fun," he said, opening the door for her.

"Not much, no," she said. She got into the backseat and leaned her cheek against the cool window. Rousing herself she said, "This typical for the first day?"

"I'd say so," he said. "They like to see how you perform under compromised circumstances."

"I'm guessing it's only going to get worse tomorrow."

Evgeni didn't respond. He only turned his head so she could see the slight smile on his face. He leaned over and she heard him open the glove compartment. "Hungry?" he said and tossed her an energy bar.

In her room at the hotel, she ordered the biggest offering of meat on the menu—a T-bone—with everything that came with it. She was so ravenous she even ordered a glass of milk like a twelve-year-old boy. When the meal arrived, she ate it much too quickly and hoped it wouldn't make her sick. She would have liked to go for a run, but she knew she didn't have the energy.

She took a hot shower, luxuriating in being completely comfortable for the first time that day. She thought about the methods that intelligence organizations used to weed people out—intimidation, stress, exhaustion. She supposed it was necessary. But that didn't mean a part of her didn't resent it. She toweled off in the steaming bathroom and fell into bed and into a deep, dreamless sleep.

CHAPTER SEVENTEEN

Capitol Hill
Washington, D.C.

Instead of climbing the steps as she usually did, Hannah rode the escalator up to street level at Union Station. She was late for her meeting with Tommy Damone. But she was in no hurry to get there. Tommy was freelance but had a regular gig for *The New Yorker* covering international politics. Lucky bastard, she thought. He'd been with Reuters—which was how she knew him—but after posting one explosive piece after another, he knew he could write his own ticket and had moved on. Hannah had called him a week before, wanting to meet and pick his brain. She figured if anyone would throw her a bone, Tommy would. What she hadn't expected was for him to start asking questions about Tajikistan. Which was why she was now standing under the cover of the west arcade of the grand train station listening to a melancholy trumpet reverberate off the high marble ceiling.

The horn was played by an old man leaning against one of the interior walls. When he finished the piece, Hannah stepped toward him.

"What was that?"

The old man lifted one milky eye to her. "That, my dear, was 'I Fall in Love Too Easily.' And I don't recommend it," he said. "The practice. Not the song."

"Good advice," Hannah said and dropped a five in his open horn case.

She slowly walked the few blocks to the restaurant on North Capitol Street. What was she willing to give Tommy of her time in Central Asia? It would all be off the record, of course, but other than the CIA and FBI investigators, who'd exhausted her with their endless questioning, she hadn't talked about that time with anyone. Most of the story she only wanted to put behind her. But parts of it were somehow hallowed to her.

Rennie. And Fareed too.

She'd have to see what Tommy had to offer.

At the restaurant, she made her way through the dining room where a five-piece band was trilling out yet more moody jazz. A round-faced boy singer who looked like he was wearing his first-ever tuxedo was pulling off a passing imitation of Chet Baker gushing out sadness and heartache from every pore. Enough with the heartstrings, she thought.

She found Tommy at a table on the roof terrace, though it was almost too cold for sitting outside. She realized she didn't have much of an appetite and ordered a dozen Raspberry Points on the half shell and a dirty martini.

"You sure that's it?" Tommy said. "The crab cakes are to die for. Really, you don't know what you're missing."

Tommy ate and drank like the long-gone generation of journalists, the ones who'd put themselves into an early grave by working too hard and giving full rein to their vices. Not that she was one to talk.

"Can I smoke out here?" she asked.

Tommy waved his fork as he chewed. "I don't see why not," he finally said.

Hannah lit her cigarette and a waiter appeared with an

ashtray. She took a few calming drags and stubbed it out. She *would* be quitting soon and for good. Just not today.

"So how are we going to do this?" she said, getting right to the point.

Tommy took a large quaff of his Gibson, capturing an onion and sucking it dry before chewing it loudly. "I've got something for you. Something that may pan out to be a front page story. I don't have one hot second to devote to it with what else I've got going on. I've got a line on a gargantuan story, but I want to do a spread on the Armin incident before I get sucked into the abyss that is and continues to be Iraq. Probably until we both retire."

"I don't know how much I can give you on Tajikistan, Tommy. Nothing can lead back to me or the Feds are going to be at my door with their fangs bared."

"Understood." Tommy leaned back and pushed his plate away. "I don't need you on the record. I just need you to steer me in the right direction."

Hannah nodded, still unsure what she was willing to give him. "Tell me what you have for me," she said, leaning forward.

"Patience, dearie, patience. I *know* you, remember. You and I go way back. Let's just say, I'd feel a whole lot more comfortable if we cover my end of things before I pass you the lead."

Hannah smiled wryly. Tommy was no fool.

Tommy heaved his bulk up and into the chair next to her, propping his feet on the seat he vacated and angling his head toward hers. "Domestic terrorism," he said quietly. "Militia wingnuts out in North Dakota. You'll love it, I promise."

"Fine," Hannah said flatly, but she was already excited about the militia angle. It was just the kind of story she was pining for.

Tommy abandoned his sprawling pose and suddenly sat up. "Good," he said, plucking a steno notebook from the inside pocket of his wrinkled glen plaid sport coat. Thrift store for sure.

"It appears that the entire team died except the lone woman who had to have made the shot. I guess you didn't see any sign of her, right, Marcus?"

"I can't recall much of anything, Tommy."

"Sure," he said, not holding back on the sarcasm. "Listen, Marcus, you've got to play nice with me here. As I said, I *know* how you are. I hate to be a hard-ass but you have to give me something, or I'm going to walk away with my Dakota story." Tommy finished his Gibson and raised a hand to the waiter. "I know who she is, Marcus. I found her." He waited for Hannah to respond but she just raised a skeptical eyebrow. "I went through the obits. In the end, I had about fifteen guys to look at. By the time I got to the fourth one, a guy by the name of Lincoln Goode, I knew I had it. Four guys. Four funerals in two and a half weeks. All FBI. I interviewed any family that would talk to me. Everyone was tight-lipped, but in that way you know they are dying to talk. Finally one did. The mother of Jonah Levin. Adopted mother, actually. She knew nothing about the assassination, obviously. But she knew about the one agent who made it out."

Hannah should have walked away from the conversation long before it had reached this point. Trading information of any kind relating to Tajikistan—if it led back to her—would bring her a world of trouble she didn't need. But it made her feel nearer to Rennie than she had since the phone call. She pushed her second martini away.

"You all right, Marcus?"

"Yeah—that whole time period…" This was always Hannah's easiest out. It didn't hurt that it was true.

He shook his head. "I can't begin to imagine. Listen, I know this probably isn't territory you're jumping up and down to unearth. But you were there. And the shooter was there. And you're the one sitting in front of me."

The shooter.

Hannah felt her stomach turn to acid as the image of the shot to Armin's head ambushed her. And Fareed. Armin's right-hand man who had wanted out as badly as she did. The shock on his face as Rennie slit his throat would haunt her forever. If only it had worked out differently. If only Rennie hadn't assumed, with good reason, that he was her guard. He would have let them go. Hell, he may have even come with them. A lump rose up in her throat and she lit another cigarette.

Meeting Tommy's eyes, she knew he couldn't wait to get back to business. She nodded. "Go ahead. Tell me what you've got."

"Okay. So, Levin's mother tells me that this woman, supposedly the fifth member of the team, attended all the funerals. Before that, Mrs. Levin said she knew her as part of the larger unit, saw her at cookouts and such, but no one knew the makeup of the team that went to Tajikistan until the funerals."

"How could they be certain then? When, surely, the other unit members also attended?"

"They knew," he said.

Hannah nodded, looking at her hands.

"Her name is Renée Vogel."

Hannah raised her head. *Renée.* Sounded like a stranger.

"She brought you out," he said, dropping the naïve act.

Hannah said nothing.

"Look, Marcus, I can imagine what constraints you're under here, but I've looked into this more than anybody and if there's one thing I know…" Tommy looked left and then right. When he spoke again, he'd lowered his voice. "This does not reflect on your competence otherwise, but there is *no* way you made it out of there on your own."

Hannah raised her eyes to him. "I barely knew her. It was chaotic. Not exactly the ideal circumstances for chitchat."

"I get that," Tommy said, nodding. Hannah could see he was almost jumping out of his skin now that he'd made some headway. "Just give me what you've got. After two months I've got almost nothing." He flipped through the pages in his notebook.

"She's local," he went on, "born and bred D.C. Capitol Hill. Working class, very Catholic parents. No known relationships with men, if you know what I mean." He glanced up at Hannah. Something in her eyes must have made him hold her gaze but he let it go and turned back to his notebook. "I can't find a clue as to what she's been up to since Tajikistan. She still rents an apartment on Capitol Hill, but I'm guessing the Feds will pull their usual funny business if they realize there are inquiries—so, I'm still holding off on approaching the neighbors."

"It doesn't really seem like you've got much."

"I know. A lot of it is circumstantial. But you know how it goes. One confirmed detail and it all falls into place." He raised his glass to her in a hackneyed show of their solidarity as reporters. Hannah forced something that approximated a smile and touched the rim of her glass against his.

"It's a great story, y'know. Aside from the obvious—more U.S. shenanigans in a Muslim country. Especially if it turns out Vogel made the kill, which everything points to that being the case." Tommy stared at Hannah, waiting for her to confirm his assumption. When her face showed nothing he shook his head. "You're a hard nut to crack, Marcus. I hate using journalists as sources. Always a pain in the ass. Anyway, it's too bad Vogel's so hard to track down. It's almost as if she knew she was going to have a career in intelligence when she was in diapers. But I did find one fairly recent photograph," Tommy said, reaching into his jacket pocket.

Hannah felt a deep calm settle over her. It was a lie that her body was able to slip into when great stress was put upon it.

Tommy produced a photograph and gazed at it, drawing his thick nail-bitten finger across its surface. Hannah couldn't read his expression but knew he was drunk, or at least on the train to getting there. Was it admiration? Respect? Lust? Whatever it was, Hannah felt territorial, something she had never experienced. Ever. Then, without a word, he offered the photo to her.

Hannah paused, thinking about what she might feel when she went home, when she was alone in her apartment. She should decline to look at it, or just pretend to look, allow her vision to blur. Then she was taking it from him.

And there she was.

Younger. The set of her mouth, perhaps more naïve. For a single, crazed moment Hannah wanted to run away with it, this unexpected treasure. Then she reminded herself she wasn't a woman who made such displays and, with one last glance, handed it back.

"I don't have anything for you, Tommy. On…Vogel. I'm sorry."

"Look, I'm offering you something here. Something

valuable. I don't want to say you owe me but…" He shrugged his big shoulders. "You owe me."

So she gave him Fareed.

Nothing about how they'd connected or how thinking about him, remembering the life pouring out of him right in front of her, made her so weak she could collapse. Nor did she tell him how kind he was, her oasis. As she, perhaps, was his. She would have liked to have told him this, so that Fareed's legacy—at least with Tommy—would be tempered by something human, but she knew he would use it. No reporter could walk away from such a gem. And he wouldn't be able to resist going on about that Stockholm Syndrome bullshit. So, she gave him the facts. Those she knew anyway.

And he told her about the Dakota Militiamen and William Keller, how they seemed to be your run-of-the-mill gun nut, government haters. "But there's something going on here. I can't explain it. It's a gut thing. I'll send you everything I've got and I'll bet you my bottom dollar you'll think the same thing."

He grabbed his bag and threw down a wad of money on the table. "But this isn't the end of the Armin conversation, Marcus. I'm being a nice guy here. I'll run with what you've given me but we're going to have to talk about Vogel. And sooner rather than later."

After he left and she sat finishing her drink, she knew that she'd been had. Or mostly. What she'd given him was as exclusive as it gets. Tit for tat. Even Steven. That was how it was supposed to be. She couldn't help but keep a tally. Call it petty, ruthless or Machiavellian—she didn't care. It was just the way her brain worked. And as she figured it, Tommy Damone owed her one.

CHAPTER EIGHTEEN

Portland, Oregon

In the ladies' locker room at Corporate Solutions the next day, Rennie draped a cool towel over her head. Dr. Marietta had pulled her aside after she stepped off the treadmill, the final exercise of the Army Physical Fitness Test—the standard test for law enforcement and intelligence officers alike. She'd eaten a small but sustaining breakfast that morning and had no trouble, breezing through the two minutes of pushups and sit-ups and the two-mile run. She'd clocked in at just under thirteen minutes when the doctor passed across her line of vision.

"A moment, Ms. Vogel."

Marietta told her Dr. Hauser, the psychiatrist, was ready for her and that she should report directly to Room 101.

"Of course, Doctor," Rennie had said, hoping her pretense of politeness was veiled.

She craved nothing more than a shower but the cool towel was better than nothing. She knew this was just another of the psychological games of the process. She would be hot and sweat-soaked when she met with the psychiatrist and they surmised, she supposed, that this might make her more vulnerable. She wouldn't be the least surprised if the air conditioning was turned on full blast.

Rennie paused in front of Room 101. *Room 101.* A coincidence? Or did the architects of the Corporate Solutions interview method have a particularly diabolical sense of humor, deliberately alluding to the torture room in Orwell's *1984* where the unlucky were presented with their worst nightmare? Rennie knocked, wondering what her own worst nightmare might be.

"Enter."

The woman inside—Dr. Hauser—was perhaps sixty years of age. Her thin blond hair was pulled back so severely Rennie wondered if she could move her eyebrows. Her razor sharp widow's peak seemed to point at Rennie menacingly.

"Sit."

Dr. Hauser wore a dated plum-colored skirt-suit. Certainly polyester, it was cinched in odd places in a misguided attempt at style. She spoke in a clipped manner as if English wasn't her native tongue. Perhaps, as her name suggested, she was German. Her office was an IKEA lover's fever dream, all blond wood and chrome accents. On the walls were art prints that looked familiar to Rennie. They were modern, exploding with color and violence. Not exactly a comfort.

"Voices," Dr. Hauser said without preamble.

Rennie took a deep breath, unsurprised that the doctor was getting to the most questionable portion of her psychological evaluation.

"Yes?" Rennie wasn't going to offer more than she had to.

"You hear voices."

"No." Rennie spoke the negative emphatically but without defensiveness.

"You answered here…" Dr. Hauser adjusted her chunky plastic glasses and peered at Rennie's paperwork. "You indicated 'True' to the statement 'I hear or have heard voices in my head.'"

"Yes, but I also checked 'False' to the statement 'I commonly hear voices without knowing where they come from.' It is true, I once did. That is, I did once. A single instance. A very long time ago when I was very young."

Years before Rennie had made the decisive error of answering truthfully to this statement in the course of her background check for the FBI. She wouldn't have answered it candidly this time around but she was certain they had access to her earlier documents.

"You have them no more?" The doctor's voice was tinged with skepticism.

"No."

"Describe."

"I can hardly remember."

"Try."

"All I can recall…" Rennie tried to cast herself back. "Is that it was like screaming."

"Screaming. What kind of screaming? Your voice? Whose?"

"I really don't remember. I'd say it was…a chaotic screaming. A woman's voice."

"Who is the woman?"

"I don't know."

"Young? Old? Can you see her face?"

Dr. Hauser spoke in the present tense, hoping, Rennie was sure, that she would slip into it herself.

"I don't recall, Doctor. It was a very long time ago."

"What were the circumstances, Miss Vogel. How old were you?"

Without thinking Rennie raised her hand to the St. Catherine medallion at her throat. "I was seventeen."

"And what was happening in your life?" Dr. Hauser used a red Bic ballpoint pen to make notes on a yellow legal pad.

"I…" Rennie swallowed.

It doesn't hurt anymore. It was a long time ago.

"I was about to leave for college." She paused. "And my father died."

"Suddenly?"

"Yes."

"And you found him?"

"No. A stranger found him in the street."

Rennie distinctly remembered the sound of the doorbell. It was old and had some kind of mechanism inside of it—a tiny hammer ringing a tiny bell. It was the classic two-tone chime except that something had gone wrong with the second tone. It had become dampened somehow, and its pitch was both muffled and off-key. Her father had kept saying he was going to take it apart and tinker with it.

She'd been sitting on the floor in her room with the door ajar playing solitaire—a complicated version involving four decks of cards—when she heard the atonal chime. And then, her mother, gasping. And a deep comforting male voice. The horror of a policeman at the door with bad news. Rennie hadn't risen but continued moving cards about on her carpeted floor, trying to free the aces. She'd always hated that carpet with its long synthetic tendrils that made her cards lie askew. She hadn't heard what the policeman said but she knew it was something horrible. Horrible and permanent. It was at that moment when the screaming began.

She'd discussed it thoroughly with a Bureau psychiatrist before she was hired. That doctor had determined with certainty that it was not a psychotic episode at all. Merely a very vivid fantastical expression of loss of control for a personality that thrived on control, as well as an explosive internal articulation of deep pain. She had no confidence that this doctor—or the next—would come to the same conclusion.

Rennie took a deep breath, the effort of speech suddenly difficult. "He was on his way home from work. He'd begun to walk instead of taking the bus. The doctor told him he needed more exercise after diagnosing his heart condition."

"So, you were at a vulnerable position in the life course and the primary male figure in your orbit left you."

"I suppose you could put it that way." Rennie detested the language of psychology.

"No boyfriend at the time?" Hauser lifted the cover of a file next to the pad. "Or now, I see." Dr. Hauser looked up at her and set her chin on her threaded fingers, elbows on the desk.

"Really, Doctor, I don't think we need to go there," Rennie said, anticipating the digression the woman was about to take.

Rennie thought she saw a trace of a smile on Dr. Hauser's lips. "I agree, Miss Vogel, I agree. Our time would be spent more fruitfully trying to get to the bottom of these voices."

Rennie said nothing.

"That medallion you keep reaching for, what is it?"

Rennie put her hand back in her lap, self-conscious.

"St. Catherine."

"And your father gave it to you?"

"He did."

"Are you a believer, Miss Vogel?"

"No. At least mostly not."

"Then what does it mean for you?"

"I would think that's obvious. It's a remembrance of my father."

"Merely that? Or does it have some other function as well?"

Rennie was beginning to feel provoked. She wanted it all to be over but she considered the question. "I think…" She reached to the medal again, felt its contours with her fingers. "I think it allows me to appeal to my better self. And it gives me courage."

Dr. Hauser looked contemplative. "I wish we had more time together, Miss Vogel. I would find it interesting to examine those notions more thoroughly. Totemism is one of my special interests."

Totemism. Rennie raised her eyebrows at Hauser's interpretation. "Are we nearly done then, Doctor?"

"We are getting close." She referred to her notebook. "So you say there has been no reoccurrence since then, when you were seventeen?"

"None."

There had been though. Only once. On the plane home from Tajikistan. Not the ideal place to have what some doctors would consider a psychotic break. In the moment, it felt alarming, but it only lasted ten, maybe fifteen minutes when she felt that a portion of her brain had been hijacked and she was powerless to do anything but listen. She'd sat very still and very quietly and waited for it to pass. And when it did, she felt more at ease than she had in a very long time.

Dr. Hauser finally seemed satisfied with Rennie's responses and the rest of their time together passed uneventfully. Dr. Hauser apparently did not have clearance for the Tajikistan information and for this Rennie was thankful.

"I have what I need from you, Miss Vogel. You are free to go."

Rennie stood.

"I noticed you observing my prints," Hauser said, her aspect less arctic now that her questioning was concluded. "I adore the modernist period. I find it sublimely beautiful in its very hideousness. These are *entartete Kunst*. A selection of pieces from the 'Degenerate Art' collection assembled by the Third Reich." She stood and walked with a pronounced hitch in her step around the small office, rapping the knuckle of her index finger next to each print. "Kirchner. Dix. Grosz. Kokoschka. The Reich toured the exhibition in hope they could inspire distaste for the works, foment suspicion against modernism which they associated with the Jews. I'm quite certain they engendered just the opposite in many viewers."

Rennie nodded, disconcerted by the doctor's change in tone.

"Those men. They heard voices too," she said, peering at Rennie. "The artists, I mean. Not the Nazis." Then she smiled broadly for the first time. "They hear voices, they see visions. All great artists touch the divine. So to speak," she said, waving her hand.

"I'm no artist, Doctor."

"No, I suppose not."

Dr. Hauser leaned in close. "But neither are you mad," she said quietly in Rennie's ear.

Rennie saw that her lipstick had strayed onto her front teeth, giving her a ghoulish look. She wouldn't have been surprised if it was intentional.

Rennie stepped back into the hallway, glad to escape Room 101. Then Dr. Marietta appeared and placed a hand on her elbow.

"Ms. Vogel, it so happens our polygrapher has a block of time just now that he can devote to you."

"No time for lunch then, Doctor?" She failed to keep the irony from her voice.

"I'm afraid not."

Good. Let's get it over with.

Marietta steered her down a network of hallways and into a stairwell. Two floors below they exited into a dimly lit corridor, stark and cold and reminiscent of a submarine. The doors on this level were not those of a typical office building. They appeared to be reinforced steel with high-end fingerprint door locks. The door they stopped in front of was padlocked as well for extra measure. Marietta removed the padlock before placing his index finger on the panel and Rennie heard the tumblers slide into the open position.

"Mr. Song will join you momentarily," Marietta said as Rennie entered the room. He closed the door behind her and the lock snapped closed. She tested the handle just to make sure.

The room was small, closet-sized. A single lightbulb on the ceiling covered by a wire frame emitted a thin, sickly glow. The room in its entirety was concrete and the walls, floor and ceiling were all painted the same gun-metal gray. Rennie sat on the cold metal chair next to the metal table. She still wore the shorts and lightweight V-neck T-shirt from her morning fitness test. Her perspiration had long since dried and now she was freezing.

This will be the worst of it. Just get through this and you're home free.

Then she heard the foreboding sound of the lock opening. As much as she hated being confined in the tiny room she dreaded whatever was coming next. The door cracked open a few inches. She could hear hushed voices in the hallway—were they angry?—but couldn't make out any words. Then the door was slammed shut. Rennie flinched.

They're just playing with you. Don't let it get to you.

A moment later the door swung open and a man entered the

tiny room carrying a laptop and a rectangular case. He neither addressed her nor made eye contact but set to arranging his equipment on the table alongside her.

He was Asian—Korean if she had to guess—five-foot-eight, five-foot-nine tops and very fit. She could hear the whirr of the hard drive and the familiar triple-tone of the operating system booting up as he began to unpack the rectangular case—cables, straps, cuff.

With everything arranged on the table, he paused, his forearms evenly spaced on the surface, his head bowed, almost hanging. He turned to her then, just his head. His eyes were very dark, almost black.

"I am Hyun-Kyu Song. Let's begin."

Great, Rennie thought. He must have studied at the Dr. Hauser school of communication.

Song was sitting on a wheeled chair and shifted it around the corner of the table toward her, the wheels squeaking over the uneven concrete floor. First he attached the chest strap—careless of whether he touched her breasts in the process, though she detected no hint of salaciousness. Then he affixed the bands around her index and ring fingers. Finally, the blood pressure cuff. Rennie remembered this being the most physically uncomfortable part of the test, but nothing could have prepared her for how tightly Hyun-Kyu Song cinched the cuff. She immediately felt the blood rush to her hand and saw it become red.

Here we go.

"Rennie, are you comfortable?" Her name sounded odd coming from his lips, robotic.

"As much as I expect to be."

"You've taken the polygraph before?"

"Yes."

"How did you find that experience?"

"I passed."

"Do you expect to pass today?"

Rennie's hand had already begun to throb. The pain traveled from her upper arm in a direct searing line to the tips of her fingers. But the pain didn't matter. Nothing mattered but getting through the next few hours. Rennie turned her head to her polygrapher and met his eyes, holding his gaze.

"I do."

Hyun-Kyu Song rolled toward her and tightened the cuff even more.

"We will see."

Across town in a penthouse suite alcove on the twenty-seventh floor of the Crane Technologies Building, Sam Crane and Peyton Virgil sat in the near dark—the windows had automatically dimmed once the video feed began. They watched as Kyu tightened the blood pressure cuff on Rennie Vogel's bicep.

"I think we ought to cut her loose now. Why put her through this? I mean, after Hauser's report—" Virgil began, but Crane cut him off.

"I'm not that concerned with the report."

"She hears voices, Sam. Our careers, your legacy..." Virgil said, pointing at Crane, "...is riding on whether we can trust these people and not only trust them, but trust them not to crack up."

"I'm comfortable with it. Hauser clearly says there is no indication of psychosis, that it's a quirk."

"I can think of another word that begins with Q and ends in K."

"Drop it, Virgil. Let's see what Mr. Song can do with her. Then we can revisit this."

Virgil's gut told him that Vogel would be fine, an excellent addition to the team. But this was too important to rely on instinct. His time in the CIA had taught him to ignore such subjective mumbo-jumbo. When critical decisions were being determined only cold hard analysis sufficed.

Crane turned the volume up on the video feed and the two men heard Vogel say, "I do."

"What did he ask her?" Crane said.

"If she thinks she will pass."

"Any thoughts on that matter?"

"Not a one," Virgil said, cutting his eyes at Crane.

"Ha—since when?"

They turned back to the screen and watched as Kyu Song began to run through the control questions where the subject is instructed to lie so the examiner can log the physical reaction to the lie.

"Did you enjoy watching Ahmad Armin die?"

"That boy doesn't mess around, does he?" Virgil said to Crane.

Vogel responded flatly, "Yes."

"Yes, what?" Song said.

"Yes, I enjoyed watching Armin die."

The stim test was intended for the polygrapher to adjust the machine. The subject's direction to lie usually only encompassed a few questions and was never this brutal. Besides, Song *wasn't* adjusting the machine. He wasn't even looking at the reflection of her responses on the monitor. He was angled away from it, gazing at her with his black eyes.

"And the boy that you killed—you described the incident, 'I sprayed him across the chest and the force threw him off his feet.' You didn't *have* to kill him did you? You could have disarmed him, couldn't you?"

"I could have disarmed him. I didn't have to kill him," Vogel said.

"You like to think about it, isn't it true? The time when you killed that boy. How old was he? Ten? Eleven?"

"He was at least thirteen. And, yes, I like to think about it." Vogel's voice was barely audible now.

Crane turned to Virgil. "I think I liked it better when all we had to worry about was whether anyone had leaked the details of our latest security OS."

"If you're having second thoughts, say so now."

"No, let's do this thing. When do we cut him off?"

"Soon. We'll let it escalate a little further."

Anger and sorrow welled up in Rennie in equal parts. She wanted to rip off the cuff and the sensors and dig her thumbs into Song's throat. But she had to get through the stim test. Then he went too far.

"It arouses you, thinking about it. Doesn't it, Rennie? Isn't it true that thinking about the life draining out of that child arouses you?"

Rennie didn't respond. She couldn't. It was too much.

His voice rose. "Look at me." Rennie turned her eyes to him. She couldn't discern his pupils from his irises. He seemed distinctly less than human. "Isn't it true that thinking about your murder of that boy turns you on."

There was something about hearing that very American idiom in the polygrapher's accent that made it sound even more horrific. Rennie clenched her jaw and held his gaze. She said nothing.

He brought his fist down hard on the table then and the laptop jumped. He swiveled quickly toward her and had just gripped the sides of her chair when a telephone on the wall rang. Song looked at her with pure hatred as the phone continued to ring, reverberating off the concrete walls of the tiny room. Finally he pushed away from her and, rising, went to lift the receiver. He listened for a moment, nodded once and hung up.

Someone is watching. Rennie wasn't surprised but wondered if the call had been orchestrated or if the watcher thought Song had gone too far.

Song took a step toward her and she steeled herself as he reached out to her, thinking suddenly, irrationally, that he was going to strike her. But he merely loosened the cuff on her arm. Not enough to completely relieve the pain but enough that she could think clearly. He sat back down again, tapped on the laptop's keyboard and, without turning toward her, said, "In the course of your work—if you are hired—you may be called upon to do things that may not precisely conform to the letter of the law. Where would you draw the line?"

And with the directness of that question, she knew the stim portion of the test was over. So it went until he released her two hours later. He asked question after question seemingly designed to sketch out the precise outlines of her moral compass. Others pointed to whether she completely understood the absolute necessity of secrecy—this last accompanied with barely veiled threats. Rennie wondered how she could be expected to pledge undying loyalty to an organization about which she knew next to nothing. But she went along, sensing that this was base-covering and would hopefully segue into the conclusion of the interview.

It didn't. Song revisited Tajikistan but without the hectoring and the tormenting. It was still uncomfortable but he was no longer persecuting her as he had during the stim test.

"Do you blame yourself for the deaths of your teammates?"

Rennie paused. Easy answer. "I do."

Song glanced at her and their eyes locked for a brief moment but she couldn't read his expression. She expected him to mine this territory more thoroughly but he switched tactics.

"And Hannah Marcus. Isn't it true that you flouted protocol to rescue Miss Marcus, thereby compromising the success of the mission?"

"Yes, but I determined that the safety of an American citizen was worth risking the mission."

"Even though it wasn't your role to make such determinations?"

"Correct."

Song stood and went out into the hallway. Again, she could hear his voice muffled by the heavy door. She hoped this would be the end of it. And she was right. Song came back in and snapped shut the laptop.

"That's it."

He efficiently released her from the sensors and fitted them back into the case.

"You can see yourself out," he said, his accent so much less marked that he almost sounded American.

Rennie massaged her arm as the blood flowed back into the area where the cuff had been. She watched Hyun-Kyu Song as he gathered his equipment.

"What part of Korea are you from?" Though a part of her still stung from his treatment during the exam, she knew it was irrational to be angry with him or his tactics and found herself wondering what his story was.

"Hoeryong," Song answered without looking at her.

Rennie squinted, scanning the Korean peninsula in her mind's eye.

"Hoeryong? But isn't that near the Chinese border?"

"Yes." Song put his hand on the door handle, seemingly wanting to escape the horrible, tiny room as badly as Rennie did.

"North Korea." Rennie's eyes traveled over his features which betrayed no emotion. Perhaps that stoicism was what had saved him. Song glanced back at her one last time and was gone.

Evgeni was waiting for her out front as before. He raised his hand to her.

"Another fun day?" he said.

"You might say so, if by fun you mean torturous and possibly lobotomizing."

"That's what I figured." He was holding a cell phone in his hand and held it out to her. "A call for you."

Rennie frowned, curious, as she put the phone to her ear.

"Ms. Vogel, it's Dr. Marietta. Mr. Virgil is here with me. I'm passing you to him."

Mr. Virgil?

Then Rennie heard the resonant bass of the imposing black man she'd met in Marietta's office that first day.

"Ms. Vogel, may I call you Rennie?"

"Of course."

"Welcome aboard. I look forward to working with you if you decide to join us. Let's set something up for next week. You can come by the house, meet my wife, Jackie. We'll have dinner."

"Sounds good," Rennie said, surprised at the personal turn.

"Your cover title will be Domestic Terrorism Analyst. I'll send you the details in your new encrypted email account. Evgeni will give you the login and password. You'll meet the rest of the team soon."

Rennie caught a glimpse of herself in the window of the Suburban. She looked stunned.

Evgeni smiled and opened the door. "Where to?"

"How far are we from the Pacific?" she said, already feeling the weight of the day lift from her as she sat in the backseat.

"Two hours. An hour and a half in no traffic."

"Would you take me? I'd like to have dinner by the water."

Evgeni crossed to the driver's side of the enormous vehicle. "You got it."

Evgeni passed Rennie a file before they got on the road. "I'll have to have that back when you're finished," he said. "Hope you don't get car sick."

"Me too," Rennie said, laughing lightly. *Finally. Some answers.* Embossed on the cover of the file was a round seal.

The Foundation for Liberal Democracy.

Rennie read how Sam Crane, the computer security mogul, had decided to involve himself and his vast resources with domestic security. She wasn't surprised at the revelation of the organization's benefactor, being in Portland after all. And such a venture would take an exorbitant amount of capital and an entrepreneurial ego accustomed to high-stakes risk. She'd even wondered if he could be behind what she now knew was called the *Special Projects Section* of the Foundation.

Before leaving for Portland, she'd pulled up the Crane Technologies website and skimmed his bio. She'd read that he'd been fascinated by language and codes ever since he could talk. He had the kind of genius that can translate complex information, data points, into alternative presentations. Once he discovered computers and code languages he felt he'd found his home. Before he graduated from high school he'd begun writing his own program languages. And while still in college he was developing the most innovative network security the world had ever seen.

But the most interesting section in the file was the part that outlined the Special Project Section's mission statement. There was the pledge that no innocents would be considered expendable and that each agent would be expected to follow a code of honor.

Maybe this will work out after all.

Rennie dropped the file on the front seat and talked with Evgeni as they drove west along Route 6. Their conversation avoided the personal, though she learned that he was Ukrainian born. She wouldn't be surprised if there were a spy or two in his ancestry. The Foundation was starting to seem like a bunch of misfits, she thought.

Once out of the city the last of the tension drained from her body. Torturous, indeed. She dozed for the remainder of the trip.

An hour and a half later, she sat on the patio of a cliff-side restaurant. She finished eating as the sun was beginning to set, streaking the enormous sky in orange and pink. About a half mile from shore, three rocks—islands, really, though nothing could have been less habitable—emerged from the sea. Rennie leaned back in her chair and sipped her wine. Something about the rocks made her think of Galapagos. She'd never been there—she'd had little time for pleasure travel. What she'd seen of the world had been in the service of her country. She envisioned Darwin scrabbling over that inhospitable rock, surely in a coat and tie. She envied him. His occupation existed upon the plane of unexplored theory. Her own choices had kept her yoked tightly, almost suffocatingly, to the practical and, worse, the pragmatic. And now the practical, pragmatic course she was signing on to would likely get her arrested if it fell apart.

I hope these people know what they're doing.

Rennie swirled the wine in her glass, taking in the rich crimson in the fading light. It wasn't ideal, this new position. It seemed a certainty that she would never be allowed to work for the government again. This was a way to serve her country. And she was more than ready to get back to work. She only hoped she could do some good. And maybe have a sliver of space for a personal life.

Hannah. What are you doing right now?

Rennie laid her hand on her cell phone and stroked the glass with her thumb.

Will I ever see you again?

Rennie shook her head. She hardly knew the woman. Then

she remembered the promise to herself that she would at least find out that she was well. Beyond that she hoped for nothing.

"Pipe dreams," she said aloud.

"You don't strike me as a woman who finds much beyond her reach."

Rennie flinched. Evgeni stood at her elbow, his bald pate shining, a slight smile on his face.

Rennie *did* feel her belief in her abilities returning. And that was a very good feeling. She returned Evgeni's smile.

"Are you ready?" he asked.

Rennie nodded and drained the last of her wine.

Yes, I'm ready.

CHAPTER NINETEEN

Devils Lake, North Dakota

Cainkiller sat down at the bar.

"What'll it be, bud?" The bartender was well over six feet tall, bearded and barrel-chested.

"Jack and Coke."

Waka waka waka.

The razor blades weren't gliding through his veins anymore. Now, the drug wanted out. It wanted to stretch its legs and stroll about the world.

"What's this place anyway?" Cainkiller said. He was in the mood to poke a big dumb animal.

"This here's Big Eddie's. There's a sign out front." He set the drink on the fake wood bar. "That'll be two-fifty."

Cainkiller raised an eyebrow and slapped down a twenty. "Run me a tab."

Waka waka waka.

"Where I come from big dudes like you who are into other dudes and wear all that leather go to fag bars." Cainkiller drained the Jack and Coke. The burn of it going down his gullet felt too good and he detected his brain shifting down a notch. "This isn't a fag bar, is it?" He set the empty Collins glass on the bar and smiled. "Hit me again."

The bartender blinked and then his meaty hand shot out, nearly knocking Cainkiller off his stool as he took him by the shirt, yanking him toward him over the bar. The Collins glass tipped over and rolled to the floor with a crash.

"You better not have said what I think you said," the bartender growled, his face centimeters from Cainkiller's.

If only he'd taken the drink before he opened his mouth.

"Hey, hey, hey, no harm done. I was just fucking with you."

The bartender glared at him and let go. Then he leaned in. "I don't know where you're from but jokes like that can get you an ass whupping around here."

Cainkiller held up both hands. "Seriously, man, my bad. I just got outta the pen. Things can get pretty rough in there, you know? We're good, right?"

The bartender grudgingly turned away and began making another Jack and Coke.

Cainkiller shook his head. He finally had the perfect balance of meth and drink pumping through him and he'd nearly ruined it all by apologizing. Never apologize.

You did apologize.

"No, I didn't."

"You say something?" The bartender had turned and was squinting at him. Cainkiller had seen that look before. When somebody pinged on him when he was acting crazy.

"I said, I need a flint." Cainkiller flicked his empty Zippo without success. He smiled. The bartender nodded toward the bowl of matches a few seats down.

Just then thunder sounded and the door of the bar burst open. A man hurried in followed by a gust of wind that sent the cocktail napkins flying off the bar. The man was old—old enough to be his father—and wore a corduroy sport coat with patches on the elbow.

"Hey, Professor, come join the party," Cainkiller said. One side effect of the drug was it made him not want to be alone. And it made him talk.

Just don't say anything you'll regret.

"I had to get out of the storm. I've got a headlight out and you can't see anything out there," the old guy said.

He seemed like a baby to Cainkiller. A middle-aged baby who'd never strayed more than a few feet from his mother's knee. "Have a seat. I'll buy you a drink."

The old guy looked uncertain. "Well…" he said, settling himself at the bar and brushing water droplets off his coat.

"Come on, live a little. What's your poison?"

Two hours later, Cainkiller had enough bourbon and enough meth in him that he was starting to feel like himself—the quintessence of Cainkiller. Just the way he liked it.

"I am he," he said reverently.

"What's that?" the old guy said.

"Nothing." Cainkiller exhaled forcefully, suddenly bored. "So what's your name anyway, Professor?"

"Ken. Ken Yates," the old guy said, offering his hand.

Outside the storm still raged and his new friend, Ken, was still nursing his first beer.

Pathetic.

"You know, Ken," Cainkiller said, leaning in close. "Don't take this the wrong way. But there's something about you that makes me want to rip your head off."

Cainkiller grinned when he saw the fear in the quiver of the man's Adam's apple. Then he stood up on the rungs of his bar stool and raised his arms in the air. "It's story time," he yelled. The big ugly bartender glared at him but let him be. Cainkiller squatted back down. "You ready for a story, Ken?"

Ken stared straight ahead.

Good. The old guy was getting nervous. Nothing Cainkiller

loved more than being the guy in the room who was making everybody uncomfortable.

Ken took a tiny sip of his beer. Cainkiller slowly got off his stool and stood behind him. "Ken?" he said in a sing-song voice. "Are you listening to me?"

"Yes…"

"I asked you a question. I asked if you are ready for story time?" Cainkiller put his hands on the old guy's shoulders. "It might be prudent to think of it as a rhetorical question."

He was so close to the old guy he could see the beads of perspiration in his hairline at the back of his neck. Ken's shoulders lifted, almost imperceptibly, in an attempt at a shrug.

"I'll take that as a yes." Cainkiller reached around Ken and took a drink of his Jack and Coke, then he resumed his position behind Ken and began to speak, nearly whispering in his ear.

"Once upon a time, there was an old man who lived like a king in a big house by the river. He had two sons. And one of those sons—we'll call him Winston—could do no wrong. And the other son—we'll call him…" Cainkiller put a finger to his lips. "We'll call him Cain."

The old guy flinched hard. Cainkiller burst out laughing and capered around him. "Oh! Ken! You're just *too* much," he said in a falsetto. Then he dropped his voice to a growl and spoke directly into his ear. "I actually *saw* the shiver travel down your spine under your nice tweed jacket. I *saw* it. Your fear is like a small scared animal that lives inside your body, isn't it?"

Cainkiller met Ken's eyes in the mirror behind the bar. He shook his head uncertainly. "Listen," the old guy said, starting to stand. "I really ought to get back on the road."

Cainkiller put his hand on the old guy's shoulder and shoved him back onto the stool. "I don't think so, Ken. What about the storm? What about your headlight? Besides, I haven't finished my story." Cainkiller tipped his glass to his mouth but there was only the merest hint of bourbon left on the dwindled ice cubes. He raised his hand to the bartender.

Waka waka waka.

The razor blades had woken up.

Cainkiller lit a cigarette. He held the match until the flame reached his fingers and went out. He took a long, leisurely drag off the cigarette.

What are you doing? You shouldn't be talking. Not about this.

But sometimes the drug had a will of its own. As he began to speak again, Cainkiller felt very far away from himself.

"Cain and Winston were only a year apart, and when they were boys they spent all their time together. Even though Winston was younger, he was bigger. He was braver too."

Not anymore.

"One day, they walked through the woods to a house that was for sale. It was empty and Winston said they should break in and explore."

You hadn't wanted to.

"So they did. Once they were inside Cain trailed after Winston through the house watching him break windows, kick holes in the drywall. Destroying everything he could. But fate was against them."

That's right—fate.

"They had tripped a silent alarm and soon the police were there. Before they were delivered to their father, Winston convinced Cain to take the blame."

You were pathetic, wanting his approval, your stupid little brother's approval.

"Cain said, 'It was my idea, Father. Winston only went along with me.'

"Daddy was enraged. And he took Cain by the collar in front of the smirking policemen, in front of his mother, in front of Winston, in front of the maid. 'Say you're sorry, goddammit.'

"And Cain *did* say he was sorry."

But you weren't sorry were you?

"I was," Cainkiller barked. The bourbon and the meth were no longer working in concert and confusion and craving took over. He glanced sidelong at the old guy as he tossed back yet another shot of bourbon.

"And after that Cain was the one who suggested the bad things. And he was made to say he was sorry again and again. And again. Forevermore."

Enough.

Cainkiller stubbed out his cigarette. "What do you think about that?"

"It's...a sad story."

"No. It isn't. It's a beautiful story. Because great men *always* have hard beginnings. Just like in the comic books."

Waka, waka, waka.

"Hey," Cainkiller slurred, his eyes glassy, the bourbon suddenly hitting him like a sack of bricks. He tried to focus on the man sitting next to him but could only see vague outlines, the most prominent of which was his silver beard. Time collapsed then and the man before him melded into the one he'd met in Wisconsin that morning at the crack of dawn. "You lied to me, you piece of shit?" Cainkiller said to Ken Yates, baring his teeth at him. "You *promised* me you had the grenade launcher."

Ken Yates let out a high-pitched yelp as Cainkiller lunged at him. But Ken Yates, who wasn't addled by bourbon and crystal meth jerked out of his way before he came crashing down hard. And that's where Cainkiller stayed, unconscious on the floor of Big Eddie's as Ken Yates, with his lone headlight, shaken to his very core, made his way back onto the rain-drenched highway.

CHAPTER TWENTY

Portland International Airport

Evgeni handed Rennie her carry-on at the departures entrance.

"Best of luck..." He paused.

"Rennie."

"Yes. I know. Best of luck, Rennie," he said, shaking her hand.

She smiled. She was well rested and glad to be going home. "Thanks."

Through security and walking toward her gate, she veered into a newsstand and bought *The Economist* and *Foreign Policy Magazine*, a bottle of Evian and a package of peanut M&Ms. She checked her watch and saw that she had forty-five minutes before boarding. She navigated her way to the nearest bar.

With her carry-on nestled against her knees, she ordered a

Bass and flipped through *The Economist* to the Middle East and Africa section.

"Who knew what a scholar you are."

Nobody could do irony quite like Martin Garrison. He pulled out the stool next to her.

"May I?"

"Help yourself," Rennie said without enthusiasm, not entirely surprised to see him.

Garrison raised a hand to the bartender and asked for a perfect Manhattan. He politely averted his gaze as the young man consulted his *Mr. Boston's* cocktail manual.

Rennie couldn't think of a thing to say to Garrison. Since his unexpected visit to her apartment on Capitol Hill, she'd given a lot of thought to what their working relationship would be like. Garrison was impossible to read. And from what Virgil had indicated they were essentially to be partners. *I guess he's the brains and I'm the muscle.* She would have preferred to work alone—after her last experience working with a team she'd rather just rely on herself.

"What are you doing out here anyway? I thought you leapt gracefully through all the rings of fire ages ago," Rennie said.

"Indeed."

"Well?"

"Did you have fun with Mr. Song?" Garrison asked, deflecting her question.

So far, Rennie had encountered two Garrisons. Both had the same emotionless sense of humor. But one was arch and made her want to leap at him, take him by the head and press her thumb deep under his jaw until he collapsed. The other Garrison could speak the exact same words but so flatly they made Rennie's blood run cold. She wondered how many more iterations of Martin Garrison lurked beneath his placid exterior. She had a sick feeling that he may have been watching her during her polygraph session along with whoever had made the call to Song. Maybe he'd been watching her throughout all her trials.

"Loads. How about you? Enjoy your time with him?" Rennie wouldn't have been surprised if he had.

"I take a certain enjoyment in watching Mr. Song ply his trade."

Was he talking about himself? Or her?

"But I was also in town to take part in planning meetings." Garrison lowered his voice and leaned toward Rennie. "It's an interesting prospect, this thing we're being offered. Our benefactor has the ultimate last say in our choice of assignments but we, along with the analysts of course, will have more influence than we could ever have dreamed of in our former endeavors."

And just like that, Garrison had shifted their dynamic from adversarial with a hint of sadism on his part to collegiality. Rennie wondered if it would stick.

"So, what do we have on the table now?"

"Plenty to keep us busy. A gaggle of congressmen meddling in African politics. A variety of factions on the political left and right. And elements of the militia movement that indicate they could pose a potential and real threat."

"What will we focus on first?"

"The analysts will be looking at all of it and anything else that emerges. On the operational end, you and I and Song and the rest of the team will be looking at a short list of groups that fall under that giant umbrella that encompasses the militia movement."

Rennie snapped her head toward Garrison. "Song is part of our team?"

"I see you didn't know."

"I did not."

Hyun-Kyu Song had struck Rennie as the kind of employable sociopath who could control himself and was perfectly suited to carrying out the institutional torture that is the role of the polygraph operator. But little else. She couldn't imagine him able to fit into any kind of team.

"You'll find he has skills other than interrogation."

"He's North Korean. What's his story?"

Garrison glanced at the departures display on the monitor above them. Rennie sighed as she saw that their flight was delayed.

"Looks like we'll have time for another drink," Garrison said.

Six hours later Rennie wheeled her bag across the broad, shiny tile floors of Reagan National Airport. Exiting the jet bridge into the terminal always made Rennie glad she was home. The cool, spare expanse with its civilized ranks of Eames chairs was the perfect counterpoint to the chaos typical of most airports. Crossing the raised walkway, she swung left, waved her SmarTrip card over the turnstile reader and caught the blue line train just before its doors closed. Moving to the back of the car, she slumped into a seat.

She was glad she and Garrison hadn't been seated near one another during the flight. And neither had looked for one another after they'd landed. But their discussion at the bar in Portland had been informative.

Hyun-Kyu Song.

Rennie still felt unsure about his involvement.

According to Garrison, Song had come of age during the worst of the North Korean food shortages. Kim Jong Il had put all the country's resources toward the military, weapons, his nuclear program, anything but feeding his people—all to ensure that his father's failed political experiment would continue. The few luxuries that slipped across the borders were gobbled up by the upper echelons of the party. The average party members got along by denouncing their neighbors while the rest of the people starved. And died. George Orwell would have shuddered had he lived to see it.

Rennie wondered how Kyu had managed, how bad it had gotten for him. North Korea barely had electricity let alone the Internet. Looking at a satellite image of the world all aglitter at night, North Korea was a blank, a black hole. How did Kyu see the larger world now that he was a part of it? His eyes were the coldest she'd ever seen—even colder than Garrison's. And then there was his cruelty. How much of it had been an act? All in a day's work for the effective polygrapher?

Abandoning that avenue of thought, Rennie propped her knee on the back of the seat in front of her. The train rattled as it crossed the Potomac, shining and dancing under the bright afternoon sun. Yes, she was very glad to be home.

A half hour later in her apartment, Rennie stepped from the shower onto the worn mat. She had left the door to the bathroom open to let the steam escape and the mirror above the sink was clear of condensation. After alternating the shower from hot to cold to soothe her strained muscles, she felt rejuvenated. Confronting her image in the mirror, she saw that she had become lean again. For two months she had rowed and run and lifted and the true contours of her body had finally begun to emerge.

She sighed heavily, in relief. This was what she had been lacking, what she needed to set her mind in order. She needed to be able to recognize herself. She peered closer. There were new lines around her eyes she hadn't noticed before.

"You're lucky that's all you brought home from Tajikistan."

The sound of her voice startled her. She'd avoided looking at herself for so long. The set of her mouth was, perhaps, a bit grimmer too. But her eyes were clear.

Okay. It's time.

Mandate or no, Rennie was going to find Hannah Marcus.

Rennie slammed the door on the ancient Saab. The air conditioning had quit working years before and she rolled the windows down, front and back, to get the air flowing as she gunned the engine and pointed herself in the direction of I-95 and Baltimore.

She had never spent much time in the curious city to the north. Built upon industrialism instead of politics, Baltimore always felt more real than D.C. Just thirty miles away, the city was unique enough to have its own accent.

Hannah's parents lived in a crumbling apartment building in the oldest part of the city. The neighborhood, once good, had grown less so over the years with businesses decamping for more traveled streets and Rennie found a parking space easily.

She hadn't thought of what she would say to them. Sometimes

there are things that matter so much that rehearsals aren't necessary. The words just come, in the only way they can.

After a short ride in a dank elevator, Rennie rang the bell of apartment 405. Inside a small brass fixture on the wall beside the ringer was a yellowing card written in a spidery foreign hand—Ira and Alma Marcus. After a long minute, the door cracked open, its security chain straddling the two points of door and jamb, a handful of forged links between safety and danger.

"Yes?" The old woman's questioning voice was laced with a trace of fear that made Rennie sick to her stomach.

Rennie cleared her throat. "Mrs. Marcus, I'm Rennie Vogel. I know your daughter. From Tajikistan." She paused. "I'm trying to reach her."

The door closed and Rennie wondered what she had said wrong. But then she heard the slide of the chain and the door opened again. Hannah's mother, perhaps under five feet tall, with pure white hair twisted at the nape of her neck and secured with pins, reached out her small knuckled papery hands, taking Rennie by the wrists.

"I know who you are. I will never forget your name and what you did for our dear Hannah."

Rennie felt strange, had never imagined that this woman would have any conception of who she was. Did she know everything? About the ambush, about the assassination, about Rennie and Hannah?

"Come, come," she said, leading her into the small living room. "Sit. Ira, look who's here. It's that girl with the German name who brought Hannah home."

Hannah's father, sleeping in an overstuffed recliner with a lever on the side to raise his feet, roused for a moment, fixing his unfocused eyes on Rennie before drifting off again.

"That's fine," Mrs. Marcus said, patting him on the shoulder. "Can I get you some tea, my dear? I was just about to fix some myself."

"Yes. That would be nice."

Rennie sat on the hard sofa watching Ira Marcus and looking for traces of Hannah in him. There were stacks of newspapers on the floor around the room. Black-and-white photographs sat on the end tables, relatives, perhaps lost during the war.

Mrs. Marcus returned with the tea on a small rectangular plastic-glazed tray, a pattern of flowers on its surface. She sat by Rennie in a low upholstered chair.

Smiling, she said, "I always wondered what became of you. Hannah can be so mysterious. She said things were such that she couldn't see you."

"Yes, that's true."

"'Things were such.' So she said and left it at that. As if Ira and I are fools and just accept such things."

"I don't think she could say more."

"Yes, yes, I understand," she said, waving aside Rennie's explanation. "But you are here now," she said, patting Rennie's knee, "and that is just lovely."

"I was hoping you could tell me where Hannah is. I know she has left the *Post*." Tapping an old contact, Rennie had readily learned that fact along with her parents' address.

Mrs. Marcus's expression changed, growing serious.

"I *can* tell you where she's gone. My foolish, brave daughter."

Tension crept up Rennie's spine. She wanted to be patient, but found it impossible.

"Where is she, Mrs. Marcus?"

"You are right, she has left the newspaper. She was not happy there, her assignments too small and inconsequential, so she said." Mrs. Marcus swatted the air as if Hannah should have been happy with what she had. "But I am very worried for her, I have to tell you. She has become her own employer and says she is driving to North Dakota." Her eyes grew wide as if she couldn't envision that a place such as North Dakota even existed. "She's investigating…what do you call it?" She put a finger to her lips. "A group of angry people who believe the government is against them."

Rennie leaned forward. "A militia group?"

"Yes, that's it. My dear, I am very afraid for her. She is all we have and these people have guns. And ideas." Again she waved her hand in front of her, this time as if batting away something ugly and could say no more.

Yes, she is all we have.

Rennie could hardly speak. "I'd like to go see her and make sure all is well. Do you know where she'll be in North Dakota?"

"She promised to call me when she arrives. I'll ask her then."

Mrs. Marcus set down her cup delicately on its saucer. She gripped her chair by its legs and, rising slightly, moved it toward Rennie. When she raised her eyes to her, instead of brown eyes cloudy with age, they were clear, clear of social graces, clear of the barriers we put up to separate ourselves from one another. Rennie saw in those eyes the purity of long-gone youth, youth that had witnessed horrors and made it out alive. A cold sweat beaded above Rennie's lip as she remembered the atrocities she herself had seen and knew what she had experienced had merely scratched the surface of all that was vile in the world.

Mrs. Marcus took Rennie's hand.

"I'm an old woman and there are too many things I still don't understand. You saved Hannah once. I am too ignorant to know if she needs saving now." Mrs. Marcus looked at Rennie imploringly. "If she does, do what you need to do."

Rennie gripped Mrs. Marcus's hand firmly in her own.

"You can count on it."

CHAPTER TWENTY-ONE

Washington, D.C.

The Militia movement. It seemed to be on everyone's mind, Rennie thought, remembering her conversation with Garrison in the Portland airport as she drove back to the city. Tension crawled around her chest and gripped her so tightly her breathing became shallow. She scanned the highway for the next exit. Now that she had the cell phone number, an impulse to call Hannah Marcus came over her. She was seized with the need to act. Since Tajikistan she had mostly quashed her impulses. She wouldn't anymore. It was time to rejoin the world. But something held her back from steering the Saab into the exit lane. She hadn't known Hannah Marcus but for five days and much of that time had been spent picking their way silently through dark forest. She wanted to talk to her now, yes, but most of all Rennie needed to know that she was safe. And she *knew* that Hannah would reassure her if she called her. But without seeing her for herself and without seeing this compound in North Dakota, worry would continue to nag. And she wasn't going to forget her promise to Alma Marcus.

A week later Rennie dressed in the dark—gray cotton trousers, white T-shirt. How odd it felt to be getting up and going to a job again. How normal. Before turning on the coffee pot and getting into the shower, she'd rowed for forty minutes, hard, feeling like she was purging herself. Now, she sat in the Adirondack on the roof deck as the sun rose behind her. She looked at her watch. She'd wait until the first rays touched the top of the Capitol before leaving for Virginia. She'd probably be early. Better that than sitting in traffic on the parkway.

The drive took forty-five minutes. The Foundation had hired offices for SPS in the Center for Innovative Technology, right across the highway from Dulles International Airport. The upside down, parallelogram-shaped building seemed an ominous presence to commuters traveling the Dulles Toll Road, a dark, hulking behemoth rising from the trees. Its reflective windows, tinted black, green and gold, were almost blinding at this time of day with the sun slanting low. Rennie steered down the ramp into the underground garage and couldn't help but think she had just been swallowed.

Pressing the elevator button, Rennie took a deep breath and squeezed her eyes shut.

Here we go.

Riding to the third floor, Rennie couldn't help but think of her first day of classes in college, the day she started as a field agent in the big FBI building downtown, and other times when her stomach fluttered and her mind darted in countless directions as if looking for cover. In each of those situations, once she was finally present in the moment, something settling had kicked in and her mind and body would calm. But today there were no butterflies. She was excited, hungry to get back to work and ready for whatever the world planned on throwing at her.

Rennie knew from Garrison that the third-floor offices at

twenty thousand square feet housed an executive suite, conference rooms, private offices, a kitchen and all the accoutrements needed to carry on business. It was much more than SPS needed but Crane was envisioning a robust force and believed the space would be filled soon enough. Rennie saw Garrison through an open door at the end of the hallway and raised a hand to him. Behind him, a tall, thin, extremely pale man with longish black hair sat at the table, tapping on a laptop, unaware of anything going on around him. He was very young.

"Rennie." Peyton Virgil stepped in front of Garrison and smiled at her as she entered the conference room. "Good to see you again. Coffee?"

"No, thanks." Rennie's attention was caught by the young man with the laptop muttering to himself in a low voice.

"Damn," he said, stretching the word into multiple syllables. "This database is fly."

Rennie detected an accent she would usually associate with hip-hop. Virgil, towering over her, leaned down close to her ear, an amused smile on his face. "Our young computer genius identifies," Virgil whispered, making air quotes, 'as black.' He hasn't quite gotten the hang of it yet."

Rennie was thinking she was glad she wasn't better at math as Kyu Song came through the door of the conference room. She stiffened at the sight of him. He was wearing close-fitting khakis and a navy polo shirt over his muscular frame. He extended a hand.

"No hard feelings, okay?" he said, his voice free of any trace of his Korean accent.

Rennie nodded slightly, grasping his hand, surprised at its delicacy. She'd have to take him at his word since what she saw in his eyes was the same cold, flat expression he had when he was tightening the cuff on her arm.

Virgil stood at the head of the conference table and cleared his throat. The young long-haired man finally looked up from his computer as a woman in a gray suit entered the door and, nodding to the group, sat in the chair nearest to Virgil. "Sit down anywhere you like," Virgil said to everyone.

Rennie chose the nearest seat; there were three coil-bound

sheaves of paper at each chair. Virgil continued, "Most of you have met before, even if it wasn't under the best of circumstances."

Kyu's face twisted into something that approximated a smile.

"I am your Operations Director," Virgil said. "Which means that I am your commander, as well as your liaison between the analysts and Crane. This," he said, indicating the woman who was the last to enter the room, "is Ursula Banford. She is our chief analyst. We have Mr. Garrison to thank for helping us lure her away from the NSA."

"I'm looking forward to working with all of you," Ursula said. She spoke precisely, every syllable enunciated.

"And this is Logan Caldwell." Virgil gestured toward the young man with the laptop.

Logan nodded and lifted his long-fingered hand, all while keeping his gaze on the laptop screen.

"After too much of the wrong kind of scrutiny, Mr. Caldwell has decided to forsake his career in computer security and seek justice with us."

Logan continued staring and nodding.

Virgil made brief introductions to Banford and Caldwell of Rennie, Garrison and Kyu. All a formality since the analysts would have access to the files of the operations team.

"You," Virgil, said stretching his long arms in a wide embracing gesture, "are our core team."

So this is it. A bit of a motley crew.

Virgil turned to their chief analyst. "The reins are all yours, Ursula. Take it away."

Ursula Banford was, on closer scrutiny, perhaps sixty years old, her tanned face deeply lined. Her short, bright blond hair was shot through with silvery white strands, and when she stood her head appeared to glow under the soft recessed lighting. She picked up the three bound documents in front of her. "I've spent much of this past week in briefings with the rest of the analysts," she began. "We've looked hard at a plethora of domestic threats to national security. Unsurprisingly, it is clear that Islamist factions and the militia movement loom the largest."

"Where and how are we getting our intel?" Rennie asked.

"Good question, Rennie," Ursula said, glancing at Virgil. "Frustrated insiders in FBI, CIA, NSA and other intelligence clearinghouses. That, in conjunction with Logan's expertise in network security, hasn't quite allowed us full access, but let's just say that we have at our disposal a treasure trove of confidential information that would make the CIA Director quake in his boots."

Network security. Rennie figured that was code for an early career in hacking. Logan couldn't have been more than a teenager when he started. A boy genius indeed.

"At this stage," Ursula continued, "we've decided to focus on the militia movement. We're also keeping our eye out for any intersections between American nationalist or religious crusaders and the Islamists."

"Intersections? What do you mean?" Kyu spoke up.

"I mean that it's not impossible these groups may have similar goals even though the roots of their ideologies appear wildly divergent."

"Indeed," Virgil said.

Rennie had the sense that Virgil's attention had rested upon her a little too long and wondered why. Something flitted through her mind but it slipped away before she had time to pin it down.

"All right, let's get down to business," Ursula said. She moved to the wall and flicked a switch that tinted the large windows at the end of the room. Rennie scanned the room, taking a moment to scrutinize her new colleagues in the dimmed light. Garrison sat slightly pushed away from the table with his legs loosely crossed at the knee, one hand stroking his beard, the other fingering the stack of documents. An image flashed in her mind and she was reminded of the rogue Valmont—the way he casually arranged his body, and something else too, but she couldn't put her finger on it. He certainly shared his duplicity.

Kyu Song stared at the wall, his back as straight as a rod, both hands splayed on his knees, waiting for an image to appear. One finally did.

Projected on the wall was a page from what looked to be an ancient manuscript. Handwritten Greek letters surrounded an image of a snake. It was arranged circularly, its tail in its mouth.

"The snake that eats its tail," Ursula said ponderously.

Garrison uttered something under his breath.

"Please speak louder," Kyu said in his direct way.

"Ouroboros." Garrison turned his head only slightly as he spoke.

"Quite right," Ursula said.

The image of the snake was replaced by a field of black and then the words *Project Ouroboros* filled the screen.

Ursula continued, "I promise I won't always be so esoteric, but the ouroboros has always been a favorite symbol of mine—I studied the classics before my time at the NSA. The symbol has had many meanings over the millennia. But it is its imagery that has been most enduring, and I am going to co-opt that imagery to stand as an emblem for the militia movement which seems intent on devouring the very thing that it proclaims to revere— the primary ideals of what it means to be an American."

She touched a key on the laptop and the Gadsen flag appeared—a coiled rattlesnake above the words: *Don't Tread On Me.* "Another powerful and enduring image. This early American flag that predates the Stars and Stripes has been adopted by many in the militia community as a symbol representing their stance that the U.S. government has become an entity that has lost touch with the intentions of our Founding Fathers."

"Who they believe were of a monolithic mind," Virgil said.

"That's right, Mr. Virgil. These are people who don't see the world as one filled with nuance. There is black. And there is white. And not a shade in between."

"And they are invariably white," Logan said. "The supposed supremacy of Caucasians is an accident of migration and geography." Rennie saw a slight grin on Virgil's face as Logan's hip-hop sensibility was overtaken by the pedantic.

"Almost exclusively, yes, Logan. Many of the groups adhere to some variety of racial theory. White men are more evolved, black men became as they are as a punishment by God. Some groups are purely political, some have a religious component— the most prevalent being Christian Identity, a sect that began benignly, though perhaps wackily, in Britain and picked up speed in the late nineteenth century. They believe they are one of the lost tribes of David and at one time even aligned themselves with the Jews. Once the ideology took hold in America, however, it became ugly. Now, Identity believers are the 'true Jews' while the Jews themselves are devilish imposters."

"Are these..." Logan turned his long fingers in the air. "... believers dangerous?"

"Most are not. *Most*..." Ursula emphasized the word, "...of the entire movement is not. Frankly, the lion's share of these groups are populated by working-class men who feel they've been left behind by our quickly evolving economy."

"As they have," Logan said with a tone of self-righteousness. Rennie suspected their boy computer whiz typically sided with the little guy against "The Man."

Ursula continued without acknowledging Logan's editorializing. Rennie could see that her patience with him was wearing thin. "They also feel threatened by immigration and how quickly the country's demographics are changing. Regardless of their ideology or their catalog of grievances, this is where we come in. Where we see a need. FBI has historically dropped the ball in dealing with these groups. And they continue to do so."

"I personally never had any dealings with these groups during my time at the Bureau," Rennie said. "But I recall that limited resources were thrown at them. Primarily since there are just too many of them to keep track of."

"That's exactly right," Ursula said, nodding at Rennie. "And most of them mouth off in what turns out to be just a show of bravado. We've drawn upon data from FBI, from local law enforcement, from the Southern Poverty Law Center and other organizations that track hate groups."

"How large are these groups?" Garrison asked.

"It's not clear. It's standard practice for them to muddy or inflate their numbers. We've selected three groups to turn the brightest rays of our analytic spotlight upon. The first is a skinhead organization."

A photograph appeared on the wall of a group of men wearing SS uniforms and marching in tight formation in a parade.

"This is 'Ohio 88'. They've come onto our radar because they used to be a bunch of disorganized gangbangers harassing the homeless and loitering in alleyways. Then Franz Geiger came onto the scene."

Geiger's face appeared next, stern and chiseled and wearing an orange jumpsuit.

"That's one mean-looking motherfucker," Logan said. Rennie was getting the sense that Logan had never felt the need to hold his tongue. "He looks like one of those badass Germans in Hitler movies."

Ursula turned a cold eye to Logan. "Except he's Jewish. Curiously, it's not an entirely uncommon phenomenon to see men with Jewish ancestry as leaders in the movement. We're concerned with Geiger because—as you can see from the photo—he spent time in prison for a series of vicious attacks. Now that he's heading the 'Ohio 88' he's been so disciplined and so quiet that we suspect he might have something big in the works."

The next image was of a man in camouflage and a black ski mask carrying an AR-15, a big semi-automatic military weapon.

"We don't know who this guy is but we'd like to. He was posting inflammatory videos on the Internet for about six months. His videos—which are full of racial rhetoric—get hundreds of thousands of hits. We know he's somewhere in the Four Corners region, where Colorado, New Mexico, Utah and Arizona share a border. There were a series of ugly racial attacks that local law enforcement believe he was responsible for, but they've had no luck in getting a line on him. In part, because of coordination. There have been incidents in all four states.

"Lastly are the 'Dakota Sons of Liberty'."

Rennie's heart hammered and she could feel a vein throbbing in her neck that must be visibly pulsing.

Hannah.

She tried to focus as an aerial satellite image of a rural compound appeared on the wall.

"This one is a curious amalgam. Its leader, William Keller, recruits locals, many of them down and out. He lets them live at the compound as a community if they choose to. He spouts a fairly vehement version of your standard antigovernment stump speech while keeping his nose clean and staying away from anything nefarious. If it weren't for the speechifying he might be seen as a kind of independent social service."

"What makes him interesting?" Rennie asked.

"It isn't him necessarily. We think there may be a connection between the Four Corners suspect—who goes by the handle 'Cainkiller' on the Internet—and Keller's group. We've been tracking Cainkiller's activity on chat groups. He's had on-and-off communication with Keller on his website's forum. Cainkiller was making noises about a trip up to North Dakota, suggesting he and Keller might join forces."

"Did Keller seem interested?" Kyu asked.

"He was noncommittal, said everyone was welcome to visit his camp and that he'd look forward to meeting Cainkiller. Keller strikes us as wanting to be a kind of parental figure to these kids who have too much rage and nowhere to put it."

"What's with 'Cainkiller'?" Rennie chimed in. "Cain killed Abel,"

"Right," Ursula confirmed, half-smiling. "Cain killed Abel. Cainkiller's into Christian Identity. Beyond his handle, we're not sure how much he's involved in it or why he's chosen to name himself after the world's first murderer." Ursula brushed her hair out of her eyes and pressed the button on her remote to advance to the next screen. "This is the only physical description we have of him."

What appeared before them was a tattoo on the back of a man's neck. It was obviously done on the cheap. It had no color and Rennie had to scrutinize it before being able to make out the image. Its primary component was a shield. At the top was a crown. Out of it emerged a sword which bisected a sideways Z that Rennie knew was an ancient German runic symbol called the Wolfsangel and had been used by the Nazis during World War II.

"Is he a skinhead as well?" Rennie asked.

"Many skinheads subscribe to Christian Identity so he may have dabbled in it," Ursula said. "It's prevalent, too, among white inmates in prisons now and it's likely he's been picked up somewhere along the way."

"That's the only image we have of him?" Garrison said.

"That's right," Virgil spoke up. "We know it's him because he uses it as his avatar image on chat groups and he's discussed it online."

"All right, let's wrap this up," Ursula said, powering off the ceiling projector and snapping her laptop closed. "Take the next week and consider these cases from an operational standpoint. We'll meet back here next Wednesday, let's say ten thirty a.m.— my commute from Maryland was hell this morning," Ursula said, making a stab at a joke. "Oh, and to bring things full circle—so to speak—let's do our damndest to keep the snake from striking."

Rennie stood, slipping the three bound files into her messenger bag. Thoughts of Hannah in North Dakota set her mind abuzz. She wondered why she had selected this group and if she had a line on Cainkiller. She was turning to leave, thinking she might get in a run before settling down to the files when Virgil laid a hand on her shoulder and said, "Rennie, have a moment?"

Three hours later Rennie sat on her roof deck in her Adirondack, a cup of coffee growing cold on its arm. She'd already booked her flights and wondered how she was going to focus on the militia files while trying to process the revelation Virgil had dropped into her lap. She'd have to shelve them till she got back.

He'd pulled her into his office, and the expression on his face—it was too kind—told her she was about to be given bad news.

"I'll get straight to the point," he said. "The Iranian defector I mentioned..."

The shred of thought that flitted through her mind during the briefing scrabbled upward toward consciousness but Virgil spoke before it completely arrived.

"It's Nasser Armin."

Rennie frowned in confusion. Was this what her neurons had

been trying to piece together? How could it be? Ahmad Armin's brother was dead. She had seen the photographs. And, perhaps most importantly, Ahmad Armin had only existed as a target for assassination for CT3 because of the threat he posed in taking retribution for the CIA murder of Nasser Armin.

Virgil answered her unspoken question. "CIA staged the murder after picking up Nasser—against his will of course. That way the Iranian leadership would be in the dark as to how much knowledge CIA had of their nuclear program."

Rennie put her head in her hands, feeling the bones along her temple. They surely couldn't contain the explosion that was occurring in her brain.

"I'm sorry." Virgil would understand the implications of what he was telling her. That her team had died, that she'd killed—*Oh God*—seven men, and for nothing. And all because CIA and FBI couldn't figure out how to talk to each other.

"Damn, damn, damn," she said quietly. Nausea coursed to her throat and the terrible pressure in her brain gave way to light-headedness.

Virgil stood and poured her a glass of water. She took it dumbly from his hand, hardly knowing where she was, blackness crowding out her vision. As the glass began to slip through her fingers he took it from her and she felt his big hand rest lightly on her back.

Rennie took a deep breath and sat up, her vision slowly returning. She took the glass of water from the desk and drank, forcing her throat to work and her stomach to accept relief.

"If you need to talk about it we have approved counselors on staff."

Rennie shook her head.

"We wouldn't stick you with Dr. Hauser."

Rennie laughed weakly.

"Thanks—"

"Call me Peyton."

She looked at his handsome brown face, his gentle eyes. "Thank you, Peyton."

"We need you to talk to him. It's the condition he's requiring to agree to work with us. To talk to you first."

Christ, can this get any worse?

"He's in Chicago now and we've arranged for you to meet him. Tomorrow."

Rennie shook her head again. "Why would we want him? What could he possibly bring to the team?"

"True, he has no experience in our world. But his language skills are robust—fluent in Arabic, French, German and English in addition to his native tongue. And having someone in our ranks who can pass as a multiplicity of ethnicities will be useful."

Rennie frowned at his use of the present tense—it was a foregone conclusion. But something wasn't hanging together. She said, "Clearly, with just those two components, we could easily find someone more appropriate and with intelligence or operations experience."

Virgil stared at his hands, his lips pressed together. He finally looked at Rennie. "When Nasser Armin was at Harvard, he and his brother both used their mother's maiden name and took on English first names. They were being groomed for Iran's nuclear program and the leadership insisted they mask their identities in case the IAEA was keeping an eye on Iranian physics students. Nasser was known as Nate Hamidi. And Nate Hamidi was a friend of Sam Crane at Harvard. They used to argue theoretical math together. For fun."

"I'd think some role at Crane Technologies would be a better fit," Rennie said drily.

Virgil shrugged. "This is the way it's going to be."

Rennie exhaled. She could see that Virgil wasn't entirely on board with Crane's decision.

"Can I bargain with you?" Rennie said.

"Perhaps."

"I need a few days—there's a friend I need to check on."

Virgil looked at her questioningly, but Rennie knew she couldn't tell him that she was going to be sneaking around the compound of a group they were beginning an investigation on.

Finally he nodded. "Take a few days after Chicago."

Rennie took her coffee cup into the kitchen and poured a finger of bourbon into it. She drank and it burned. She drank again and it finally reached her brain.

That's enough.

She poured the rest down the drain, rinsed the cup and poured fresh coffee. The thought of checking up on Hannah had been getting stronger, making sure she was safe. Or maybe just seeing her. But Chicago first. She would fly out in the morning.

CHAPTER TWENTY-TWO

Chicago

Rennie rode on the stinking El from O'Hare Airport. She held onto the cracked vinyl strap. The train was crawling along but she didn't have far to go. And the strong scent of urine made her think it probably prudent to stand. Growing up in D.C., with its nearly pristine metro, she was always surprised at the condition of other cities' trains.

It had taken longer than she had hoped in baggage claim. Always a problem when she was traveling with a weapon. Even after 9/11 the airlines were surprisingly rational about their passengers flying with a handgun. As long as it was registered and in a locked case in luggage that would be checked. She'd been ambivalent when Ursula had handed her the box with the new Sig Sauer P239. She hadn't held a gun since the night she wound up in jail. But that was all over now and she would never allow that person to be resurrected.

She could feel a hole in her sock with her toe and focused on the nagging discomfort. How such a little worrying thing could capture the attention and drive all else away. But nothing could abolish the real worry. She was to meet Nasser in the bar of the Fairmont Hotel.

Chicago. A neutral city.

To meet the brother of the man she had shot in the night, far away, three years ago.

Her orders were to submit to his questioning in hopes that he would work with them. Why on earth the Foundation wanted him—other than his Sam Crane connection—she still couldn't divine. He had asked to meet with her. She knew he wanted something, an explanation, a catalogue of details, the final intimacies of his brother's end. Or, maybe, the Why? The How? Or her own psychological rendering of the event.

What was she required to give? His brother had died. She had killed him. Who required more of an explanation? Comparing traumatic experiences is always cheap, better kept to oneself because, ultimately, some things can never be understood. Who was to explain to her how she should assimilate the consequences of the contract she'd made with her country? Like so many before her, countless boys, patriotic or drafted, had died in wars they'd likely never considered, firing upon other equally naïve boys. How was she supposed to sit across a table from the blood relation of a man she never met but whose life she had ended with a bullet in his brain?

She checked her watch. She'd have just enough time to check into the hotel, shower and work herself into a panic before meeting him.

The night before, late, just after she'd finished packing, there had been a knock at her door. This time she wasn't as alarmed to see Garrison's shadowy outline through the warped panes. They'd sat in her living room, she on the couch, he in a chair. He snapped off the lamp next to him.

Her anxiety had felt like a separate entity, a creature inside of her, determined to crawl its way through her innards, up her gullet and take up permanent residence in her throat.

"What is he expecting?" she'd asked.

Garrison seemed more relaxed than she had ever seen him, perhaps a reaction to her palpable tension. Or maybe he'd been drinking. He crossed his legs and rested his head against the back of the chair as if this was some remote theoretical question they were discussing.

"I don't know."

Rennie tossed her head in disgust.

"Well, what do the analysts"—she emphasized the word with derision—"at the Foundation think?"

Garrison, who always seemed at first glance like the quiet uncle it was too easy to forget, uncrossed his legs, swiveled in his chair and turned his cold blue eyes on Rennie.

"You will not do this. If we are to work together, and it appears that we are, you will not approach me as if I am the oracle at Delphi. There are no easy answers. You tell me. What is it that Nasser wants, what is it that he requires from you?"

Rennie thought back to when she fought Garrison in the hallway in the boarding house in Tajikistan. And overcame him. And wondered if they were always to battle with one another or if she should accept him as someone she could physically overpower but should defer to in this new place of psychological warfare. She wrapped both hands around her ego, on the verge of saying or doing something that couldn't be retracted, and appealing to her reason, responded to him in an even and measured voice.

"He's an intellectual. Or a scientist at the very least. His understanding of violent political necessity is remote even though he was forced to consider that the result of his good work for his country would be the annihilation of innocents. He is secular and Western educated. He does not view our—my—action in black and white." Rennie sat forward running her vision across the nicks and scratches of her coffee table as she thought. "No, this is personal, not political, for him. He may not even be sure what he wants from meeting me." She turned her head and looked at Garrison. "He wants to see the agent of his brother's end. And to know the details. He is curious by nature and guilt ridden that he, somehow, could have changed the course of events."

A sneaky smile spread over Garrison's face, almost, but not quite, reaching his eyes.

"The Foundation analysts would be proud."

Rennie stifled the desire to say, good for them, and just nodded her head once.

Rennie walked from the El instead of taking a taxi. Talking to Garrison the night before had momentarily calmed her about the meeting with Nasser. But none of that palliative had made it onto the flight to Chicago. She turned into the Fairmont's circular drive, brushing by the bellmen waiting to take her bag.

She checked in, rode the elevator up to her room and didn't bother unpacking. She'd be in Chicago less than twenty-four hours and living out of her carry-on suited her fine. She crossed the room to the window and opened the heavy curtains. The city was too bright to see any stars in the sky but the glittering Gehry bridge shone in the dark like a golden oasis.

Rennie hadn't had much time in recent years to linger in museums and galleries but she'd traveled to Spain for a conference soon after she became an agent and had been overwhelmed by the Guggenheim in Bilbao. Coming upon the façade suddenly as her taxi rounded a corner she felt her heart actually begin to beat faster. Gehry's twisting and curving planes of burnished metal were otherworldly, something perhaps fit for the gods of Olympus. She hadn't known he had work in Chicago but recognizing it buoyed her mood, if only for a moment.

She looked at her watch and took a deep, uneven breath.

Just get it over with.

The ride down in the elevator from the eighth floor was much too fast. As she walked across the cold marble tiles to the bar where she was to meet Nasser, a shiver traveled over her scalp.

Oh God, I hope he's not here yet.

The bar was chill and modern and ashtrays lay on every table. She was fifteen minutes early. Nasser wasn't there yet. Rennie approached the bar and ordered a beer and a pack of cigarettes.

Just today. And then no more.

She sat in the corner and sipped the beer. She shouldn't have ordered it. She knew it looked bad, but she wasn't confident she'd be able to utter a sound if she didn't ease some of the tension in her throat. She was thinking about smoking a cigarette when he entered the bar. He was taller and thinner than his brother, but their features were similar and for an instant all Rennie could see were her crosshairs just above his ear. Suddenly the bar didn't seem quite so cold and she wished she'd worn something even lighter than the thin cotton V-neck sweater that was now much too warm.

Then he was in front of her. She got up and had to force herself to reach out her hand to him, knowing it might not be welcome.

"Rennie Vogel," he said.

Nasser's eyes seemed to be taking all of her in, consuming her in leisurely gulps. Then he noticed her hand, still hovering. He nodded without taking it and sat down.

Rennie sat too. Just then—the bartender must've put on a CD—a cool muffled trumpet filled the silence between them. Rennie recognized Chet Baker's slow, languorous hand fingering *My Funny Valentine* and wondered if the bartender thought they might be on a very awkward first date. If Nasser recognized the tune, he didn't appreciate the irony. He crossed his legs and stared at the table. "Smoke," he said, nodding at the pack of cigarettes. She held the pack out to him—she recognized the look of longing. He waved it away and she realized he was giving her permission. Without looking up, he said, "I'm not certain why I'm here." She lit a cigarette, drew on it deeply, and laid it in the ashtray.

Rennie allowed his silence to become weighted, seeping into her before she spoke.

"Perhaps you just needed to see."

"Yes." And then after another silence, he said, "I feel like a traitor. First, colluding with the United States who has never supported my country's right to autonomy. And now with the woman who killed my brother."

The woman who killed my brother. Hearing those words from Nasser—though she had never blunted the truth of them to herself—felt like a sharp spike entering her brain. Rennie was ashamed to find solace in her cigarette, ashamed to be a witness to this man's desperation, ashamed she'd ever had any part of it. But it was what it was. She took another deep drag and a long pull on her beer.

"I don't know what to say." Rennie rubbed her forehead. "I wish you weren't here in this position. I know things went very, very wrong in regard to your brother and I will regret it for as long as I live. But I have to believe that my country as the only large power left on this earth has the ability to do good." It's an easy position to be in, isn't it? she thought. The only large power on earth. Even when you're wrong you can justify that you're right.

"Good luck in that. What is the expression? You're batting a thousand…" Nasser said, a thread of anger stitched through the words.

Rennie just wanted to take it all back. Her career and all the rest could just go to hell. Women make poor killers, she thought as her empathy for him overran everything else. She wanted to get away from him then. To run as fast as she could. She didn't know if he was looking at her and she couldn't bring herself to raise her eyes to his.

Coward.

She forced herself then. He was looking at her but the coldness had left his eyes.

"I will never forgive you."

She didn't think he had intended to say it and she could see that he hated himself for it, though what it implied for him she didn't know. His shoulders seemed a little less close to his ears and he leaned forward and drew a cigarette from her pack on the table, reaching farther yet to take her Zippo and light it.

"I wouldn't either," she said.

He nodded.

CHAPTER TWENTY-THREE

Annandale, Virginia

After the Friday night service Kyu Song walked to his car. The church was in a crumbling 1970s structure that had previously housed a mega-Laundromat. The Friday service wasn't nearly as packed as the one on Sunday mornings. Kyu didn't listen to the sermon. He just wanted to sit among other Koreans and hear his native tongue.

None of the other churchgoers knew he was from the North. He hadn't wanted to navigate their questions so he'd said he was from Seoul. He'd spent a year and a half there after escaping his home country over the Chinese border. He had a natural ear and was able to disguise his accent. After their initial interest they'd learned to let him be.

Kyu drove the few blocks back to his apartment and settled himself on his sofa, the TV tuned to one of the countless cop dramas, the volume muted. He was worried about his new position. Not that he wasn't up to the task. Kyu had been a member of the secret police for ten years; he was a more than capable operative. What he worried about was not the shadow element but that it lacked the imprimatur of any government entity—that if something went wrong, he could have his green card revoked and be sent home.

Eego oowe hanya?

Why are you doing this then?

But he had raised this concern during his interview process and the Foundation had assured him that he would be protected from deportation.

Subterfuge. Lies. He didn't know how to live any other way. At least now he could feel like he was one of the good guys. If the entire thing wasn't a ruse. He shook his head, trying to throw off the paranoia that was bred into him. Although that wasn't entirely true. His father had tried to shield him from the horrible psychology that came with being a North Korean. But he could do only so much. Kyu was a young man before his father had confessed to him his own story. The confession had been a risk. It was common for family members to denounce one another. Kyu had even considered it. But in the end he saw that his father meant more to him than Kim Jong Il. And the story became something like a drug to him, so much so that every few months he would ask his father to tell it to him again. He wanted to hear it a million times. To have it forever imprinted on his mind. Now that he was so far away, surely to never see his father's gentle wrinkled face again, he would recite the amazing details of the story to himself, at those times when he felt most at sea.

Kwan Kyu Choi ran. As fast as he could. For three days he traveled by night and hid himself during the day.

He could never say what amalgam of reasoning and emotion caused the old couple to reach out to him in generosity when the very act would have brought ruination down upon them. Kwan knew he would never forget their faces even as they kept their eyes averted, out of shame or fear he didn't yet know, as they locked him into their chicken house. For two days he slept and listened to the gentle clucking of the hens when he woke. The old couple would carry steaming bowls of rice and broth across the patchy piece of ground that lay between their ramshackle house and Kwan's shed. On the third day they unlocked his door and motioned for him to follow. His stomach seized in fear. Perhaps all this time he'd unknowingly been their prisoner as they waited for the authorities to arrive.

Once they were inside the little falling down house, the woman said to him, "Take off your clothes." The house was a single room with a dirt floor. A poorly ventilated woodstove warmed the room but made Kwan's eyes sting from the smoke it spewed. The woman must have read the fear in his eyes. She glanced at her husband, then they bowed their heads to Kwan in unison and turned their backs to him. It was only then that he saw a set of clothes on the low, rough table.

He quickly disrobed, wishing he were nearer to the smoky stove. Unfolding the first garment, he instantly recognized the rough gray fabric as the battle dress of the North Korean infantryman. Above the left pocket, a white patch of cloth had been stitched and upon it was written "Song."

Kwan slipped the shirt over his head and hurried into the baggy drawstring trousers. He cleared his throat.

The Songs turned to him but kept their eyes fixed on the floor. Then Mrs. Song withdrew a blade hidden somewhere in the folds of her clothing. She bent to his discarded threadbare uniform, the last physical evidence of his identity, and cut it into strips, feeding them bit by bit into the fire. After, as they sat sharing their first and final meal together, Mr. Song spoke.

"Our son, Hyo Jin, was released from duty ten days ago. He had a wound to his leg. By the time he arrived home to us, his blood was poisoned from the infection. His flesh was so hot it nearly burned to touch it. He died after two days. We buried him near the stream where he loved to fish."

Kwan bowed his head in an offering of sympathy,

"You cannot make it across the border alive."

Kwan couldn't think about the consequences of this fact, of all that was lost to him, his family, his life. He would have to think about that later. Then Mr. Song turned to Mrs. Song who dipped her head in assent.

"You will now be Hyo Jin. We've had no visitors. No one knows of his death."

They told him that he must leave the next morning before anyone who had known Hyo Jin could discover him. He was to go north, nearly to China, to a mining town called Hoeryong. He was to carry a letter addressed to Mr. Song's cousin who would take him in.

Kyu often thought of the old couple. He had never asked his father if he was tempted to contact them. He wished he had thought to ask him that. Kyu massaged the back of his neck and snapped off the TV. Then he lay back on the sofa and went to sleep. He was awakened ten minutes later by the ring of his cell phone. He didn't recognize the number and let it go to voice mail. A moment after he listened to the message, he jumped up, grabbed a notebook and transcribed it:

"Mr. Song, my name is Tommy Damone. I'm a reporter for *The New Yorker*. I understand that you work for the Foundation for Liberal Democracy and I'd like to speak to you for an article I'm writing about an incident in Tajikistan in August 2001. Please give me a call when you have the chance."

Vogel.

Kyu jotted down the reporter's number. "This isn't good," he said aloud in Korean. "Not good at all."

CHAPTER TWENTY-FOUR

Devils Lake, North Dakota

Hannah was parked along the street in her rental car. She was looking over her notes with all the windows rolled down, hoping the cold air would wake her up. It was early still and the street was deserted except for an old man in overalls walking slowly toward her down the sidewalk, past shops that looked like they hadn't changed much since Kennedy was in office. She supposed the town was quaint. Quaint had never done much for Hannah.

The old man halted as he came alongside her car. Bending his bony frame, his hands on his knees, he cleared his throat.

"Lost? Need directions?"

Hannah smiled the friendliest smile she was capable of. "I'm okay. Thanks."

The old man peered at her a few beats longer, then nodded crisply, straightened himself and continued his slow shuffle down the sidewalk. Hannah returned to her notes. Then her head snapped up. *Your instincts are going to have to be better than this.*

She hopped out of the car, hurrying after him.

"Sir, do you mind if I ask you a few questions?"

He turned back to her slowly.

What a horror getting old is.

"No, ma'am, not in the least. How can I help you?"

Hannah explained that she was a freelance reporter doing a piece on William Keller and the Dakota Militiamen. He agreed to her switching on her recorder.

"Will Keller is a good man. This country's gone to pot and he's got the right ideas. I know a few of his boys—all good boys, they are. Don't cause any trouble. Just looking out for our best interests."

"What about your local political leaders? They're not addressing the problems?" Hannah asked.

"Politics is as mean and dirty as a bag full of rattlers. There's no future in the system. The power needs to go back to the people. Natural rights of man and such," he said with a wave of his bony hand.

Back in the car Hannah watched his retreating form in her rearview mirror. She exhaled forcefully. "Christ, everybody's got an opinion."

Hannah knew a great reporter had to be not only objective but empathetic, with the ability to stand in her subject's shoes no matter how roughshod and ill-fitting they may be. She had to be able to see past her own prejudices and assumptions to get to the essence of the man's discontent.

"But, Lord, people are a nightmare."

Enough. Push all the bullshit away.

She needed to be ready for her meeting with Keller later that morning. She knew she was rusty but she *had* to make herself open to ideas she'd otherwise consider repellent. To be able to see what more, perhaps, banal resentment those ideas might be a stand-in for.

Hannah lifted the lever under her seat to make room for her PowerBook on her lap. Her battery was running low so she turned the key in the ignition without starting the engine and connected her battery charger to the cigarette lighter. The radio came on with it, a deejay chattering. She turned down the volume so that it was only a whisper. She clicked open the file on her desktop labeled "Tommy."

Tommy Damone had emailed her scans of everything he had on the Dakota group and she had downloaded them before she left D.C. As she paged through the PDF file, she was again struck by how much material was here, more than she'd hoped for. She would approach this piece as a standard investigative profile. At this point she couldn't hope for any bombshells; at first glance Keller's group didn't look like they were up to anything illegal.

Tommy's info on Keller seemed pretty thorough though. Unfortunately, since he hadn't been out to Dakota, he had next to nothing on his men. But the final page of the document was curious. It was a scanned page of handwritten notes—Hannah recognized Tommy's scrawl—he'd had taken on ruled paper.

WK CIA ?

weapon

MW WV pen

DoS connection

Very curious indeed. Hannah made a note to email Tommy once she found an Internet connection.

She ran her hands over the driver's seat until she found the right lever and reclined two notches. Then she reached behind her and pulled from the backseat a book of Walker Evans' photographs she'd bought on a whim at a bookstore in Madison, Wisconsin. She flipped through the black-and-white images of old blighted towns, of dirt-poor people. Though she had seen poverty at its worst in Central Asia, in Iran and in Africa, she'd been shielded from it in her own country. At first glance, Devils Lake didn't appear to be crushed by poverty but she knew the region had its share of economic hardships. Besides, poverty in America didn't have the same face it had in the rest of the world or even in the forties when Evans was driving the dirt roads of the South with his camera equipment in the back of his truck. Nowadays, it might mean you skip or scrimp on a meal so you don't have to cut the cable access for your TV. Though poverty looked different, that didn't mean it wasn't a struggle. Nor did it blur the inequalities. Somebody always had more. And it always stung.

This area of the country had been hit particularly hard. Preparing for her interview with Keller, Hannah had combed through Lexis-Nexis, reading stories of entire areas becoming ghost towns as Big Agriculture gobbled up family farms. There was just no way for them to compete. Hannah suspected that this monumental transition, which had been taking place for decades, in no small way accounted for the appeal of the militia groups.

She closed the book of photos and turned up the radio. The deejay was talking about, of all things, the Beach Boys. But with a kind of reverence usually saved for the Sunday pulpit. Hannah had always avoided the conventional, and the sixties surf band represented little more than a corny cliché whose time she was glad to see had come and gone.

But something about the deejay's tone roused her curiosity. He was talking about an album, a supposed masterwork by the leader of the band, left to founder forty years ago as he descended into mental illness. It had been anticipated by the audiophiles as a thing of genius and those lucky enough to have heard a bootleg recording had been lusting after it ever since. Brian Wilson had eventually reined in whatever it was that had felled him. Maybe, the deejay speculated, good and appropriately prescribed pharmaceuticals had done the trick. Now, he had resurrected the album and, finally, it was available. Some were calling it the finest, the most perfect, the most American album of the rock era.

The deejay sounded absurdly proud as he announced that he would be playing the album in its entirety. Hannah was about to snap off the radio when the first track began. She paused at what sounded like a choir in a cathedral emanating from her speakers. Yes, it sounded like the Beach Boys, but like nothing she'd ever heard from them. The piece segued into a little shuffling doo-wop interlude and then the second track began. It was called "Heroes and Villains."

Simultaneously, the title and the jangly rhythm she'd dismissed as clichéd and irrelevant reached out and grabbed her by the throat and then slipped down and seemed to rouse something in her heart. Feeling welled up from someplace deep and burned her nostrils.

Yes, there *was* ambiguity in life. It *was* often difficult or even impossible to distinguish the good from the bad. But sometimes ambiguity slipped off into the shadows in the face of cold, stark reality. Sometimes there *were* heroes and villains—she'd seen them firsthand. Something seemed to pop inside of her and her cheeks flushed in anger as a lump of unwelcome emotion formed in her throat. She punched the steering wheel with the flat of her palm.

What the hell is wrong with you?

The music was trite and naïve. And meant to manipulate. But she found she was shaking, completely taken up by it. *Was this what the militiamen heard? Was America a holy thing?* And then her thoughts suddenly coalesced and she snatched a pad and a pen from the passenger seat.

The harmonies were as gripping and as reaching as any oratorio. This was something more than secular music, but its religiosity was not the kind that reached to the sky. It stretched its arms wide and plunged its hands into the earth, new world earth that birthed the beginnings of a brand-new political system, one that gave the lone man and the lone woman a kind of autonomy they had never known. A system that wormed outward and was finally hailed as the seminal shift in human political relations, where the animal in us, hard-wired to behave hierarchically, sat down on its haunches, dropped its ears and stepped forward, ready to engage the modern world with reason at the fore.

Hannah tossed the pad aside and leaned her head back, exhausted. Maybe she *could* commune with this world but had *chosen* not to. Something rose up in her then and she envisioned herself upon her knees, her head in her hands, sobbing. Sobbing for all that she'd never opened herself to. And for all that she knew she never would.

This is as close to an emotional purging I can come to, I suppose.

When the music stopped, Hannah snapped off the radio and pointed the car toward the hotel. She felt foolish for all she had felt while listening to the album. And Hannah Marcus hated feeling foolish.

Later that morning, after she'd settled into her room and had breakfast and two strong cups of coffee, Hannah spoke to Keller on the hotel phone. For an hour he spoke with the politeness of a man used to having a certain dynamic with a woman, where the woman was something precious, a hothouse flower to be shielded from every danger. He suggested when she left the hotel that she come prepared to stay for a few days, that there was a cabin available and she would be comfortable there.

"I'll consider it," Hannah said, though she had no intention of doing so. It seemed sheer lunacy for a lone woman, and a Jew to boot, to put herself in the hands of a man with an angry and violent ideology. But something in Keller's manner put her at ease and as they talked more he struck her as only wanting to be understood. By the time they hung up, she had decided to take him up on it. A perfect opportunity to see the daily operations of the compound firsthand.

CHAPTER TWENTY-FIVE

Devils Lake, North Dakota

William Keller rinsed the last of the shaving cream off his chin. He stared for a moment at his reflection and compared his strong features with the slighter ones of his father in the creased black-and-white photograph he kept wedged into the corner of the medicine chest mirror. There was something in the shape of the lips and in the deep-set eyes. Yes, he was his father's son.

Keller checked his watch. A few minutes after 10:30 a.m. The woman journalist was supposed to get here at eleven. He had misgivings about talking to her. Lately, he had misgivings about a lot of things. Since he'd begun the Dakota Militiamen three years ago, he'd been so deep inside the little world he'd created he'd felt neither need nor desire to interact with the larger world. The phone call from Hannah Marcus had reminded him that real people existed outside of his dominion—real people with their own unique opinions instead of the monolithic mindset he usually attributed to outsiders. It had set him to thinking. Was he doing the right thing?

Keller sat down heavily on the edge of the old claw-footed tub and pulled the worn wallet from his back pocket. The letter his mother had given him on his sixteenth birthday lived in one of the transparent sleeves. He removed it gingerly and unfolded it. He had read it so many times he could recite it by heart. But handling the now yellowed notepaper made him feel nearer to the man he'd never known. As he read, his lips silently mouthed the words that were his mantra.

Dear son,

Though your mother and I have not had a chance to discuss it, I'd like you to be called William after your great-grandfather.

Will, I fear I may never meet you. My work for this great country of ours may require that I make a sacrifice I am both loath and honored to give.

Remember, my dear son, that I am with you. And remember always,

Honor your mother,
Honor your country,
And tell no lies.
Your father, Donald Keller.

Keller remembered how keenly he'd felt the absence of a father. He'd needed a strong guiding hand to help him navigate the choppy waters of adolescence. His mother, silent and withdrawn, only seemed to flit about in the shadows of the dark and dreary house. By the time he was eight years old, he was already taking care of most of his own needs—heating cans of Campbell's soup for his meals and using the big washer and dryer to clean his clothes.

After she'd given him the letter, his mother had told him that his father had been an undercover CIA officer and had died in the line of duty. And that the government had thrown him over to shield its involvement in his assignment. From that day forward, Will felt ensnared in a wet, clinging net. How could he honor his country while despising its duplicitous government? He never appealed to the CIA for confirmation or more information about his father's death—his mother convinced him that none would be forthcoming, that it would be a futile endeavor. Thus, brick by brick, an image of that organization and the U.S. government itself as a ruthless behemoth was built in his mind.

The letter appeared to have been written hurriedly and Keller had often tried to imagine the scene that was unfolding around his father, ultimately leading to his death. He'd even wondered if Donald Keller hadn't paused to take the time to write his son, would he have lived?

Keller returned the letter to its home. Would his father see the work he was doing as honoring his country? Since the call from the reporter this question had been eating at him.

Before heading toward the camp entrance to wait for Hannah Marcus, he stood on his porch—the only original structure on his property—and scanned all that he had built. It was after he'd finished his tour of duty in the Marine Corps, with medals of valor and bravery pinned to this chest, that he decided he would assemble his own band of brothers. But he soon realized that his antigovernment, anti-CIA stance was not enough to rally those willing to flout the law and—when the time came—wage war on the real enemies of their country. His father's final words in the letter always ate at him, a conundrum he couldn't puzzle out.

Tell no lies.

But his father *had* told lies, had assumed an entirely different identity.

Will had told lies, too, accepting that sometimes a man had to. For the greater good. He told lies to his followers, whose rage at the government had more to do with its lax position on immigration and the rights afforded to minorities who they believed were no better than animals.

Will walked slowly down the porch steps to the dirt lane. He was beginning to question whether he had gone too far, if he should have taken the more conventional route to make change. Maybe that was why he was willing to meet with the reporter. He was ready to be judged.

CHAPTER TWENTY-SIX

Hannah turned her rental car off the highway onto the dirt road "seven miles outside of town on the right" as Keller had indicated on the phone. She still felt unsure about meeting the man on his own turf. At the very least she should have told someone where she was.

Most people have at least a few close friends. And you don't, so what? She'd never been one to have a best friend to confide in. That kind of intimacy just never interested her. Though few would agree with her, she believed that such relationships were formed out of weakness and insecurity. And she didn't consider herself to have much of either quality. She didn't need anyone to commiserate with, to unload her fears onto. That never solved the problem anyway—it just made you feel less alone and she wasn't afraid of feeling alone.

Hannah checked the odometer. Only half a mile more. It was beautiful country but the woods and the isolation reminded her too much of Tajikistan. An unruly thought flitted into her mind. *Maybe you are deliberately putting yourself into a potentially dangerous situation to try to prove you're actually safe when nothing bad happens. If you had that best friend, she might point that out to you.* "Well, we'll soon find out," she said aloud.

A tall, well-built man stood at the entrance to the camp lifting his hand in greeting.

Keller had mentioned in their initial conversation that he'd been a Marine and she could see it in his bearing as she got closer. He stood with a wide stance, hands behind his back as if at parade rest. He wasn't the proverbial jarhead but his hair was cut very short. The military had figured out how to get into a man's brain and stay there. *Therein lies power,* she thought.

She pulled the car up next to him and lowered her window. "Mr. Keller. Hannah Marcus," she said, reaching out her hand to him.

"It's pretty exciting, you coming out here to talk to us," he said, leaning down to her. "I think the whole town is talking about it."

"Really?" Somehow just that knowledge made Hannah feel safer.

Keller directed her to where she should park her car.

With the exception of an old farmhouse, the compound had the look of a rough outpost in some remote land—which in a way it was—with a touch of the Wild West. Keller drove her along the dusty, rutted road in his own vehicle, a Jeep with oversized wheels, pointing out the buildings where the men slept when they stayed at the compound. They parked alongside Keller's house and continued their tour of the camp on foot.

Outside the simple building where Keller indicated the men's meals were cooked, two slaughtered deer were tied by their back legs to a frame, their blood draining into a basin. Hannah took the sight in fully, feeling a quiver just below her navel. Two men had just hung a third animal by its back legs.

"Ever dressed a deer?" Keller asked, looking amused.

"Not lately," Hannah said in attempt to show good humor.

"That's Buddy Olsen. And that's Marshall Wallace." Keller

pointed to the two men. Buddy was small, slight really, and had the type of complexion that could become nearly purple with embarrassment, as it was now. Hannah supposed not too many women turned up at the camp.

Marshall Wallace, by contrast, was tall and wiry and pale with dark, deep-set eyes. Hannah thought of Tommy's handwritten diagram and the arrow connecting two sets of initials. WK and MW. William Keller and Marshall Wallace?

Keller introduced Hannah to the two men as the journalist he'd told them about. Buddy stammered and nodded, but Wallace only glared at her as he sharpened a lethal-looking knife on a leather strop. There was something almost hypnotic about the way the knife hissed over the leather. A tattoo encircled the man's wrist. Black gothic letters. Hannah could make out a 'C' and an 'A' but nothing else. Then Wallace let go of the strop and with a glance at Hannah turned and plunged the blade of the knife into the deer, up to the hilt. Then, backing off a few inches he jerked the blade upward, from the rib cage to just short of the place where the animal's back legs met. The intestines tumbled out, a slithering mess, at his feet.

"Easy there, Wallace. Careful not to puncture those guts or you'll be in a fix."

Wallace's eyes bore into them as they turned away and walked on.

"Do any of the men live here full time?" Hannah asked.

"A few."

"Those that live here full time, do they work? How do you support yourselves?"

"We don't require much," Keller said as they made their way along the road. "All my men are trained in advanced survival techniques, so we can provide a lot of what we need for ourselves. But we are wired. We have electricity and even an Internet connection. Most of our revenue comes from the magazine we produce—*Survival Kit*—or through donations routed through our website or our radio show."

Hannah had listened to all of the archived Internet radio programs—this was a new venture for the militiamen and she had gotten caught up quickly. Like the magazine, the radio show was concerned mostly with survival tactics, rarely venturing into anything controversial. It was in the chat rooms on his website where things got interesting.

Hannah jumped as she heard the crack of a weapon firing.

"Target practice?"

Keller nodded. "Want to check it out?"

"Why not?"

A few hundred yards further they came upon a line of ten or twelve men shooting at makeshift targets—the outline of a man painted on a tree, cans set up along the top of a sawhorse. And most ominously, a kind of scarecrow set up on what looked like a broomstick.

"Want to give it a go?" Keller said, smiling.

The last time Hannah had handled a weapon was in Tajikistan. "No thanks," she said.

Later, after she'd seen the rest of the camp and collected more background material on Keller and the organization he had built from the ground up, Keller showed her to her cabin, suggesting she get settled in. The cabin was comfortable and clean. Keller seemed so proud to be able to offer it to her that she was embarrassed for him. He stood with his hands stuffed in his back pockets of his jeans. She knew he was hoping she'd be pleased, impressed. She forced herself to say, "It's very nice," though she had a difficult relationship with the word "nice," finding it to be insidiously useless. But he didn't detect anything amiss and his lips parted in a smile.

She held up her cell phone. "Doesn't look like I'm getting a signal out here."

"No, the big companies haven't made it out our way. You really have to be with a local service to get a decent signal."

"You said something about an Internet connection?"

Keller chuckled. "Well, just in the farmhouse. But I'll bring a modem over and get you hooked up for dial-up. But I'll warn you now, it doesn't always work so well," Keller said before leaving her alone in the cabin.

Hannah supposed that would be better than nothing, thinking it was like living a decade behind the rest of the country out here. The cabin suited her well enough. It was small but she was long accustomed to small spaces, growing up in the claustrophobia of a two-bedroom apartment. If anything, that had helped when she was confined to her ten-foot-square stable in Tajikistan, allowing her to keep her sanity.

When Keller came back she powered up her laptop and almost felt nostalgic when they finally heard the familiar strangled sound of the modem connecting to the ISP server.

"There you go," Keller said, clapping his hands.

When he was gone she opened her email—it took an eternity to load—and wrote Tommy with some questions about his diagram. She clicked 'Send' and the hourglass indicating that the program was working appeared and continued to hang for the next twenty minutes as she made herself a drink and finished settling into the cabin.

The next day Hannah left the compound early, driving the rental back into town. She needed to pick Tommy's brain sooner than later and since she wasn't having much luck with Keller's modem, she decided a stop at the public library was in order.

Hannah glanced at the sky as she drove. It was deeply blue but the clouds were what caught her attention. They seemed not so much ethereal but more like a mountain of white and gray sitting upon an invisible shelf in the sky. After stopping for a quick breakfast at a diner Keller recommended, she pulled into the library parking lot as the first raindrops began to fall.

The library seemed new and was nearly empty this rainy morning. A group of children sat in a circle at the back listening to a librarian read. A few patrons were browsing the stacks and a few sat at the two banks of computer terminals that faced one another. A bearded librarian behind the reference desk nodded at her.

Hannah chose a terminal at the end of the row, facing the entrance. She popped her floppy disk into the drive and pulled up the notes document Tommy had emailed her. AOL Instant Messenger was already installed. She logged in and pinged Tommy who wrote back that he was watching baseball but there would be no greater pleasure than to multi-task with Hannah.

Damonerep: My boys need to get the lead out of their ass.

MarcusH07: They should be glad you didn't go into coaching.

Damonerep: They sure as shit should. You got trouble in River City?

MarcusH07: It's a lake and a damn big one. No trouble so far. Just lots of unanswered questions.

Damonerep: How can I help you?

MarcusH07: The diagram—I emailed you about it but didn't have any luck with the local technology.

Damonerep: You mean they have computers out there?

MarcusH07: Funny. How did you get a line on MW? Marshall Wallace, right?

Damonerep: I didn't but it looks like you have. I didn't have a name for MW. Just initials in Keller's chat room. MW was sniffing around about acquiring some big illegal weapon. Never said what it was. But it got me hungry to find out more.

Hannah glanced up from her monitor to see Wallace himself settling into the chair opposite her. She froze for an instant and then nodded at him.

"It's Wallace, isn't it?" she said to him. "From Keller's camp?"

He was wearing a band T-shirt, wet and plastered to his chest. It was printed with a gaping-mouthed skull and crossbones with Skullhead written underneath in gothic script.

Wallace glared at her. "No comment," he finally said.

Hannah shrugged.

Damonerep: You there, Marcus?

MarcusH07: Guess who just sat down across from me?

Damonerep: Our boy, MW?

MarcusH07: You got it.

Damonerep: Keep your wits about you out there. That's one kid that's looking for trouble.

MarcusH07: Noted. The diagram. What's with the DoS reference? Department of State.

Damonerep: I don't know. There's something funny with MW. I guess it wasn't in my notes, but he goes by "Cainkiller" on the Internet. I have an NSA source who ran it through his databases. There was an entry for Cainkiller but it had been locked down tight. All he could tell me was someone at State had done the locking down.

C.A. Cainkiller. Hannah thought of the tattoo with the gothic letters encircling Wallace's wrist.

MarcusH07: So what do you think is going on with State?

Damonerep: I don't have a clue. Could be anything really. Without more we're just barking up every tree in the park. Probably not a good use of our time.

A long, low peal of thunder rumbled overhead. Hannah looked up to see Wallace get up and head for the exit.

The entrance to the library was typical of modern buildings, with an airlock vestibule and two sets of glass double doors enclosing a space between them to maintain temperature. Wallace had just passed into the airlock, the first door still slowly closing, and was about to push through the second when the librarian called to him.

"Young man?"

She saw Wallace turn. He stood in the airlock, staring through the glass, his face a mask of anger, the cords along his neck so taut they looked like they could break through the skin. Hannah couldn't read the librarian's expression as he entered the intimate space, but her instinct, too late now, was to stop him.

Damonerep: You there? Or did they have to send the Internet to the shop—

MarcusH07: Something's up here. Signing off.

Damonerep: Stay safe, Marcus.

MarcusH07: Will do.

Hannah logged out of the computer and ejected the disc from the drive. When she looked back to the scene unfolding in the airlock, she could see it had already escalated. Wallace's back was to her but she could almost see the rage wafting off his body as the librarian talked to him. His shoulders were pulled back and his fists were clenched at his sides. The librarian's face became more unsure by the second. Then Wallace raised his arm and jabbed the librarian in the chest with his index finger before pushing through the outer doors and running down the walkway through the rain. He jumped into the green Explorer she'd seen parked by his cabin, his tires screeching against the wet pavement as he tore out of the lot.

The librarian stood stunned, frozen in the airlock, gaping after him.

Hannah gathered her things and headed for the exit.

Right place, right time, she thought. She couldn't even count how many breaks in a story had happened this way.

The librarian locked eyes with her as she entered the airlock. "You're the reporter staying at the Keller compound?"

Lord, I'm glad I don't live in a small town.

"That's me," Hannah said.

He said his name was Yates. His anxiety was palpable.

"I can't afford for anyone to see me talking to you but there are things you should know, that someone should."

"About the man that just left?"

He nodded. "I told him I was thinking about going to the police." He paused. Fear had pushed his voice up high in his head and he had to catch his breath before he could continue. "I hadn't meant it. I was just trying to get him to talk to me. I just wanted to help him. He seems...troubled. Now I'm thinking I *should* go to the police though it might be more prudent for me to talk to you." He paused again. "But not here. I probably shouldn't be talking to you at all."

"What happened exactly?" Hannah asked.

"I think I saw things I wasn't supposed to see. While he was online."

"What did you see?"

He shook his head. "I overstepped my bounds."

"Does he know what you saw?"

"Yes." Yates looked terrified. "He said that I just made the biggest mistake of my life."

"Can you get away now?"

He shook his head. "Come by my house. Tomorrow night. After work. Say six o'clock?"

He pulled a card from the inside pocket of his tweed coat and jotted his address on it. The card was old, yellowed, and had a perfectly round hole in the bottom. Must have been from an old card catalog. She flipped it over. The card read: *The Psychopathology of Everyday Life* by Sigmund Freud.

Back at camp, walking from her cabin down the road now muddied from the rain, Hannah was glad to be left to her thoughts. She didn't plan on telling Keller about the incident at the library. At least not yet. She wanted to see what he would offer about Marshall Wallace without prejudicing him in any way.

Hannah was beginning to get a feel for the layout of the camp. There were three other cabins across from her own and all appeared to be occupied. A jeans-clad young man with a buzz cut sat on the front step of one of them. He eyed her as he arced a buck knife under his fingernails. She raised a hand to him. She'd need to interview some of Keller's men at some point if they were willing. Other than receiving the occasional belligerent eye from Keller's men, Hannah hadn't seen anything amiss at the camp. But she still couldn't shake the unease she'd felt since she'd gotten there. She couldn't put her finger on it, but it was almost as if there was a malevolent undercurrent vibrating through the camp.

Don't be absurd.

Hannah hated catching herself succumbing to superstition. A dark cloud passed in front of the sun then and the camp was plunged into a murky gloom. Hannah felt a gust of clammy air on the back of her exposed neck and turned her head sharply to convince herself that nothing was behind her.

"You have to get it together," she said, gritting her teeth.

"You're early."

Hannah started at the sound of Keller's voice calling to her, surprised to find herself only a few paces from the steps leading to his porch. Sitting there with him at an unfinished table a few minutes later, drinking instant coffee, with the sun sinking toward the horizon, Hannah tried to shrug off the foolishness she felt for her moment of panic on the road. She opened her line of questioning, pressing record on the digital recorder that lay between them on the table.

"Your men—do you recruit them or do they come to you?"

"Both." Keller sat with his long legs stretched before him, his hands linked and resting on his belly.

"Do you insist upon a military background?"

"I prefer it," he said. "And I prefer men who have served during wartime, particularly those who have seen combat. We're already starting to see guys who served in Afghanistan and Iraq."

"I would think military service might reinforce their allegiance to the government."

Keller barked a laugh. "No guarantee of that. It can go either way."

"Wallace. The man who was dressing the deer yesterday. What can you tell me about his background?" Hannah asked, her curiosity getting the better of her.

"Ah. Marshall Wallace." Keller sat up and leaned closer to her, lowering his voice. "Of all the men here, he was one I was most hesitant to take on. But I see promise in him and when I have more time, I plan to take him under my wing, so to speak."

Hannah thought of the tattoo on the back of his neck. "Is he a skinhead?"

Keller chuckled. "A woman to the point, I like that. Yes, I guess you could say that."

"And how do you hope to influence him?"

"I hope to make him see what is truly important."

"Which is what?"

"That the administration of this great country has grown corrupt over time, that it has lost sight of its true purpose."

Keller spoke emphatically and Hannah could see that he was gearing up to make an argument to her. "And what is its true purpose?" she said, handing him the question he expected her to ask.

"To protect and support its people—especially the downtrodden."

Hannah wondered if he knew how much he sounded like a liberal. "So, the racial question is not important to you?"

Keller paused. "It is what it is."

Hannah didn't press him further, afraid to alienate him.

"Is Wallace ex-military?"

"In a sense. He enlisted at eighteen but didn't get beyond boot camp."

"Discipline problems?"

"You could say that."

Hannah remembered the diagram in Tommy's notes. *MW.* And next to it—*WV pen.*

"Has Wallace ever served time?"

Keller looked at her, frowning. "Not that I know of. I have all the men fill out paperwork when they join the Militiamen. I don't do background checks or anything like that so I wouldn't swear to it, but he never admitted to anything like that. I mean, he was a skinhead so I'm sure he's been hauled into the county lockup a time or two."

Hannah nodded. "Your platform, so to speak, is that usual trinity in militia groups—antigovernment, white racial superiority and Christian supremacy."

"Yes," Keller responded without hesitation but Hannah saw a slight shift in his eyes, a slight tightening of his jaw. "But I don't focus on the racial stuff."

Hannah nodded. "Your writings suggest your primary concern is corruption and lack of transparency in government. The other two elements seem less important to you."

"That's correct."

"It seems to me that what you're doing here, what you've accomplished, is very much the same as political organizing, community organizing. I wonder if you wouldn't get further in your cause by dropping the racial and religious elements and focusing on the government issues by more traditional means. Say, by running for office."

Keller shook his head, scratching at a splinter on the table. "It was something I considered, but judging by others who attempted the same thing, support was lacking."

"Would you say that you have appealed to the community's desire for these other elements—the racial and religious elements—as an expediency and that you, personally, have no real passion for them?"

Keller was a handsome man. He smiled shyly, dropped his eyes and said, "No comment."

Hannah had to wonder if she was being played. There was something…charming about Keller—a word she despised. But he seemed to be trying to telegraph to her that he was less hard line than he proclaimed himself to be.

Keller slapped his thighs suddenly. "Look at that sunset. Just gorgeous, isn't it? Why don't we walk over to the rise where there's a better view," he said, standing.

Hannah would have preferred to keep going—she felt she was beginning to get somewhere, but she switched off her voice recorder and slipped it into her pocket as she followed him off the porch. The evening was chilly but the air was so crisp and fresh she didn't mind.

"Big storm coming, you know." Keller said, modulating his long stride so that his pace matched Hannah's.

Hannah looked at the sky. The clouds were churning in the fading light and just then she saw a flash of lightning in the distance.

"Don't worry—it won't get here for an hour or more. We'll have you safe and sound back in your cabin by then."

Hannah glanced up into his smiling face. She could sense that he was attracted to her. "Beautiful, isn't it?" Keller said.

Hannah nodded. "It is."

"God's country. I bet you don't get much of that in Washington, D.C."

"No, I suppose we don't."

"It's important to keep in touch with the land. Human beings get too far away from it and they don't know what they're about anymore."

Hannah wondered if that was true. "Would you say the militia men agree with you? What draws them to join up?"

Keller stared into the sky. When he finally spoke, he didn't look at her. "Honestly? A lot of these guys, most of these guys, just want to feel important, to feel that finally they have one up on the college-educated assholes who think we're nothing but a bunch of rednecks. They want to dress up and fool around in the woods and act like they've figured everything out. Some guys are into sports, wearing their team gear, spouting stats. These guys are into survivalism." He turned to her finally. "Think about it. On some level they feel their very existence is threatened. And you know what? They're right. How many more corporations will come in here and remove any chance they have to live as independent men instead of as some jerk killing cows with a bolt gun all day long in some godawful stinking slaughterhouse? These guys are convinced they're going to be the last ones standing when the end comes—they like to imagine something apocalyptic, something huge and explosive, when really it's been happening for decades, bit by bit, with every lost farm, every lost small business, every little town left to die. This," he said, sweeping out his arm to encompass the camp, "gives them something. Being a man in America today is more complicated than it's ever been—especially if you're not already standing on the top of the heap."

Hannah scribbled in her notebook, trying to encapsulate the gist of his argument. His analysis seemed dead on from everything she'd read as she prepped. She hadn't expected Keller to be so lucid.

If she didn't find the bombshell in Keller's group that Tommy suspected she'd find, she was beginning to imagine a different slant for her piece. Instead of an investigative story, she could envision a feature on Keller's camp, viewing it through a socioeconomic lens. "In the seventies was the farming crisis—"

"Was?" Keller interrupted. "Farmers in this country have been screwed over for years. The world is passing them by.

Their livelihood has been sold out to Big Agriculture. Where do they see themselves reflected in the media other than as doltish rednecks? Rural people have few options and I suspect you know that men need to feel like they have a purpose."

"What's your purpose, Mr. Keller?"

Keller ran his hand over his cheek. "I want these men to know that they're the real American men. I want them to know they have a place in this strange new world."

"Why strange?"

"Because it's unnatural."

"Unnatural how?"

"Men weren't meant to sit in offices all day playing with imaginary money."

"But all that is natural isn't necessarily good. Nature is brutal," Hannah countered.

"I don't mean that. I mean that you get away from yourself when you only live in a world of concrete and glass and plastic."

Keller was looking at Hannah with passion lighting his face. But it wasn't her role to prop up his ideas. She decided to return to the racial question.

"What about the charges of anti-Semitism?" she asked.

Keller looked away from her. "I feel bad about it. It's not my thing but it's expected. If somebody brings up the Jewish conspiracy in international banking or some of the more extreme Biblical interpretations, I'll say, 'We all know what's what but it only hurts to focus on it.' That works for a lot of them. The truly entrenched bigots either keep their mouths shut or go find a more radical group."

Hannah wanted to tell him that here was his opportunity to lead, to change minds. But it wasn't her place and the thought of allowing anti-Semitism to fester as a stratagem made her stomach turn. The sky was darkening again with storm clouds and only a few traces of light remained from the day. "Shall we wrap it up for today?"

"Sure," Keller said and then he paused. "Are you Jewish?"

Hannah nodded, curious where he would take this. But he only nodded back.

CHAPTER TWENTY-SEVEN

Devils Lake, North Dakota

Rennie paced along her rental car. She'd pulled over a half mile short of the entrance to the Dakota Militiamen compound. She'd hoped to catch Hannah at her hotel. The front desk clerk, apparently unconcerned with privacy regulations, had said she wasn't there. It hadn't taken much prodding for him to offer even more. "Why, Miss Marcus was barely here an hour before she checked out. She's a reporter, you know," he'd said, leaning on the glass-topped desk and getting comfortable. "I hear she's staying out at the Keller camp."

Now Rennie was so ramped up she was nearly jumping out of her skin. She needed to *do* something. She speed dialed Hannah's cell phone for, probably, the twentieth time since she left the hotel. And for the twentieth time it went straight to voice mail. Hannah might not have a signal. She might have turned the phone off. Or someone might have taken it from her.

Not much of an optimist, are you?

One way or the other, Rennie was going to find out. She reached in the open window and grabbed the Dakota file from the passenger seat. Splaying it out on the hood of the sedan, her penlight between her teeth, she flipped to the map of the compound.

Two miles.

She needed more detail. She switched on her Garmin GPS. Her signal was weak but the image finally loaded. She zoomed in close and followed the road to the compound with her finger, scanning for places where she could hide the car. There were two possible spots. One a mile and a quarter in. The other was further, only a few hundred yards from the compound and too close to risk someone hearing her engine or her tires on the road. Lightning jagged across the sky to the west and was followed by a distant rumble of thunder. Rennie hopped back in the car hoping the rain would hold off.

It was fully dark by the time she pulled back onto the highway. There was very little traffic coming or going and when she turned onto the compound road and killed her headlights, there wasn't a soul as far as the eye could see.

The dirt road was in better shape than she expected and since it had rained recently she wasn't wary of kicking up dust. So she didn't waste any time and only slowed when she got near the spot she'd targeted on her GPS. As she backed the rental off the road—in case she needed to get away quick—she could see it was a good place to hide the car. It wasn't far from a creek—a spot probably used by fishermen so they didn't have to trek in from the compound humping their gear.

Rennie eased the car over the uneven ground, the suspension of the certainly on-road sedan rocking hard. She backed in as far as she could and killed the engine. She stepped out and leaned her weight against the door until finally hearing the latch snap into place. Crouching next to the car to get her bearings, she felt her adrenaline running at high pitch. Just the way she liked it.

But any pleasure she might have taken in it was blunted by her worry for Hannah.

And something felt wrong. A tremor of dread settled in the pit of her stomach. Still crouching, she leaned back against the car and slipped the Sig from her waistband. She held perfectly still and listened, opening every sense to its fullest capacity. She could hear the chittering of crickets and the katydids, the strange siren song of the cicadas. The woods were alive and electric with activity.

Just sounds of the night.

She'd been buffered from it. In Istanbul. In D.C. That aspect the world takes on when nature reigns. She shivered hard.

Let it go.

This wasn't Tajikistan. And as long as she could do anything about it, it never would be.

Stop thinking and get moving.

Rennie stood, feeling exposed, and moved toward the road. She walked in the grass where her footsteps would be muffled and where she could take cover in the woods if a car came along.

No, this wasn't Tajikistan. Nothing like it. She was able to think this once her brain had calmed down. But Hannah *was* at the end of this road. Her stomach burned for a moment. Was she being presumptuous? Turning up without an invitation, meddling in her professional life?

Yes. She was being presumptuous. But she had to make sure Hannah was safe.

Once she resigned herself to that fact, Rennie picked up her pace and was at the edge of the compound in less than ten minutes.

Buddy Olsen eased open the door of the cabin he shared with Marshall Wallace. His walkie-talkie had burped with Wallace's code that meant Buddy should go find him. He'd been all over the compound looking for him and figured he should check their quarters before signaling back to him which would piss him off. And there wasn't much worse than Wallace pissed.

"You in here, man?" he asked. It was pitch-black inside the cabin.

"Over here and keep your voice low."

Wallace was lying on his bunk by the window with a cloth draped over his head. Only a few centimeters of a pair of night vision goggles protruded.

"You trying to catch that reporter lady in her skivvies, you perv?" Buddy laughed, hoping he'd get a turn.

Wallace ducked from under the cloth and turned his cold eyes on Buddy. Though he'd stopped shaving his head soon after he'd shown up at camp, he was still the scariest dude Buddy had ever seen. Nobody had crazy eyes like Marshall Wallace. Buddy shivered.

"Do you have the message ready?"

"Yes." Buddy had written out Wallace's message before he'd gone into town for a roll of duct tape.

"You have your weapon ready?"

"Yes."

"It's time for us to do something."

Hannah stared at her laptop screen. Her dial-up connection was still mind-numbingly slow, if it worked at all.

"Finally," she said when the Lexis-Nexis article loaded. She alt-tabbed back to the Word document where she was typing in her notes from the day. Though she was still fully entrenched in the information-gathering element of the story, her brain automatically entered into formulating the narrative. She'd worked on deadline too long for this kind of multitasking to be anything but second nature. It also meant she had something. Something compelling. She typed the final page of notes, saved the article as a text file and closed the laptop.

She leaned back in the chair, lengthening her spine and enjoying the stretch. She went to the kitchen and looked through the cabinets until she found a glass. She was glad she'd taken Keller up on his offer to stay at the compound. She'd have a much more intimate view of the rhythms of the camp and her piece would be richer for it. And she was growing comfortable with the cabin, especially since she'd made a small fire in the grate. Though rough hewn, the cabin had most of the elements that constituted civilized life—stove, refrigerator, coffeemaker, microwave. The bed and sofa were comfortable enough. The presence of carpets covering most of the plank flooring somehow set her at ease and made her think she wasn't completely in no man's land.

She poured two fingers of Chivas into the glass and went out to the porch. It was at the back of the cabin—away from the dirt road that ran through the center of the camp and away from the eyes of anyone who might be curious about the "lady reporter"—Keller had the unfortunate tendency of introducing her this way. There weren't any chairs on the porch—it was an entirely rudimentary structure—and Hannah sat on the edge, her feet in the grass. It was close to being, but not quite, too cold. The full moon and the ever-approaching lightning lit the huge sky. A field of several acres separated her from the line of the woods.

The view, the crisp air, the failing light—it was lovely. Though she never craved nature Hannah appreciated it when it was offered to her. She felt her muscles relax, the Chivas softening the edges of her brain.

She thought about the conversation she'd had that morning with her mother. She'd been eating breakfast in the organic café Keller had recommended—the only escape in town from grease and batter. Her coffee had been served in a mug that read, *Your breath is the voice of your soul.* She'd rolled her eyes and then her cell had rung. She cringed when she saw her parents' number on the screen. She'd forgotten to call when she arrived as promised. Her mother had sounded unusually excited and said she had news. Hannah sipped the Chivas and shook her head.

Rennie. In the apartment she grew up in, that Hannah had tried and failed to move her parents out of—with the newspapers and the floral prints and the dead relatives.

She couldn't envision it.

Hannah didn't like collisions. There was work, there was her private life, and there were her parents. It was as if each were a planet that existed within the same solar system, but she would only ever travel to one at a time. Overlaps were not only anathema but impossible. How could she exist in two places at once?

Her mother and Rennie talking. About her. She didn't like it. But she also had the strange sense of Rennie coming closer, as if she were homing in on her. She wasn't sure whether or not she liked *that*. She'd never liked the idea of being watched over. But there was something—what was it?—enveloping, perhaps, that Hannah couldn't say she disliked.

She thought to go back inside and check if Tommy had responded to her email. In his hand-drawn diagram, there was an arrow between MW and WK—Marshall Wallace and William Keller. And in the middle was the word "weapon." Keller certainly had plenty of weapons at the compound. That was a given and Tommy would have known that too, so why mention a weapon unless it was something out of the ordinary? Or illegal? She'd meant to ask him about it when they were IMing but the altercation between the bearded librarian and Wallace had distracted her.

Hannah heard the snap of a twig and jerked her head to the right.

It's nothing. Enough with the jitters.

She couldn't see anything in the dark and had convinced herself that it was a nocturnal creature or just a rotten branch giving way when a form began to emerge out of the shadows. Hannah wanted to stand, rush inside and bolt the door but she couldn't seem to move. The silhouette took on substance, now in the light of the moon, and she saw a tall, slim figure walking slowly toward her. Her heart began to pound as the figure came nearer.

It can't be.

And then Rennie Vogel was right there in front of her, emerging out of the moonlight. Hannah began to shiver.

Rennie stepped up onto the porch and sat down behind her, slipping her arms around her waist. She kissed her lightly on the neck. Hannah leaned her head back.

"Are you a ghost?" she whispered.

CHAPTER TWENTY-EIGHT

"No, I'm not a ghost," Rennie said quietly. She could have sat on that porch forever, her arms around Hannah waiting for the storm. But Hannah wriggled out of her embrace, conveying her urgency by pulling Rennie to her feet and into the cabin. She closed the door behind her, pushing Rennie against it.

"You're here," Hannah said, her eyes filled with emotion.

Thankfully, it wasn't an accusation. "I met your parents—"

"I know."

"I just had to know you weren't in trouble."

Hannah shook her head. "No, I'm not in any trouble."

"You have to be very careful." But Rennie knew even before she said it that Hannah would not want someone worrying over her.

Hannah pressed her lips together. "What do you mean? Is there something you know?"

Rennie paused. She knew she shouldn't... "Have you come across a man called Cainkiller?"

Hannah frowned. "I have," she said, looking at Rennie intently. "He's here. Marshall Wallace."

A name.

"How do you know about him? Who are you working for?"

Rennie told Hannah what she could and was vague about the rest.

"I think you should leave with me," Rennie said.

Hannah smiled. "That's not an option. Nothing has happened to suggest I am anything but safe. I'm not a cop. I'm not going to go breaking into his cabin or doing anything to make him focus on me."

"But—"

Hannah interrupted Rennie by placing a finger on her lips.

"Enough," she said as she moved toward her.

The only illumination came from the fireplace and the moonlight streaming through the windows. Rennie's eyes met Hannah's and she expected to feel her lips upon hers again. Instead, Hannah slipped her arms around Rennie's waist and laid her forehead on her breastbone. Rennie stroked the back of her neck.

"What is it?" Rennie asked. She couldn't tell what Hannah was feeling.

Hannah didn't respond. Then whatever had gripped her passed and she tipped her head upward and captured Rennie's mouth. It was neither gentle nor patient. Rennie felt consumed as Hannah's hands moved over her waist and hips, every inch of her body alive with sensation. It had been too long ago and too many miles away and a part of her wanted to weep with relief. She had promised Hannah that they'd be together again. But she'd hardly believed it herself. It had seemed too much an impossibility. But now, Rennie couldn't imagine anything that felt more right.

Hannah broke their embrace then and without a word pulled Rennie's shirt over her head. Rennie wore nothing underneath. Hannah paused only a moment to reach out a finger and trace a line between Rennie's breasts and across her abdomen. Then she slowly encircled Rennie's waist with her hands, finally dipping her fingers beneath the waistband of her pants. Rennie shivered at her touch. Hannah leaned into her then, touching her lips to Rennie's collarbone before slipping Rennie's pants and underwear off her hips, letting them drop to the floor. Rennie shifted out of her shoes and stood naked before her. Hannah's eyes shone. Resting a hand lightly on Rennie's hip, she stretched up and put her mouth close to her ear. "I'm glad you were in the neighborhood."

Then she took two steps away and stood loose-limbed, a half smile playing on her lips, as if she were offering herself for inspection. During their harrowing time together in the dark woods of Tajikistan, Rennie had seen many elements of Hannah Marcus. Fear and courage. Exhaustion and determination. But it was only when they were finally alone and safe in a hotel room did she see the first flicker of boldness, something she suspected then was Hannah's true nature. Now, standing before her, supremely confident, that boldness almost verged on bravado. With one hip thrust out like Donatello's bronze David, Hannah was secure in her own power. Rennie's pulse thudded in the presence of it. Hannah began to undress then, making no show of it. As the last of her clothes slid to the braided rug, Rennie stepped forward until they were only inches apart. Rennie felt as if the very atmosphere was charged, every particle around them quickening in response to their desire, so palpable it emanated off them in waves of heat.

Then Hannah backed away, catching Rennie's hand as she went. She clasped a corner of the thick duvet as they passed the bed and pulled it along with them, draping it thickly over the floor in front of the fireplace. Rennie took her by the wrist and pulled her into her, her other arm around her waist.

"I've got you." Rennie hadn't meant to say it aloud.

"Do you?" Hannah said. Her tone was playful but Rennie could detect an undertone of willfulness.

"Don't I?" Rennie felt the heat from the fire against her thigh and hip.

The sound of thunder invaded the cabin then. Even the fire seemed to respond to it, the flames suddenly darting higher as if they were trying to escape. Hannah kissed her again, deeply, before breaking off with a laugh. Her arousal was unambiguous. It was almost a living entity in the room and her voice was rough with it. "Looks to me like *I've* got you," she said breathing into Rennie's neck. She raised her thigh and held Rennie tightly. "Yes, I've definitely got you."

Rennie awoke. She hadn't intended to sleep. She hadn't wanted to cede a moment of their time together to slumber. But once they'd moved from the fireplace to the bed, sleep had overtaken her.

Hannah stirred. "You're awake."

"I should go," Rennie said. "Can't afford to get caught sneaking in and out of your cabin."

Hannah stretched and slipped her arm over Rennie's hip. "Reminds me of summer camp."

Rennie tried to picture Hannah as a teenager and couldn't conjure the image.

"Did you charm all the girls?"

Hannah's head was on Rennie's shoulder, her eyes closed, as she stroked the sharp bone of her hip with her thumb.

"No girls then."

Rennie paused. "Am I your—"

"Oh, no, no." Hannah rose up on her elbow, looking down into Rennie's face. Rennie couldn't read her expression. "But you're one of the few." Hannah kissed her gently. Then she got up suddenly and trod into the kitchen. She poured a glass of water and then turned, leaning against the counter, watching Rennie. She seemed completely unselfconscious in her nakedness. It both aroused Rennie and made her slightly anxious, so exposed she was.

The sheet had slipped from Rennie's own body. She felt the need to cover herself but didn't move. Hannah's face softened into the more gentle, vulnerable expression she remembered from their time in Tajikistan. "You're very lovely," she said.

Then Hannah came to her, sitting on the edge of the bed,

offering her the water. Rennie sat up slightly to drink. Hannah set the glass on the table next to the bed and put her hands along Rennie's jaw, working her fingers into her hairline. She dropped her hands to Rennie's shoulders. "Stay forever."

But the words sounded empty. There was no forever here, in a borrowed cabin on the compound of a heavily-armed militia group.

Rennie forced a smile and hesitated, constructing and deconstructing her words, before she finally said, "I want to see you again."

Something hard flickered over Hannah's features before they softened again. She leaned down and kissed Rennie on the forehead, the softest of kisses.

"Yes. You will. I want that too."

Hannah watched from the back door as Rennie slipped again into the darkness, raising her hand before she disappeared into the woods.

Yes. She is a lovely woman.

She continued standing at the open door, feeling the cold air slip through her thin robe. The storm was nearly above the compound now, the clouds scudding across the moon which was at turns blazing or shrouded in the darkness.

But then flashes of lightning lit up the field and the woods as if a moment of creation were trying to break through. The thunder, when it came, booming, felt like a physical presence and the door rattled on its hinges, as if quaking in fear. A shiver ran over Hannah's skin. In the silence after the roar, she thought she heard a voice. Or voices maybe. And then the rain began and she closed the door.

Hannah slipped off her robe and put another log on the fire. She added a finger of Chivas to her glass and sat on the tangled duvet in front of the hearth and let the heat soak into her. Her brain felt a blank. She tried to work up a kernel of anger at Rennie's sudden intrusion. But she couldn't. She pulled the blanket over her shoulders, curling it around herself.

Why had she lied when Rennie asked if she'd been with another woman? Hannah shrugged as if the question had been posed aloud. She'd felt too much at that moment and was afraid of what her face might betray.

When are you going to stop being afraid?

Hannah shrugged again and took a sip of the Chivas. Was it fear? It never felt like fear. If her parents had taught her anything it was to be careful of what or who you loved. To be cautious about who you let in because in an instant, *poof*, they can be taken away. But Hannah hadn't ever been particularly cautious. Whenever she'd felt an outpouring of "love" from someone she was dating, she'd always chalked it up to a momentary glitch, a temporary collision in the brain, a pheromonal imperative that would fade as soon as the first glow wore off. And the first glow always wore off. So, she'd never encouraged it. She supposed it was cruel but she had just never felt like playing along.

But why hadn't she felt it? That, she imagined, was the real question. There had been nice boys, sexy boys, smart boys. And occasionally there was one who was all three. *Fareed.* But Fareed was anything but a boy. She *had* cared for him and wondered what they might have found together if he hadn't made the swerve into terrorism, if he hadn't been her captor, if they'd just happened to meet. On the street, in a café, at a conference. If, if, if. None of it mattered because Rennie Vogel had seemingly fallen from the sky onto that little dusty ridge and changed everything for all of them.

Hannah stoked the fire, watching the flames dart and leap, hungry to consume ever more. Thunder crashed above and the world sounded like it was being rent. The storm was fully upon them. Hannah stood and, dragging the duvet around her, crossed to the door and checked that she had locked it. The rain was pouring in earnest. She was thankful she wasn't out in it, like Rennie. She remembered being so drenched and cold when she was in Tajikistan that she thought she'd never warm again. And then Rennie had put her arms around her just as she had tonight. Sitting behind her, encompassing her in warmth.

Screw it.

Yes, she felt something for Rennie Vogel. There, she said it.

Outside the cabin the sky had become cloudy and churning. Rennie's mind too was awhirl. She should have insisted that Hannah come with her. But she knew it would have been futile. And Hannah was right—there was no sign that she was in danger.

You need to stop being overprotective.

Aside from the worry, Rennie still felt unsettled about their time together. Though she was in no doubt of Hannah's passion, her emotions puzzled her. Rennie couldn't parse them out. She took a deep breath and tried to clear her head. This was no time to be off her game. She'd have to figure out what Hannah's emotional reticence might mean later. Now, she focused on her surroundings, opening her ears for any unusual sound.

She couldn't detect anything amiss—the chittering of insects, a distant rustling in the woods, probably deer or fox. The storm was coming fast though. She tilted her face to the sky where the clouds were swirling and darkening as she made her way toward the woods. She turned and saw Hannah still standing at the door. Rennie raised her hand to her and felt a nagging pull, wanting to go back, pretend they were anywhere but here. But this wasn't the time or place for a more prolonged reunion. So she pushed on, hyperalert now that she was out in the open.

She felt the legs of her pants dampening from the dew-laden field grass. Then thunder shattered the near silence so completely Rennie could feel it in her bones. Once she entered the woods it was very dark. Her penlight would make her going easier but it was safer to leave it off. She figured she'd trek the quarter of a mile through the woods before making her way to the road and her car.

The clouds hadn't overtaken the moon yet, and picking her way over fallen logs and broken rock was easier than she'd expected, but she felt more at ease when her GPS indicated she should veer right and she made her way out onto the road. She had just spotted her rental when she saw what looked to be the outline of a box truck parked in the road beyond.

Shit.

Then something hard thudded against the back of her head. She felt herself falling, her vision already blotted out. When she hit the rock solid ground the rest of her mind went blank.

CHAPTER TWENTY-NINE

Buddy stood over the woman on the ground, looking back and forth between her and Wallace.

"What the fuck, man? Who is she?"

"I don't know. A cop or a Fed or something. And look what we have here." Wallace pulled the Sig Sauer from the back of the woman's pants and held it up.

"Nice piece."

"No shit, Sherlock. Check her for ID."

Buddy ran his hands over the woman's body.

"Take your time why don't you?" Wallace kicked Buddy's foot.

Buddy grinned up at him. "She's clean."

"Clean, huh? You got some jargon now?"

Buddy's grin faded.

"Come on, Buddy boy, we're getting drenched out here. Wipe that stupid look off your face and grab her legs. We've got to get her into the truck and then you can have a good look at her."

"Shouldn't we get Keller?" Buddy said uncertainly.

"Fuck, no." Wallace grabbed him hard by the sleeve.

"What are we going to do with her?"

Wallace smiled. "We're going to have a little fun. And you're finally going to see some combat."

Rennie awoke, her head pounding. She opened her eyes to nothing but darkness. She couldn't place herself in the world. Was she in Tajikistan? Turkey? D.C.? She closed her eyes again and tried to arrange her broken perceptions into something coherent.

She was lying in the back of a vehicle, moving fast over uneven terrain. Her wrists and her ankles were bound with what felt like duct tape. And she was naked.

Naked.

She could feel debris on the floor of the vehicle—maybe some kind of a box truck—adhering to her skin.

Christ.

Rennie began frantically moving her arms and legs, working on loosening the tape, when the truck came to an abrupt stop. She heard the cab doors open and men's voices—laughter. When she heard the scrape of the latch on the door to the back, she positioned her body as it was when she woke and closed her eyes. Then she heard heavy boots on the corrugated metal bumper and felt a steel toe knock hard, once, into her ribs.

"Wake up. Now."

Two men stood above her in full forest camouflage. One was tall and thin, his hair cut close. He had a small duffel bag slung across his chest. The other was much smaller, almost slight. Both carried silenced H&K MP5s, one with a night vision scope—the same deadly submachine gun favored by special forces that she had carried in Tajikistan.

The taller man looked at her hands and feet and Rennie hoped he couldn't tell that she had made some progress in loosening the tape. The smaller man stared at her breasts, a stupid expression on his face.

"Whaddya think, Buddy? You think she's a Jew? Or maybe a nigger lover? Or better yet, these lady cops tend to be dykes. What do you think, Buddy? Maybe she's a nigger loving Jew dyke. That would be perfect." Then he knelt down to her and placed a finger under her chin. "But there's one thing I'm sure of. She's some sort of cop."

Rennie opened her mouth to speak and became aware of the throbbing pain in her head. "I'm not a cop. I just came to check up on my friend," she said, speaking slowly and gently in a voice she had never heard before.

The tall man came closer and gripped her around the jaw with his long-fingered hand. He squeezed and raised her head closer to his.

"Then why do you have this?" He shoved her face away from him as he stood. Her head hit the floor of the truck hard and she almost blacked out again. Then he turned back to her, her Sig in his hand.

"I—"

"Shut up."

The boot came down on her again, harder this time. She tensed her body and took the blow in her strong obliques, spared from hearing the sharp snap of her own ribs.

"You better save your energy, sweetheart. If you're lucky, you're going to need it. Let's go, Buddy."

"Yeah."

The tall man pulled a dark hood from his duffel bag and turned his back to her. Rennie saw the tattoo on the back of his neck.

Cainkiller.

Every shred of her being wanted to cry out, *No, No, No,* as he slipped the hood over her head and darkness came over her again. And then they were lifting her by the arms and legs, carrying her awkwardly out of the truck. The cold hit her bare skin and chilled her instantly. The two men carried her for a long time, stopping occasionally to shift her roughly. Branches clawed at her skin. They were in the woods.

The men hadn't carried shovels. Were they just going to shoot her and leave her? Something about their behavior, their manner, seemed manic and she wondered if they were high.

Rennie tried to measure how much ground they were covering. They had been on foot for, maybe, twenty minutes. A slow pace, no more than two miles per hour. Which put them about half a mile from the truck. They splashed through several steps of water, a creek probably, and then the terrain changed, became softer and they dropped her to the ground.

Sand.

The hood was ripped from her head. The men stood above her. Cainkiller was smiling. She was on the beach of an enormous body of water.

Devils Lake.

"You can tell us who you are if you want." Cainkiller's expression changed, rage rippling along his jawline. "But it doesn't matter. Everything has been set into motion. And neither you nor that reporter or anybody else is going to stop it."

He paused and then seemed to remember Buddy's presence. He cleared his throat.

"The sin of man," he said haltingly. Then, bizarrely, he began to giggle.

"What's so funny, man?" Buddy said, looking worried.

"Nothing, nothing," Cainkiller said, regaining his composure. "The sin of man is upon you." He reached down and slipped the hood back over Rennie's head.

Rennie struggled then, thrashing her arms and legs, further loosening the duct tape. But she was stopped as Cainkiller's boot came down hard on her again. Her hip screamed in pain.

"Wait," she heard Buddy say softly.

"For what?"

Buddy's voice sounded desperate. "Maybe we could, you know, do her first?"

Rennie heard a quick movement and the distinct sound of an automatic pistol being cocked.

"Even we have a code of honor, asshole," Cainkiller said. But then he giggled again. "Besides, there's no time."

At that moment, as they were focused on one another, Rennie rolled, blind, toward the water, the sand which had seemed soft now gripping and chafing her.

"Grab her!" she heard Buddy say and just as her skin touched the lake's edge, she felt their hands on her arms and legs again, lifting her roughly. This time they walked fast, hurrying.

"Okay, we're set, right?" Buddy asked. He was breathing hard.

"We're set."

Then, their hard boots sounding on three wooden steps. And then more wooden, hollow footsteps.

The pier. They were carrying her down the pier.

God help me.

Then they stopped. All was quiet but for the sound of the water lightly slapping against the piles.

"Okay, on the count of four," Cainkiller said.

Rennie took great gulps of air inside the hood as they began to swing her body, laughing like schoolboys, losing their rhythm and beginning again.

"One, two, we've got you..." they sang together. "Three, four, you're no more."

She held her breath.

"And, *heave*..."

Airborne, Rennie knew it wouldn't last long.

She entered the water inelegantly, her body slapping the surface hard. The water was freezing, unforgiving. In an instant she was under and the hood, already loose, floated away from her face.

Thank God for that.

She sank, quickly, feeling the deep, numbing cold, willing herself to remain calm. She concentrated only on systematically moving her arms and legs hoping the water would render the glue of the tape less effective. She worked to find the most efficient motion in this thick, wet environment. The awareness that her lean body was sinking like a rock made the adrenaline course through her veins like rocket fuel.

Rennie felt something heavy and slick slither across her back and tried not to imagine what manner of sea creatures would soon be nibbling on her inert body if she didn't save herself.

Just concentrate.

Back and forth she worked her arms and legs until her muscles started to burn. Then, at last, her legs came free. Exhilarated by this first success, she undulated and kicked strong and sure toward the surface, working her hands as she rose. Her lungs were shot through with pain and she wanted nothing more than to open herself, to take something, anything into them and kill the ache, but she kept her mouth shut. When one hand finally slipped from the tape secured around her wrists, she reached out her arms and took vast, arcing motions toward the barely perceptible light at the surface.

Buddy Olsen had always imagined himself in heroic situations. Foiling plots, rescuing the girl, saving the day. That's why he'd joined the army. But his diminutive size—he was only five-six and very thin—ensured him a technical position. He'd made it to Iraq but never once left the Green Zone.

In Keller's organization, he had hoped for more—even if it killed him. He fantasized about that too. He knew all about Ruby Ridge and Waco and saw himself as a new kind of warrior, one not beholden to the usual chain of command. But his supposed bravery had never actually been tested and when Wallace smacked the woman hard on the back of the head, so hard he thought she might be dead, all he could think to do was to run to Keller.

He was glad his better instincts had won out. As Wallace said, Keller was small potatoes. And Wallace had great ideas, ideas that would be put into action. Soon. Any day he'd said. This thing with the woman—whoever she was—was just a test. A kind of training ground. To show that Buddy was ready to join Wallace on the mission.

Buddy felt the meth Wallace had given him wearing off and a sliver of doubt crept into his brain. He was crouched just inside the woods peering through the high-powered night vision scope of his submachine gun at the surface of the lake. It seemed impossible that the woman would be able to get out of the tape in time. He scanned from the shore to the end of the pier and beyond. The moon was full. Smoky fog hung over the water. It seemed dark and primeval and lightning spread tentacle-like fingers across the sky. Buddy heard the rain begin again and the first few drops hit the brim of his cap. One droplet fell onto the back of his neck and slid slowly down his back until it soaked into his shirt where it felt like a cold bony finger. He turned his head slowly just to make sure.

Nobody there.

Steam continued rising off the lake as the rain fell. Buddy looked away from the scope again and saw the forest filling with fog as well. It almost seemed like it was moving toward him, coming for him, and he had to force himself not to jump up and run out into the open.

Maybe she's already dead and that's her ghost.

"I don't believe in that crap," he said aloud. Or did he? He pressed his eye back against the scope again, scanning the surface of the lake. With the raindrops hitting the water it looked alive, like something was bubbling up from underneath.

Buddy remembered camping on the north side of Devils Lake when he was a kid. Boys sitting around a campfire roasting fat marshmallows and telling scary stories. But the one that stuck with him was the one about the sea monster and the legend that it lived in a river that supposedly ran underground all the way to the Gulf of Mexico and opened up near the bottom of the lake. There'd been many reported sightings of the primordial, fire-breathing sea creature, monstrous in its proportions, even a few grainy pictures on the Internet. Buddy had always liked the idea of a Loch Ness monster lurking in Devils Lake. It was fun and he'd imagined a big grinning cartoon like Puff the Magic Dragon. But tonight his mind took him to some darker place and as he watched the steaming, bubbling lake he could almost see the creature assembling itself out of the amorphous mist. But this beast was no cartoon. It was hulking and begrimed with slime, its mouth a gaping, blood-dripping maw.

Suddenly Buddy had a thought. *Devils* Lake. Maybe that's

how it got its name.

Then, he saw the surface of the water begin to move and felt himself rooted to the ground, expecting to see the monster at any moment. The lake was rippling more deeply—*something* sure as hell was coming up. Buddy shook with fear. The lake's surface was finally rent with such ferocity that Buddy jerked backward. Unable to tear his eyes from it, he kept his scope transfixed on it.

It can't be.

She rose from beneath, near the shore, taking long lumbering steps, water cascading from her body, lean and perfect, shimmering in the moonlight. Her arms were wrapped around her as if against the cold. And then she stopped—with the water at her knees—stood tall and tossed her head. Through the strange light of the scope, Buddy could see her hair lifting and arcing in a corona, pregnant droplets of water slipping off the ends. Her body shone before him—but just for a moment. She strode purposefully toward the beach, looking left and right. Buddy flicked the safety of the submachine gun to the off position and put his finger on the trigger.

CHAPTER THIRTY

Breaking the surface of the lake, her mouth gaping, Rennie took in air in huge hungry gulps. So much that she almost submerged again with the relief of it, it was so divine. Then she found her footing—slippery, blessed sand under her feet—as oxygen flooded back into her brain. The cold hit her hard and she sank in on herself. Only one thought coursed through her.

Alive.

She righted herself then and flinging her hair out of her eyes, trudged toward shore. The oxygen continued its restorative work and her mind began to hum.

Men. Guns. Cainkiller.

She dropped down onto one knee, letting the water touch the tops of her shoulders, so that only her head emerged from the water, and took in her surroundings. It had begun to rain and the light of the moon blinded her after the desperate, unholy dark of the lake's depths.

Rennie tried to think. What the hell was happening? Thunder crashed and she dropped a few inches lower into the water. The storm was in full force now. Thunder, lightning, rain streaming over her face.

Had they left? Or were they hiding?

It didn't matter. The water was freezing. Her teeth were chattering. Her body temperature was plummeting and she felt her limbs becoming numb. She *had* to get out of the lake now. Men with guns or no.

As she moved toward shore, keeping her body submerged, lightning cut the atmosphere and for two seconds the world around her was bright as day. In that moment she saw, just a few feet beyond the water's edge, the glint of steel. A weapon lying in the sand.

A trap.

She looked left and right but could see nothing in the dark. Dread settled over her.

One of the men had a night vision scope and she knew she might rise from the water only to be met by a barrage of bullets, tearing her flesh.

But she couldn't stay in the water or she would freeze to death.

She reached to her throat and found the St. Catherine medallion still there. She gripped it, tight in her fist and closed her eyes.

Now.

Rennie bolted from the lake, loping as fast as she could through the sand.

Struggling forward, she saw that a silenced MP5 was lying atop a foot-square piece of cardboard. On it written in heavy, rain-smeared black magic marker was:

YOU HAVE 60 SECONDS.

What kind of game are they playing?

Her clothes lay beside the note and the weapon. She noticed a hole in the shirt near the collar. She knelt down and slipped her finger into it and then it dawned on her. Another bullet slammed into the ground next to her, throwing sand over her foot. She grabbed the shirt and pants in one hand and the MP5 in the other and ran, firing a shot toward the dark wood line. She tore barefooted through the sand for the woods, away from the spot she thought the shots were coming from.

Rennie entered into the woods, right-flanked sharp another twenty feet, ready to fire at any sound or movement. She hit the ground and listened intently but could only hear the rain biting into the soil and the thunder rumbling overhead. She popped the thirty-round magazine out of the subgun. Ten bullets nestled against one another. She hoped it would be enough.

She struggled into the sodden shirt and pants feeling immeasurably better now that even a few millimeters of soaking fabric separated her from the world. Her feet were already damaged though, maybe even bleeding. That could pose a problem eventually but for now it was meaningless. First and foremost, she needed to know how many men were in the woods. At least the two she knew of. Cainkiller. And Buddy was the other man's name, she remembered now. But that didn't mean there weren't more already in position when she was flung into the lake. In a tree stand, she thought, scanning above her. Or hunkered down around the next bend in the creek. They could be anywhere, waiting her out. Or worse. Already stalking and hunting her.

Rennie's eyes were quickly becoming accustomed to the dark. She listened again and still heard only the rain. But there was something…

What was it?

She cocked her head toward the sound, angling the muzzle of the MP5 in the same direction.

There it was again.

Yes. Feet moving slowly through leaves. If it was the man with the night vision scope, she was in trouble. She lay as flat as she could, her finger on the trigger, the contours of the weapon comfortingly familiar.

She heard the sound again and then saw the glint of a scope.

Cainkiller carried his MP5 nose down, angled snug across his body. He paused, listening, before reaching for the driver's side door handle of the truck. He chuckled as he swung into the cab and fired the ignition. Buddy and the lady cop could keep each other busy for a while. Of course, the lady cop's end of that deal was her dead and sunk in a few inches of ooze at the bottom of the lake. He'd told Buddy to wait at least two hours. That a good soldier made no assumptions. That some people can hold their breath for hours to be sure. He'd almost laughed at Buddy nodding his dumb head at that one.

Leaving the note and the subgun by the water's edge was just for fun. Something for Buddy's simple mind to latch onto. Cainkiller just hoped he wouldn't forget the gun when he headed back to camp. Or the cop's clothes. That was even more crucial.

Cainkiller held the wheel steady with his knee as he tapped out a quick text message to Buddy. If only he could have figured out a way to get rid of them both in one go.

Nope. Nopers. Nopest. He didn't need Buddy anymore. He didn't need him at all.

You never needed him. You don't need anybody. You're the Lone Fucking Ranger. The Lonest Fuckinest Ranger that ever was.

Cainkiller produced a manic whinnying sound from high up in his throat.

He could have shot Buddy, he supposed. He'd be zipping out of town in twenty-four hours and by the time anybody caught up to him it would all be over. And his name would be forever enshrined among the likes of Timothy McVeigh and Eric Rudolph. Though he suspected historians would find him, Cainkiller, *way* more interesting than those white trash blockheads.

Immortality.

He wanted to imagine the headlines, the twenty-four hour news coverage on CNN and MSNBC and FOX News, but details kept nagging at him. They should have weighted the woman's body. But then Buddy would have wussed out on him knowing she had no chance of ever getting out of that lake. He should have thought it all through more systematically. He should've cut back on the meth days ago. He'd meant to. But the razor blades were always lying in wait for him.

Waka, waka, waka.

Cainkiller put the drug out of his mind and checked his watch. He tried Buddy again on his cell phone, this time calling instead of text messaging since Buddy hadn't really gotten the hang of the new form of communication yet. The rain was coming down in a torrent and the truck sloshed through deep ruts that had quickly filled with water. Buddy didn't answer but Cainkiller couldn't worry about it. He had to get to camp and get the hell out of there before Buddy got back. Even though he hadn't gotten the weapon from the douchebag in Wisconsin, like the Einstein he was he'd figured out a way around that little problem. Now there was just one more thing to tidy up and he'd be rolling east, en route to all that he was destined for, now and for always, amen.

Rennie kept her eye on the winking reflection of the scope. She had to make a decision. Shoot now and reveal her position or wait and see.

Wait and see what?

That was the question. She had her bead on one man and couldn't afford to lose it. She wasn't sure what the parameters of this game were, but she wasn't going to wait to find out. The scope was pointing directly at her, had been for at least five seconds.

What are you waiting for?

All he'd have to do was change the angle of his weapon and he'd be swallowed by the darkness again. And then he did just that.

Dammit.

Rennie lined up her sights, aiming where she last saw the glint of the scope. She controlled her breathing and put her finger on the trigger. At the final instant before she fired, a light appeared. Her eyes were able to make out the man's form. He had been walking toward her but had stopped. His cell phone screen was glowing through his pants pocket and he was looking at it dumbly.

Now.

Rennie fired twice and leapt to her feet. She ran, zigzagging through the trees, in search of better cover, until the earth arced down to the creek. She jumped down, slipping in the mud until she found traction and crouched behind the incline. It was only then that she heard the man screaming.

"My legs, my legs!"

Buddy.

She lay still, her subgun pointing up. Where was Cainkiller? Rennie's vision was more penetrating now, accustomed as it could be to the dark, and she scanned a 360-degree arc around her. Other than Buddy whimpering and squirming on the ground, she neither heard nor saw any movement. Then Buddy stopped whimpering. She couldn't decide whether she hoped he was dead or alive. She heard motion again and leaned into the bank of the streambed, peering over the edge. It was rocky and sharp and slimy. Her knees and feet sank into the mud.

She heard the sharp crack of a branch and saw the glint of Buddy's scope waving to and fro. Somehow he was on his feet again and moving toward her. He was sobbing and in the midst of it, she heard him saying, "You bitch, you fucking bitch." Then it was as if the night exploded. Lightning split the sky as multiple flashes erupted from the man's muzzle, bullets pounding into the trees, biting into the ground, as he unloaded the MP5 blindly.

This can't go on.

Rennie rose up, just enough for a clear shot, and fired. A trio of double shots, in a structured pattern where she saw the muzzle flash. Ducking back down, she heard him fall. She scrambled backward, changing her position slightly and with care. She lay in the mud, still and alert, for twenty minutes.

Where in the hell was Cainkiller? Had he run off when he heard the first shots? Not likely. He didn't strike Rennie as a coward. Anything but.

Rennie had found that there were times in dire situations

when the commonplace intruded. Depending on your personality, this could be a source of comedy or heartbreak. Rennie supposed she didn't have much of a sense of humor. As in Tajikistan, when she glimpsed the Nike logo on the bottom of the teenage boy's sneakers as her battery of bullets blew him off his feet. Nor now, when Buddy's cell phone ringtone reached her ear through the racket of the storm. Mick Jagger crooning "Time Is on My Side." She thought there must be a demon of irony residing over one of the circles of hell.

Rennie waited for the phone to stop ringing and then waited another five minutes before making her way slowly out of the creek bed toward the fallen man. For an instant a thought flitted across her consciousness.

You killed again.

A part of her wanted to curl up on the cold, hard, wet earth and go to sleep.

How had it come to this?

When she'd joined the FBI, she knew she could someday be faced with ending the life of another human being. When she was accepted onto CT3 that likelihood became exponentially greater. But she'd always imagined it in the context of a rescue operation. Or unavoidable collateral damage—a phrase only the most soulless of bureaucrats could have invented. Tajikistan, and all that happened there, was a total catastrophe. And now this. Whatever *this* was.

She was only a few yards from Buddy now. He was still, too still.

After this, no more dead. No more, please. By my hand.

But then she was jerking the weapon away from his reach. Going through his clothes. Pocketing his cell phone, his wallet and checking for any other weapons. Then, using the light from his cell phone, she looked at his face—her shower of bullets had caught him in the neck and chest—just long enough to confirm he was carrying his own, and not someone else's, ID.

Buddy Olsen. You should have stayed home tonight.

Then she moved away from him as quickly as she could.

CHAPTER THIRTY-ONE

Rennie sat on the bed in her motel room wrapping her wounded feet with tape. She occasionally lifted her head to watch Garrison's shadow passing back and forth through the filmy curtains. They'd been at a stalemate since he'd rapped on her door forty-five minutes earlier. That was six hours after she'd picked her way out of the woods, hitched a ride back to town and found a phone. She couldn't have risked making a call from Buddy Olsen's cell, now resting accusingly on her nightstand.

The storm was showing no sign of letting up. Garrison had driven that point home when she'd reluctantly opened the door to him.

"This is on track to being the storm of the century in North Dakota. We have less than twenty-four hours to figure out what damage you've done before that lake rises and traps us here for days."

So he'd said in his frigid voice.

Just when she thought that whatever loomed between them might be thawing.

Their impasse, which had devolved into silence and the occasional glare, had been interrupted by Garrison's cell phone. No Rolling Stones ringtones for him. And he'd decamped with his umbrella to pace along the concrete walkway that ran along the front of their rooms.

Rennie finished taping her feet, slipped on dry socks and shoes and took a few tentative steps. Sore, but not too bad. A few superficial cuts and plenty of bruising but it could have been much worse. She shook her head and glanced at Buddy Olsen's cell phone again.

We're coming for you, Cainkiller.

Now they had both a name and a number for Cainkiller, his number handily supplied to them by Olsen's cell phone. Rennie had tried to reach Hannah too but it had, for the millionth time, gone to voice mail. Rennie was only set at ease by the thought that Cainkiller had no reason to target Hannah.

Then she'd made the dreaded call to SPS. Once she'd gotten hold of Virgil and admitted the debacle her trip had turned into he'd taken it in stride. And though they were now able to put a name and face to Cainkiller, she knew he couldn't be happy with this turn of events.

Garrison opened the door, his umbrella dripping a pool of water onto the liquid-resistant industrial carpet. As usual, his face betrayed neither his emotional state nor indicated anything about the phone call. He didn't take off his windbreaker and she could see the outline of his weapon of choice—the sleek black Beretta 92FS—snug under his left arm. She knew he had another piece tucked into the back of his waistband and he produced it now, handing it to her butt-end.

"Compliments of Mr. Virgil."

It was a replica of the Sig P239 that Wallace had taken off her. She released the magazine—eight rounds—and replaced it, engaging the safety.

"Are we going somewhere?"

"We've got a location on Cainkiller. He's not far but we've got to move if we're going to catch up to him."

So the call had been from SPS. Rennie wondered why he'd needed to take it outside. Some team they were.

"Logan tracked his cell?"

Garrison nodded. "But the towers in this region are too far apart so he's unable to keep a constant line on him."

"Where was he when they caught up to him?" Rennie asked, slipping her rainproof anorak over her head.

"Buying a pack of cigarettes in a convenience store. Logan was able to hack into the store's security camera. The feed is routed through the web to the owner's online account. We got lucky."

"Something to be said for bad habits, I guess," Rennie said.

Rennie's anorak could only do so much and in the time it took them to dash to the car, her pants were soaked to the knee. The motel was right off the highway and Garrison jammed the gas pedal to the floor, the windshield wipers slapping double time. Soon they were pushing the rental to ninety miles per hour. The road, like so many in this part of the country was straight and flat and looked like it might be able to touch the horizon. When it wasn't raining. Now they could barely see ten feet in front of them.

Rennie hated being a passenger under even the best of circumstances and there was perhaps no one she'd rather have less as her driver than Martin Garrison. She felt her tension ramping higher. It had been raining steadily for almost ten hours now and water had begun to pool in places on the highway where it would suddenly pull their tires toward the shoulder. Garrison was doing a good job correcting, jerking the wheel when he needed to, finding purchase on the pavement for the tires, but they were driving much too fast for the road conditions.

"So what have we found out about Cainkiller?" Rennie asked, trying to prevent her foot from yet again pressing the imaginary brake pedal on the floorboard.

"I could ask you the same. What did Marcus give you when you saw her?"

They hadn't gotten into this territory yet—Rennie's unsanctioned visit to Hannah.

She paused. "Not much. Just that he struck her as an angry, aggressive skinhead."

"That's all?" Garrison said. "I wonder what you found to talk about all that time."

Rennie ignored his remark. "The analysts? What do they have on Wallace?"

"Not much so far. But Logan was able to find out he's not long out of a prison stint in West Virginia."

"West Virginia? I thought he was from somewhere around the Four Corners region. What was he doing out there?"

"He wasn't up to any good. Federal weapons charges. He tried to buy a cache of automatic weapons off an undercover ATF agent."

Rennie nodded. She cranked up the heat in the car, directing it at her feet. "I guess tossing a bound and naked woman into a lake sufficiently violates the conditions of his probation."

Garrison glanced at her. "Naked? That's a decidedly diabolical twist."

"You sound impressed."

Garrison shrugged.

"Any idea what he wants the weapons for?"

"Not a clue."

If Cainkiller was smart, he'd get away from Devils Lake as far and as fast as he could, Rennie thought. She peered through her rain-streaked window. Occasionally she could see a house from the highway. Rennie couldn't help but think of the Laura Ingalls Wilder novels she'd read as a girl. She'd loved the resourcefulness of the little family that lived in the middle of nowhere. Only occasionally had their isolation filled her with dread. Even now, the thought of throwing away her cell phone and microwave oven and everything else and just living somewhere far away from the traffic and noise and constant human press of modern life was deeply appealing. She didn't think she'd want to do it forever, but she craved a short respite.

She'd never lived anywhere but cities—her whole life in D.C. except for the time in Istanbul. She wondered if she should have tried harder in Istanbul. Bucked against the Bureau's desk sentence by going over and above, worming her way back into more interesting assignments until Tajikistan was a distant memory. But she knew there was no getting out from under that time. It suited them to blame her presence on the team for the debacle the mission had become. If they budged from that, they would have had to admit their own culpability.

Garrison's cell trilled again. He listened intently for a few moments. "Okay," he said finally, closing the phone. "That was Logan. He was able to get another triangulation point on Wallace. We should be on him any second."

"What's he driving?"

"An older model Explorer. Black or dark green or navy. They ran him through the motor vehicle registration database but there's nothing attached to his name."

"It's green," Rennie said, spotting it as they came around a slight bend in the road. "SUV parked on the shoulder."

Garrison handed her a pair of Vortex tactical field glasses and a radio transmitter the size of a box of matches, along with a wireless earbud and microphone. "I'll pass him and double back. You ready to follow him on foot if need be?"

"As ready as I'll ever be." Rennie pocketed the field glasses and transmitter and clipped the tiny microphone under the collar of her anorak. She slipped the earbud into her ear canal and tapped it once. "Hear me?"

"Loud and clear."

They blew past Cainkiller's Explorer. Rennie turned in her seat, squinting through the pounding rear wiper.

"He's just exited the passenger door and hopped the fence into a field. He's carrying something, something big." She turned back around in her seat once she lost sight of him. "Where the hell could he be going?" She turned to Garrison. "We need to find out what's across that fence."

Garrison flipped open his cell as he made a U-turn. By the time they passed the Explorer again, Cainkiller was nowhere in sight. Garrison jerked the rental off the road and into a drive a few hundred yards past the Explorer, pulling to a quick stop and sliding on the wet, loose gravel.

"Go," he said sharply. "He doesn't have more than two minutes on us. I'll feed you information as I get it."

Rennie put her hand on the door handle.

"And, Vogel…" he said, his hand on her forearm as she opened the car door. "Just follow him. No heroics."

Rennie glanced at him and without acknowledging what he'd said bolted from the car and across the highway. The rain had let up somewhat but by the time she ran the short distance to the fence every bit of her the anorak didn't cover was soaked.

Rennie braced one hand on a post and vaulted over the fence. The woods at that spot weren't dense—towering pines and flat ground. It was still about an hour to nightfall but it was much darker in the dripping woods as she made her way in—the canopy of overlapping limbs reducing her line of sight to a hundred yards or less. She moved cautiously, avoiding fallen branches, toward the light of the open field, her eyes constantly scanning for any motion since Cainkiller may have decided to shield himself as she was, abandoning the field for the woods.

Another fence, joined at a ninety-degree angle to the one she just crossed, separated the field from the woods—this one also of wooden planks but reinforced with a mesh of thick wire rods indicating the likelihood that the field was or had been in use for cattle. At that fence, she put the toe of her shoe on one of the wire rods and leaned over. She could see the back of a figure moving fast about a quarter mile ahead. And she could see now that it was a duffel bag he carried, its straps over his shoulders. She hopped down and tapped her earpiece, moving away from the fence in case Cainkiller decided to look back.

"He's a quarter mile in, sticking to the edge of the field. I'm going ahead through the woods to make up the distance." Rennie bent down to quickly retie her shoelace. "Any intel on what's back here yet?"

"A Kenneth Yates owns the property. Single-family residence on a ten-acre lot. That's all we've got for now. I'll keep an eye on Cainkiller, let you know if he changes his course into the woods."

"What's that?" Rennie wondered how he could manage that from his position in the car.

"I'm right behind you."

Rennie turned and saw Garrison fifty yards behind, standing stock-still in the rain, arms at his side. Their eyes met for only a second before she turned away and broke into a run.

She picked up speed and settled into an easy rhythm, skirting around or over rocks and downed limbs. She knew she'd gain on Cainkiller soon—he couldn't move nearly as fast with the duffel on his back—and likely outdistance Garrison as well.

What was Cainkiller up to? He should have been hightailing it out of Devils Lake. And why leave the Explorer on the road where it could be so easily seen?

Rennie slowed her pace, certain that Cainkiller must be near. "What's his status?" she said, thumbing on her audio.

"Still following the fence line."

"I'm going to check our relative position," she said.

"Good. You'll see the house off to the right."

"We know anything more about Yates?"

"Nothing yet. But do nothing, Vogel. Understand? Just keep up with him."

Something about his insistence on this point set off an alarm inside her head.

"What do you mean, do nothing?"

"Based on what we know already, the analyst's assessment indicates that Cainkiller may not be working alone. And since he's all we've got, we need him alive and a free agent. If he's working in tandem with a partner or a team, then we've lost our only thread. Cainkiller can't be sacrificed for the sake of whoever he's after."

"Who says?"

Garrison paused. "Our supervisor."

Rennie didn't have time to think through the implications of this revelation but wondered why he hadn't shared this information when they were in the car. She found it very hard to believe that Virgil would be so cavalier with a civilian's life.

She began to jog again, intent now on getting ahead of Cainkiller—and Garrison. If Cainkiller swerved toward the house—otherwise where could he be heading?—she'd be in better position.

"Vogel. Affirm your orders." Garrison's soft voice was in her ear again. He meant the 'do nothing' order. She could hear by the slight increase in his breathing that he was moving fast.

"I heard you." But something still nagged at her. She didn't want to promise him anything.

"Not what I said. Affirm your orders."

Bastard. Rennie felt tension rise from her neck and settle into her jaw.

"Affirmed."

Rennie switched off the audio and ran, her breath even, but she was less mindful of the crash of her feet through the undergrowth. She felt her adrenaline ramping up as she set her pace at something just short of a full-on run. Cainkiller would need cash now that he was on the move. It was possible that he knew whoever lived in the house and planned on hiding out there. Or he might be targeting it for a burglary.

Rennie slowed slightly and cut back toward the field to check Cainkiller's progress. She crouched as she edged toward the fence—no time for mistakes now. Her breath caught as she saw Cainkiller no more than a hundred and fifty yards ahead. He was bent low. He slipped the duffel off his back and tossed it over onto her side of the fence. Rennie tried to see the house but from her position she didn't have a clear view.

As soon as he put a boot on the plank to climb over, she cut back deeper into the woods. She'd have to move fast but silently. The landscape here was so flat there were no natural land formations, only trees not nearly wide enough to use as cover. But that meant Cainkiller wouldn't have that advantage either.

Rennie slowed her breathing and focused intently on each step. Cainkiller was apparently less concerned with being heard and was moving quickly. Then he stopped. He'd reached the point where the fence line cut ninety degrees toward the house and then another ninety degrees before forming a U-shape that encompassed the property.

Cainkiller dropped the duffel and bent to it. Rennie stayed put, watching, her view of his activity obscured by his back. She turned her head but saw no sign of Garrison. Rennie raised her field glasses to her face, rain dripping into the gap between the anorak and her neck. Cainkiller was well covered with a long dark green trench-style raincoat but she could see the Christian Identity tattoo clearly at the nape of his neck. Then he shifted slightly and she saw the weapon. An M40 sniper rifle. The standard issue sniper gun for the Marine Corps.

Where in the hell did he get that?

Rennie tapped her earbud as Cainkiller checked the assembly of the weapon.

"He's got a sniper gun," she whispered.

There was a pause before she heard Garrison's voice in her ear. It sounded too intimate. She didn't like him that close. "Just watch him, Vogel." She remembered Garrison's promise then that nothing would be hidden from her in this new organization.

"Did you hear me, Vogel?"

"Affirmative," she said and tapped off the audio. She heard him but that didn't mean she wasn't going to take action she deemed necessary.

Cainkiller was moving now, bent low. He left the duffel bag at the turn of the fence and was soon out of sight. Rennie moved fast, covering as much ground as she could before slowing to a crawl fifteen yards from the corner. She had a clear view of the house. It had a large rambling deck on the back that curled around the far side of the house. A man—Kenneth Yates?—stood at the corner of the deck holding an umbrella. Rennie raised the field glasses. He was middle-aged, bearded, and he was talking to someone who stood just around the corner where the deck wrapped around the far side of the house. Worry creased his features.

Cainkiller sure as hell wasn't crawling around the woods in the rain with a high-powered sniper gun if he had anything but malevolent intentions. Whoever the man on the deck was—and whoever he was talking to—Cainkiller wanted one or both of them dead. And Rennie wasn't going to let that happen no matter what Garrison said.

She slipped the Sig Sauer from her waistband and crept forward. The ground was muddy and she moved on her forearms to keep her hands clean. Reaching where the fence angled right, where Wallace had left the duffel bag, Rennie fingered the outline of the St. Catherine medal underneath her T-shirt.

Just let everything go right this time.

Safety off, she raised the Sig close to her face, ready to train it on Cainkiller when he was in sight again. Peeking around the duffel, her knees pressed against it, she scanned the fence line and the woods it enclosed. A flash of color caught her eye. Cainkiller was flat on his belly, only his head was raised as he moved forward on his elbows. But the bottom of his shoes were bright yellow and she was able to keep him easily in view.

Gotcha.

Rennie pulled back around the corner where she had cover, flicking the audio on her earbud. Garrison spoke before she had a chance to.

"Status?"

"Adult white male talking with someone who is out of view on the deck."

"Subject?"

"Getting into position now. Can we take him in?"

Rennie rifled through the duffel as she spoke to Garrison.

"Do nothing. Stay on him and don't let him see you."

"He's preparing to take a shot. I won't let that happen."

"We're letting this unfold."

Unfold?

"I didn't sign up for this. Out."

Rennie thumbed off the audio. When she edged her head back around the fence, tension formed immediately in Rennie's throat.

Gone.

Cainkiller was nowhere in sight. Rennie scanned the woods frantically. She couldn't have spoken to Garrison more than fifteen seconds, twenty at most. Had Cainkiller heard her? Impossible over the rain. Or had he only found he needed to change position to have a clearer shot? He might only be using the scope to watch the man. But Rennie had seen a pair of high-powered binoculars in his duffel. They'd offer more than enough clarity if his intent was benign.

Rennie moved out from her cover, knowing Cainkiller might have the advantage, might be lying in wait for her. Moving so she was nearly parallel to the house but no closer to it, she could see the man on the deck, gesturing as he spoke to his unseen companion. His hands seemed to be moving in slow motion. If she called out to him in warning, would he heed her or only stand frozen in confusion? The only way to save him was to find and stop Cainkiller.

The woods here were chaotic. Piles of brush and cut logs and limbs provided much needed barriers. Rennie skittered from one to the next. The rain had picked up again, only adding to the chaos. Behind the last pile before more open woods, she heard rustling and the distinctive sound of metal against metal. Rennie stood frozen before crouching and moving toward the edge of the pile. She stuck her head out and saw Cainkiller, again stretched out and preparing for a shot.

The man on the deck was still talking, oblivious to the danger lurking behind him. But Rennie was there to make sure this day did not end terminally for him. She had good cover behind the pile and fixed the sight of the Sig Sauer at the nape of Cainkiller's neck where the crown and sword tattoo marked him. How far along he was in his setup would determine whether she would have to fire on him or could make use of the cuffs in her back pocket.

Watching, she saw that he'd had time to settle in. She'd already heard him bolt the cartridge into place. Now, he was still, waiting.

Dammit. Dammit. Goddammit.

She had to take him out. Now.

Rennie inhaled and took her finger off the trigger guard. She studied her sight again along Cainkiller's jawline. Garrison's orders came into her head—had they really come from Virgil?—but she pushed them away. Cainkiller didn't have a tripod and was using his elbows to steady the weapon. He kept shifting, having difficulty getting the right position. Rennie lowered the barrel of the Sig slightly. She'd go for a body shot—she didn't want to risk missing and it was too far for a head shot with a handgun. Then just as she put her finger on the trigger she felt a hand clamp across her mouth. In the next moment she heard the retort of a weapon.

No.

She felt another hand gripping her belt, pulling her, her body twisting as she fell. Then a body underneath her. Everything was a blur of motion, sound and wet. She felt legs beneath her own and was about to bring her knee between them when the hand that had covered her mouth clutched her by the hair. She was staring into the eyes of Martin Garrison. And she knew that the weapon that had sounded was not her own.

CHAPTER THIRTY-TWO

By the time Rennie heard the second shot, Garrison had levered her onto her stomach and pinned her with all his weight. With his knee bearing down on the small of her back and one hand on her wrist, the other pressed her face into the muddy ground. Dead leaves plastered to her cheek tickled her nose. She beat down the instinct to throw him off her, tackle him and shove the barrel of her gun into his eye socket. She just stopped struggling. She felt him lessen his grip on her and finally let go. As he turned to look toward the house she swung her arm, the butt of her Sig catching him just behind the ear.

"You stupid bastard, you let Cainkiller shoot him."

Garrison bent over, his hand covered in blood from the blow to the thin skin on his scalp. They glared at one another and then an eerie howl broke the silence.

"What the hell was that?" Rennie said.

"Cainkiller. Exulting over his kill."

For the briefest moment, Rennie thought she saw a flash of fear in Garrison's eyes.

"Head back to the road and tail him if he goes for his car." Garrison pulled out his cell phone. "Now!" And then he spoke into the phone. "Logan, make a 911 report from a number with a local exchange. There's been a shooting, at least one man shot…"

Rennie tore off through the woods before he finished speaking, anger coursing through her. Garrison had likely prevented her from saving a man's life, maybe two men. This wasn't the way it was supposed to be. The Foundation was supposed to be different. No senseless deaths. And she couldn't see this as anything more than senseless. Her instincts told her that Garrison had done this on his own. He had a history of going rogue. And she wouldn't believe Virgil would have made such a ruthless decision until she heard it from his own mouth.

Rennie ran hard, the cold air going right through her as it hit her wet clothes. She'd bet there was the addition of cold sweat too from her confrontation with Garrison.

What in the hell what was Cainkiller up to? First, he pulls his weird game with her and now this. Was he unraveling? During her career she hadn't had much experience with completely unhinged minds. It would make everything that much more complicated if that's what they were dealing with.

Rennie slowed her pace as she neared the road. She'd prefer to wait out Cainkiller from the shelter of the car but she needed to have visual contact. The woods weren't dense here but it was nearly dark. She lay down flat on the ground. She was so wet and cold at this point she didn't even notice the damp. She could hear the occasional car on the road but there wasn't much traffic. She suspected there was never much traffic in this part of the state.

Rennie began to shiver from the cold. Then she heard movement off at a distance. Her chills subsided and she became perfectly still. The sound became more distinct even over the rain. Leaves rustling, the snap of dead branches on the forest floor, a man moving quickly but not quite running. She brought her forearms up underneath her shoulders, ready to move quickly if need be. The Sig was in her hand, safety off. The lights of a car coming along the road illuminated the woods for a moment and she glimpsed him. Cainkiller, with the duffel on his back again, was intent on his course, angling away from her en route to his vehicle, seemingly unconcerned that he might have company in the dark woods. When he was far enough from her Rennie darted the short distance to the shoulder of the road, vaulted the fence and ran hard for the rental, the cold air hitting her wet clothes again like a fist.

The rain had waned to a drizzle. Jumping into the driver's seat, she turned the key one position so she could lower her window. The night was eerily silent and a shiver ran over her as she listened intently. A quarter of a mile. Probably too far to hear the sound of his engine, she thought. Then she saw a flash of red light and knew it had to be his brake lights as he started the car. She turned the key fully and pulled out onto the road, no headlights. She reached down to flip on the seat warmer when the headlights of an oncoming vehicle hit her windshield, flashing them at her to turn on her own. The car was going fast and she barely made out the make. An Explorer. *Shit.* Cainkiller had made a U-turn and was now speeding back toward town.

"Goddammit, what else can go wrong?"

Rennie accelerated around the bend as Cainkiller's taillights disappeared and made a quick reversal, her tires sending the gravel on the shoulder flying. The Explorer was out of sight and Rennie pushed the rental up to eighty-five. She could hear sirens in the distance, hopefully en route to the site of the shooting. Maybe the men on the deck weren't dead. Then she heard the low tone sounding from her earbud. She fingered on the open transmission.

"Vogel, you there?" Garrison said, his voice as flat and calm as always, as if they hadn't just come to blows with each other in the woods.

"I'm here. What do you have there?"

"Are you on Cainkiller?" he asked, ignoring her question.

"He just blew past me but I think I can catch up with him." She could see taillights up ahead and hoped it was the Explorer.

"Keep on him. I've got things covered here."

"Have you ID'd the vics?"

"Kenneth Scott Yates. He took a head shot."

Rennie committed the name to memory. Then she swallowed a combination of anger and bitterness. "He's dead?"

"He is," Garrison said lightly, as if she'd only asked if Yates would be meeting them for brunch.

Soulless bastard.

"What about the other guy?"

All Rennie heard was the faint static of the open transmission.

"Garrison?"

"It's a woman, Vogel. She's alive. Just a hit to the shoulder." He paused. "It's Hannah Marcus."

Rennie's breath drained from her body and the road swam in front of her before she remembered to inhale. She looked at the taillights, not far ahead now, one last time and thought of her promise to Hannah's mother before she slammed on her brakes and jerked the steering wheel right onto the shoulder and then left in a tight curve, her tires skidding, before she was headed back toward the shooting site and to Hannah.

"Vogel? Stay on Cainkiller. Marcus is going to be fine. Vogel?"

"Son of a bitch, son of a bitch, son of a bitch." And then she cut the transmission.

Cainkiller slowed as the ambulance approached, lights flashing and sirens wailing. He turned up the Explorer's stereo to drown it out. Buddy had a good system, he had to give him that. He rapped the knuckle of his index finger on the steering wheel feeling the angry mechanical synth worm its way through his body.

He felt high. So high he thought he might not need the drug any more.

"Hahahahaha!" he laughed manically. "You are one funny cowboy."

What a rush it was.

"Yee haw!" he screamed.

His father always told him he needed to get more exercise, burn off some of his intensity. But running around a track or doing a bunch of pushups would never compare to what he'd just done.

All right, settle down, cowboy.

He had to ramp it down. And think.

He knew Yates had to be dead but he wasn't sure about the journalist. The light had been too poor for him to be certain. And the success of the first shot had filled him with such adrenaline that he'd begun to quiver with pleasure. It had been a stroke of luck that she'd been meeting with Yates at the perfect moment. If he'd aced her too, he'd be having a very lucky day indeed. It probably didn't matter though. Whether she was dead or alive. Everything was in motion and it would all be over soon. He just had to stay one step ahead of them. Two days and it would be done.

Cainkiller reached into the console for a cigarette and increased his speed. He'd always had a lead foot and would have to watch it—he couldn't afford any stupid mistakes at this point. A simple traffic stop could ruin everything. He would do what he had to do, but a dead cop was a complication he didn't need at this stage of the game.

Why are you even doing this?

This was why he took the drug. Sometimes his brain started whispering stupid questions to him. Besides he *knew* why he was doing this. He had two points to make. A political point. And a personal point.

Since when did you care about politics?

Cainkiller slammed his elbow into the door. "I do have a political point! Two points. Not one, but two."

And as luck would have it, he could make both points in one fell swoop.

"Swoopie-doopie-doop."

Right.

A car came into view behind him and then swerved onto the shoulder before making a U-turn. Cainkiller shrugged and lit his cigarette. He hadn't had a smoke in hours and let the buzz sink into him, his body becoming weightless as the nicotine shot through his bloodstream. He wished he could get royally fucked up one more time before this big job, maybe even find a hooker. Out in these boondocks she probably wouldn't even have a full set of teeth. But there was no time. When he was in the pen he'd read a book about the 9/11 hijackers and how before the big day those stupid self-righteous fuckers had taken advantage of America's loose morality, the thing they were supposedly giving their lives to destroy. If he made it out of all of this he would treat himself. He had no desire to be a martyr. If anything was anti-American, that was. No, he might have to sacrifice himself but he wouldn't do it willingly.

Cainkiller turned onto I-90 heading east. His Mapquest directions told him it was seven hundred miles to Iowa Falls where he would acquire the final component of his little project. Then another thousand miles to D.C. With plenty of Red Bull and a steady supply of ephedrine he could be in D.C. in two days and still have time for a nap before doing the deed. He'd stay away from the meth for a while. It was jet fuel for his brain when he needed just regular old unleaded gasoline right now.

Are you sure?

"Yes!" he roared and slammed his elbow into the door again.

That's going to smart tomorrow.

"Please. Quiet," Cainkiller whispered almost inaudibly.

He took one last deep pull off the cigarette and flipped it out the window, watching the orange glow extinguish behind him on the wet road.

Rennie rattled across the cattle grate and tore down the rutted, potholed dirt road to the shooting site, not caring that she was wrecking the suspension on the rental. Two sheriffs' cruisers and another ambulance had passed her on the highway. Her stomach roiled with anxiety. She didn't trust Garrison's assessment of Hannah's injuries. He'd have said anything to keep her on Cainkiller's trail.

You should have kept on him.

She hoped she didn't regret that she hadn't. She wanted ten minutes alone with a pen and a pad so she could work out what they actually had on Cainkiller. See what it added up to. Regardless of his ultimate intentions he was a dangerous motherfucker, as her old SAC used to refer to the worst of the criminals they encountered. She herself had only come across his type once before. A true sociopath. Vicious and completely without empathy. Enough to make your blood run cold. Before being assigned to counterterrorism she had worked on a case involving the serial murder of prostitutes. Brutal, gruesome crimes. When she and her team had finally tracked down the guy, he was a lamb, making no attempt at resisting arrest. But the room they found him in, the room where he committed his handiwork, was the most horrific spectacle she'd ever seen. Foul and rank with carnage and death. And he sat in its midst as calmly and comfortably as if he were lounging on his sofa watching the Sunday football game. It still sickened her to think of it. His depredations seemed akin to Cainkiller's, to the satisfied, cold and somehow subdued rage she'd witnessed when Cainkiller had hauled her off to the lake.

Rennie slowed as she approached the house. There was only a fine mist under the dark and cloudy sky, the stars obscured, but she knew this wasn't the last of it. Another wave of the storm would be upon them any moment. She could smell the smoke of a fireplace somewhere not far off and craved warmth, her sodden clothes clinging to her.

The strobing lights of the cruisers and emergency vehicles flashed luridly on the white planks of the house. A young sheriff's deputy approached her car, his Maglite shouldered and pointing at her as she pulled to a stop.

"What can I do for you, ma'am?"

His kindness was a balm. Maybe she wasn't a city girl after all. She realized she had no idea what to say to him.

"A friend…" Emotion welled up from someplace deep. "A friend of mine has been injured here."

He stepped closer shining the light in her face. "And how do you know that, ma'am?" Whatever had been soothing in his tone was less so now.

"I got a call. I'm not even sure who from."

Get it together, Rennie. You sound like an amateur.

The deputy narrowed his eyes at her. "What's your friend's name?"

"Hannah. Hannah Marcus." Rennie struggled against her throat catching.

"That's her. The boys are getting her into the ambulance. You can follow her to the hospital in your car."

"Is she conscious?"

"She's in and out, but it looks like she's going to be okay."

Rennie wondered where Garrison was. "Is anyone else here with her?" The investigator in her unable to resist the question.

The deputy ran his hand along his chin, his eyes filling with emotion. "Just Mr. Yates and he's gone."

"I'm sorry," Rennie said. Small town, everybody knows everybody. "She's not from here—any idea what she was seeing him about?"

The deputy's emotion passed and he narrowed his eyes at her again, this time taking in her soaked and muddied clothes. "I have no idea, ma'am. Could I see some ID please?"

CHAPTER THIRTY-THREE

Rennie pressed the transmission button on her earbud as she followed the fast-moving ambulance en route to the county hospital thirty miles east.

"Garrison? Come in."

She tried a few more times getting no response.

Coward.

It was possible they were out of range but she hated to give him the benefit of the doubt. She shifted her hip and pulled her cell phone from her back pocket and speed-dialed Garrison's number.

"Yes?"

"Where are you? Why did you leave the scene?" She tried to keep the tension out of her voice. Working with Garrison, accepting the job with the Foundation, the whole thing was beginning to look like a bad idea.

"Obviously because it's imperative that local law enforcement doesn't get a bead on us."

"And it's imperative that we don't lose any more people." *Christ.* She knew she'd built her own trap as soon as she said it.

"Hannah Marcus isn't with us. She's peripheral. And now we've lost Cainkiller's trail."

"People aren't peripheral. And as far as Cainkiller is concerned, we have his cell number. Logan can triangulate him again."

"He's trying. All we know is that Cainkiller is heading east. He can't place him with any more precision than that at this point."

A sick churning began in Rennie's stomach. Flashbacks to Tajikistan. Everything being her fault. But, no. This was different. She'd done the right thing. Or at least tried to.

"I'm en route to the hospital. I won't be there long. Where are you? We need to meet. What happened in those woods can't happen again."

Silence.

"Garrison?"

"I'm at the motel. I'll be waiting for you."

Why did almost everything that came out of Garrison's mouth sound like a threat? Rennie suddenly had an image of Margot Day, Garrison's CIA colleague whom he'd interrogated in Tajikistan, gagged and strapped to a chair, a line of blood bubbling along a shallow cut he'd made on her chest.

Rennie pulled into the emergency entrance of the hospital behind the ambulance and hopped out of her car. The deputy she'd spoken to at Yates' house was standing by the ambulance doors as they were opened. He was holding an enormous black umbrella and indicated she could join him beneath it.

"Can I just have a minute with her? I can't stay but she should know someone is here for her." It was oddly intimate standing with him in the little circle of shelter under the umbrella.

"She's not conscious, ma'am," he said kindly. "Blood loss. She wouldn't even know you're here."

"Out of the way," a paramedic barked at them as he pulled the wheeled stretcher onto the pavement. Rennie's breath caught as she saw Hannah. Her left side drenched in blood. An oxygen mask covered her nose and mouth but didn't hide the pallor of her skin. And then she was gone, sailing through the doors of the emergency bay.

She'll be okay.

"Will you be here?" Rennie said to the deputy.

"Yes, ma'am. We'll want to interview her once she gets out of surgery and can talk to us."

"Will you call me when you know something?" she asked, offering him her Beth Forrest business card. "About her condition." Rennie felt stripped bare, exposed in a way she wasn't used to.

The deputy looked skeptical but also curious. "I suppose there'd be no harm in that."

Garrison opened the door to his motel room holding a cup of steaming coffee, his hair still damp from a shower. Rennie craved nothing more than a hot shower.

"How did you get back here?" she asked, aware suddenly of the anger boiling inside her.

"I hitchhiked," Garrison said matter-of-factly.

"Not very smart. Whoever picked you up might connect you to the shooting once it hits the news."

Garrison shrugged. "And yet I should have stayed on the scene holding Marcus's hand until the boys in blue rolled up?"

Rennie didn't answer. He was right of course.

"Coffee?" Garrison offered.

Rennie took a deep breath and nodded, frustrated by his ever present calm and hating to take anything from him.

"How's Marcus?"

"Heading into surgery."

"She'll be fine, you know."

"You don't really know that. Besides, it never should have happened. Look me in the eye and tell me that we were following Virgil's orders and not your own."

Garrison turned to her and handed her the cup of coffee. His eyes seemed blacker than they had just a moment before.

"Sit down." Garrison directed her to one of two chairs at a flimsy kitchen table against the wall. He sat in the chair next to her. Rennie thought again of Margot Day and a shiver touched the back of her neck.

"We're not allowed to participate in the lie. We can't afford to," he began.

"What?" Rennie spoke sharply, irritated. She didn't have time for riddles. "What lie?"

"The lie that Americans tell themselves so they can feel safe at night, so they can have hope for their children's futures."

"I have no idea what you're talking about."

"*Listen* to me," he said, emphasizing the first word in that unsettling way he sometimes did when he spoke. He leaned forward and took Rennie by the wrist, holding it tightly, just short of inflicting pain. "Before the World Trade Center, this country was lulled into a false sense of security by an unprecedented period of peace. It was not only unprecedented but unnatural. Violence and chaos are always lurking just beneath the surface of any so-called civilized society. Civilization is merely a veneer, a thin veneer always riven with cracks."

He leaned closer to her. "And it's our job to look at those fine cracks under a microscope and mend them before they become gaping holes that make the whole thing fall apart. It's our job to circumvent the natural state of disorder."

Garrison seemed possessed. Rennie had never once heard him speak at such length. She was tired and freezing in her wet clothes and in no mood to be lectured to. He continued, hardly taking a breath, "*We...*"— he punched the word, gripping her wrist harder—"have to look things in the face directly. *We* can't pretend that everything is okay, that the world is a benevolent place, that people are ultimately good-hearted. *We* cannot participate in the lie. And *we* sometimes have to do ugly things, things that fall outside of the morality that your average American is allowed to pretend exists. We do these things so that *they* can believe that it exists. That is our gift to them and that is what today was about. And *you* fucked it up."

Rennie wrenched her wrist from his grip. "That's bullshit." She stood and walked to the window. "No one can do this work with that kind of nihilism running through their veins. It makes you like Cainkiller. Like the ones who will do whatever they have to do to achieve their ends. Where everything and everybody is just collateral damage. I won't be that way. And I don't believe you are either." She turned back to him. "What about your son? You gave up everything for him."

Garrison sat back in his chair, his palms on his thighs. The fire had gone out of his eyes.

After a long silence, he said, "My son writes to me in language punctuated by flourishes, speaking of the Greeks. Of truth and beauty. Of exiting the cave into the light. What do you think of that?"

"How can I think anything of it?" Rennie said, pacing in front of him. "You're right, some of us are afforded a place to think of such things and some of us are charged with doing the dirty work so others can have such freedom. If our mandate, our destiny, is clear and true and we are up to the task, we must accept it and leave philosophy to others."

"Yes. I agree."

Rennie stopped pacing and leaned down to him. "But not at the needless expense of innocent lives. I can't take it that far. I can't and I won't. And for that matter, Virgil would not be on board with your position. If we're going to work together, we have to be on the same page. Why did you sign on knowing the goals of the Foundation if you don't agree with them?"

Garrison didn't answer.

"I don't believe that you aren't more hopeful. For our country. For humanity…" Were they really having this conversation? It was the last thing she needed to be thinking about.

Garrison stood. Rennie had an impulse that he was going to grasp her by the shoulders but he didn't. "I think you are talented," he told her. "I don't say that about many people. But this job is going to ruin you unless you learn to have *two selves*. Yes, we make connections, relationships. We go to Thanksgiving dinner, say grace, eat the turkey and the pumpkin pie and allow ourselves to forget for a moment all we know. But, *here*, if you conflate the fiction of that fantasy, with this, the real, you'll be dead. We are here to preserve the fantasy that human beings can coexist and not murder each other in the streets without compunction. But the rub is that we can have no share of that fantasy."

Rennie had turned away from him again as he spoke. She wanted to scoff at him but his words burrowed into a place in her mind that she needed to keep safe and an overwhelming emotion made her throat begin work as she fought to keep it down. *Not now. Not in front of him. You can think about all of this later.* But she couldn't help but note that Garrison never affirmed or denied that the orders to only follow Cainkiller, and not fire on him, came from Virgil.

She heard Garrison refilling his coffee cup and felt the tension in the room dissipate. When she turned back to him she could tell his brain was elsewhere, that he'd left their fraught conversation behind.

"We need to meet with Keller," he said facing her, his face placid again. "I want access to Cainkiller's quarters—see what we can find there. And you'll need to talk to Marcus once she's able. Find out why she was meeting with Yates and anything else she has."

Rennie swallowed, feeling nearly free of the emotion that had almost overtaken her. Garrison stood and his knees cracked. She sometimes forgot his age. He had twenty years on her. She knew he'd been through a lot during his time underground with the CIA. That life would have taken its toll on his body. She hoped she could rely on him if she needed to. She finally nodded assent to his plan.

She thought for a moment. "I should see Hannah before we meet with Keller. Better to have all her info before we go in."

"Agreed. And we've got our ace in the hole with him." Garrison tapped a file on the coffee table. "It should make him cooperative."

CHAPTER THIRTY-FOUR

Rennie exited the elevator onto the third floor of Mercy Hospital. Hannah had come out of surgery, been upgraded from critical to stable condition and had been resting comfortably since noon. This according to the helpful sheriff's deputy who'd called her with updates throughout the day.

After a blessedly hot shower and with the chill finally out of her bones, Rennie had gotten a bite to eat in town and finally had that ten minutes with her pen and pad. Except the ten minutes had stretched into an hour and a half as she made notes, sipping coffee, crisscrossing the pages with arrows signifying possible connections and questioning every assumption. She was left with more questions than answers. Hopefully Hannah would be able to fill in a few of the gaping holes. And then Keller. Garrison was interested in getting a look at Cainkiller's room. But her sense was that Cainkiller had known he wouldn't be coming back. She thought finding any evidence there was a long shot.

Rennie scanned the corridor for signs to Room 307. She wondered if hospitals were designed to be intentionally confusing. After coming upon the nurses' station a second time, she stopped and asked for directions. A scowling, stolid woman in scrubs patterned with oversized flowers directed her down a hall she had somehow missed. Hannah's door was ajar a few inches. Rennie took a deep breath and rapped lightly on the door frame.

When no answer came, Rennie peered inside.

The room was dark and Rennie could barely make out her small form in the bed. She approached slowly. Hannah no longer wore the oxygen mask and her color had returned. Her shoulder was bandaged and she had an IV drip attached to her opposite hand. Seeing her so vulnerable brought back their time together in Tajikistan. There they had relied on one another, knowing at any moment they might be hunted down by Armin's men. When Rennie had seen Hannah at the compound, it hadn't been the same. In Tajikistan, Hannah had been completely open to her, but here, though she had welcomed Rennie into her cabin and into her bed, there was a deep and seemingly impenetrable reserve that she hadn't seen before.

Maybe that's how she always was. She needed you in Tajikistan in a way she's not likely to ever need you again.

Just then Hannah opened her eyes as if she could read Rennie's thoughts, and reached out her hand to her.

"You always seem to appear when I need you." Hannah's voice was slurred from the painkillers.

Rennie's stomach burned with the guilt that she *was* there when she had needed her and had still been unable to prevent that bullet from entering Hannah's shoulder. She touched the St. Catherine medallion at her throat. *Thank God it wasn't worse.* Rennie took Hannah's outstretched hand and pressed it gently.

"I can't seem to keep myself out of trouble, can I?" Hannah said.

Rennie felt her eyes filling with emotion.

"You have a soft heart." Hannah's eyes were heavy-lidded

and not entirely focused. "And I have a stone where mine should be. And it's always been that way..." Her words trailed off and her hand became slack in Rennie's grip as her eyes closed.

Rennie wondered if it was true. Is that what she was sensing when they were together in the cabin?

Rennie met a nurse as she stepped out into the hallway.

"It's nice to see her have a visitor other than a cop," the woman said. She looked mature, competent. "Is she awake?"

Rennie shook her head.

"Come back in a few hours." The nurse laid a hand on Rennie's arm. "She's still full of drugs from the surgery and would probably be talking nonsense if she were awake. She'll be more herself this evening."

Rennie took a walk around the hospital grounds while she conferenced with Garrison, Kyu and Virgil on her cell. All agreed with Garrison's planned course of action. After finding out what else Hannah knew, Rennie and Garrison would head out to Keller's camp.

Kyu and Virgil had been researching Cainkiller's background. They already knew he'd been released from a state penitentiary in West Virginia three months before on weapons charges.

"We found a guy who was buddies with Cainkiller in prison," Kyu said. He sounded like he was in a car. "He's out now but he's already violated his probation and is sitting in the county lockup in some little town in West Virginia. I'm driving out there now to talk to him."

"What about Cainkiller's family?" Rennie asked.

"There isn't much. Or much that cares," Virgil said. "His parents wrote him off years ago and want nothing to do with him. Apparently, Bob and Janie Wallace weren't surprised they hadn't heard from him since his release and hoped they didn't. But his live-in girlfriend is another story and she isn't happy about it. Kyu talked to her on the phone a couple of hours ago, and he'll be flying out to Utah tomorrow to interview the girlfriend in person."

"She was difficult on the phone," Kyu said. "Was suspicious of me but sounded like she wanted to complain about Cainkiller to anyone who would listen. She said she couldn't afford the rent on their two-bedroom garden apartment on her own. She's planning on setting all of his stuff out on the curb and moving in with her sister. I asked when and she said, 'Real soon', but she agreed to wait until we talk in person."

Rennie laughed under her breath at Kyu's imitation of the woman's accent.

"Garrison and Vogel, anything new on Yates?" Virgil asked.

"Not much," Garrison said. "He was the director of the county public library. Never married. No record. You'll have to see what you can get from Marcus, Vogel."

"Will do," Rennie said.

After they signed off, Rennie wandered around the hospital. She finally stopped off at the cafeteria and ate an overcooked piece of meat and nursed a few cups of sludgy coffee. When she headed back to Hannah's room, the same nurse was clearing her dinner tray as she entered the room.

"See, what did I tell you? She's as perky as a robin after a rain."

Hannah looked surprised and pleased to see Rennie before she raised a skeptical eyebrow at the nurse.

"I'll leave you—just ring if you need anything, Ms. Marcus."

"Feeling better?" Rennie asked.

"You were here earlier?" Hannah shook her head. "I have no memory of it. And, yes, I feel better." She still looked perplexed. "Did we talk?"

Rennie nodded. "You said you have a stone for a heart."

Hannah turned toward the window. The sun was nearly down, coloring the sky in streaks of purple and orange. "Pretty, isn't it?"

"It is. Trying to prove yourself wrong?"

"Maybe." Hannah turned back to her, a trace of a sad smile on her lips.

Rennie crossed to the other side of the bed and sat in an armchair. "How's the pain?"

"Uncomfortable when I move the shoulder, but otherwise the drugs seem to be doing their job."

"Do you mind if I ask you some questions?"

Hannah shrugged and winced. "Go for it."

"The man you were meeting at the farmhouse—Yates—why were you meeting him?"

"I witnessed an altercation between him and Wallace—a.k.a Cainkiller—at the library. I talked to him after Cainkiller left."

"Did Cainkiller see you talking to him?"

"I don't think so but he knew I was there. Yates said he wanted to go to the police. But he was having second thoughts." Hannah shook her head. "But that wasn't the first time he'd met him."

Hannah told Rennie about the librarian taking refuge from the storm in a roadside bar. Cainkiller was already at the bar and very drunk, based on Yates' description. Yates thought he might be high as well, though he said he didn't have much experience with that kind of thing.

"Cainkiller told him a story."

"What kind of story?"

"Yates couldn't remember all of the details. He was pretty terrified and he said Cainkiller was acting crazy, but the gist of it was that he had a beef with Daddy."

Rennie nodded. "From what we know, he's been alienated from his family for some time."

"From what Yates said, it also sounded like he came from money."

"That doesn't jive with our information," Rennie said, frowning.

"He could have delusions of grandeur," Hannah offered. "He wouldn't be the first."

"No kidding."

"Right at the end of their conversation, Cainkiller was so wasted, he mistook Yates for someone he'd tried to buy a grenade launcher off of."

"And there's the motive for silencing Yates."

"That's not everything."

Hannah went on to describe the encounter between the two men in the library. The information was key and might mean Yates' death wouldn't be in vain.

Rennie gazed out the window. The sun had dipped below the horizon, leaving the view bathed in that eerie twilight hue that always made her feel slightly off-kilter. She finally turned back to Hannah.

"There's something I have to tell you." Rennie took a deep breath. "We were there. I was and Garrison was. But...we were unable to stop the shooting."

Hannah's gaze gripped hers intently. She finally nodded slowly. Rennie knew she had more questions but understood that Rennie had said all that she was going to say.

Hannah sighed forcefully. "Can't we just get out of here? Run away and go someplace quiet, secluded. Nobody for miles." She glanced down at her bandaged shoulder. Rennie couldn't read her expression. "Journalists don't get shot at in this country. I just wanted an interesting story. One that mattered. But I don't want any more of the chaos that I had in Tajikistan."

Rennie took her hand. "Maybe no more pieces on men with guns."

Hannah smiled. "We'll see."

Still holding her hand, Rennie said, "You know, after this is all over, after you're better, we can go somewhere. Take some time..."

The look in Hannah's eyes cut her off. Tension filled Rennie's throat.

"You know you shouldn't expect too much from me."

The jumpy, panicky feeling inside her stilled. *Finally, something direct.* Hannah had spoken flatly, unequivocally. She hadn't softened it or sugarcoated it.

Rennie smiled. "Okay. I won't. But, listen." Rennie leaned in close. "I'll be coming for you anyway."

CHAPTER THIRTY-FIVE

A fine mist was coming down as Rennie walked across the hospital parking lot to her rental. Sitting in the car, she watched as fine droplets on the windshield trailed together and dripped slowly toward the wipers. She started the engine and reviewed her notes. Yates had been shot just as he was telling Hannah about Cainkiller. Yates wasn't a local. Fifty years old with thinning hair and a beard going gray, he'd only been in Devils Lake six months. He wore wide-wale corduroys and a sweater vest. A tweed coat with suede patches on the elbows rounded out the look of the quintessential librarian, so Hannah had said. Which was what he had become after abandoning his career as a safety manager at a power plant in Cleveland. He'd made good money and decided he'd "retire," go to library school and move west. With his lack of experience, he didn't have many options, but Devils Lake took him on as Library Director—with a staff of five—for the Lake Region Public Library. He'd bought his farmhouse for a pittance compared to Cleveland prices.

Since the library had such a small staff, Yates would regularly perform reference duties himself. From his position at the reference desk he could clearly see the bank of patron-use computers. Libraries have strict privacy policies. Even when patrons call up objectionable or offensive material they are generally left alone. He'd told Hannah that Cainkiller had come in one day and gone straight for the computers. He hadn't seen—or at least hadn't recognized—Yates yet.

"So, what was he looking into?"

Hannah shrugged her good shoulder. "He was very uncomfortable talking to me about it. Yates took his librarian's ethics seriously, but it seemed to me he hadn't known what it would be like out here. All the guns and bravado. He was trying to take it all in stride but Cainkiller tipped him over the edge. Once I got to his house—he called it a ranch—he spent most of the time we had before the shooting trying to justify to himself what he was doing."

"Did he ever tell you what he saw?"

"Weapons-related sites. Grenade launchers. Homemade bombs. But most interesting, he was looking up mosques."

"That's not good. Did he say where the mosques were?"

"He couldn't tell. One website was titled The Islamic Center. It had a picture of what he described as a grand mosque."

"Nothing like that around here I wouldn't think."

"I wouldn't either."

"Anything else?"

Hannah shook her head, her eyes vacant. "A moment later his blood was covering my face and chest."

Rennie finished reading through her notes, set the pad on the passenger seat and headed out of the hospital parking lot toward the motel. *This wasn't what we were expecting.* Nothing they had learned about Keller's group had indicated targeting

Muslims, Rennie thought as she drove. Their primary grievance was with the government. But Cainkiller seemed an outlier in Keller's group.

Pulling into the motel lot she thought about poor Yates. He really hadn't known what he was getting himself into. It was a different world out here. And like a lot of victims, he had the bad luck to be at the wrong place at the wrong time.

Aside from Rennie's and Garrison's rental cars, the motel parking lot was filled with oversized pickup trucks with boats hitched to them. Fishermen and hunters were the usual clientele. An enormous hand-painted sign on the side of the building advertised free Internet. Conveniences here were much more utilitarian. As if nature reigned supreme and they had to trumpet any small victory against it. Maybe Garrison was right. The thin veneer of civilization...

In her room, Rennie powered up her laptop and had just logged onto the motel's network when there was a rap at her door. Garrison came in and sat on the edge of her bed while she updated him on the Yates development. "There's an Islamic center in Fargo but I can't tell how big it is. Seems like the most logical, closest target." She thought for a moment. "But I don't think that's what he has in mind. He'd want something more high profile."

Garrison said nothing at first. Then he announced, "I arranged a meeting with Keller for tonight so we can get a look at Cainkiller's quarters."

"Tonight?" Rennie looked at the time on her laptop. Almost 10 p.m. "Who does he think we are?"

"He doesn't. I told him we have information on his father and that was good enough to get us an invitation to the compound."

"Okay." Rennie was ready for a break in their search for Cainkiller. "Let's do it."

The rain was coming down in a torrent again by the time they steered the car back onto the highway. Along the way, they stopped for coffee at one of the many bait shops that doubled as convenience stores. This shop, like the others she'd been in, seemed cobbled together. A couple of drink coolers, a grill and a counter with Slim Jims, Peppermint Patties, Chapstick. And a fish cleaning station. The pervasive odor came from the fish cleaning station and not the grill. At least the coffee was hot and fresh.

Keller was waiting at the entrance to the compound. He sat on a folding chair, wearing an enormous poncho, rain pouring from it. When Garrison pulled to a stop he stood and leaned down to the driver's window.

"Blattner and Radley, right?" Keller said.

"That's us," Garrison said, confirming their aliases.

"Mind giving me a lift to my place?"

"Hop in," Rennie said.

When they sat down at Keller's kitchen table he seemed nervous, his forehead furrowed in worry as he eyed the folder Garrison carried. Garrison's greatest gift, his uncannily placid demeanor—Rennie still wasn't sure if it was for real—was firmly in place. That placidity could be threatening or benign at will. This meeting called for benign and he supplied openness and a grandfatherly kindheartedness in heaping spoonfuls. Not that it seemed to set Keller at ease. His kitchen was spartan, entirely practical with nothing decorative though Rennie could see several mounted heads—a bear, a buck, a mountain lion— through the door to the living room. There was also a well-lit fire burning in the hearth.

"Gets chilly up here at night," Rennie said. "Mind if we move into the living room?"

Garrison shifted his eyes to her but she couldn't tell whether or not he approved.

Keller nodded and led them to his sofa. Garrison took the armchair. She wondered if there were lessons in tradecraft on seating dynamics—he always seemed intent on a particular spot. Regardless, she thought Keller might be more open with them if he was seated where he was accustomed to relaxing.

"So, Henry Blattner and Ellen Radley?"

"That's right," Garrison answered him.

"Are those your real names?" Keller asked.

Garrison spoke evenly. "No."

Keller shook his head. "It's not clear to me who you are and it's becoming less clear to me every minute why I agreed to meet with you."

Garrison didn't miss a beat. "Because we can tell you things you have long wanted to know."

"Why would you do that?"

"For your peace of mind."

Keller raised an eyebrow.

"And because you have something we want."

"You're CIA," Keller said. It wasn't a question.

"No. But I used to be."

"And now?" Keller didn't seem concerned with Rennie.

"I can't tell you that—"

"FBI?" Keller cut Garrison off.

"No. We have no affiliation with the United States government."

"Then why do you care?"

"Because in many ways we are like you. Patriots who believe in our country but believe we can best serve it in a separate role."

"I don't believe you."

"Let me make myself more clear." Garrison didn't change the position of his body. He sat leaning back in the padded chair, legs crossed at the knee, his arms loose. "We are affiliated with an organization that contends it can do more for our country by working outside of any official capacity, where we are not hampered by corruption. Or legality."

Rennie stared at Garrison, alarmed that he was giving away so much.

Keller looked at Garrison for what seemed like an eternity. Rennie could see that hard-won skepticism was fighting against a gut feeling that Garrison was being straight with him.

"What do you know about my father?" Keller's voice wavered as his emotion rose at the mention of his father.

This is going to be too easy. Rennie had been around Garrison long enough to feel his tension, deeply concealed, ramp down at this first victory.

He leaned forward then, mimicking Keller's position, their heads close together, *mano a mano*. "Your father was a hero, Mr. Keller. He knew he would never have any kind of public acknowledgment for his service to his country, and he knew that if things went wrong, he would be disavowed. This is a rule of the game that every operative accepts. It is an ugly and necessary rule for those who are caught up in it. It is the ultimate sacrifice to country, the sacrifice of identity and sometimes reputation."

And family. Rennie knew that this fiction had nearly destroyed Keller's mother and had driven him to the kind of chest-beating, ill-conceived nationalism he was practicing on this compound. She wondered if he knew he was playing with fire, or if it was his intent to flame out in a blaze of glory.

"What happened to my father?"

"You know the story up to the time when your mother left the country?"

"Yes."

"Your father was ordered to stay on."

Keller dropped his head as he listened to Garrison recount the story of Donald Keller's bravery and his death. And how his country had perverted the facts about how and why he died.

"He was never honored for his duty." Keller spoke with bitterness.

"Not publicly, no. But he wasn't forgotten."

Garrison picked up the folder he'd laid on Keller's coffee table. He handed Keller a photograph.

"This is an image of the Book of Honor in the lobby of CIA headquarters."

Keller looked at the photo of the book locked inside a case of polished metal and glass. On one side of the page, in succession, was a vertical column of stars. A few of the stars had names written next to them. But most did not. On the other side of the page was a column of dates. "These are the dates of the deaths of CIA operatives killed in the line of duty," Garrison continued. Then he pointed to a place on the photograph. Underlined in heavy black marker was June 27, 1965 and across from it, a star.

"That's the year I was born. And the day my father died,"

Keller said. The skepticism was draining from his face leaving behind only grief.

Garrison handed Keller another photograph, also taken in the entrance lobby of the CIA. The image depicted a marble wall upon which was engraved:

In honor of those members of the Central Intelligence Agency who gave their lives in service to their country.

Beneath that were five rows of stars that had been cut into the wall. One was circled on the photograph.

"This is your father's star."

Keller dropped his head and closed his eyes.

"Your father knew what he was getting into. He knew that a country as great as ours in a world that hasn't caught up with it has to have an organization that engages in ugly acts for the greater good. He knew he might be called upon to sacrifice himself. He was willing and he did it."

Keller looked as if something were collapsing inside of him. He looked around the room as if he expected the walls to crumble around him.

"All of this…" Rennie knew he was seeing beyond the walls of his humble farmhouse to the compound he'd created.

He put his hand to his head. His words came out barely a whisper. "I've made a mistake."

CHAPTER THIRTY-SIX

Devils Lake, North Dakota

Nasser Armin's plane touched down midafternoon. He'd taken a Northwest Airlines flight out of Minneapolis—the only airline and the only city that served the Devils Lake Regional Airport. He waited twenty minutes outside the terminal for a taxi that took him to the City Center Motel, an ugly brick and vinyl L-shaped building that nevertheless had an old neon sign affixed to its corner that appealed to the love of noir he'd had when he was a boy. Though it had been difficult for him to get his hands on them in Iran, he'd devoured Raymond Chandler and Dashiell Hammett novels whenever he could. Life had seemed so much simpler then.

Nasser's room was surprisingly pleasant. Modern in contrast to the motel's exterior. He'd come to hate the Midwest. So provincial, so dowdy and dour. Such was his lot. He felt adrift—

had felt this way ever since his long slumber in Denver had ended so abruptly. The Foundation kept trying to convince him that he had a place with them—a place where he could feel useful again. But all he could think about was the past. And here he was, still stuck in the Midwest, intent on meeting the woman whose life his brother had interrupted.

He wasn't sure what meeting Hannah Marcus would accomplish. When he'd hatched the idea and received the approval as well as the woman's whereabouts from Peyton Virgil, he'd been consumed with the notion of apologizing to her. Now it just seemed absurd. It was the Iranian in him talking when he needed to bury that part of himself and become an American. Since he was stuck here.

He thought about his meeting with Rennie Vogel, remembering the look in her eyes. What part of him had required that meeting? He shook his head and rooted in his travel bag for the pint of rye he'd brought with him, something to still his churning stomach. His real self. That was who had needed to meet the woman who'd killed his brother. Not the Iranian or the American in him. Just his real self. And now he felt guilty for putting her through it. He'd seen how haunted she was. And yet what he'd said to her was true. He couldn't forgive her.

Several hours later after he had showered and settled into his room, Nasser walked to a diner a few doors away from his motel. He was nearly fifty years old and he was growing much too stodgy in his habits. He wanted his own food, his own things around him. There'd be no Middle Eastern grocer in this tiny town, let alone a restaurant. In the diner, he ate a plate of meatloaf and mashed potatoes all covered with a glossy, overly salted gravy. He paid his tab and pushed through the heavy door and headed toward the hospital. He liked a cigarette after a meal but the diner hadn't allowed it and he craved one now.

He'd always found it fascinating the way America struggled with its two strongest strains—Puritanism and an unquenchable thirst for freedom. Now the puritanical thread had turned its disapproving eye upon the smokers and everywhere it was becoming less and less common to be able to smoke with dignity. Nasser didn't believe in smoking while he walked. He considered it uncivilized. Smoking should never be about *multi-tasking*—a horrible modern word he despised—unless, of course, it was to facilitate thought. So, he walked the seven blocks to Mercy Hospital and then sat on a bench to smoke before visiting Hannah Marcus.

He took the stairs to the third floor—not for the exercise but so he could think of what he might say to her. She should be expecting him. Virgil said he would inform her of his visit. But then Nasser hadn't expected to arrive until the following day. He'd wanted too much to put this meeting behind him. Now he only wanted to avoid it. He paused outside Room 307.

A nurse approached him as he stood, indecisive. "May I help you, sir?"

"I'd like to see Miss Hannah Marcus."

The nurse tilted her head, her eyebrows raised. "You're a visitor?"

"Yes, I am a visitor."

"Visiting hours are almost over, she said, looking at her watch. "But, go right ahead."

Hannah typed on her laptop, awkwardly, with one hand. She had expected to be released today but there had been no sign of the doctor who would sign her discharge papers. Her dinner tray, which she'd mainly left untouched, was assaulting her both with its odor and the sight of it as it congealed. She was considering calling for the nurse to remove it when the door to her room moved slightly.

"Jenna?" She'd grown fond of the nurse on the evening shift as she mostly left Hannah alone. The door stopped moving. "Is someone there?"

A man with olive skin wearing a tweed coat and a tattersall shirt with a spread collar pushed into the room. A series of images flipped through Hannah's mind. The one she settled on—even though she knew it couldn't possibly be true—nearly took her breath away.

Fareed.

"Miss Marcus, I'm sorry. I didn't mean to…"

Hannah didn't know what her face had betrayed but the man held both hands palms out in a show of peace. He certainly was *not* Fareed, whose life she had seen drain out of him before her eyes. But there *was* some aspect of Fareed in this man and it made her throat catch to see him.

"Who are you?" she asked as he neared her bed.

His eyes were wide in what nearly looked like fear. "Mr. Virgil didn't inform you of my arrival?"

"I don't know what you're talking about."

He looked back toward the door as if he were considering leaving. He put both hands to his cheeks. "I don't know what to say. I fear this will come as a horrible shock."

He looked in shock himself. Hannah wanted to take him by the collar of his clearly expensive tweed and shake him.

He circled around the bed and sat in the armchair. He ran his hands through his hair, slightly receding though very black and thick. "I don't even know how to begin. I expected you to have been forewarned of my visit. But then I am a day earlier than I expected. It is my fault."

Though it was unlike her, Hannah began to take pity on him. "Why don't you start with your name?"

He raised his hands in an expression of futility and his eyes filled with emotion. "I'm not even supposed to be alive."

Hannah's heart began to hammer. She leaned across to him with her good arm and gripped his hand, hard. "Who the hell are you?"

"I am Nasser Armin."

They stared at one another for a long beat as Hannah absorbed the implications of what he'd said. She let go of his hand. It meant that she would have never been kidnapped. It meant she wouldn't have engaged in a gun battle in the highlands of Tajikistan. It meant she wouldn't have shot three men. Because if Nasser Armin was alive, none of those things would have happened. But he was and they had anyway.

"What a fucking joke," she finally said. And then she began to laugh. At first quietly, and then as it gained more force she tamped it down before it turned into tears. She continued to laugh quietly as shivers traveled over her so strongly her shoulder wound began to ache. "I mean, seriously, what a fucking joke. There's got to be a word in Yiddish for this. I should call my parents. They're the only ones I know who'd appreciate it."

She felt Nasser take her hand and jerked her head toward him.

"*I* appreciate it," he said quietly. He was ashen, his brown eyes pained and glassy.

In Tajikistan Hannah had had only a single face-to-face encounter with Ahmad Armin. And though the man before her was his brother, she could barely glimpse the resemblance. She noticed how soft his hand was before she disengaged her own. Small and soft as a girl's, as if he'd never done any sort of manual labor in his life. As she remembered his biography, she supposed he hadn't.

They talked for more than an hour. Gradually, the feeling that a cruel joke had been played on her passed. The collision of the Armins with the CIA—and eventually the FBI—was a tragic one. And Nasser was living, breathing evidence of a certain kind of American hubris.

"I have a friend, an investigative journalist, who could really do something with this story."

Nasser shook his head. "The CIA made it clear I should not go to the media. That I would regret it."

"Saying it doesn't make it so," Hannah said. "Think on it."

Jenna poked her head in the door.

"Looks like you're going to be a free woman. Dr. Woolf is doing late rounds. He can discharge you tonight. Unless you want to wait for morning."

"Finally," Hannah said.

She looked at Nasser. It was ironic but, somehow, the fact that Nasser Armin wasn't dead made her feel more alive than she had in a long time. It was as if, out of the debacle that was Tajikistan, there was finally a little bit of good news.

"Why don't you come back with me to my hotel. We can talk more and get some decent food."

An hour later, they both sat in matching, overly plush armchairs, a selection of cheeses and a crusty baguette on a tray between them that they had finagled from the hotel kitchen's staff as they were cleaning up for the night.

"So, you're finished with CIA?" Hannah asked.

Nasser nodded. "Yes, thank Allah." He spoke with more than a trace of irony.

"And now you're with the mysterious Foundation?"

"It seems so." Nasser topped off their glasses from the bottle of Sauternes in the bucket next to him.

"And this Virgil you mentioned has some sort of leadership position?"

"Yes. A fine man. Very imposing." Nasser raised his bushy eyebrows and chuckled. "I don't know how they intend to employ me. My skills are very specific, you know. But it is becoming clear I'm no natural at any of this covert business." He shook his head. "I should never have mentioned his name."

"Your secret's safe with me."

Hannah stretched, careful of her shoulder. "It looks like they've recruited everyone from the Tajikistan incident but me. Maybe I should beg them for a job."

"Maybe you should."

Nasser told her then about his meeting with Rennie. At the mention of her name something in Hannah's heart leapt. She was beginning to realize that Rennie was taking up residence in her mind in a way no one ever had. She would have thought it would have made her feel trapped. But it didn't. A thought strayed into her mind—*I do want to be wanted and loved.* She wanted to roll her eyes in revolt against such a hackneyed and conventional idea. But it was true all the same. She'd have to grow accustomed to it.

Can a person really change?

Nasser had been sitting quietly since she'd stopped speaking, caught up in her own reverie. "You have something heavy on your mind?"

"Not so heavy," she said. "I was thinking about someone I care for. That I shouldn't keep it quite so hidden."

"Love should never be kept hidden," he said, a faraway expression on his face. He smiled. And then he leaned over and patted her arm. "I wish you all the happiness this world can give you, dear Hannah."

CHAPTER THIRTY-SEVEN

"Things will have to be different from here on out," Keller said.

He'd been sitting with his arms on his knees, his hands clasped together, staring into the fireplace. Rennie suspected Keller's organization would take an altogether altered form over time. That would undoubtedly drive some of the men away, to more extreme groups, but perhaps some would evolve with him and exchange a stagnant ideology for one more productive to their community.

Keller shook Garrison's hand and then Rennie's. "Thank you," he said. Then he seemed to come back to himself and the vulnerability that had made his eyes shine throughout their discussion faded. "Now, what is it that I can do for you?"

Twenty minutes later they stood before Cainkiller's cabin.

Keller paused before fitting the key in the door. "I wouldn't do this under any circumstances but these. I want you to know that. I'll never waver in the belief that a man's property is sacred."

"It may turn out to be nothing," Rennie said, looking up at Keller, "but if something *is* there, it could save lives."

Keller nodded and turned the key in the lock.

When they'd first mentioned Cainkiller back in Keller's living room his expression showed that the young man was on his radar too.

Then they filled Keller in on all that happened since Cainkiller and Buddy had knocked Rennie unconscious. Buddy's death. The shooting of Yates and Hannah.

"I wanted to give him a chance," Keller said, speaking of Cainkiller. "It's his type that my organization was supposed to try to keep on the straight and narrow."

The straight and narrow on the road to Armageddon, Rennie thought.

"Did he set off any warning bells?"

"Not at first. But there was something. I couldn't put my finger on it. Something inconsistent about the way he spoke. Mostly he spoke plainly like all the guys here. I mean, we always have a few who try to use big words when they're arguing about their theories, but this was different. Sometimes words would appear in his regular conversation that made me think he had more education than he'd said."

"Anything else?" Garrison prodded him.

Keller leaned back and stared at the rough-hewn beams on his ceiling. "It's one of those things that's hard to put your finger on, but sometimes I just had the sense that he was lying."

"Lying about what?"

Keller shrugged. "Hard to say. Maybe just his commitment to the Militiamen. Almost like he thought he was above us."

The hinges on Cainkiller's door cried out as Keller pushed it open and pulled the string for the bulb on the ceiling. A thin whistle escaped from his lips. Cainkiller's cabin was absolute chaos.

"Have you had any reason to come in here since he took up occupancy?" Garrison asked.

"Not really. I've been to the door a few times—I didn't see anything like this."

It was a small room with two metal cots along the two side walls, a toilet and shower stall at the back. Clothes were strewn on the floor, some stained with blood and mud. A stack of books on the skinhead movement, the militia movement and Christian Identity were tipped over on the folding table that served as a desk. And papers, some printed but most handwritten in blue Sharpie, were everywhere—under and on top of one of the beds, sticking out of the books and littering the desk. It was cold in the room, the one window up a few inches. Underneath it was a ceramic pot, mostly filled with ash.

"Looks like he burned some papers," Garrison said, poking through the remnants.

"I've got something here," Rennie called from the other side of the room. "Printouts and photos of the Islamic Center. But it's not the one in Fargo." She turned and held up a high resolution photograph. "It's the D.C. Islamic Center."

"Christ," Keller said.

"Not there, no," Garrison said dryly. "But maybe Cainkiller intends on introducing him to the good Muslims of the District with a bang."

"We're going to need to take this stuff with us," Rennie said.

Kyu Song checked the time on the dashboard of his black Volkswagen GTI as he exited the highway toward Buckhannon, West Virginia. His flight to Utah was taking off from Dulles in six hours. He'd have less than an hour with Rodney Powers. With more information coming in from Vogel and Garrison in North Dakota on Cainkiller, he and Virgil had been scrambling to develop more leads on their end. They'd tapped their sources at the FBI, but all the Feds had on Cainkiller was the same data SPS already knew. This meant that until Kyu interviewed Cainkiller's girlfriend, Rodney Powers was their most valuable asset.

After being cleared by the front desk, Kyu set the bezel on

his watch as he waited in a room empty but for a few tables and a refrigerator. He suspected it was the break room for the sheriff's office.

Rodney Powers was led into the room by the same deputy sheriff he'd seen at the front desk. This was a small operation.

Rodney had the bearing of a man apt to get beaten up on a regular basis. He embodied the word cocky, strutting and popping his hip with each step. He slumped into the chair across from Kyu.

"Tell me who you are again," Rodney said.

"My name is Kyu and I'm a private investigator. Marshall Wallace aka Cainkiller is missing and I've been hired to track him down."

"Who hired you?" Rodney said, squinting his eyes.

"I can't say."

Rodney shrugged. "I'm mad at that douchebag, you know. He said he'd send me smokes."

"Oh?" Kyu said, noncommittally, encouraging him to go on.

"Yeah, we were buddies for a while. But then he got all tight with Zoid."

"Zoid? What is this…Zoid?"

"Hey, man, I like your accent. You kinda sound like that guy on *Kung Fu*." Rodney slapped Kyu on the shoulder.

"Keep your hands to yourself, Powers," the deputy sheriff said, taking a step forward.

Kyu stared at the place where Rodney had touched him before turning back to him. "I'm not Chinese."

"Naw, man, no offense. I know you got your green card or whatever."

"Wallace," Kyu said, getting Rodney back on topic.

"Yeah, so, the Zoid was this freaky dude—Zoid, freakazoid, get it?—and him and Wallace got pretty tight. I didn't hang too much with him after that. I mean, Zoid wasn't his real name." Rodney scratched his chest where the skin showed pale and hairless in the V of his jail uniform. A multicolored tattoo covered him to the collarbone. "I can't remember what that dude's name was." He shrugged. "Everybody called him Zoid. Even him. Hey, man, you know karate?"

"I know karate but I am not Japanese." Kyu leaned forward. "I am Korean." He emphasized each syllable.

"Kor-e-an." Rodney repeated after him, his lips curling around the sounds like he was tasting something new. "That's cool."

"Wallace's friend. This Zoid, what else do you remember about him?"

"He was freaky. Real skinny like a junkie. Like this…" Rodney forced his chin out and engaged the muscles in his neck so that the cords along his throat and the veins that ran down along the side were pronounced. "His eyes were way back in his head. You know, he had, like, a shelf, like those guys who do too many steroids."

"Was he doing steroids?"

Rodney shrugged again. "I doubt it—the rest of him sure didn't look like he was doing roids. I think he was a meth head before he got sent up."

"What else?" Kyu said.

"I can't remember nothing else." Rodney twisted his mouth and looked at the ceiling. "But he kinda talked down to everybody. Lucky he didn't get his skinny ass kicked."

"Do you know what he was in for?"

"Arson."

"What did he burn?"

"Beats the hell out of me."

"Let's get back to Wallace," Kyu said. "What was he into?"

"He was a good guy. Pretty much your standard skinhead. You know what separates a skinhead from your run-of-the-mill gangbanger? Principles. And that was Wallace through and through. He hated the ragheads, I mean, *really* hated them."

Mushikhan kaeseggi.

What a jackass.

Kyu looked over at the deputy. He wanted nothing more than a few minutes alone with Rodney. But that wasn't his job anymore. He wondered how Rodney would have handled prison in North Korea.

"Did he ever talk to you about any plans to do anything about the Muslims? Any sort of public action to get his points across?"

"Wallace had lots of ideas. I don't rat people out but I'm still pissed about those smokes. Speaking of…"

Kyu glanced at the deputy who nodded at him before he reached into his bag and handed Rodney a carton of Marlboro Reds.

"Can I smoke, Harlan?"

The deputy rolled his eyes and carried over an ashtray from a shelf on the wall. Rodney went through a whole ceremony of opening the carton, rapping a pack repeatedly against his hand and finally stripping off the cellophane. He tapped the bottom and two cigarettes shot up from the pack. He held it out. "Want one? What did you say your name was?"

"Kyu. And no."

"Q. That's cool. Like that James Bond gadget guy."

"Wallace," Kyu reminded him again.

"Oh yeah." Rodney dug in his pants pockets for a match and lit his cigarette, drawing on it like it was his last breath. "He had all sorts of ideas. It was nine-eleven that really got to him. He was more against the Jews before that. But with the Ay-rabs, it was like he'd found his life's calling. He wanted to do something big. He even thought of going to flight school and then hijacking a flight to Saudi Arabia and crashing it into that place all those Muslims go."

"Mecca."

"That's it," Rodney said, slapping his hand on the table and making the ashtray jump.

"Ramp it down, Rodney," the deputy said.

A light came into Rodney's eyes. "Yeah! Ramp up the debauchery!" he shouted.

The deputy advanced on him and gripped him by the shoulder. "Cut the shit, Rodney, or your visit is over. And I'll take your smokes."

"All right, man, jeez." Rodney twisted away from him, his mood soured. "We used to say that, me and my crew, when we were cruising around town. We'd go, 'Ramp up the debauchery,'" he said in a high-pitched elevated whisper. "Everybody would laugh their asses off."

Kyu glanced at his watch. He needed to be back on the road five minutes ago. Hopefully he could make up the time.

"What else? What other plans did he have?"

Rodney crushed out his cigarette in the ashtray and lighted another. He looked like he had grown bored with the conversation.

"I don't know. He thought about going over there somewhere, somewhere in the Middle East, and kidnapping somebody, like one of their preachers and then make a video with a black hood over his face. He'd say some stuff about the Muslims trying to take over and then he'd waste him. And he talked about going into some big mosque strapped with explosives. You know, basically do the same thing they do but do it to them."

"Was he only talking? Or was he really planning on doing something? Did he have someone he was working with?"

"He might have been working with the Zoid. They were pretty secretive. And they both got released about the same time."

Kyu stood abruptly. "Thank you for your time." He jotted his cell number on a blank card. "If you think of anything else at all, please call this number."

CHAPTER THIRTY-EIGHT

Rennie finished filling a duffel bag with evidence from Cainkiller's cabin. She zipped it closed and set it outside the tiny room on the rudimentary porch. She'd scanned the papers as she was filling the bag but hadn't seen any details about when Cainkiller might terrorize the D.C. Islamic Center. But something was up. Ten minutes before, Garrison's cell had rung and he stepped outside Cainkiller's cabin to take the call.

Her own cell had vibrated a moment later. Hannah. Her worry over Hannah's condition was more subdued now that she knew she'd been discharged. But, bizarrely, Nasser Armin was in Devils Lake. Hannah said she'd explain later.

Keller joined her on the porch. He shook his head. "It's hard to believe all this was going on right under my nose."

Rennie wanted to say, Well, that's what you get when you

invite a bunch of skinhead conspiracy nuts onto your property. But Keller was feeling bad enough as it was. She said, "I just heard from Hannah. She's been released from the hospital."

"That's a relief. Nice woman," he said, a thoughtful expression on his face.

Rennie glanced at Garrison.

"Okay, send the file and we'll talk in the morning," he said, and pocketed his phone.

Rennie raised her eyebrows as he joined them on the porch.

"Can you give us a minute?" Garrison said to Keller.

He nodded and stepped back into the cabin.

"What file?" Rennie asked.

"Everything the analysts have on Cainkiller. Not much new in it but Virgil's sending it anyway."

Rennie nodded. "Nasser's here."

"I know. A call from him came through to Virgil just as we were hanging up."

"When did you know?" Rennie asked sharply.

"Relax. Virgil just told me. Nasser turned up a day sooner than planned. Apparently the poor sap wanted to apologize to Marcus." Garrison's tone suggested he thought this to be a pathetic gesture.

Something cold settled in the pit of Rennie's stomach. "I thought the Armins would be out of my life once I got away from Tajikistan."

"You could always shoot him," Garrison said dryly.

Rennie didn't bother with a response. She asked, "What else did Virgil say?"

"Kyu made some headway with Cainkiller's prison buddy in West Virginia. Key points are that he mouthed off about targeting Muslims. Hijacking planes, kidnapping imams, blowing up mosques. And he said Cainkiller had a particular friend who was released about the same time. Buddy Olsen never served jail time so it wasn't him. But that doesn't mean he hasn't been working with someone else who's not on the scene. We need Cainkiller alive to lead us to this guy and whoever else."

Rennie ignored Garrison's return to his justification for not protecting Yates and Hannah. "If the target is the Islamic Center in D.C., we're going to have to bring FBI in on this sooner than later."

Garrison nodded. Rennie knew he hated to agree with her. This was the worst part of their position with the Foundation. If they discovered a real threat, an imminent threat, their mandate was to report it through their contacts to the proper authorities. It would make for a less than satisfying end to a case.

"We'll have to eventually," Garrison said. "But Virgil's giving us a bit more time. He's got some contract boys watching the mosque and he's been inside himself getting the lay of the land. We'll all be conferencing in the morning."

"Okay, better get moving then." Rennie picked up the duffel. "We should get back to the motel and go through these papers. We're going to need a scanner so we can send copies to the analysts."

"We're not done here yet."

"Oh?"

"I saved the best news for last. Virgil just heard from a contact at ATF. They busted an arms dealer in Iowa. They're bargaining with him as we speak. His most recent transaction was a trade of a batch of C4 for a grenade launcher to a skinny guy with a tattoo on the back of his neck."

"Cainkiller."

Garrison nodded. "Sounds like our man." He shifted his eyes toward the door of the cabin and called, "Mr. Keller, could we have a word?"

Ten minutes later the three of them, huffing cold breath as they hurried, approached a corrugated metal shed with three heavy locks on the door. Fortunately Keller was being cooperative. He admitted outright that he had weapons he wasn't supposed to have, that for him it was a hobby and it legitimized him in the eyes of his followers as well.

"I always have the keys on me. And it's the only set," he said.

Keller heaved open the creaking door and flicked the power unit switch on the floor. Rennie looked at Garrison. A smile twitched at the corner of his mouth and his eyes glowed.

"Beautiful," he said quietly.

Keller had installed a network of lights that ran along the

walls at shoulder height and cast the lovingly mounted and hung weapons in a soft illumination that approximated the cinematic.

Rennie looked back at the scene. Keller stood ahead of them, his broad back outlined against the diorama of the weapons. He turned only his head to them. "It's gone."

Cainkiller drove nine miles over the speed limit. As fast as he dared. He'd packed the C4 in the interior wall of his spare tire, which sat in the well and was covered with firewood he'd bought along the road. Even if he were pulled over, it was unlikely the officer would want to unload four hundred pounds of wood. The bitch was, he was burning through gas like crazy being so weighted down. But with all the Red Bull he'd been drinking, he needed plenty of piss breaks.

He was behind schedule and his heart felt like it was about to explode. At least the trade not far outside Iowa Falls had gone well. He began to laugh and then hiccupped and laughed harder, his body shaking so violently he nearly lost control of the Explorer. He lit a cigarette as his laughter subsided.

"One you make it out alive, two you don't. Three you make it out, four you don't. Five you make it out, six you don't." A Camaro shot past him then, the first number on its license plate a three.

"Woo hoo," he hooted and pounded the dashboard with his fist.

He'd been playing this game off and on since he'd packed the C4 in the tire. He wasn't suspicious and he didn't believe in magical thinking but as he got closer to D.C. he felt forced to consider the possibility of his own death. *But nothing can kill you, cowboy. You're immortal.*

Cainkiller heard his cell phone chirp and hunted for it in the debris that littered his passenger seat. He took his eyes away from the road for a moment to glance at its screen.

"What the fuck?"

The phone was cycling through its menus faster and faster as he watched. And then it stopped and his usual display screen appeared normally. "Piece of shit," he muttered and tossed the phone onto the floor of the passenger seat. He wasn't expecting any calls anyway.

The next morning Virgil walked into the analysts' room at the SPS offices carrying a tray of coffees and a box of doughnuts that had just been delivered.

"We've got him, boss," Logan called to him. "He's finally reached an urban enough environment to triangulate him. He's about a hundred miles south of Chicago and, depending on his route, we should be able to keep pretty good tabs on him. Regardless, if we lose him and he's on his way to D.C., we should be able to grab him at least fifty miles outside of the metro area which will give us an hour or so to get into position."

Virgil was so relieved he almost cried. "Good work, Logan. That's our best news yet."

Virgil was growing increasingly concerned with how Project Ouroboros was going. Regardless, he had an instinct that this thing was going to resolve and soon. He only hoped it ended with Cainkiller in a cell and the good people of D.C. safe and sound in their homes.

Rennie pulled the curtain aside. "Have you looked out here lately?"

She was in Garrison's room where they would receive the conference call. Garrison stood at the stove in the kitchen making breakfast.

"I have not," he said.

"It's getting worse," she called over her shoulder. She could barely see through the window. The rain was pelting it so hard the water ran down in a sheet. "We need to get out of here soon or we're not going to be able to get out."

She let the curtain fall as Garrison set two plates of eggs and toast on the table. "Coffee?" he offered.

"Please."

Rennie disliked being around other people in the morning and she especially disliked participating in a scene of faux domesticity with Garrison at the crack of dawn.

"I don't see anything else to keep us here," Garrison said.

"I don't either. Though it'd be nice if we had a better idea where Cainkiller is."

"It would, indeed."

"Let it go."

Ten minutes later they sat together in front of Garrison's laptop looking at a split screen with video feeds of Virgil in D.C. and Kyu in a Starbucks in Idaho.

"Can everyone see and hear?" Virgil asked.

They all assented.

"Kyu's in a coffee shop and will be typing his communication. Okay, everyone should be up to speed through the network, but let's just cover the key points."

Words began to rapidly appear in a box at the bottom of Kyu's screen: *I'm meeting Cainkiller's ex-girlfriend in twenty minutes—she agreed to see me before she goes to work.*

"That's fine, Kyu—we should we done by then. We have to get Garrison and Vogel on a plane while the road to the airport is still open."

"We've already missed the morning flight and there's not another one until this afternoon," Rennie said.

"No problem. We've had one of our benefactor's aircraft in position for a few days. As long as you make it to the airport you can fly out as soon as air traffic control clears you for takeoff."

"This aircraft comes equipped with a pilot?" Garrison said.

"Yes, Mr. Garrison," Virgil confirmed.

Rennie glanced at Garrison. She would not describe him as a man with a sense of humor, at least not one that most people would recognize. She supposed his occasional non sequiturs at least amused himself.

"Can we bring Marcus out with us?" Rennie asked, turning back to the screen.

"Yes, as long as it doesn't prevent you from getting out ASAP. The lake is rising fast and Route 2 is already spotty. But, yes, bring Marcus and Armin both," Virgil said and turned away to address someone off screen. "Dana, call Marcus and Armin and tell them to leave for the airport immediately." He wrote something down on a pad. "First, a new development that we haven't gotten into the network files yet—we have Cainkiller on our radar." Virgil turned away from the web camera. "Logan, what's his location?"

A disembodied voice came through the speakers. "We don't have him at the moment. Lost him soon after he entered Ohio. We're getting blips of data but nothing we can narrow down precisely. We think he may have stopped."

"Good, we need the extra time," Virgil said, turning back to the webcam.

"Okay, so we've got Cainkiller, presumably, en route to D.C. The evidence we have now is that he's armed with four pounds of C4, which he traded Keller's grenade launcher for in Iowa Falls. From the papers Vogel and Garrison found in his quarters, we are looking at the Islamic Center of Washington as a possible target. Other than his recent reckless behavior there's no reason to believe he plans to hit it as soon as he returns to the area. That said, tomorrow is Friday and that means *khutbah*—the Islamic corollary to the Sunday sermon—and the mosque will be at full capacity. If we haven't located Cainkiller by tomorrow morning we're calling in the Feds so they can warn the imam and get into position."

"What are we expecting Kyu to get off the ex-girlfriend?" Rennie asked.

"We don't have high expectations," Virgil said, rubbing his chin. "But it's a base we can't afford to leave uncovered. Kyu, report in as soon as you finish with her and catch the first flight back here."

Kyu raised his hand in acknowledgment.

"Okay, let's move." He turned away again. "Dana, did you get hold of Armin and Marcus?"

"They'll be on their way in a few minutes." Another disembodied voice in the background.

"We're good to go then. Happy travels, everyone. Be safe."

Virgil's screen went black and then Kyu's a moment later.

"How much time do you need?" Garrison asked.

"I'm ready. Just need to grab my bags."

"Meet me in the lot in five."

CHAPTER THIRTY-NINE

Provo, Utah

Kyu turned off the engine of his rental in front of Charity Finch's apartment and took time to get a feel for the neighborhood. Several of the apartments had American flags affixed to the railing. One even had a Confederate flag. This was not a nice part of town.

Though Kyu believed that nothing was more important in American society than the freedoms enshrined in the Constitution, it was, perhaps, the most difficult thing for him to get used to in the United States. That those freedoms were extended to speech and other forms of expression—even when they were shouted from the rooftop in direct opposition to that Constitution—was something he understood only theoretically. But the cult of individual expression would never sit entirely right with him. There was an ineradicable vein of despotism that coursed through him and made him want to shove the Constitution down the throats of those Americans who spoke against it. He took a few deep breaths. In through the nose, out through the mouth. *No need to think about such things now.*

Kyu flipped open his laptop and located the file on Charity Finch. Twenty-two years old. Moved to Provo with her parents from San Diego when she was ten. Enrolled in a course at BYU in business administration but quit before the semester was over. Worked a variety of low-paying jobs—mostly as a clerk in convenience or grocery stores. Began dating Cainkiller off and on after he moved to Provo for work from southeastern Utah, near the Four Corners region. Kyu closed the laptop and slipped it into his messenger bag. He checked his other supplies and got out of the car.

Charity Finch lived on the third floor, facing the street. Kyu jogged up the three flights of stairs and rapped on her door.

"You're the investigator?" she verified before letting him in.

Charity Finch was rail thin with wispy, winged hair. She wore sandals that were once white with skinny jeans that had a glittery pattern stitched down one leg.

Inside, the apartment was small and shabby. An enormous television dominated one side of the living room. The carpet was stained and there were cigarette burns on the coffee table. The only place to sit in the room was a puffy sofa covered in a lavender sheet. This, at least to the eye, was clean. Kyu sat on it next to Charity and opened his laptop on the coffee table.

"You said on the phone that the last time you spoke to Wallace was two days before he was released from prison," Kyu began.

"That's right. He always called me after evening mess on Tuesdays." Charity looked at Kyu warily. "I've been worried sick about him but if he's just going to disappear on me like that then I'm gonna have to move on. I can't cover this dump on my own."

"Why do you think he hasn't contacted you?"

"Beats me. I mean, he said he was gonna go on up to some group in North Dakota, South Dakota, something like that," she said, waving her hand. "But he was definitely gonna come home first."

"Did you know any of the people he was close with in prison?"

"I didn't *know* them. But he sure talked about them a lot. He talked about Zoid all the time."

"Do you know Zoid's real name?"

"Nuh-uh. He didn't never say," Charity said, smoothing the sheet over the arm of the sofa.

"What can you tell me about Zoid—where he was from, what he was in for?"

"Marshall was real impressed with him, said he was the smartest guy he ever knew and they were going to go to Dakota together. He said Zoid was from somewhere nice, I can't remember where." She put her finger to her lips. "California, Florida, Maryland, something like that."

Kyu raised his eyebrows. "Those are very different places. They aren't even near one another."

"Look, I said I can't remember, okay?"

"It's okay," Kyu reassured her. The cordial interview was not exactly where his expertise lay. "What else do you remember?"

She picked up a leather cigarette sleeve with a clasp at the top. It had a pocket on the side for the lighter. "I remember asking him what religion Zoid was. I mean everybody around here is Mormon. Like, I mean, everybody. I'm not. I grew up Catholic but I'm Christian Identity now, like Marshall. I had to convert or he wouldn't go out with me." She giggled into her hand and lit her cigarette. "It's not like they baptize you or anything. I just had to say I believed and that was it." She took a drag off the cigarette, her lipstick making a dark smudge on the white filter. "But he said Zoid was Episcopalian which got me thinking he must be wealthy. Or come from a wealthy family. A lot of Episcopalians have money, you know." Charity sat up straight and crossed her legs as if she were trying to elevate her bearing and show that she was qualified to make such pronouncements. A thought appeared to occur to her and she leaned forward, jabbing the air—much too close to Kyu—with her cigarette. "And Marshall said he was educated too. Bachelor's degree and all."

"Do you know where he went to school?"

The phone on the wall just inside the kitchen door rang.

"Hold on a sec," Charity said and jumped up.

She said "Hello" and then began speaking in Spanish.

Spanish was the first Romance language Kyu had learned after English. A much simpler language than English, he appreciated its more regular structure. Charity was telling someone named Juan that a *chinito*, a generically Asian male, would be exiting her apartment in fifteen minutes and that Juan should grab his wallet.

Charity hung up and smiled sweetly at him. "Can I get you a glass of water or something?"

"Do you have a Coke?"

Kyu was addicted to Coke and figured it was safer than betting on the cleanliness of Charity's glassware. While she rummaged in the kitchen he took a turn around the tiny room. One wall was covered in cheaply framed photographs. Most were of Charity as a child, gray complexioned, her eyes too far apart. In a few, Charity was a teenager, leaping into the air, pom-poms held high.

"I put it in a glass for you," Charity said, handing him the Coke.

Kyu frowned as he took it from her.

"Who is this?" he said, pointing to a photo of Charity seated next to a young man who stood above her with his hand on her shoulder in front of an artificial wooded scene.

"Why, that's Marshall." She sounded affronted.

"*That* is Marshall Wallace?"

"Of course it is. Who else would it be?"

"Who goes by Cainkiller?"

"Yes, though I've never called him that myself."

Kyu turned quickly and sat down to his laptop, mousing until he had the right file open. The photo of Cainkiller that Garrison and Vogel had just gotten from Keller—Keller kept files on all his men, mainly in case of emergency—opened crisply.

"Who's this?" he said, swiveling the laptop around to her.

Charity leaned down to it. "Hell if I know. Kinda looks like Marshall a little, but it sure isn't him. Hey, wait a minute. Maybe that's Zoid. Marshall said they kinda looked alike. Some of the other inmates even called them the 'twins'."

"I have to go," Kyu said, snapping his laptop shut and swinging his messenger bag over his head.

"What's wrong?" she said shrilly.

"More than you know," Kyu said.

He snatched the eight-by-ten photo of Charity and Wallace off the wall.

"Hey, you can't do that," she yelled.

"Yes. I can," he said, opening the door. "And one more thing. I'm not *chinito*. I'm Korean."

Kyu became hyperalert as he moved toward the stairway, adrenaline coursing through him. He opened his nostrils and breathed deeply. He'd spent his whole life knowing that danger always lurked around every corner. There was, perhaps, no other developed society as brutal as North Korea. At least not since the Soviet Union fell. Nothing felt more natural to Kyu than sniffing danger nearby. It was comforting.

He took the stairs slowly and silently. He could feel another man's dark attention on him. Juan must be very close.

The stairs terminated at the back of the building. Kyu felt the air around him charged, crackling with energy. He was wound tight and craved a confrontation.

He stepped off the bottom step. The edge of the open-air stairwell was just a few feet away. A person could be hiding around either corner.

He had rounded the railing heading toward the front of the building when the man made his move, darting out from the edge of the building and rushing him. Kyu rounded with lightning quickness. Juan already had his knife in his right hand, a fixed, serrated hunting knife.

Juan was about to speak—demand his money, Kyu supposed—when Kyu caught him on the ear with a roundhouse kick. Juan went down hard, the knife flying out of his hand. Kyu leapt on him but he was out cold. He gripped the limp man by the throat and leaned down to his ear. "Korean," he said. He would have carved it into his chest if he'd had the time.

CHAPTER FORTY

Garrison drove while Rennie gripped the hand strap above the window. They were headed north on Route 2, the lake on their left. While one of Crane's private aircraft stood on the tarmac waiting for them, Cainkiller was churning east. With luck, if they could get cleared for takeoff they'd beat him back to D.C. But they had to get to the airport first. And traffic was crawling. It was still raining hard, so hard their windshield wipers could barely manage the volume. The lake was surging, waves crashing hard against the banks and spraying violent gusts at the foolish drivers who had waited until this last possible moment to get away from the soon-to-be-flooded land around it.

Rennie dialed Hannah's cell phone. Rennie needed to be damn sure she'd be on Crane's plane when it took off. But her call went directly to voice mail.

"Marcus?" Garrison asked.

Rennie nodded.

"Aren't you concerned with Nasser's well being too?"

It was a rhetorical question but Rennie responded anyway. "I just don't know what use he'll be to the Foundation."

Garrison nodded. For once they were in agreement.

A cacophony of car horns erupted and Rennie turned her head to see the lake rushing toward them and heard a *whump* as a foot of water slammed into the car. "We're going to have to turn off," Rennie yelled.

"Not yet."

Garrison stared straight ahead, gripping the wheel hard. As their tires churned through the water, the engine began to sputter. Garrison jerked the wheel to the right, steering the car partially onto the shoulder where the water wasn't as deep. Traffic was heavy, cars ahead and behind as far as she could see. "This isn't good," Rennie said. Then the drivers in front of them braked and they were at a standstill. "We have at least a mile or more to go—this is going to get a lot worse."

"I looked at the map," Garrison said. "None of these turns go anywhere—a quarter of a mile, maybe half a mile inland. Turning off isn't going to do us any good."

Traffic was moving again, but slowly. Garrison edged the rental forward, water spewing up from its tires.

"You're going to flood the engine."

"Not yet."

"Wishful thinking."

"Yes."

Rennie touched the St. Catherine medal at her throat and unfastened her seat belt.

"I remember, once," Garrison began. "I was in Novgorod when the Volga flooded. On one of those torturous winding roads that hug the river. I was driving a Fiat of all things." He chuckled to himself. "It wasn't well maintained, of course—the road, that is. Everything was eroding at that time in Russia. Water was rushing down the mountain onto the road. One moment it would be clear and the next you'd be fighting a foot of water. I knew it was hopeless. The only salve was that the Soviet bastard holding a Ruger to my head as I drove probably wouldn't be able to keep it there when the car was carried into the river."

"And was it?" Rennie asked in spite of wishing Garrison would turn his brain to their current problem.

"It was."

"Well, you're obviously here to tell the tale. How did your Russian fare?"

"Not so good. When I exited the Fiat, he had the nerve to reach his hand out to me to save him." Garrison glanced at her, a small smile playing upon his lips. "I declined to take it."

Rennie sighed. Garrison could never resist reminding her what a cold-hearted bastard he was. She looked past him out her window. They'd come to a dead stop again. The water hadn't receded and she knew it could rise again at any moment. Then she heard a loud sluicing and jerked her head toward the lake, her fingers curling around the door handle, just in time to see a wall of water crash against the side of the car.

Feeling the car shift sideways she knew it was too late. She should have bailed out the moment she heard the roar of the water coming toward them. But then she felt Garrison's hand on her wrist. For an awful moment, all she could think was, *He wants to take me down with him.* Then the sheet of water drained from the glass and an enormous black truck filled the window. Garrison lowered it and there was Keller, leaning across to the passenger window and shouting over the storm, "Where are you going?"

"Airport," Garrison shouted back.

Keller shook his head. "You're never going to make it in that thing." He was looking at the low-profile rental and back to them like they were crazy. Rennie thought he was right. "Pull off the road and jump in."

Garrison nosed the rental onto the shoulder and popped the trunk.

Rennie jumped out of the car, sloshing through water up past her ankles, beating Garrison to the trunk. She handed him his bag, the rain pelting down on them, and grabbed her own. A moment later they sat together a bit too snugly on Keller's big bench seat.

"Glad I saw you," Keller said. He looked warm and dry and like he was enjoying playing the hero.

"You out for a pleasure ride?" Garrison said. His thinning hair was plastered across his scalp. He looked like a drowned rat.

"Figured I'd come out and see if anybody needed a hand. This baby can get through most anything," Keller said, slapping the dash of the truck.

And it was. The big truck tore through the foot of water traveling in the deserted oncoming traffic lane, shearing it to either side.

"And Moses stretched out his hand over the sea," Garrison said.

Keller grinned as the truck finally passed beyond the lake. The airport wasn't far and when Keller pointed the truck down the road that led to it, he said, "You know, you'll have a long wait for the next flight. *If* there is another flight out of here today."

"We've got it covered," Garrison said.

"Thanks for the rescue," Rennie said. "You couldn't have had better timing."

"Glad I could help." He looked away then, through the windshield with its chunking wipers trying to keep up with the rain. "I know you all didn't come all the way out here just to tell me about my dad." He turned to them then. "But I appreciate it all the same. Things are going to be different now." Keller shook Garrison's hand and leaned across him to shake Rennie's.

Rennie hoped it was true.

"I almost forgot," Keller said. Releasing his seat belt, he lifted his hips and rummaged in the front pocket of his jeans. "I was cleaning out the rest of Wallace's cabin, going over it with a metal detector. It's a little hobby of mine—never know what you'll find," Keller said sheepishly. "Anyway, I found a coin that had slipped under the floorboards."

"What kind of coin?" Rennie asked.

"I don't know. I can't even be sure it's Wallace's but I figured you'd want to see it anyway." He handed an envelope to Rennie.

"Open it," Garrison said.

Rennie opened the flap and tipped out the large coin. "It's

one of those commemorative coins. On the front it reads, 'Founding of the United Nations, 1944.' It shows a group of men sitting around a table." She flipped the coin over. "And on the back, 'International leaders met at Dumbarton Oaks in 1944 to form the United Nations.'"

"United Nations?" Garrison said. "Was Wallace into that New World Order nonsense?" He directed the question to Keller.

Keller looked taken aback. "No offense, but that's one thing I think we need to keep our eye on."

Rennie cringed. After everything Keller had said, this was unexpected. From her experience, arguing someone out of a conspiracy theory was impossible. No appeal to logic or good sense ever seemed to make any difference. But it rankled that Keller bought into such an absurdity.

He continued, "One world government seems inevitable. The Federal Reserve, the Council on Foreign Relations, the United Nations and now globalization. It's hard to argue that it's not where we're headed. Just wait and see. Next will be the North American Union. Once that happens there'll be no stopping it."

"Is that a yes?" Garrison said, reminding Keller of his question about Cainkiller's beliefs.

"I'd say most of my guys were on board with that. Wallace?" Keller rubbed his chin with his hand. "I can't say I remember anything in particular."

Rennie and Garrison ran across the tarmac and up the jet stairs at the Devils Lake airport. Rennie threw her laptop bag onto a seat at the back of the plane. Hannah wasn't there yet and a cord of tension encircled her chest. Trying her cell phone only took her to Hannah's voice mail again. Rennie crossed the aisle to peer through the rain-spattered window. No sign of her.

"The pilot says we're cleared for takeoff now," Garrison said, leaning over the seat in front of her. "But conditions are unstable and that could change at any moment."

Rennie stared through the window again. "Let's give Marcus fifteen minutes."

Garrison looked at Rennie coldly. He shook his head and turned away toward the front of the plane. Rennie slumped down in the seat and laid her forehead against the cool window, watching the back of the terminal. But she was so tired and wet and exhausted that she was soon asleep. She jolted awake when she felt a hand on her arm.

"Hey," Hannah said. She was wearing a gray wool turtleneck and black pants. "Can I join you?"

Rennie smiled in relief and glanced at her watch. She'd been asleep ten minutes and now the plane's engines were rumbling to life.

"You doing okay?" Hannah said.

"Better now." Rennie looked to the front of the plane and her eyes met Nasser's. He nodded once before dropping into his seat. "So, you've met Nasser."

Hannah nodded and ran her hand through her hair. "It's funny. You just never know, do you? We both lost something in Tajikistan. It makes us oddly compatible."

"Compatible?"

"I've grown fond of him. You may as well." Hannah took Rennie's hand. "You know, I'm not used to talking about how I feel. I think it's overrated generally." Hannah looked away. She took a deep breath as if she were marshalling her thoughts. Or her courage. "Even though I never knew him, he loomed as such a large figure at Armin's camp. The camp wouldn't have existed without him as a symbol. And then he turns up at my hospital door. It was like he'd been resurrected. And then I felt resurrected. I keep things shelved—it's the way I work—but something broke through then. We went back to my hotel room and talked. And I realized something."

Rennie held her breath as Hannah turned back to her.

"You remember what you said in the hospital? You said, 'I'll be coming for you anyway.'" Hannah leaned over and kissed her on the cheek. Rennie felt her lips brush her ear. "I don't want you to stop showing up," she whispered.

Rennie began to tremble, her heart pounding in her chest. She drew away from Hannah and put both her hands along her jawline. "I won't." Then she kissed her lightly on the lips.

"We're going directly to Virgil's house in Shaw," Garrison said as they exited the corridor that led from the jetway into the terminal at Reagan National. "There's a car waiting for us—leave the bags."

After finally being cleared for takeoff in North Dakota, the Citation X took only a little over two hours to fly back to D.C. But they were forced to land at Reagan National—Dulles could not accommodate their landing at such late notice and that meant meeting at the Foundation offices would take time they didn't have.

Rennie looked for Hannah as she bypassed baggage claim but could see no sign of her. Thinking of their conversation, she tried to keep a smile from forming on her lips.

"Let's go, Vogel," Garrison said.

Rennie nodded. She'd call Hannah when she had a chance, see if they could grab dinner after she finished with the SPS meeting at Virgil's.

Rennie and Garrison were silent as they rode down Fourteenth Street away from the airport. But it was a companionable silence. Rennie leaned her head back against the seat watching the lights of the city. As they crossed Pennsylvania Avenue she gazed at the Capitol, illuminated and glowing against the evening sky. When she was in Tajikistan, she never forgot for a moment that her actions were in direct service to her country. Later though, she came to realize her time there was in service to her government instead of her country. It was harder, now, to keep her mandate in mind. In some ways she was acting as an enforcer of the law as she had in her pre-CT3 time with the FBI. Except no evidence was collected according to the legal protocols. The United Nations coin Keller had given her and that now sat in her pocket would have been bagged, labeled and eventually dusted for fingerprints. No, the work she was doing now felt like a no-man's land.

She glanced over at Garrison. Something had changed between them after they'd fought in the woods. And after he'd offered her his world view in his motel room. She couldn't subscribe to his outlook, at least not in the way he did. But she had to admit there was some truth in it. They were easier with one another now. And that was a good thing.

The car finally turned onto T Street and then again at Twelfth and pulled to a stop. Virgil and his wife, Jackie, whose successful career in legal advocacy had led her to her current position as chief counsel for a prominent New England senator, lived in a three-story Victorian in the Shaw neighborhood. Rennie had been there once before for dinner soon after SPS had formed. She had found Jackie to be a formidable presence. The intensity of her gaze could be unsettling. That night as they ate, Rennie and she had connected over their mutual interest in middle-period jazz. They gently sparred over the respective merits of cool versus bebop, Rennie in the camp of the former and Jackie fully committed to the latter.

Jackie was opening the door as she and Garrison jogged up the steps. She was dressed in a long red gown and a thin black coat. A filmy cream scarf was knotted at her throat.

"I'm not happy with him," she said, jerking her head toward Virgil who held the door behind her. "But welcome, I'm glad to see you both again." She descended the steps and entered the car Rennie and Garrison had just exited.

"Come on in," Virgil said. He wore an evening suit, his bow tie loose. "Once again work has gotten in the way of fulfilling my role as Mrs. Virgil's escort. But she'll get over it."

Rennie and Garrison settled themselves at Virgil's dining room table, setting up their laptops and filling their plates from the leftovers Virgil offered them.

"We have new developments," Virgil said. "We alerted FBI through our contact about two hours ago. They will be covering our suspect as he enters the city. They'll have men at the mosque as well, though it's mostly empty now," he said, looking at his watch.

"So, Cainkiller is off our hands now?"

"No, but Wallace is off our hands because he's dead."

"What?" Rennie said, frowning, "I don't understand."

"The man you know as Cainkiller was assuming Marshall

Wallace's identity as well as his Internet handle." Virgil passed a sheet of paper across the table. It was a morgue photo of a twenty-something white man with a shaved head and two SS tattoos under his collarbone.

"How do you know this is Wallace?" Garrison asked.

"Kyu." He passed them another photo of the same young man, this time very much alive and standing next to a woman in a Sears-type portrait.

"That's Wallace's girlfriend," Rennie said.

"Right."

"So, who was the guy who threw me in the lake in North Dakota, our Cainkiller?"

"We're working on that as fast as we can. We think it's a man who befriended Wallace in prison and the man who ultimately killed him. He was called Zoid if you remember from the case file. He was released around the same time as Wallace. And Charity Finch—that's Wallace's girlfriend—said they were planning on going to Keller's camp together. Kyu is still in Utah—he and the analysts are simultaneously working to get the prison records."

"Now what?" Rennie said.

"We wait." Virgil gestured to their untouched plates. "Eat before it gets cold."

CHAPTER FORTY-ONE

Potomac, Maryland

Cainkiller turned down the drive off River Road. The wooded drive was a quarter of a mile long and terminated at a house that overlooked the river. His brother, Winston, who'd followed a more appropriate career path for a diplomat's son and hadn't wound up in prison, lived alone in the house at the end of the drive—at least Cainkiller hoped to find him alone. His brother. After all this time. His stop in Iowa had transformed his blocks of C4 into a wearable explosive with a remote device for detonation. Now all he needed was his ticket in. And that's where Winston came in. He heard his cell phone chirp.

"What the fuck?" He slowed to a stop.

Cainkiller reached over and ran his hand under the passenger seat until he found the phone. He flicked it open and saw that it was cycling through its menus again. Could someone be tracking him? He should have thought of it the first time it happened. He lowered the window of the Explorer and hurled the phone into the woods.

He didn't bother with any stealth as he approached the house. His brother's 1967 Jag was parked by the front door. He loved that car. His father had promised it to him. But then things had gone wrong for him and Daddy's perks went away. It would be a pleasure to drive it again. He pulled the Explorer behind the Jag and rang the front doorbell. No answer. He looked around, wondering if he'd missed him. *That would be very bad.* Then the door opened.

"Oh my God. Devon." Winston Randolph wore a tuxedo shirt open at the neck over a pair of gray sweatpants. "What on earth are you doing here? I didn't know you were out of..." His voice trailed off at the end, unwilling to speak of something as distasteful as prison.

How long had it been since Devon Randolph had heard his true name?

"I've come to replace you, dear brother," Cainkiller said as he stepped inside the door, closing it behind him.

"Replace me? What do you—"

Cainkiller drove the heel of his hand into Winston's eye socket and leapt on him as he hit the Persian entryway carpet. He dragged him to its edge and slammed his head against the hardwood floor until he lost consciousness. Before allowing himself to think, he unbuttoned the tuxedo shirt and wrestled it off him, tossing it out of the way. Then he pulled the fishing knife he'd stolen from Buddy Olsen out of his pocket and plunged it into Winston's neck. "Goddammit, you always had to side with him didn't you?" He turned the knife until it hit the artery and the blood rushed out of him.

In the shower upstairs, as the water washed away Winston's blood, Cainkiller was unprepared for the rush of emotion that overcame him. Tears mixed with water as he leaned over sobbing for his brother.

What the fuck, get your shit together.

By the time he stood before the bathroom mirror, surprised that he remembered how to tie a bowtie, the moment had passed.

He'd let his hair grow and though it was still short, he no longer looked skinhead-shorn. He looked like Winston. The two brothers had always resembled one another closely. In high school at Landon, they would fool the headmaster who could never keep them straight. Though he was only a year older than Winston, Cainkiller's years of taking drugs and drinking, of getting into fights, and his time in prison had taken their toll. But they still looked enough alike for him to pass. He held Winston's Maryland driver's license next to his face in the mirror. He nodded, a grin taking over his features.

"Move in slow," Ben Whitman whispered. He thumbed the transmitter on his com device and directed the outgoing audio so that only the command center could hear him. "Any luck in getting hold of the ambassador?"

"Negative," Whitman heard through his earbud. "His cell phone is switched off—it goes directly to voice mail. We're doing our damnedest to track down a member of his staff."

"Does he have a security detail?" Whitman asked.

"Not when he's in the U.S."

The team of five had left their vehicle with one man inside along River Road. The other four were humping it through the woods to the house. Two on either side of the drive. They were in full SWAT gear and moving quickly but stealthily, two pairs of silent but deadly FBI agents homing in on their target—the residence of the French ambassador's son. Whitman led on the south side of the drive, Scott Hempel covering him from behind. He switched his feed back to the team. "Okay gents, we're almost there. Spread out as we near the edge of the woods where the lawn starts. Hold there until you get my go-ahead."

A trio of ten-fours came through his earbud.

He could see the house now. He squatted down fifteen feet from where the woods terminated. Hempel moved into position to his right thirty yards away. Whitman scrutinized every inch of the house and the surrounding grounds. No movement at any of the windows. "Move forward in tactical positions. Skirt the drive. One man on each corner of the house." He didn't have to give more specific instructions. Their tactical roles were well defined. He knew Hempel would take the back corner while Whitman, himself, covered the front. O'Brien and Cohen would mirror their positions on the opposite side of the house.

"Let's go, boys."

The team set off toward the house, avoiding the white gravel of the drive that might announce their presence. Cohen carried the two-handled steel battering ram.

As Hempel edged down the slope toward the back of the house, Whitman crouched and moved slowly toward the front door, checking each window as he went. Cohen matched his progress on the other side, each communicating to the other with hand signals. There was no movement in the rooms Whitman could see. The front door had narrow panes of glass running along each side of it and a fan of low steps leading up to it. He and Cohen edged up to the door simultaneously. Whitman took a calming breath, his MP5 at the ready, and peered into the window.

Fuck.

"White male injured in entryway. Call in a 10-43, O'Brien. Anything at the back?"

"Negative," Hempel whispered.

"We're going in," he said quietly. He gave Cohen the signal to open and clear. Cohen stepped forward, drew the battering ram back and slammed it into the door just above the handle. The door exploded open and each man, his weapon raised, entered the room.

"Entryway clear."

Whitman knelt down to the man on the floor. His throat ravaged, he was clearly dead. He and Cohen moved systematically through the rest of the rooms on the first floor. Then he heard Hempel's voice through his earbud. "Second floor is clear. And I found Winston Randolph's passport in a drawer in the master bedroom."

"Let's take a look at it," Whitman said.

Whitman turned as he heard the heavy footsteps of his colleagues on the stairs. Hempel looked at the dead man on the floor and shook his head. "Looks like the ambassador will be getting some bad news," he said as he tossed the passport to Whitman.

Whitman opened it and crouched to the victim. "That's him." He looked up at Cohen. "Winston Porter Randolph."

Whitman radioed into the command center "The suspect is not, I repeat, is not on the premises. He must have dumped his phone. We probably walked right over it in the woods." He listened for a moment and nodded. "We'll begin a search of the rest of the property."

CHAPTER FORTY-TWO

Rennie paced along the bookshelves in Virgil's library. She had tried and failed to concentrate on the titles so she just paced.

"I wish you'd sit down," Garrison muttered.

He'd already complained that her leg was jumping when she had been sitting in one of the leather club chairs that flanked the fireplace. They expected to hear back from the analysts at any moment, hopefully with news on Zoid's identity.

Virgil strode into the room holding a sheet of paper fresh from the fax machine. "We've got him." He handed the paper to Rennie.

It was a prison intake photo. Rennie looked up at Virgil. "That's him." It was undeniably the man who'd thrown her into the lake in North Dakota. She passed the paper to Garrison.

"Devon Randolph," Rennie mused aloud. She went to the long table in front of the bookshelves where her laptop was set up. She quickly pulled up Wikipedia and typed "Devon Randolph" into the search box. There were no results. Then she tried entering his full name: Devon Blyton Randolph. Again, there were no page results.

But there was a cross reference to a single entry.

Rennie clicked on it and scanned the page. Her heart was already racing as she read. Garrison peered at the screen over her shoulder. "Franklin Phillips Randolph is the current United States Ambassador to France. He has two sons. Devon and Winston."

Rennie's head snapped up. "The story that Cainkiller told Yates in the bar. He referred to a brother named Winston." She shook her head. "Is it possible that Cainkiller is the son of the French ambassador?"

Virgil frowned deeply just as his cell phone rang. He looked at the display. "It's the analysts."

Rennie watched his face as he listened.

"Got it," he said and hung up. "Good work, Vogel. The analysts just confirmed your find." FBI tracked Cainkiller's cell to his brother's house in Potomac. Winston Randolph is dead." He frowned again, the expression on his face indicated he was trying to think something through.

"What is it?" Garrison said.

"The function my wife just left for…Ambassador Randolph will be attending it as well."

"What is the function?" Rennie asked.

"It's the anniversary of the founding of the United Nations. *Everyone* will be there. Ambassadors, heads of state. The President would have been but his emergency appendectomy is keeping him away. The First Lady will be there though."

Rennie reached into her pocket and pulled out the coin Keller had found in Cainkiller's cabin. She flipped it over to its reverse. A chill traveled down her body.

"Is it at Dumbarton Oaks?"

Virgil's head snapped toward her. "How did you know?"

"We didn't think this was relevant. But right before we got on the plane Keller gave us this." She handed Virgil the coin.

"He found it in Cainkiller's quarters."

"Oh my God."

The tires of Virgil's roadster screamed as he made the slight left onto Florida Avenue. Dumbarton Oaks was only a little less than two-and-a-half miles from his house in Shaw but with D.C. traffic, that could mean ten minutes or an hour.

"Try my wife again," he shouted, handing his cell phone to Rennie.

"It's still going immediately to voice mail," Rennie said. "Is it unusual she would have it turned off?"

"Not when she's with the Senator at a function."

Cainkiller handed the Jag's keys to a valet as he stepped out onto Thirty-second Street in Georgetown. He'd loved driving the Jag again, tearing along the winding roads that hugged the Potomac on the route into the city. His pleasure in the car had only been mitigated by the pressure of the C4 where it rested against his back. It was bulky and uncomfortable but not so bulky that it showed through his evening jacket.

There was a short line at the door of the Dumbarton Oaks house which now housed its museum. Security had been set up outside for the commoners. The dignitaries were ushered past and dealt with inside. Cainkiller nodded to the older couple in line in front of him.

"Lovely evening," the woman said. She wore a knee length ermine over a sapphire colored dress.

"It is," Cainkiller said. "A lovely evening for a lovely event."

You always could turn on the charm in a pinch.

When he reached the pair of Secret Service men flanking the brick walkway, he said, "Evening, gentlemen."

Don't get cocky, cowboy.

"Ticket and ID, sir," the one on his left said.

Cainkiller handed him Winston's driver's license and the

ticket to the event that had taken him nearly twenty minutes to find. After frantically searching the house, he'd finally found it in the glove box of the Jag.

The Secret Service agent marked his clipboard and handed him back his ticket and ID. "Enjoy your evening, Mr. Randolph," he said.

Cainkiller nodded and ascended the steps into the house.

He'd been to Dumbarton Oaks many times as a child. It was one of his mother's favorite places in the city. She'd take both boys there on nice days where she would sun herself on a blanket while the brothers tossed a football or explored the gardens. He was less familiar with the interior of the house. Artifacts didn't interest him then and they didn't now.

Old, dead junk. Who gives a shit?

He approached a docent explaining the provenance of a pre-Columbian mask.

"Toilet," he said, his voice too loud.

Rein it in, cowboy. You've come too far to screw things up now.

"Yes, sir. Through the next gallery and to the right."

Cainkiller snagged a glass of champagne from a waiter's tray. It was possible he could be recognized by a friend of the family, even after all these years. He pushed open the door to the men's room and flinched as he glimpsed a tuxedoed man with thick silver hair standing at the washbasin. The man turned and nodded at him as he exited the bathroom.

Cainkiller exhaled forcefully, trying to calm his wildly beating heart. If it *had* been his father, what would he have done? He still held the glass of champagne. He downed its contents and set the glass on the ledge below the mirror. He leaned on the sink and stared into his reflection.

"Pull yourself together, dipshit."

Another man in evening dress entered the bathroom just as he slipped into the farthest of the two stalls. He shrugged out of his jacket and hung it on the hook on the back of the door. He flushed the toilet and reached down to cut the water to the tank. He waited until the man left the bathroom and lifted off the ceramic lid and set it on the floor. He quickly unbuttoned his vest and hung it over the hook. The interior of the vest had been altered to hold the C4 in place. He unzipped the pouch and eased it out. He knew it was stable—that was one of the benefits of C4. Jarring or dropping it would not cause it to detonate, but he didn't want to take any chances.

Cainkiller could hear the galleries outside filling with guests, their voices carrying through to him. He secured the linked blocks of C4 to the side of tank and put the lid back into place. He quickly redressed. The vest was only a touch looser now. He delicately plucked the detonator from his inside jacket pocket.

It was a simple device and had only two components. First, the on/off mechanism which made the detonator active. He took a deep breath and switched it to the on position. The tiny red light in the housing began to pulse. The second component was the detonator itself. Now that the device was live, all he had to do to detonate the bomb was to flick open the lid and press the button. He put the detonator back into his pocket, took another deep breath and opened the door to the stall.

You have five minutes.

That's all he was going to give himself. It would probably take longer for the now inoperable toilet to be attended to, but there was always the chance that some enterprising guest might try to fix it himself.

Here we go, he thought, and stepped back into the museum.

You're not really going to go through with this are you?

Cainkiller stopped and cocked his head. He ducked back into the men's room and took a tiny snort of meth. Just enough to silence his weakness.

That's better.

Now, to make sure Daddy's on the premises. Cainkiller maneuvered through the crowd scanning faces. Just as he accepted another glass of champagne from a waiter, he saw him and froze. Franklin Randolph stood in the first of the Byzantine galleries chatting with a man Cainkiller recognized as the previous ambassador to France. Keeping his face averted, Cainkiller made a beeline for the exit.

Just a few more feet and you're home free.

An imposing black man with graying hair was talking

emphatically to one of the Secret Service men. The black man's back was to Cainkiller as he made his way through the entryway. The Secret Service agent met his eye and though his heart was in his throat, Cainkiller gave him a casual, friendly smile.

And then he was out on the street, handing his stub to the valet.

"It'll be just a minute, sir."

"That's all right. I'll walk with you. I could use the air."

You did it, cowboy. You sure as shit did it.

Inside the Jag, Cainkiller rested his head on the steering wheel.

This is too easy.

He took a moment to take another small hit from the vial of meth before he started the engine and eased out of his spot. The valet had parked the Jag a block away around the corner—much too far from the museum to detonate the bomb. The detonator's range was only two hundred yards, which meant he'd have to drive right by it.

He turned onto Thirty-second Street and could see a stream of people exiting the museum.

What the fuck?

Someone must have found the bomb or maybe that black man… Cainkiller punched the accelerator on the Jag, his tires squawking as they gripped the pavement. Heads turned toward the sound and two men pointed at him. Ten seconds later he was at the corner of the house. He stopped the Jag in the street and pulled the detonator from his pocket.

This is it, baby.

He popped opened the housing, turned to look at the house and pressed the trigger. Then the silence of a quiet Georgetown evening exploded into a cacophony of light and sound and shattering glass.

CHAPTER FORTY-THREE

I wish I knew what the hell was going on in there.

Rennie sat behind the wheel of Virgil's roadster keeping her worries to herself. Garrison sat next to her in the passenger seat, so quiet and still she almost forgot he was there. She hadn't figured Virgil for a gearhead. She had to admit that the 1963 Alfa Romeo Spider was an alluring vehicle. She just hoped it would perform if they needed it to.

She checked her watch. Virgil had been gone for ten minutes. They were parked on Thirty-second Street about mid-block. They had tried getting closer but a Secret Service man had rapped on their window and told them to move. On top of it, they hadn't had time to get any sort of radio contact in place. So they were stuck. Waiting.

"How much longer do you think we should wait?" she said, turning to Garrison.

Just then, an explosion rattled their windows and glass rained down on the cars parked ahead of them. Sparks showered the street and smoke billowed into the night sky.

"Shit!"

"No more waiting," Garrison yelled.

Rennie reached for the door handle as an early model Jaguar blew past them. Garrison's cell phone rang a second later.

"The Jag. Go!"

Rennie turned the key in the ignition and the engine roared to life.

Thank God.

She backed out of the space in a quick movement and kept turning the wheel, forcing the roadster into a tight U-turn. But Georgetown streets were narrow. The back fender of Virgil's pride and joy dimpled the side door panel of a Lexus SUV. Rennie grimaced and threw the car into first, tearing off after the Jag. Cainkiller was moving fast but she could still see his taillights.

"Don't let him go this time," Garrison said.

"Don't worry."

Rennie sounded her horn as she approached stops signs and blew through them. Ahead, the Jag turned right, going straight for the congestion of Wisconsin Avenue.

Rennie squealed around the corner just in time to see the Jag catch the light and turn left onto Wisconsin.

"No," she yelled and threw the Alfa into fourth. She laid on the horn as she neared the intersection and pushed her way through the stunned traffic before seeing Cainkiller disappear onto P Street.

"I hope he knows what he's doing," Garrison said chuckling.

"And I hope he doesn't."

She almost laughed herself as she turned onto P and saw the Jag rattling down the street.

P was one of two streets in D.C. that still had trolley tracks running down the center. What surrounded the trolley tracks—

which were an inch to several inches high—were cobblestones, which would wreck your alignment if you drove over them too quickly. Cainkiller was neither going very slow nor saving his suspension as he bounced along.

Rennie turned the wheels of the Alfa directly onto the tracks. Instantly, every vibration, every rattle evaporated as the wheels sailed along the perfectly smooth rails.

"Don't fall off," Garrison said, still amused.

Rennie glanced at him and accelerated. In a few seconds she was upon the Jag. Garrison already had the window down and was leaning out with his Beretta in hand.

"What are you doing?" Rennie yelled.

Garrison fired and the back window of the Jag shattered. He leaned back into the car.

"Should I kill him?"

"No!"

Just then Rennie's cell phone rang. She snatched it up and heard Virgil's voice on the line.

"Capture. Don't kill," she shouted.

Garrison shook his head as he leaned back out the window and aimed to fire at the Jag's tires. But his angle was all wrong and the tires were tucked too deeply under the chassis.

"Can't do it," he said, dropping back into the car.

Rennie heard the faint sound of a voice and plucked her cell phone from between her legs, realizing Virgil was still on the line. She tossed the phone to Garrison.

"We're at P and Thirty-fourth," he reported.

Rennie could hear the buzz of Virgil's deep baritone as she shot off the end of the trolley tracks, sticking close behind Cainkiller who was quickly picking up speed now that he was on pavement.

"Okay." Garrison turned to Rennie. "Just stay on him. Metropolitan Police is converging."

Cainkiller swung a left and Rennie followed after, tight on him.

"Didn't this guy live here? I hope he's not planning on taking Thirty-fifth all the way down to M."

Perhaps the steepest hill in the city, the final block of Thirty-fifth Street was a harrowing pitch covered in cobblestones. It was daunting to drive down even in perfectly dry conditions. Rennie could hear sirens in the distance as the Jag tore down the narrow street. Cainkiller wasn't even pausing at stop signs. She continued to sound her horn upon approach and blew through them nearly as fast. Once they hit the hill, the Jag bounced wildly over the cobblestones and showed no sign of slowing as it neared the bottom.

Rennie held her breath as he tore around the corner, expecting at any moment to hear the sound of a collision. She paused at the bottom just long enough to see that traffic was clear and followed him.

Garrison turned in his seat. "Metro Police have cut the entrance onto Key Bridge."

Rennie glanced in her rearview mirror and saw a cruiser pull out after them.

"Cainkiller's turning onto Whitehurst," she shouted, pointing at the elevated freeway that ran under the Key Bridge and along Georgetown by the waterfront.

Rennie followed him onto the freeway. Suddenly, Cainkiller slammed on his brakes. Rennie could see flashing lights in the distance. Cainkiller leapt out of the Jag and ran directly toward them. Rennie and Garrison both sprang from the Alfa in the same instant. Cainkiller looked psychotic, running toward them in his tuxedo and brandishing a hunting knife. Rennie heard screams and the crunch of cars knocking into each other as they tried to escape the violent scene in the adjacent lane.

Then Cainkiller abruptly stopped running, his attention riveted on Rennie.

I'm supposed to be dead.

"Toss the knife away and raise your hands," Rennie shouted to him.

Cainkiller just continued to stare at her.

"Enough of this. We have to disarm him," Garrison said.

"Let's do it," Rennie responded. Just as she took a step toward Cainkiller, she heard the sharp crack of a gunshot. Cainkiller staggered backward gripping his thigh.

"This is how you disarm a suspect?" Rennie shouted at Garrison.

Rennie turned back in time to see Cainkiller put a hand on the railing.

"He's not going to jump," Rennie said in disbelief. She ran toward the railing just as he went over.

He can't possibly...

Peering over the railing, Rennie saw that it was only about an eight-foot drop from the freeway to the top of an old stone ruin. From there it was a short hop to a set of stairs built alongside it that wound down to the street. Cainkiller was already halfway down.

"Tell Virgil to get uniforms on the towpath and on Water Street," she yelled to Garrison. "And don't shoot anyone," she felt compelled to add.

Tucking the Sig into the back of her pants she vaulted over the rail. She landed well, legs bent, and hopped down to the top of the stairs.

Cainkiller was already out of sight. Rennie ran for the opening of the aqueduct tunnel, palming her Sig and slipping off the safety. As she neared the tunnel entrance she saw that it was shrouded in darkness inside. Rennie slowed and edged up to the stone arch.

Go slow. No mistakes now.

Tendrils of ivy clung to the stone. Rennie tried to listen for footsteps but traffic noise from above drowned out any subtle sound. She took a breath and craned her upper body around the corner. Double gripping the Sig, she swung it first left and then right in an attempt to cover the entire interior space of the tunnel. She couldn't see a thing.

The street wasn't well lit on the other side of the tunnel either but Rennie could see the shadowy skeletal underside of the freeway, its steel supports stretching down to the street. Waiting for her eyes to adjust, she heard a sound from within the tunnel. A faint scuffing.

Rennie's eyes were slowly adjusting to the dark of the tunnel but the ambient light on the other side was throwing her off, playing tricks on her vision. She kept thinking she saw movement.

A shape or a form in the darkness. But just as she trained the Sig on it it faded into nothing.

Then she heard, "Aren't you going to help me?" A whispered voice seemed to sneak out of the tunnel and touch her on the ear. A shiver coursed over her body.

Look at what a failure you are, Devon. Begging a woman for help.

Cainkiller pressed his hand against the hole in his pant leg trying to keep the blood inside where it would do him some good.

Arteries bring the drug to the brain.

"The drug," Cainkiller whispered.

That's right. Remember? Waka, waka, waka and all that. The drug is the only thing that can save you.

"The drug."

Look at you, Devon. Lying in the dark in your own filth. Despicable.

Cainkiller had to stop the voices fracturing and colliding. He needed the drug. That would make everything right. Just like it always did. But he was so tired, his eyelids full of lead. And the vial was in his trouser pocket, trapped by the weight of his body.

"This is your last chance."

Your last chance.

But wait. The voice hadn't come from inside his head this time. He turned to the left and forced himself to see. A human form, a horrible black cutout, hovered at the entrance of the aqueduct.

"Oh. You."

"Come out with your hands up and you won't get hurt," the form said.

"Too late for that," Cainkiller said weakly.

With every ounce of his strength, he rolled off of his left side and inch by inch scooted toward the stone wall. Partially upright, he dug in his pocket for the vial. His heart leapt when his fingers finally brushed the cool glass.

"You're supposed to be at the bottom of Devils Lake," Cainkiller said, his voice stronger now in anticipation. He unscrewed the cap of the vial.

"I came back to get you," the form said.

A shiver shook Cainkiller's body.

She's going to get you, Devon. She's going to lock you up again and you're never going to get out.

"We'll see about that." Cainkiller tipped the contents of the vial into his palm and snorted as much of the powder as he could.

A light exploded in his brain and his eyelids shot open. The pain in his leg evaporated and he could feel the blood being drawn back into his body. He could feel his muscle fibers multiplying too. Cainkiller leapt to his feet and screamed.

Rennie jumped as the scream erupted, bouncing off the stone walls.

What the hell?

She gripped the Sig harder as she saw Cainkiller emerge from the far side of the aqueduct, running fast. Very fast. Faster than should have been possible.

"Police! Drop the gun!"

Rennie turned to see two big Metro cops running awkwardly down the bank. The two cops were lumbering toward her, weapons drawn. There was no way they were ever going to catch Cainkiller.

"FBI! I'm going after him!" she yelled and took off running. Her lie might get her in trouble but she'd worry about that later.

Rennie ran hard, tearing down the street after Cainkiller. Sirens were getting closer. Water Street was edged on one side by buildings and on the other by the river. There was nowhere for Cainkiller to get away until he reached Thirty-fifth Street and he was gaining on it fast. She was closing the gap between them but not nearly fast enough. Cainkiller was looking frantically to his left and right. Looking for a place to hide or a place to escape. But Rennie was there to make sure he didn't find it.

The sirens were getting closer. She had to cut Cainkiller off before he had more options. Rennie pushed her lungs and legs to their breaking point.

Fifteen yards.

Red and blue lights patterned the street. Metropolitan Police were very close.

Ten yards.

Cainkiller was nearly at Thirty-fifth. He jagged to the left to cut the corner tight. Just then a police cruiser—no lights, no siren—shot from Thirty-fifth and slammed on its brakes, nearly running Cainkiller over. He'd barely stopped himself from running into the side of the vehicle when Rennie dove, hitting him around the chest, sending them both skittering across the hood and onto the pavement on the other side.

Cainkiller was frantic, thrashing his arms and legs as she tried to get a hold on him. Time seemed to slow as Rennie heard the sirens getting closer and the doors of the cruiser opening. Then an image of poor Buddy Olsen flashed through her mind. And Hannah, bloodied and unconscious. Filled with rage, Rennie reared up and brought all her weight down on Cainkiller, driving her elbow into his chest. She heard him gasp as the air rushed out of his lungs. She drew her Sig and slammed it against the side of his head.

Cainkiller lay inert as Metro cops gathered around them, weapons drawn on both of them.

"You're done," she said.

EPILOGUE

Petersburg, West Virginia

"I'd have thought you'd had your fill of the woods," Hannah said.

Rennie smiled, taking in the view, languorous and vast, that stretched out before them as they sat on the cabin porch, each armed only with a glass of Rioja.

Twenty minutes earlier they had dropped their bags just inside the heavy oak door of their rented cabin and locked it tight. Rennie had taken Hannah's hand and maneuvered her against the wall where they had kissed, slow and sure.

They sat close together on the porch, the cabin overlooking a winding river, its far bank rising to a dense forest of pine and fir. Hannah tipped her head onto the back of the chair. She reached over and trailed her fingers over the back of Rennie's hand. "I'm glad we have a few moments to get away and become reacquainted." She cocked an eyebrow.

"You plan on having a full dance card when we get back?" Rennie asked, unable to stop herself.

The flirtatious look on Hannah's face faded into one that was simple and kind. She stroked Rennie's hand with the flat of her palm, insistently. She smiled, but sadly.

"I don't. Nor do I plan to. But let's just be easy with each other."

Rennie looked into her eyes. She often couldn't fathom what Hannah was thinking. But she understood that she was offering what she could.

"Okay." Rennie turned her hand over to grip Hannah's and they held on tightly, letting the gesture speak for all that was left unsaid.

Rennie smiled.

"I don't think I've ever seen you this relaxed," Hannah said.

Rennie turned to her. "I have news."

Before Rennie decided to take a few days away, Virgil had called the team together for an unscheduled meeting. They'd assembled at his house in Shaw. Virgil was keeping a close eye on Jackie who was lucky to escape the bombing with just a turned ankle.

"What I'm about to tell you will likely come as a very big surprise," he'd said once the doors to the library were closed.

And it had been. Something close to amazement even flickered over Garrison's features.

"Wait," Kyu had said. "So, you're telling us that SPS is a covert arm of the FBI?"

"Not exactly. It would be more accurate to say that FBI has *sanctioned* SPS."

"Splitting hairs," Garrison scoffed. "Essentially we're working for them but will pretend we're not if anything goes wrong. Classic plausible deniability. They let us do their dirty work off the books and everyone goes home happy." He raised a questioning eyebrow.

Virgil didn't look amused. "I'm not going to dispute Mr. Garrison's assessment. But I do want to say that the fact that he's hearing this news at all means that he will not be fired. And he is very lucky that he is not going to be fired," he said, looking pointedly at Garrison. "But let me make myself clear," he went on. "From this day forward, he is on permanent probation. I hold him personally responsible for Kenneth Yates' death. Arrangements have been made for Mr. Garrison to quietly compensate the Yates family. If I had it my way, I'd have him charged, but it turns out he has some very influential connections. That said, he has assured me that nothing of the sort will ever happen again."

Garrison had given a single nod.

Rennie had hardly been able to take it all in. But as she drove home to Capitol Hill, a smile had broken out over her face much as it was now.

"This is better for you, yes?" Hannah asked.

"It is. It's a lot better," Rennie said. "I feel...legitimate again. Plus, the chastisement of Garrison was particularly satisfying."

"Oh, I bet it was," Hannah said. She ran her hand through Rennie's hair. "Being back with the FBI—or at least having their stamp of approval—must feel a little like you've come full circle. And like you've been vindicated."

"It does." Rennie thought for a moment. "It's funny. Around the Bureau you'd always hear rumors that groups like these exist. Black ops. I just never imagined I'd be involved in one."

"Are you having ethical qualms?"

Rennie thought of her conversation in the motel room with Garrison.

Sometimes we have to do ugly things, things that fall outside of the morality that your average American is allowed to pretend exists. We do these things so they can believe that it exists. That is our gift to them.

"No." She met Hannah's eyes. "I'm not having ethical qualms."

"Good." Hannah stretched. "This trip really was a stroke of genius. What shall we do with ourselves tomorrow? Venture out into the world or stay holed up in our cozy little cabin?"

Rennie pretended to consider this weighty question. "In, I think."

"Yes, in," Hannah said, holding Rennie's gaze.

Hannah was leaning over to her when whatever was to come was interrupted by the chime of her cell phone.

"I swear I meant to turn this damn thing off," she said laughing.

She fumbled in her pocket and was about to decline the call when Rennie saw her expression change as she looked at the display. She help up a finger and flipped open the phone.

"Hey, Tommy. What's up?"

Rennie's stomach churned at the thought of Tommy Damone and all that he may have uncovered. Hannah felt strongly that it was time to get the events from Tajikistan out in the open. Rennie still wasn't sure. The thought of her name bandied about in the media made her want to lock herself away.

"Oh, no," Hannah said, standing up suddenly.

Whatever peace had come over Rennie since they'd arrived at the cabin drained out of her.

"Now?" Hannah spoke emphatically. "Where? CNN? Got it." She snapped the phone shut. "Come on."

They hurried into the living room, found the remote and clicked on the TV. Hannah flicked through the channels until she found CNN.

This just in. Breaking news from the nation's capital. We now have exclusive unedited video of Devon Randolph, the French ambassador's son, being detained by former FBI agent Rennie Vogel, who we recently learned was involved in the U.S.-sanctioned assassination plot against Ahmad Armin. First the video.

The opening shots of the video were of the sidewalk and the amateur cameraman's shoes as he ran. Then an image of a car door filled the lens until the camera was finally stabilized on its roof. Audio of the cameraman came through rasping. "What the hell? What the hell is she doing?" Then there was Rennie. Running very fast. Randolph kept turning his head to check her progress. Then a police cruiser pulled out of a side street and slammed on its brakes barely avoiding running down Randolph. Rennie could feel her adrenaline kick in even as she watched. It was strange seeing herself. She felt both entirely present—as if it were actually happening all over again—and yet at a remove. She watched as she dove at Randolph, hitting him in the chest and carrying them both over the hood of the car. Her muscles tensed in the same way they had before she and Randolph slammed onto the pavement. The final frame of the video was of Randolph, his hands cuffed behind his back, being put into the back of a cruiser.

"Nicely done," Hannah said.

This story is still developing but what we know is that Devon Randolph murdered his brother Winston before gaining access to a United Nations gala at Dumbarton Oaks in Georgetown. A bomb exploded soon after Randolph exited the museum. Randolph had become estranged from his high-profile family after developing a violent right-wing ideology. It is said that he believed that a conspiracy existed among national leaders and the international banking community to form a one world order.

In a related development, we have Thomas Damone in the studio, an investigative journalist whose piece on the U.S.-sanctioned assassination of Ahmad Armin in Tajikistan three years ago will be published next week in The New Yorker *magazine.*

Mr. Damone, tell us how Rennie Vogel, who we just witnessed spectacularly capturing home-grown terrorist Devon Randolph, was involved in the Armin assassination. Is she still with the FBI?

"I think it was pretty spectacular too," Hannah said, smiling at Rennie.

A grainy black-and-white image filled the screen then as Tommy responded to the host's question. Rennie at sixteen years old. Her junior yearbook portrait. She wasn't smiling but her lips were parted enough to show her braces.

"Nice grill," Hannah said.

Rennie covered her face with her hands.

"It'll be okay," Hannah said. "At least you won't be recognized on the street."

That much was true. Not much of a consolation though.

They finished watching the segment and snapped off the TV.

"This is too much," Rennie said.

"It needed to come out."

"I know."

Shame had taken root in the pit of Rennie's stomach. She'd yet to make peace with herself in regard to her role in Armin's death and she wasn't sure she ever would. She closed her eyes and leaned her head back on the sofa. She imagined her mother, her aunt Laurel watching the segment or reading about it, and it almost took her breath away. She closed her eyes. "I should have blown this thing open myself. I was a coward not to."

Hannah shook her head. "You couldn't. It would have ruined you."

Hannah drew her legs under herself and faced Rennie. "My father, when his mind was still whole, once said that a human being never knows what he is capable of—dignity, grace, bravery, or pitiable cowardice—until he has been stretched upon the rack and forced to contemplate his own brutal end. Hannah leaned over and slipped her hand around the back of Rennie's neck. "If I know anything in this world, it is that you will always be brave, every single time."

Rennie opened her eyes again and found Hannah looking at her intensely. She thought of the first moment she saw her, through the scope the sniper rifle. How weak and vulnerable she had seemed then. But she had proven herself to be anything but weak or vulnerable. And here she was, right now, before her. Rennie would have to exorcise her ghosts some other time.

Rennie smiled. "It's going to be chilly tonight. Why don't I go get some kindling for a fire?"

"Why don't you just stay right here for a moment." It wasn't a request.

"Just for a moment?"

"We'll see," Hannah said and leaned in to kiss her.

**Publications from
Bella Books, Inc.**
Women. Books. Even Better Together.
**P.O. Box 10543
Tallahassee, FL 32302
Phone: 800-729-4992
www.bellabooks.com**

CALM BEFORE THE STORM by Peggy J. Herring. Colonel Marcel Robideaux doesn't tell and so far no one official has asked, but the amorous pursuit by Jordan McGowen has her worried for both her career and her honor.
978-0-9677753-1-9

THE WILD ONE by Lyn Denison. Rachel Weston is busy keeping home and head together after the death of her husband. Her kids need her and what she doesn't need is the confusion that Quinn Farrelly creates in her body and heart.
978-0-9677753-4-0

LESSONS IN MURDER by Claire McNab. There's a corpse in the school with a neat hole in the head and a Black & Decker drill alongside. Which teacher should Inspector Carol Ashton suspect? Unfortunately, the alluring Sybil Quade is at the top of the list. First in this highly lauded series.
978-1-931513-65-4

WHEN AN ECHO RETURNS by Linda Kay Silva. The bayou where Echo Branson found her sanity has been swept clean by a hurricane — or at least they thought. Then an evil washed up by the storm comes looking for them all, one-by-one. Second in series.
978-1-59493-225-0

DEADLY INTERSECTIONS by Ann Roberts. Everyone is lying, including her own father and her girlfriend. Leaving matters to the professionals is supposed to be easier! Third in series with *Paid in Full* and *White Offerings*.
978-1-59493-224-3

SUBSTITUTE FOR LOVE by Karin Kallmaker. No substitutes, ever again! But then Holly's heart, body and soul are captured by Reyna... Reyna with no last name and a secret life that hides a terrible bargain, one written in family blood.
978-1-931513-62-3

MAKING UP FOR LOST TIME by Karin Kallmaker. Take one Next Home Network Star and add one Little White Lie to equal mayhem in little Mendocino and a recipe for sizzling romance. This lighthearted, steamy story is a feast for the senses in a kitchen that is way too hot.
978-1-931513-61-6

2ND FIDDLE by Kate Calloway. Cassidy James's first case left her with a broken heart. At least this new case is fighting the good fight, and she can throw all her passion and energy into it.
978-1-59493-200-7

HUNTING THE WITCH by Ellen Hart. The woman she loves — used to love — offers her help, and Jane Lawless finds it hard to say no. She needs TLC for recent injuries and who better than a doctor? But Julia's jittery demeanor awakens Jane's curiosity. And Jane has never been able to resist a mystery. #9 in series and Lammy-winner.
978-1-59493-206-9

FAÇADES by Alex Marcoux. Everything Anastasia ever wanted — she has it. Sidney is the woman who helped her get it. But keeping it will require a price — the unnamed passion that simmers between them.
978-1-59493-239-7

ELENA UNDONE by Nicole Conn. The risks. The passion. The devastating choices. The ultimate rewards. Nicole Conn rocked the lesbian cinema world with *Claire of the Moon* and has rocked it again with *Elena Undone*. This is the book that tells it all...
978-1-59493-254-0

WHISPERS IN THE WIND by Frankie J. Jones. It began as a camping trip, then a simple hike. Dixon Hayes and Elizabeth Colter uncover an intriguing cave on their hike, changing their world, perhaps irrevocably.
978-1-59493-037-9

WEDDING BELL BLUES by Julia Watts. She'll do anything to save what's left of her family. Anything. It didn't seem like a bad plan...at first. Hailed by readers as Lammy-winner Julia Watts' funniest novel.
978-1-59493-199-4

WILDFIRE by Lynn James. From the moment botanist Devon McKinney meets ranger Elaine Thomas the chemistry is undeniable. Sharing — and protecting — a mountain for the length of their short assignments leads to unexpected passion in this sizzling romance by newcomer Lynn James.
978-1-59493-191-8

LEAVING L.A. by Kate Christie. Eleanor Chapin is on the way to the rest of her life when Tessa Flanaghan offers her a lucrative summer job caring for Tessa's daughter Laya. It's only temporary and everyone expects Eleanor to be leaving L.A...
978-1-59493-221-2

SOMETHING TO BELIEVE by Robbi McCoy. When Lauren and Cassie meet on a once-in-a-lifetime river journey through China their feelings are innocent...at first. Ten years later, nothing — and everything — has changed. From Golden Crown winner Robbi McCoy.
978-1-59493-214-4

DEVIL'S ROCK by Gerri Hill. Deputy Andrea Sullivan and Agent Cameron Ross vow to bring a killer to justice. The killer has other plans. Gerri Hill pens another intriguing blend of mystery and romance in this page-turning thriller.
978-1-59493-218-2

SHADOW POINT by Amy Briant. Madison McPeak has just been not-quite fired, told her brother is dead and discovered she has to pick up a five-year old niece she's never met. After she makes it to Shadow Point it seems like someone—or something—doesn't want her to leave. Romance sizzles in this ghost story from Amy Briant.
978-1-59493-216-8

JUKEBOX by Gina Daggett. Debutantes in love. With each other. Two young women chafe at the constraints of parents and society with a friendship that could be more, if they can break free. Gina Daggett is best known as "Lipstick" of the columnist duo Lipstick & Dipstick.
978-1-59493-212-0

BLIND BET by Tracey Richardson. The stakes are high when Ellen Turcotte and Courtney Langford meet at the blackjack tables. Lady Luck has been smiling on Courtney but Ellen is a wild card she may not be able to handle.
978-1-59493-211-3